Praise for

THE SKY CL

"*The Sky Club* portrays diverse, unexpected facets of the Appalachian region in the years of the Great Depression. It is a novel of climbing, social, financial, emotional, romantic, to a mountaintop, to The Sky Club, to risk and wealth, to danger, and, ultimately, to enduring love."

—Robert Morgan, Author of
Gap Creek and *Chasing the North Star*

"Ever since Terry Roberts took up writing about his ancestors in Western North Carolina, he has produced a remarkably varied and valuable shelf of novels. . . . but *The Sky Club* is the best one yet! Wildly original, this is a truly Appalachian novel all about money, sex, drinking, and the Great Depression. . . . along with the more familiar themes of place and family. I especially admire the apparent ease with which Roberts has created the tough, true, funny and unforgettable Jo Salter, an independent pistol of a woman who tells this lively tale set in a speakeasy on top of a mountain."

—Lee Smith, *New York Times*
bestselling author of *The Last Girls*

"*The Sky Club* is a wagonload of perilous fun. Terry Roberts has engaged, with customary vigor, many of his favorite themes: local Appalachian history, mountain cultures rural and urban, personal and communal courage, individuality. The resulting story is sprightly and steady in the manner of its heroine, the gifted Jo Salter. Every page here shines with truthful surprise. *Bravo!*"

—Fred Chappell,
Author of *I Am One of You Forever*

"Roberts has captured a moment in Asheville's history that to this day affects our way of life. It is a well-told tale, reminiscent of John Ehle's great novel, *Last One Home*. I think Ehle would have been proud of *The Sky Club*."

—Wayne Caldwell,
Author of *Cataloochee*

THE SKY CLUB

ALSO BY TERRY ROBERTS

My Mistress' Eyes Are Raven Black

The Holy Ghost Speakeasy and Revival

That Bright Land

A Short Time to Stay Here

THE SKY CLUB

TERRY ROBERTS

KEYLIGHT BOOKS
AN IMPRINT OF TURNER PUBLISHING COMPANY
Nashville, Tennessee
www.turnerpublishing.com

The Sky Club

Cover design by Emily Mahon
Cover photo by Jesse L. Roberts
Text design by William Ruoto

Library of Congress Cataloging-in-Publication Data
Names: Roberts, Terry, 1956- author.
Title: The sky bar / a novel by Terry Roberts.
Description: Nashville, Tennessee : Turner Publishing Company, [2022] |
Identifiers: LCCN 2021042067 (print) | LCCN 2021042068 (ebook) |
ISBN 9781684428526 (paperback) | ISBN 9781684428533 (hardcover) |
ISBN 9781684428540 (ebook)
Subjects: LCGFT: Fiction.
Classification: LCC PS3618.O3164 S57 2022 (print) |
LCC PS3618.O3164 (ebook) | DDC 813/.6—dc23/eng/20211018
LC record available at https://lccn.loc.gov/2021042067
LC ebook record available at https://lccn.loc.gov/2021042068

Printed in the United States of America

In Memory of . . .

Belva Anderson Roberts (1888–1974)
Grandma Roberts
who bade me tell the stories.

"Money often costs too much."

— EMERSON

THE SKY CLUB

PART ONE

SPRING 1929

1

YOU COULD SAY THAT MY life began with my mother's death.

For up until that time, I was slated to become one kind of woman, and after that, everything changed. Everything changed and I became another.

She passed in the first few days of February 1929, which was harsh and cold in the Big Pine Valley. Not an especially bitter winter as mountain winters go, but even so, it was long and dark, as mean a season as you can imagine. The rhododendron leaves curled tight for days and lambs born overnight froze to death in the pasture grass before dawn.

My mother's name was Mary Freeman Salter. She was fifty-eight when she died of measles. Of all the things in this solid world to die of . . . measles. The doctor, when we were finally able to get him up the icy dirt roads to home, said the measles caused her brain to swell and led into pneumonia. In the end, she couldn't breathe, the doctor said, and so she suffocated.

But you should know this, here at the beginning. None of those things killed my mother. Exhaustion is what killed her. Fifty-eight years of farm work—from before first light to after dark. Oh, my father worked, make no mistake, but she was up an hour before him to stoke the cookstove and boil the coffee; and she was darning and knitting for an hour after he was snoring by the fireplace. Fifty-eight years of that plus seven children born at home—my brothers and me.

In the last few days of January, when her head had begun to hurt her terribly but she still had breath, she called me in from the kitchen to sit with her. It was a bleak afternoon, and the whole house stank of wood smoke and grease from having been shut up since Thanksgiving. We were the only ones there as Papa had the boys in the woods felling trees to cut into railroad ties.

She stroked my hand and told me two large things. "Don't feel sorry for me," was the first. "Don't you ever feel sorry for me. I chose this life, and I loved this place. Loved your father often as not. Bottom line, I chose this right here, and I was up to the task, both the daytime of it and the night."

She paused and coughed. Not an outright coughing fit. That came later. But a hoarse rattle in her lungs that she couldn't clear. "I chose it and it's my life . . . But it is not your life." This was the second thing.

"What do you mean?" I asked. She startled me, and I asked it loud enough to be heard in the yard.

"I mean when this is finished," she murmured. "When I'm dead and buried . . . you get the hell out of here. Make a life for . . ." Her voice was shriveling up, and I leaned over her, for at that point she was no longer contagious. My chest against her chest, my ear close by her lips to hear the rest. "Make a life somewhere else . . . a life that I can't even imagine."

She made me promise her. Which I was glad to do. For it was a relief to be shut of my father and the two brothers still at home. All of whom I loved, of course, but all those men require a lot. Plus there's this: when my mother died at fifty-eight, she looked seventy at least. Her dear old face was wrinkled like a dried apple and her hair a dirty white.

We buried her in her best dress at Crooked Ridge Cemetery with fresh snow falling around us. My father did not cry or weep but neither did he speak. Stood trembling with his jaw clenched shut like a sprung trap.

The preacher talked about how we'd better get right with Jesus if we ever expected to see her in heaven. And how she'd climb up out of that grave on some last day, along with the rest of the saints. Something else about a trumpet blast. But for once, he didn't talk overlong because it was so damn cold. The boys—my brothers—had dug the grave out of frozen, rocky soil with pick and shovel, and when the preacher said amen, they filled it in again. They—all six of them—too sad and cold to even cuss the ground.

And so, at the ripe age of twenty-six, an old maid by country count, I came to live in the big, bold town of Asheville, North Carolina. Came to live by mutual agreement in Uncle Frank and Aunt Brenda Morgan's house on Charlotte Street. Twenty-six years old, I was to look for a job and pay a percentage for room and board. I was old but not a maid. I'd taken care of that little piece of business when I was fifteen.

2

"You've got a boy's body."

"Well, the . . . with you . . ."

"Don't take it wrong. I have a body like a cow. Bo-vine. I could smoke two packs a day and starve myself silly and I still wouldn't be as skinny as you."

My cousin, Sissy Morgan, was watching me unpack the trunk that contained just about all my worldly possessions, a half-dozen books and a few things to hang in the closet.

I gave her the same critical once-over she was obviously giving me. "I've had to do with a lot of cows in my time and I don't think . . ."

"Humpf." That was the sound she made. "Easy for you to say. You didn't get stuck with these mammaries like I did." She was sitting on what was to be my bed and leaned back against the headboard to heft her own breasts.

"Seen bigger," I said. "Men seem to . . ."

"Not here," she said. "Maybe up there in the holler where you come from. But it's 1929 down here, and men expect you to look lithe and lissome."

"What?"

"You know. Lean, muscular. Like you could dance all night with a cigarette in one hand and a gin in the other."

"Preacher says you'll go to hell tomorrow for dancing."

"Well then, we're going there," she said. "You and me."

I grinned at her. "Could be we will. But I have a feeling I've got a lot to learn first about . . . 1929."

"A hell of a lot," she agreed. "God, Josephine, are those really your clothes?"

I was half in the closet, slipping one of my three dresses onto a wire hanger. My best dress, really, at least what I'd worn to church on special Sundays up home. I had to bite my lip before I replied to Sissy, for I'd grown up around all those brothers, and I had a salty tongue. Didn't want to make an enemy on the first day and the dress itself was almost ten years old, a velvet number that was worn paper thin in places.

When I did turn around, Sissy was going through the clothes left in the trunk, carefully laying one dress or skirt or blouse out on the bed after another. "I said, are these really your clothes?" she repeated herself.

"I heard you," I said carefully. "Some of it's mine. Mostly my mother's."

She looked up suddenly. "I'm sorry. I didn't mean . . ."

I shook my head at her, more roughly than I intended. For I could feel my face crumpling up, and tears. A real, honest-to-God, ugly crying fit.

And you need to understand. I don't cry. Not since I was sixteen or seventeen and my mother had told me to get over myself. Oh, occasionally when it was that time of the month, I'd get a little weepy out of pure self-pity. But not like this. Not the flood out of the Bible.

Sissy stood up and put her chubby arms around me. "Josephine, honey, I'm sorry. Truly, I am. I just meant . . ." And then she started to cry. Nearly as old as me, a grown woman, and her cranking up just because I was. "All I meant was that there's no color, nothing . . . soft."

She was right. The clothes on the bed were black and brown and gray. They looked harsh almost. Weathered to the color of an old barn that has never been painted. "Well, she had a blue chiffon," I offered, trying not to sound defensive.

"Where is that?" She was standing beside me, her arm around my shoulder still. It was comforting, I admit.

"We b-b-buried her in it," I blubbered, and we were off again, crying on each other's shoulders. Had my mother actually been there, she would have told us both to dry up and wash our faces.

According to Sissy, my underclothes were the worst. In her words, "an absolute horror." I came to town with my three or four pairs of cotton step-ins and two items that I suppose you could name brassieres, one to wash and one to wear. And three slips, one of which, a cream-colored number, I was actually quite proud of.

Sissy could abide the slip, she said, and she laughed out loud at the brassiere I wasn't wearing. "This thing wouldn't hold *one* of mine," she exclaimed. "But even so, I can't imagine a man would want to touch it, let alone . . ."

"What! It never crossed my mind that a man would . . ."

She stared at me for a long moment. "Okay, Josephine . . . No, not Josephine for God's sake. What did they call you at home?"

"Josie."

She shook her head decisively. "Nope. Sounds like a cow."

The woman was obsessed with cows and had probably never milked one.

"Not Josie . . . Jo," she said. And apparently liked the sound of it.

"Listen to Sissy, Jo. This is your first lesson from the twentieth century, where you have come to live. The whole point of what you wear under your dresses and skirts and such is whether or not a glamorous young man of your acquaintance would want to, first, touch that garment, and second, remove it from your body. Understand?"

"I don't think . . . I mean . . . Jesus . . . did you actually say glamorous with regards to a man?"

She nodded emphatically. "Well, *glamorous* might be a slight exaggeration. But at least he's wearing the right clothes and his shoes are shined so that they reflect the moonlight when he's walking you home from a date."

I was trying to imagine a pair of shoes, men's shoes no less, that would reflect anything at all. And even if they did, why moonlight?

"And the point of your undergarments is that they are both an enticement and a reward to such a young man."

I laughed outright. Most of the young men I had known . . . well, you wouldn't want their hands anywhere near you unless you liked the smell of manure and black dirt. "You talk like a magazine," I said to Sissy.

"Thank you. I read a lot. And I am here to be your teacher. I know clothes the way a bookie knows horses. And what I don't know about men you could pour in a . . . a thimble."

"What's a bookie?" I asked, mesmerized.

"Never mind. Concentrate on the clothes and the men. Tomorrow, we are going shopping. Daddy says that you can start out working at the bank if you want. But not dressed in anything on this bed, not if I have anything to say about it."

"Thank you." It was all I could think of to say.

She grinned. "We're going to be friends. Real friends."

And actually, despite all odds, it turns out she was right. I could feel myself smiling back at her.

"I've told you what I know. Clothes and men. I also know a little bit about liquor. I know which brand of cigarettes to smoke.

And I'm very good at my job." She was a stenographer at a real estate development company, whatever a stenographer was. "Now, you tell me what you know. What are you good at?"

I thought of a dozen kinds of farm work. Hard work in the sun or over a smoking hot stove. None of it made sense there, in the big house on Charlotte Street. "I'm very good at numbers," is what I finally said.

3

THE BON MARCHE DEPARTMENT STORE wasn't as big as a town all by itself, but when Sissy hustled me under that red awning and through the front door the next morning, it felt like it. Four stories high and at least half a city block. Five or six years old according to Sissy, for whom even small numbers were always a little fuzzy.

I had fifty dollars folded small in a change purse and stashed in my mother's old brown pocketbook. It was half the money my father had given me to start out this new life, and I had no intention of seeing it lost or stolen. Sissy also had money—no telling how much, I doubt she knew herself—that she meant to invest in me.

She'd announced at breakfast that Monday morning that we intended to shop, and shop we did. It was exhausting. In Bon Marche alone, there were six clerks on the first floor, all dressed like they were going to church, and more clothes than I had ever seen in one place in my life. Six clerks, two cash registers, seven life-sized dummies dressed up in women's clothes, and a fancy woman with a dog who was wearing gloves. The woman, not the dog.

Things I learned that day: The smiling man dressed in a beautiful suit, who stood by the front door and spoke to Sissy when we came in, was a Jewish gent named Lipinsky, and he owned the place. The whole place, all four floors. The dummies were not dummies, they were mannequins. And the dog was not a dog but a poodle.

"Does it hunt?" I whispered to Sissy, who only gave me a disparaging look and shook her head sadly. I'm sure I would have been on the receiving end of one of her lectures about the poodle dog, but she was too busy. I was too busy.

I took off and put on my clothes more times in that one day than I had in the previous week, and in between, tried on so many different items—alone and in combination—that I lost count. And in case you haven't figured this out by now, I rarely lose count . . . of anything.

The final tally? Two *panties* (by lunchtime, I was calling them that too), two *bras*, two *slips* and one *half-slip*, three pairs of *stockings*, two *skirts*, three *blouses*, and the dress. *The* dress, chosen from the finalists by Sissy and a young salesgirl named Frances.

I paid for half this haul. Sissy paid for half and a taxicab to ferry us and the bags back to Charlotte Street.

Now, about the dress. I didn't realize it at the time, but the dress was important. The skirts and the blouses came in real colors. Blue and pink and dark red, except that Sissy and Frances named them turquoise, salmon, and blood. They were to wear to the bank, according to Sissy. But the dress was different. It wasn't colorful but rather black and silver, and it had a quality the other things didn't. Even I, as stupid as I was then, realized when I tried it on that it flowed over you like water. It was tight enough to show off your body rather than hide it, but the fabric didn't bind you anywhere. That dress moved all on its own with you inside it. Sissy gasped and muttered a curse word when she saw it on, and Frances just nodded.

It was not to wear during the day, Sissy explained. It was for nighttime.

"Why would you wear something dark as night during the night?" I asked her.

She smiled mysteriously. "Oh, you'll find out," was all she said.

I also need to describe my uncle to you at this point. Before what happened later. He was a banker, not the president, but one of the vice presidents to that exalted personage, at the Central Bank and Trust Company downtown on Pack Square. He had been a big man around town for years, and it was somewhat remarkable that my Aunt Brenda, my mother's sister, had somehow managed to snag him years before when they were both students at Weaver College.

He was always ambitious, a man on the make, and yet, by the time I came to town in February of '29, he was firmly established and looked it. He had once been tall and thin—like a heron bird—but by that winter, he was portly. In country terms, he was fat, but I came to think of him as portly because his expanse was the evidence of his prosperity.

At home in the evenings, he could be found in his shirt sleeves, but he never left the house unless he was immaculately dressed in trousers, vest, and jacket. Wool in the winter, linen in the summer. At the bank, when he was working on the third floor where no customers could see him, he occasionally took off the jacket, but I never saw him roll up his sleeves or loosen his tie. It was the style that they all aspired to, my Uncle Frank and the men of his circle. Bankers and lawyers and . . . as I came to see in time, the politicians they consorted with.

They ate well, they drank well, and they dressed well. And as the years passed, it took ever more linen and wool to cover their growing bellies.

In addition to Uncle Frank and Aunt Brenda taking on the

appearance of wealth, it was also necessary that the household put on a show as well.

Aunt Brenda was not allowed to cook or serve. There was a colored woman named Pansy for that. She wasn't allowed to be seen working in the yard. There was Pansy's husband, Raymond, for that. Apparently when she first came to town, Brenda had happily kept a cow out back, but Frank had nixed that idea after taking a job at the bank. Milk was to arrive each weekday morning on a fancy delivery truck from the Biltmore Dairy out on the estate.

But since Brenda was herself a country woman at heart, all of this leisure only made her nervous, and she tended to flutter around Frank when he was home like some kind of moth or butterfly. I almost said like a butterfly around horse droppings, for we've all seen that, but that image wouldn't be fair to Frank.

Because to be fair to Uncle Frank, he was enjoying his life immensely. In addition to his salary from the bank, he was also caught up in various real estate investments north of town, out at our end of Charlotte Street where E. W. Grove held sway before he died. He had known Grove, and Grove's son-in-law Seely personally, and, as I came to find out the second Sunday I was there, the whole family would take Sunday dinner at the Grove Park Inn on a regular basis. Sunday dinner at the Inn, where various personages, even Seely himself, would stop by our table to check in with Uncle Frank. Invariably, they would ask about the bank, and Frank would nod sagely and say, "Solid as a rock, my friend, solid as a damn rock." Even I, the country cousin, was occasionally invited and got to see this grand performance play out.

So you see, Uncle Frank's carefully groomed clothes along with his gold watch chain and his initialed cufflinks were all part and parcel of his accumulated life. His round, red, closely-shaven face, his carefully barbered, gray hair, even his one gold tooth—

all those things spoke to who he was and who he knew. He was never without a smile for the ladies or a grin and wink for the men, and after dinner, he was never without a cigar. Cuban, or so he said.

Sissy assumed her father was rich. Her brother, Frank Junior, assumed the same. You couldn't tell what Aunt Brenda thought; she was too fluttery. What I thought was wait and see.

And as things unfolded, I did see.

4

THE NEXT MONDAY MORNING I went to work at the Central Bank and Trust on the square. My uncle deigned that I should ride downtown with him in his motorcar, although that rarely happened once our different routines were established. The bank opened its doors at 9:00, and by midweek, I was letting myself in the alley door for employees by 8:30. Uncle Frank often didn't show up till almost lunchtime, depending on what sort of breakfasts and community meetings he had on his calendar.

That first morning, he turned me over to Foster Reynolds, the head cashier, who squired me around the first floor, which was all solid, white marble. Most of the space was taken up by neat little cashiers' cubicles with barred windows, through which the cashiers dealt with customers. He introduced me to various other cashiers, who were to man those cubicles during the day. I say "man" with a wink, because they were mostly men older than me, some in their thirties, and only a few women.

Mr. Reynolds then took me up to the second floor, where I was to be trained during that first day, along with a nervous young man named Joshua Breed. Reynolds himself was too important to actually teach us what was involved in the job, so he turned us over to Mable. That was her only name as far as I could tell . . . Mable. So, for the morning, it was Mr. Breed, Mable, and me . . . Josephine. And in fact, that was part of the training. When we talked to customers, we were to refer to the women by their first names, unless they were ancient wives of important men and so earned Missus status. All men were Misters. Mable winked at me for the first time that morning during this part of the indoctrination.

Mable had been at the bank for over ten years and was assistant to the head cashier. She was a short, wide, middle-aged woman with hair dyed an impossible shade of red. Everything but her hair and her attitude was what you might expect. She might have been my aunt . . . or yours. But the hair was startling. You blinked in disbelief when you saw it for the first time and for the next ten times after that. Same with her attitude. Moxie. That's what I learned to say after a few days. Mable had a lot of moxie.

She also wore a pair of spectacles pushed down on her nose. She regarded everything through the spectacles, or at least everything she didn't already have memorized. And when she stared hard at you over the spectacles, your insides withered a little whether you'd made a mistake or not.

She took us through savings accounts, personal and business. Passbook accounts that required the customer to have the passbook in hand to do business. Checking accounts, which most businesses had but very few individuals. Deposits and withdrawals. Interest.

I asked about loans and she explained that neither Joshua nor I would work those windows in the beginning. That was a different department and it required special training. "You'll get a shot at it, if you want it," she reassured me. "The loan department, even just the cashiers in the loan department, aren't having any fun these days. Mostly them hick farmers coming to offer a chicken or a bushel of apples for payment, complaining about how hard times are out in the country."

I started to mention that maybe I was one of those hick farmers and maybe times were hard out in the country, but I still hadn't got over her hair, and I didn't want to start something on my very first day. So I just nodded. And blushed.

Along about 11:00 she gave us the first of two math tests we had to pass before we could work the floor. Fifty problems: half addition and subtraction to two decimal places and half multiplication and division, also to two decimal places. Two decimal places meant dollars and cents, I figured. I did it all in my head, wrote down the answers in the neat little country-girl script that I'd learned from Miss Maud Gentry at Dorland-Bell School, and handed Mable my paper.

She looked at me appraisingly over her half-glasses and then we both tried not to stare at Mr. Breed, who was sweating like a mule in the traces. He was covering his paper and a spare sheet besides with columns of figures and then erasing half of them and beginning again. It got to be 11:30. I distinctly heard Mable's stomach rumble, and from where I was sitting, Mr. Breed looked to be halfway home. But now he was into some division and up against it.

By 11:45 and Mable was entertaining herself by comparing my paper to an answer sheet she retrieved from the desk. She held both pages carefully up to the well-lit window and stared through her reading glasses to make this comparison. After she was done, she gave me a suspicious look, and it occurred to me that she must think I'd cheated somehow. Maybe because Uncle Frank might have known about the test.

"Josephine," she muttered. "Have you seen this test before today?" That hard look over the glasses.

"No, ma'am." I said it with some spunk because I didn't care for her implications.

"What's seventeen times seventeen?"

I told her. "Two hundred eighty-nine."

"What's seventeen point seventeen times three?"

"Fifty-one dollars and fifty-one cents."

"Who said anything about dollars and cents?"

"It's a bank, isn't it?"

She almost smiled. Not quite but close. "What's one hundred fifty-six divided by twelve?"

"Easy," I said. It was starting to feel like a game. "Thirteen."

"What's twelve divided by thirteen?"

That one gave me pause, but not for long. "Ninety-two cents if you round off your amount."

She did smile then. And winked. That was her third wink of the morning.

We both turned back to Mr. Breed, who had been brought to the point of desperation by the last five or six problems in the set. "I can't concentrate with you two talking numbers," he whined and swiped at his forehead with a nice, sharply folded handkerchief from his breast pocket.

"That's alright," Mable said. "I'm sure you've answered enough to show me what you can do. Let me have your paper." And then once she had his sheets of pencil scrawl and erasures in hand, she told us "I call it lunch time. See you both back here at one o'clock. And don't be late. The head cashier wants to give you two his standard lecture."

Mable was right. It was a lecture. By Mr. Foster Reynolds, who joined us from his office somewhere on the second floor. He went on for the better part of an hour, a dapper little man whose hair was so plastered to his scalp with treatment that it looked like it had been combed with a garden rake. During his hour of public relations blather, he asked us a lot of questions and answered them all himself. I can give you the gist of it because I took notes, in the beginning because I thought there might be a test, and then later, when he got going good, it was like watching a political speech or a country preacher on full throttle. I wasn't sure at the time what half of it meant, but he made it sound important as hell.

"Who knows what Robert E. Lee said about the South?" That's how he started out.

Mr. Breed and I shook our heads; we didn't know. Mable knew but wasn't telling.

Mr. Foster Reynolds thrust his forefinger into the air. "Lee said that when to the intelligence of Southern men we have added the wholesale instinct of saving money, no race will equal us!" Reynolds stared at us triumphantly.

"Did he say anything about Central Bank and Trust?" Breed asked tentatively.

"Noooo, but only because we didn't exist when Lee was alive. We were not chartered until 1903. But we exist because of the foresight and attitude of people like General Lee, who understood the absolute value in saving and investing money."

Didn't Robert Lee manage to burn down half a continent and still lose the war? Which I thought but didn't say out loud.

"The bank is the cornerstone of civilized society, and this bank, Mr. Breed and Josephine, *this* bank is at the very center of civilization in Western North Carolina and in the thriving metropolis of Asheville. Before he died, when Mr. Grove needed money for one of his projects, where did he come to?"

"Here?" It seemed incredible to me that Grove ever needed a bank. That's how naïve I was.

"Yesss, Jospehine!" Reynolds was so excited, he hissed. "Yesss. He walked through the front door of this institution, took the private elevator up to the third floor, and stated his needs, which we were happy to fulfill, just like now when we extend the same courtesy to Mr. Seely, Mr. Grove's son-in-law. Under the leadership of men like our formidable mayor, Mr. Gallatin Roberts, we are building a new and greater city. Everywhere you look, a beautiful new building is under construction. No more log cabins out back, no more mules in the livery stable! Why, right now, there are at least thirty automobiles parked in Pack Square alone, and the street cars are running day and night.

"What is this bank?" He stared at us, Breed and me, as if we constituted a crowd.

"The cornerstone of . . . society?" Breed tried.

"Oh yes, every bit of that. And even more importantly, we . . . are . . . the . . . future. Remember that!" This time he wagged his finger for emphasis. "As the city grows under Mr. Roberts' leadership to include the surrounding areas, we will become known as *Greater Asheville*, and money will come flooding into this bank like a river, a veritable river. And you, Mr. Breed, and you, Josephine, will be a part of what makes this bank gleam like a beacon on a hill."

He suddenly switched directions. "And just who do you think should come to us at Central Bank and Trust with their money? Who?" He paused to lower his voice. "Everybody should come. Each little lady with her allowance from her husband. Each child whose parents have the foresight to teach them the wisdom of saving money. Even if it's only a pittance. Even a dollar will do! Say it after me . . ."

"Even a dollar will do." Breed and I together, mesmerized.

"Even a dollar will do . . . because a dollar deposited at Central Bank and Trust will become ten dollars, and in time, a hundred dollars, and as Greater Asheville grows and grows, that child who walked through our front doors, holding on to his mother with one hand and his dollar bill with the other, will end up living in Biltmore Forest or Grove Glen or Kenilworth and parking his Packard Roadster on Pack Square. What do you think of that?"

"How much interest does . . ." I started but Mr. Foster Reynolds cut me off.

"That child will be part of something. He will belong to our vision of a city and a region that is more modern and wealthier than any in America. Now remember this, write it down if you need to. Say it to yourself over and over so that you can repeat it to our customers when they walk in the door. *As the city grows, Central Bank and Trust grows; and as the bank grows, each customer grows. Until every man is his own Vanderbilt!* . . . Have you got it?"

What about every woman? I thought. Who is she?

"Every man his own . . . Vanderbilt." Breed was mouthing the words as he wrote them out with his pencil.

Foster Reynolds glanced at me. "Got it," I told him. "City grows, bank grows, every man a Vanderbilt."

"Yesss," he said.

The second-floor training broke up mid-afternoon. Mr. Breed and I were to return the next morning for one more session with Mable plus the second math test and then begin shadowing an experienced cashier. As we were leaving, Mable pulled me aside. She held one ink-stained finger up to her lips, and we paused to let Breed trudge wearily on down the hall toward the stairs. After a moment, she shut the door quietly behind him, leaving us alone in the training room.

"Listen, dearie," she said. "Do you want some advice?"

I nodded. "All I can get," I said.

"Well, then. Two things for now. One, don't show off. Don't let them see how fast you are with the math. It only upsets them." I started to speak but she shook her head to shush me. "Listen, Breed is a dolt. You and I know that, but he's the son of a prominent lawyer in town, and so there's a place for him at the bank. He will be paid ten cents an hour more than you for doing the same job and doing it poorly. Don't let it upset you and don't show off. Keep your own counsel and before long, they'll discover just how much they need you."

"Is that what happened to you?"

She smiled and nodded.

"You said there were two things . . ."

"Two for today." She said it as if there were a lot more lessons to follow. "Do something with your hair."

"What do you mean?" I asked. I had my mother's hair, shades of nut brown with hints of red woven in, and I was proud of it.

"It hangs nearly to your waist, dearie. And everybody in this town who sees it knows at a glance that you just climbed down off the turnip wagon from Madison County."

"What should I do?"

"For now, put it up in a bun on the back of your head. Let 'em see your neck."

I nodded, and she started to open the door.

"Wait," I said. "How do you get away with . . . that?" I gestured at the fire-engine red mass on top of her own head.

She grinned. "I get away with it because I'm an institution," she said. She gestured around us at the second floor. "I get away with it because I trained all these little cock-suckers. Including Mister Foster Reynolds."

5

I FIGURED THAT IF ANYBODY KNEW what she was talking about when it came to the inner workings of Central Bank and Trust, it was Mable the institution. Day two, I swept my hair back and rolled it up into a bun on the back of my head. Five bobby pins. After all, I'd done something similar every day when I went outside to work on the farm. Try hoeing out corn rows with your hair hanging down around your face dripping sweat and you get the idea why. I would have asked Sissy what she thought, but she was still asleep when I left the house that morning to walk to the bank. Her Realtor didn't expect her till mid-morning.

The other thing I tried was face powder. I had found a powder compact in my mother's ancient pocketbook. A little round number that she could only have bought at Penland's Store in Marshall. I'd seen her use it once or twice on a Sunday, so I had a vague idea. I took the soft little puff and threw a little on my nose and cheekbones, figuring to hide the freckles if nothing else. And then puffed a little more hoping to get something like an even effect.

So there I was. My legs freshly shaved—for the first time above the knee—my hair up, and my nose powdered. Nobody stared at me on the sidewalk while I was walking to the bank, so I must not have gone too far wrong.

As I walked along that morning, I told myself that I was going to buy myself a dictionary. The trouble with my brain was that it was chock-full of numbers—numbers everywhere and in constant motion like fish in a pond. It was the words that sometimes tripped me up and made me feel less able. Already, I'd been dealt *lithe* and *lissome*, *panties* and *stockings*, and here I was heading to day two with Mable, who had *moxie*. One week in town and the vocabulary was already etching a new wrinkle in my brain.

When Mable strode into the second-floor training room, she glanced at me and nodded. "Better," she said. I nodded back.

That morning, we talked ethics. There was a brief review of the day before: savings versus checking, personal versus business, passbook. But the most of it was our responsibility in the handling of the bank's money. Not other people's money but the bank's money. The bank's money was sacred. It passed through our hands; therefore, it was necessary that we touch it, count it, record it, but then it went on into its proper bin. We were never to be tempted to hold on to any of it, even if there was no record of our having touched it.

"Do you understand what I'm saying?" Mable was staring mostly at Mr. Breed, and for once, her tone was serious to the point of threatening.

"Thou shalt not steal," I said.

"Precisely," she said. "And if you do, thou shalt go to jail."

And again, just before lunchtime came the second math test. To me, it was just like the first test, except that now the numbers before the decimal were much larger. I recall there was *1,456.88*. I remember it because I liked the sequence 4-5-6 and the double 8s. There were a lot of numbers like that, all the way up to hundreds of thousands. *358,456.73* and such. Whoever had made the test loved that 4-5-6.

Again, I did the operations in my head and wrote down the answers as neatly as a schoolteacher. But this time, to save embarrassing poor Mr. Breed the dolt, I actually worked out the last five problems on paper, just to stall for time, and checked the answers I'd already written down. The answers were right except I'd let my decimal drift once, for which I rapped myself on the knuckles with the pencil.

I could have saved myself some time, though. Mr. Breed was mired down somewhere in the early problems, and I thought Mable and I might both starve before she mercifully took the paper from him. This time she didn't test me while we waited. This time, she knew that I knew.

THE AFTERNOON OF DAY TWO was given over to shadowing a real cashier. We'd do that for a day or more, then a few days being shadowed by Mable or some other experienced person, and then . . . on some high, holy day, we'd be on our own behind the ornate little bars that separated us and the money from the public.

I thought it was going to be thrilling, fascinating—the touch of hundreds of dollars in and out of the till, numbers everywhere. And I thought for sure it would beat the hell out of farm work. And in some ways, it was . . . and it did.

But the shadowing part, at least on that day-two afternoon, was tedious to the point where I thought I'd have to jab myself with a pencil to stay awake. I was assigned to a Mr. Sherrill, no first name that I ever heard. He was a quiet, prim little man, shorter than I was. Each time a customer came up to his window, he would greet them in a soft voice, smiling briefly, and then treat them as precisely as an adding machine. His hands were soft, his nails manicured, and he didn't make a single mistake.

He did tell me at one point that he was used to being shadowed by new cashiers and to ask him any questions I had. I stood at his shoulder whenever he had a customer, my hands clasped behind my back to keep them out of the way, and I watched his hands. He favored a mechanical pencil and he would point with this pencil to the various operations that he carried out when he recorded something in his transaction log. The pointing was for my benefit, so that I could track what was going on. And it did help, for the first half-dozen times or so, but after that, I had it. Savings and checking, personal and business, passbook.

Mostly it was children or old people who had passbook accounts. Or farmers and loggers in from the country, who were proud of the fact that they owned a bank account, with the passbook for proof. And even more proud when the numbers in the little book increased before their very eyes. They were fascinated when Mr. Sherrill recorded and initialed a deposit in their passbooks and would grin at him through the grill with the same tobacco-stained teeth as my brothers up home.

As the afternoon wore on, however, there were fewer and fewer customers of any kind. The hands on the large clock over the door—with its wooden case and Roman numerals—slowed to a crawl and began, I thought, to slip backward. My feet hurt from standing attentively at Mr. Sherrill's shoulder, but I was afraid to move and, truthfully, there wasn't much room to move in.

"Is it always this slow in the afternoon?" I finally asked him.

To his credit, he actually turned on his stool and looked over his shoulder at me, favored me with the same quiet smile he gave the customers. "Just you wait till Friday," he said. "Come Friday afternoon, it's worse than the drug store in here."

The next day, day three, I caught a break. Mable assigned me to Jezebel Rodgers, and by mid-morning, she was Jezzy and I was Jo. Jezzy was the opposite of Mr. Sherrill. She was all personality and pizzazz, which was another new word for me. Mable had moxie, and Jezzy had pizzazz.

She smiled at the women and had little candy suckers for the children. She was solemn and respectful to the older men, some of whom maneuvered the line to get to her window. You could tell they liked looking at her, and after Mr. Sherrill, no wonder.

But it was with the younger men that she worked her magic. When some young swain strolled up to her window, it was as if somebody turned a light on inside her. She would tilt her head forward and look up through her eyelashes at him. Her voice would begin to purr. And if he responded in kind, lingering at the window and smiling in at her, she would lean back and laugh, even if he hadn't said anything funny—lean back and let him see where her blouse was not so primly buttoned and get the full effect of her shaking her short hair.

She had a fine time whenever a good-looking young man came to her window, and he had a fine time too.

Her addition and subtraction, however, suffered while a good time was being had by all. Her numbers could go astray when she didn't even bother to look down at what her fingers were recording. So I got in the habit of nudging her once her customer had wandered away and pointing out where her 9 and her 16 had added up to 35.

The odd thing was she didn't mind at all. She was having too much fun. And when I asked her if she didn't get in trouble when her accounts didn't total up, she only shrugged and said she always checked them at the end of the day, and on a busy day, showed them to Mable before turning in her book. "Mable fusses," she admitted. "And tells me that Jezebel is a good name for me. Which it is, don't you think?"

I did think. But also, it was impossible not to like Jezzy, at least for me.

And then that afternoon, he appeared on the scene. He didn't come to Jezzy's window to transact any financials but rather strode right down the middle of the lobby past all the cashiers and made for the steps leading to the upper floors.

"Oh, my goodness," Jezzy muttered as he walked by. I looked up from checking her figures. "Will you look at the rear end on that man."

I did look, and his trousers were tight enough so that his hams were certainly there to be seen, and I didn't mind the looking.

"Who is he?" I whispered to Jezzy, who had begun to breathe just a little faster.

"Cameron Scott. His father's a doctor. His grandfather was a governor or something."

"I'm sure, but what's he got to say for himself?"

"He's just a flirt, mostly. And whatever he's doing upstairs, he's doing it for his father. But here's the thing, Jo . . ." She turned on her stool to face me and look earnestly into my eyes. "His family is richer than sin. Money falls out of their pockets, and they don't even notice."

"Richer than Mrs. Vanderbilt?"

"Lord no. Not even God is richer than her. But rich. They just built a house out in Biltmore Forest that looks like a mansion."

"Have you seen it?"

"Not inside, but I convinced one of my dates to drive me by it, and it's bigger than . . . than the high school."

I nodded, smiling at her. "Well, how are you going to get inside it?"

"Oh, that's easy," she said. "I'm going to marry Cameron."

I laughed outright.

Someone cleared his throat. We both turned, and then leaned forward to peer out the window and over the counter, where an ancient little man was staring up at us. "I'd like to make a deposit, please," he croaked, "in the amount of eleven dollars and twenty-five cents."

6

THAT EVENING AT DINNER—IT MUST have been a Wednesday—I mentioned that I saw Cameron Scott at the bank that afternoon, just to see what sort of response he elicited from Uncle Frank. But even before Frank had time to reply, Sissy surprised us all with an audible moan.

"Sissy, are you ill?" Aunt Brenda asked.

"No, mother, it's just that he's so dreamy."

"Cameron Scott?" I know I sounded doubtful. "The doctor's son?"

"One and the same," Sissy replied. "I think he's the best dressed young man in town. And ohhh, he can dance." More of a squeal than a moan.

Frank Junior looked up from his plate of fried chicken just long enough to shake his head at his sister's sound effects.

"That's neither here nor there, whether the boy can dance," Uncle Frank said. "It's what his father's done with the family money that's impressive."

Frank Senior laid down his knife and fork. Apparently, the Scott family money was so important a topic that he couldn't chew food and discuss it at the same time. "Money is like water, Josephine," he said. He was speaking to me, but you could tell by the tone of his voice that he meant this sermon for the whole family. "It must be kept moving, always moving. You buy a lot one day, you hold on to it for a week or a month, till the value has risen, even if only a few hundred dollars, and you sell it. You can't get attached to it; if you hold on to it, the money dies. Next, you buy two lots, hold on to one while its value grows and sell the other. You watch where the city is going to grow—north around that new lake in Baird Bottom, south into Biltmore Forest, east up in Kenilworth—where the action is, and you buy. You spend every penny to buy, so you can sell later on when everybody else in town suddenly realizes they must have that lot.

"That's what Grove did. That's what the Westall brothers do. And if I say so myself, that's what I do, but on a humbler scale." He smiled modestly.

"But what does that have to do with dreamy Cameron Scott?" I asked.

"It has to do because his father, Doctor Craig Scott, is a master of the art. He bought up property out beyond the Biltmore Station, adjacent to the Vanderbilt holding, when it was nothing but woods and played-out farms. Then he held on to it while Biltmore Village grew up around the train station and that little cathedral that George Vanderbilt constructed before he died."

"So he kept his money moving?"

"Exactly. Money either moves or it dies. Dr. Scott could have lived in that little bungalow over in Montford that he inherited from his father, but no, he took every dime that he made practicing medicine, and he spent it on real estate. And I might add, real estate that everyone else thought was worthless. I came in on the end of it, and as a young banker, I even counseled him not to throw his money away south of town. But he was right, and I was too green in the game to see what he was doing."

"And now he's rich," Frank Junior added. Obviously having heard this homily before.

"Now he's more than rich. Craig Scott, along with the Westalls and Pinkney Starnes of Imperial Life . . . the handful of local men who figured it all out. And it was Craig and the Westalls who made their money the smart way, fast with real estate. You look at the Westall boys, who started out in the lumber business, and you'd never know they had a dime, but Craig Scott, on the other hand, he knows how to enjoy his money. Just built himself a mansion on one of his own lots in Biltmore Forest, and now they're building a brand-new, modern hospital in Biltmore Village on land he sold to the town."

"Isn't that . . .?" I didn't know what word I was looking for . . . *crooked* maybe.

"Nope. It ain't nothing but keeping your money moving. Why do you think I wanted Sissy to go to work for the Asheville Development Company?"

"So she can keep her money moving?"

Uncle Frank laughed outright. "No, she doesn't have any money to move. But I do. And I figure it doesn't hurt to have a . . ." Here he lowered his voice. ". . . a spy on the inside. See where the other smart boys in town are looking at lots and putting up buildings. What's hot and what's not."

I glanced at Sissy to see how she was taking all this. She was grinning at her father.

"Besides," he said, "if she plays her cards right, she can meet a smart young man on the rise while she's in the real estate office."

"Show him some property," Sissy said. For a second, I thought she meant her boobs. And after another, longer moment, I was sure that's what she meant.

Uncle Frank was nodding and grinning. "Some property . . . But the main thing, Josephine, is that this city is growing constantly, and if I and the other men in charge have anything to say about it, it will keep right on growing. And what's more, I plan to take advantage of it. I have an announcement to make." He paused and sat up straighter in his chair, glancing at each of us in turn to make sure we were all sufficiently attentive. "Today, family, I bought one of the finest lots in Lake View Park."

This time, Sissy really did squeal. Even Frank Junior perked up.

He continued. "And this lot, I'm not going to sell. This lot I intend to build on. Oh, it may not be as big and grand as Stratford Towers or a Moorish castle like the Campbell place, but it will double the size of this modest abode." He gestured around him to make sure we knew he meant the modest abode where we sat. "I intend to do this family proud."

Shorthand for doing himself proud.

He held up one large, white hand. "This is real estate." He held up the other. "This is cash." He rubbed both hands together luxuriously and sighed. "Put the one with the other, and the friction causes an explosion."

AFTER FRANK GOT THROUGH MOANING and groaning about Lake View Park, and Sissy got through moaning and groaning about Cameron Scott, which I thought amounted to roughly the same thing, I helped Pansy clear the table, which she fussed about, but I did every night anyway.

"I hate being waited on," I told her, like I did every night.

"Don't care," she would reply, "you going to do me out of a job."

"Doubt it," I would say. "I hate frying chicken." Which would almost make her smile.

That night, when it was just the two of us in the kitchen, I asked her what she thought.

"About what?"

"All that money and property, property and money."

"What I think don't matter," she muttered, dropping a handful of silverware into a pan of soapy water, so that it splashed onto the counter. And the mood, half-playful before, suddenly shifted in a way I didn't understand. Turned ugly somehow.

"I don't mean anything by asking."

"I know you don't mean nothing," she growled, low in her throat, so that no one could hear from the dining room. "You a country gal and you ignorant of how things work in this town."

"Can I learn?"

She shook her head, slowly, still not willing to look at me, and then harder, as if trying to dislodge something from her mind. "Some things you don't want to learn," was all she would say.

Sissy and I went for a walk that night so that she could smoke a cigarette or two . . . well, maybe three . . . in peace. We strolled north along Charlotte Street, away from downtown, toward a park she knew, where the Grovewood Real Estate office was.

After a bit of aimless chatter, with her blowing her smoke out of the far side of her mouth, she slipped in a question about Cameron Scott, and I realized what she really wanted to talk about.

I liked Sissy, especially the way she had sassed her father—*show some property*—without Uncle Frank even realizing it. So I told her what little I could, including what Jezebel had told me. That Mr. Cameron Scott was in and out of the bank running errands for his father; that she had driven by the Scott place out in Biltmore Forest; that he was rich; and oh yes, her plan was to get inside the mansion by marrying Cameron.

I also added a few thoughts of my own. That unless I missed my guess, the suit the boy was wearing would have fed a poor family for a week; that the smirk on his face when he went through the bank lobby made him look downright silly; and that he seemed sinfully proud of his own buttocks.

It's a good thing that Sissy and I had already declared our friendship because she got downright testy at some of this. *Of course* he was in and out of the bank running errands for Dr. Cameron Scott Senior; the smirk was simply the smile of a self-confident man; and he was not—repeat, *not*—fair game for any lowly bank teller. Having forgotten in the heat of the moment that becoming a bank teller was my ambition.

Furthermore, one of his lovely suits would probably feed a poor family for a month, not a week; that he had every right to smile at the world, wouldn't you if you were him; that she personally would love to get her hands on his strong and manly butt. That she would know what to do if she ever did. And in sum, Cammy Scott was . . . dreamy.

"What did you just call him?"

"Dreamy?"

"No, *Cammy* for God's sake. Do you know this boy?"

She turned on the sidewalk to face me and puffed herself up like a chicken. "Not in the biblical sense. Not yet. But I've danced with him three times at the Club, and I've necked with him in the parking lot once. And upon examination, I believe I can safely say that he is not a boy. He is a man."

"Jesus."

"I know. But it's a secret. You can't tell a soul because it's all part of my grand plan."

"Which is?" We had reached the park Sissy had told me about, with the little stone building that housed the Grovewood Real Estate office. Across the street was what looked like some kind of church. It was almost full dark and getting colder. It was town cold rather than raw, country cold, but even so. We stood on the porch of the office just long enough for her to light one more cigarette and then started back. And as we walked, she told me the utterly bizarre story of the Royal Rhododendron Festival.

And when she first described it, I thought she must have been stealing liquor out of her father's cabinet and sucking it down before dinner because what she described didn't sound real.

7

Oh, my god, jo, you don't know about the Royal Rhododendron Festival, with the king and queen and the Royal Court? Where have you been?"

"Basically, in the middle of nowhere," I admitted. It was dark enough while we were walking back so that I couldn't really make out Sissy's face, and I assumed she had to be joking. "Never heard of the Royal Begonia Festival."

"Rhododendron! It started last year in June with some old garden club ladies, but the newspapers got hold of it, and all the major boosters have decided that it's the key to getting tourists into town. There will be parades and balls and events and awards. I cannot wait."

"Why June?" But even as I said it, I thought I knew. June was gorgeous in the mountains. A hundred shades of green on the hills and weather just warm enough to make a deacon smile.

"June is the start of tourist season." That was Sissy's answer. "It's like the doors open up to the mountains, and the flatlanders start to flood in from everywhere. And with the tourists come tourist money. And once they're here, they fall in love with bucolic Asheville and they want to—"

"Buy a lot?"

"Exactly. So once people like my boss and all the other real estate developers realized that they needed more people to come here in order to keep their money moving, they decided to take over the sad little garden club thing they had last year and turn it into something spectacular."

By that point I realized she was completely serious. It wasn't a joke. She was starting to sound like a real estate booster herself... bucolic and spectacular! "So what's your plan?" I asked her.

"Huh?"

"You said it was all part of your grand plan to get your hands on Cameron Scott's butt. Are you going to tackle him behind a parade float?"

"God no . . . Well, maybe. But I hope it won't be so . . . so direct as that. No, my plan is that he will be king and I will be queen. And we'll have to spend days and nights together for weeks. Or at least we'll both be in the Royal Court, so we'll still be thrown together all over town, and he will have ample opportunity to get his nice, sweet hands on me."

I started laughing. "Nights together?"

This time she was so excited that she blew the smoke from her Lucky Strike straight in my face. "*Royal* nights together!"

I couldn't sleep that night, not after the first few hours. I dreamed I was up home, cooking a meal with my mother. My mother of several years ago, when she was younger, and in the dream, we were almost the same age. I don't know, thirty or forty maybe, but still mother and daughter, for she was directing things as she was wont to do in the kitchen.

She burned herself on the woodstove and said "damn" right out loud, which I had only heard her do once or twice in my whole life. This alone was a sign that our relationship in the dream was somehow mixed up in time, for she would never curse in front of me if I was just her daughter. I was the one with the wicked tongue, not her.

We were roasting a chicken along with pans of biscuits and a big old pot of green beans. Baked apples. And some kind of pie.

I knew what it was in the dream but had trouble remembering when I woke. Blackberry maybe. Papa favors blackberry.

And as we were working along, both of us sweating from the heat of the woodstove, she was telling me about some boy she knew before Papa. And by all that's holy, she was talking about his hips and his thighs. I was astonished that she should know about such things, should think of such things even if she did know about them. His thighs were as tight as a bow string, she kept saying.

Well, good God, Mama, what did you do about his bow strings? I said in the dream. Another sign that our relationship was folded up in time, for I never could have said anything like this to her in life.

Why, honey, I did everything nature required and then some, she said. And kept right on doing it for one whole summer. Did you not ever stop to wonder why your oldest brother, William, doesn't favor the rest of you?

Well, where did you do it? I said, not stopping to bother about William.

More than once't in a barn loft, she said, matter of factly, wiping the sweat off her forehead with her apron, but the hay itched him and his fine, pale skin to death. We found the church was the best place, for nobody goes there during the week except of a Wednesday.

The church!

In amongst the pews, honey. On a pallet of your clothes. And when she said this, she leaned over and tapped me on the shoulder with an ancient wooden spoon she was using to stir the beans. You should try it, she said, but use some padding'.

As you can imagine, this dream brought me fully awake, aching with how much I missed her. Though we never really talked like this when she was alive, apparently, we could now that she was dead.

When I pulled up out of that dream, I started to weep like a baby lamb who can't find her woolly mama and that nice, warm teat. Wept till I hiccupped there in that still-strange bed in that foolishly large house on Charlotte Street.

I tossed and turned for thirty minutes or so, and then I decided to find myself a tonic. A tonic is what eases you to sleep when your worries are too much to bear. Some people swear by warm milk, as did my mother. But my father favored a stronger fix.

When mama was laid up with her final sickness and then again after she died, neither he nor I could sleep through the night. I would get up and go to him, where he sat by the midnight fireplace, rocking and rocking. I'd complain to him that I couldn't sleep and he'd grunt and fix me what he called a toddy.

His receipt for the toddy was a quarter glass or so of his white corn liquor, with honey from the bees and a quarter glass or so of hot water from the kettle. He'd add a little sugar too, if there was any on the table. He took *his* medicine—the corn whiskey—straight with a thimbleful of water for he was a tough old codger, or so he said.

He would sup his and I would sup mine, and we didn't need to say much of anything, for our knowing was intertwined, so much a fabric of kinship that we knew each other's thoughts well enough. Each pain, each ache, each sudden wish. Sometimes he'd grunt and I'd nod, or I'd sigh and he'd wink, and that was all it took to make up a conversation. Once or twice I cried, and he held my hand, his own hand a bony web of calluses and crooked fingers.

So what was I to do this night, when he was thirty miles away, by himself, without his only daughter to comfort him? And here I was at number 46 Charlotte Street with neither a mother nor father except in the haunted fields of my dreams.

Here's what I decided. I decided that I was my father's daughter, damn it, and my mother's. I decided I could make my own toddy. So I crept along in my nightgown, which also had been my mother's, a warm flannel number that stretched almost to my feet. Crept to the head of the stairs, paused to listen, and then eased on down, taking care to sneak along close to the wall, where the treads wouldn't creak.

The house was as dark as an Egyptian tomb, which I imagined to be pretty damn dark.

I found the doorway to Uncle Frank's study, where I knew he kept his liquor in a decanter on the sideboard. Tennessee Bourbon, he called it, which sounded foreign to me—decanter and bourbon both—but of the same general principle as Papa's mason jar and corn whiskey. I inched open the door to the study and tiptoed along barefoot till I came to the sideboard.

There was moonlight in through the high windows of the study, so I could see quite well. Well enough to put my hand on a glass and pour it half full of this bourbon Uncle Frank was always going on about. I sipped it but had to stop to blow like a horse for a long moment. By taste, it already had the honey in it, which I found convenient, but it needed some water or something to cut it.

So I eased along to the kitchen and with a splash of water, fashioned what I later learned was called bourbon and branch at the club, which then as now, I like just fine. Especially the word *branch*; I know first-hand what a branch is.

I walked all over the house that night excepting the bedrooms, step by step, sip by sip, and discovered anew what I'd suspected all along. It was big by daylight, but it loomed larger and larger in the dark. Three or four times the size of the Rock House on Big Pine Creek where I'd grown up.

This house was huge and empty and dark, excepting where shreds of moonlight plus the glimmer from a streetlight or two filtered in past the curtains. It felt devoid of anything truly human, once the Morgans were all asleep and Pansy was gone for the night.

Thirty miles to the north, my Papa was sitting alone by the old, stone fireplace, savoring his own medicine along with the heat from a bed of hot coals. Flickering light from a stick of oak or maple thrown on to blaze. He was missing Mama, and he was missing me, his Josie. And I wondered had he slept at all.

I was the same, missing all that had ever mattered to me, especially him now that he was as lonely as I was. Lonely as two old stumps in the middle of a field, the both of us. Except that he was in his own chair, rocking before his own hearth, sipping whiskey he'd stilled himself.

Here I was making do with bourbon from Tennessee—or was it Kentucky? Made by some fool old men I'd never meet nor know. Somewhere far away from my real home and my true family.

And when I finally lay back down, yawning in the wee hours, I couldn't imagine why this family I'd come to live with would want a larger house—a much finer estate, Uncle Frank had called it—when this one was so dark and empty.

8

DAY FOUR AT THE BANK, and Mable assigned me again to Jezzy Rodgers, which was just fine with me. You could learn more about the town from eight hours of Jezzy than you could from eight days of taking the newspaper.

When I look back on it now, I also wonder if Mable—she of the flaming red hair—didn't also want to see how I would react to Jezzy's account keeping, which could be just as freewheeling at times as her commentary.

During the morning, I heard about the other bank employees that we could see from our little cubicle or who walked through the lobby on business. I learned to call the junior members who worked the windows—mostly women—tellers, and the senior members—mostly men—cashiers. All the way up to the head cashier, Foster Reynolds—he of the plastered hair—who wasn't really a cashier at all but a manager who spent all his time on the second floor.

The highlight of the morning for me was when the front doors of the bank swung open and in strode none other than Uncle Andy Robbins. Uncle Andy was not my blood uncle but rather honorary uncle to everybody on Big Pine. He was headed back toward the two cubicles that handled loan transactions and wouldn't have seen me at all if I hadn't broken a dozen bank guidelines and called out to him.

He bent over to peer in at the row of cubicle windows, and when he saw me, his eyebrows rose up dramatically, and he pointed a finger to mime aiming a pistol, which was how he always greeted me even as a little girl. He strode on toward the back of the lobby, but I knew he'd stop to visit on the way out. Uncle Andy would visit with a lamppost.

"Who in the world is that?" whispered Jezzy.

I told her his name.

"How do you know him?"

"Know him! I grew up a half mile from his farm on Doe Branch. Everybody in Madison County knows him."

"But he's wearing overalls."

"So what? Those are his going-to-town overalls." It was true. The overalls were clean and ironed, plus his good white shirt was buttoned up to his neck. "You should see what he wears six days a week," I said to Jezzy.

A half-hour by the bank clock passed, and here he came back again, and just as I suspected, he stopped at our window to visit. There was a nice town lady in front of our window and he paused politely in line behind her. I say politely, even though he was entertaining Jezzy and me the whole time—first by making antic faces and then, when the lady's transaction went on for a bit, by yawning comically and scratching his head. Finally, by pretending to fall asleep standing up.

When the lady eventually shuffled away, he stepped up to our window big as life, grinning all over his face. He reached one big, calloused paw between the little bars to grasp my hand warmly and then shake Jezzy's as well, his big, rough mitt swallowing her white fingers whole.

"What are you doing here?" I whispered, for by now it was obvious that he was drawing a lot of attention, something like having a bear wander out of the woods into a cocktail party.

"I come into town to pay on my boy's loan. This here bank holds the note on his tobacco acreage, and his wife is so pregnant that he dursen't leave her. So I came in to pay on his note, see if they'd front us another five hundred so we could add some land further up Doe Branch . . ."

This was big news in our part of the world, but I could tell Jezzy was losing interest fast.

"Did they give you the money?" I whispered.

"Hell no," he said. "First time they ever turned us down. And money up home as hard to find as a . . ." He paused, staring at Jezzy, and I knew that all his *hard-to-finds* were vulgar.

"On the way home, will you stop off and see Papa? Tell him I miss him."

Uncle Andy nodded. "Yup. I'll come in next month as well. See if them tight-asses in back . . ." He nodded toward the loan section, ". . . have loosened up any."

I nodded at him so hard that I could feel the pins in my hair loosening. Country women don't cry in public, you understand, but my eyes were damp, just at the sound of a familiar voice, talking the language I'd grown up with, the way English was meant to be spoken.

Uncle Andy nodded to me and winked broadly at Jezzy. "Pleased to meet you, Miss Jezebel," he said and shambled on off, his brogans squeaking on the polished floor.

"Did he just call the loan officers tight-asses?" Jezzy whispered to me.

I nodded, smiling.

"Well . . ." she giggled, looking down at her account book. "They mostly are. But, Jo, what was that smell?"

"Vicks. Ever since the flu epidemic, he rubs it all over his chest from November till spring. Claims he never gets sick."

After lunch, there was the usual lull, and for some reason I can't recall, Jezzy began telling me about her previous Saturday night, when she'd gone on a date with a man she'd been seeing off and on. A real estate agent, of course, on the make, and because he'd just sold a house, he had some cash. You have to imagine her telling it, getting more excited as she went.

"He had some ready money for once and had borrowed his boss's auto-mobile. You'll never guess in a thousand years where he took me!" She paused expectantly. "The Sky Club, up on the mountain."

"Never heard of it," I whispered, trying by example to get her to lower her voice.

"Oh God, the Sky Club, Jo! It's the best, most mysterious, most fun place in the world, or at least in this burg. There's jazz most every night up on the second floor, and dancing. Steaks to make your mouth water. An honest-to-God bar, despite all the laws, and a bartender who never speaks, just smiles. Did I say there was dancing already?"

I nodded.

"So Billy took me and another couple up there. We had a table all to ourselves, and it was glorious. We saw that old chief of police, not with his wife but some other woman. We saw one of the Directors from the bank, a dentist, and him sitting at the end of the bar, turning his face away whenever anyone got close . . . And we saw *him*."

"Who's him?"

She gazed at me in expectation. "Arrowood . . . We actually saw him."

"I'm sorry . . . Arrowood?"

"Oh, Jo. I promise we're going to get you out and about. Next time, I'll make Billy take you with us. Somewhere, anywhere. Arrowood owns the Sky Club. Or at least he manages it for the gangsters up north who really own it. He always wears a tuxedo, plus he always has a cigar in his hand but never smokes it. Anybody tries to speak to him, he only nods and smiles. The women, oh, my God, Jo, the women throw themselves at him, but he only smiles and slips away. And he's beautiful."

"I don't trust your notions of beautiful. You said Cameron Scott was beautiful."

"Yeah, well. Maybe Arrowood isn't what you'd call beautiful, but he is thin and hard and . . . They say he's killed at least three men. Men who made trouble at the club or tried to cut in on his bootlegging operation. He disposed of them. And whenever there's a fight, he and the bartender put out the lights and thrash whoever caused the trouble."

"*Thrash* them, do they?" I had to smile.

"And throw them out into the parking lot."

"Do they thrash the women?"

"No, they slap them silly and stow them in the backseat of their cars. I've seen it."

"Really?"

"No, but I heard all about it. Nobody knows where Arrowood came from and nobody knows who he really is. He's a . . . a legend."

"Does he have a first name?"

Jezzy shrugged. "Nobody knows that either. He's just Arrowood. Dark and wicked."

But neither Uncle Andy Robbins nor the legend of Arrowood, dark and dangerous, was the keynote of that day. Jezebel's ledger book . . . that was the item that sang out.

You see, the problem was that Jezebel Rodgers couldn't add and subtract. Or at least not numbers greater than 100 and especially not when she was excited. As for the decimal, it skittered around in Jezebel's math like a little black bug, showing up first one place, then another.

In short, Jezzy had her own brand of style and dash, but so did her math. Shadowing her was perfect training for me.

When I first began with her, a small electrical shock would zip down my spine every time I watched her write down the wrong number from a customer's passbook or record one sum here and another there, or—worst of all—confuse her addition and subtraction in a way that would hopelessly snarl her day's totals. I had a physical reaction to that as well. The numbers that I knew at a glance were in error seemed to pulse slightly when I looked at them and then change color slightly from the black lead of the pencil to a shade of brown, and if I didn't correct them, a faded red or pink.

It had always been thus for me with numerical notation. From the time I was a small child, I had written numbers in the dirt with a stick rather than letters or words. Secretly, I thought numbers were sacred, and to see them go astray was almost painful.

I learned quickly how to silently and tactfully correct her mistakes, first by pointing and nudging, then by quickly, quietly erasing and correcting, and then finally by going over each transaction when there was a lull. But truth to tell, I needn't have been that subtle. She was fine with me checking her work as we went and then quickly, quietly auditing it both before we broke for lunch and then at the end of the day. She was justifiably terrified of Mable and grateful when I assured her that her book was perfect when I went with her at 5:30 to turn it in.

All the account books ended the day in Mable's office in back of the first floor, and when Jezzy and I went to hand in her account book, she signed and Mable countersigned the register noting its safe return. Then the oddest thing happened. Mable motioned Jezzy on out of the office and crooked her finger at me to stay.

I figured I was in trouble, and at first, it appeared I was right. Mable sat me down on the other side of her worktable and made me wait while the other tellers and cashiers turned in their accounts. And when everything was in, she told me to get myself up and shut the door.

Door closed, she asked, "how much did you help Jezzy with her book?"

I didn't know what to say, for I didn't want to get the girl in trouble.

"I know you helped her. I'm just curious when and how."

So I told her straight up. Nudging and pointing, erasing and correcting here and there. Auditing before lunch and after closing.

"How do you mean, *auditing*?"

"Checking every number against every other number that it's related to, and then running all the math again, quickly so as not to embarrass her."

"Do you do it all in your head?"

"Most of it. I use a folded piece of paper as a rule and make notes on it where I need to."

She smiled and shook her head. Then she picked another teller's account book out of the pile on the table and turned it so it was right-side-up to where I sat. "Show me," she said.

I opened the cover of the accounting record book in front of me and turned to the last page with writing, dated that day. I let my eyes roam down the columns of figures and notations. Some of the numbers, several in fact, vibrated gently, and in two places, the black lead from the penciled marks was turning that aggravating pink. Bleeding beyond pink to red.

Mable hauled herself stiffly to her feet as though she'd been sitting for several hours and walked around the table to stand beside me. I pointed to the places where I sensed the book was in error.

"Mistakes?"

I nodded. "What do you want me to do?"

"I want you to correct the mistakes while I watch. I want to see how you do it." She reached across the table and placed a large, gum eraser and a couple of pencils in front of me. "Do you need an adding machine?"

I shook my head no. "It'll slow me down."

I turned back two pages in the ledger to the beginning of the notations for that day. I folded a sheet of lined paper into what looked like a paper ruler an inch wide or so, to use as I worked my way down each page, making quick calculations and drawing lines connecting one set of numbers to another. I also let my mind go blank, so I could concentrate on each set of numbers in turn and not be distracted by the whole page. This way, I could let my eyes roam over each little thread in the weave, both vertical and horizontal.

There were three pages of notations for that day. I found mostly simple things: passbook or account codes that didn't match the overall pattern because they had one number too many or too few, missing decimals, such as that. Only three mistakes in the calculations, all on the final page, two of which (the numbers that had seemed to change colors when I first saw them) had thrown off the day's final totals for cash by $9.47.

I underscored the errant account numbers lightly with my pencil, and corrected all the math, so that each column on the three pages was precise, tight and neat, the numerals themselves folded into proper relation with all the other numbers on the page.

I looked up at Mable when I was done. At that moment, it reminded me of the simple exams she'd given Mr. Breed and me, as though this too were a test. She smiled faintly and nodded. I closed the book and stared at the cover. It belonged to one of the senior cashiers, a man named Thomas.

"He got tired at the end of the day," I said randomly.

"Is that what the numbers tell you?"

I nodded and almost giggled, but not quite. She was serious.

"Well, Jo, that took you . . . a little over two minutes. Do you know what that means?"

"I need to get faster."

She laughed outright. It was a wonderful sound that reminded me of a cowbell ringing. "Hell no," she said when she could catch her breath. "God no . . . But don't you see. This man's book is one of our cleanest. And trust me, we've got some that will slow you down." She paused, her hand on my shoulder in a friendly way. "Or maybe they won't. We'll find out."

It was dark that evening when Mable turned me loose. Six-thirty perhaps or a little later. I'd corrected three separate accounting books for her, including one that was a spider's web of mistakes. Now, when I say spider's web, I mean something sticky in your hair and in your brain, but also something with a careful and intricate pattern. I could see the pattern because most of the numbers that made up the web quavered ever so slightly within their little boxes on the lined accounting paper. When I touched it with my pencil, the web itself seemed to shudder ever so slightly as if an insect had flown into the mesh. The errors in this book were not mistakes but something else, something intentional. And the final totals were off by exactly twenty-five dollars, not a cent more and not a cent less.

It was clear the person who'd sculpted these numbers knew exactly what he was doing. Too precise, too neat, too pretty really. I said something to that effect, but Mable didn't comment, only nodded.

"Do you want me to do this every evening?" I asked her when she let me out the employee door in the alley.

"Maybe," she said. "I need to think. We'll talk tomorrow."

9

ON FRIDAY RIGHT AFTER LUNCH, the head cashier, Foster Reynolds, handed out paychecks, and I got one. I'm not sure what I expected to happen, or when, but there it was in my hand. Pay came in the form of a beige piece of paper, with the fancy logo of the Central Bank and Trust Company of Asheville, North Carolina, in the upper left corner . . . a check. I had never seen a check addressed to *Miss Josephine Salter* before in my life, but there it was, my first. Made out for the grand sum of *twelve and 50/100 dollars*, or *$12.50*.

"Is this for a month?" I whispered to Jezzy, when no one was looking.

"No, you country goose, it's for a week. We get one every Friday, rain or shine."

"That's five hundred dollars in a year. How the hell do they stay in business?"

Jezzy shrugged. "Don't know and don't care. What are you going to buy with yours?"

"Nothing. I'm going to save it."

She shook her head impatiently. "Wrong answer. You're going to buy a pair of shoes. Look at those pitiful things on your feet. Please buy a pair of shoes."

Later that afternoon, right before they locked the front doors, I took my check over to the window of Mr. Sherrill, the first cashier I'd shadowed, and opened a passbook savings account. He showed me how to endorse my paycheck on the back and hand it over, for which I received my precious little embossed passbook.

It was only months later that I realized that all I'd done that day was give the bank's money right back to the bank without ever even touching it.

Friday at closing time I went for the last time with my new friend Jezzy—who was by the way, wearing very stylish shoes—to turn in her account book. It was perfect. I'd seen to that. And like the day before, Mable waved Jezzy on out the door and into the mysterious delights of her weekend.

And, like the day before, she kept me behind. This time, she gave me six account books to check, all of which were the work of the older, more experienced cashiers. On that Friday, she stood behind me and watched everything I did, shadowing me rather than the other way around.

There were five men and one woman represented in the stack. Four of the six were all but perfect, except for a few hasty and erroneous account numbers. Of the other two, one man's handwriting was hard to decode, and you had to replicate his math to be certain of the actual numbers he had penciled in. In particular, his 4s and his 7s were hard to distinguish, as were his 6s and 8s. But once you caught the pattern, his book, too, was all but perfect.

The last book, of course, was from the same man whose spider web I'd deciphered the day before. He'd painstakingly created the same pattern within the accounts and hidden his work just as neatly. This time the final totals for the day were off by twenty-five cents rather than twenty-five dollars.

"He's playing with you," I whispered to Mable, after I pointed out what he'd done. "Just to see if he can get away with it."

I turned slightly to look up at her. She was scratching her head with the eraser end of a pencil. The pencil had pushed the famous red hair slightly askew, and for the first time, I realized it was a wig.

"I'll deal with him on Monday," she muttered. "He'll wish he never added two plus two when I get through with him."

"Do you want me to keep doing this in the afternoons?" I asked.

She nodded and smiled ruefully. "You better. I don't know how much longer I can see the damn numbers."

AND SO I BECAME A working girl. Up home in Madison County, I was a woman of twenty-six, but in town, the whole point was to be a girl. To be sillier, to be dreamier, to be . . . younger.

On Big Pine Creek, there was nothing to make me ashamed of my age or my shoes or my hair. I often wore overalls when I worked in the fields beside my brothers, and my shoes were made to go to the barn and back in wet weather, not to the streetcar stop and back while looking like I was dancing. I tramped up the old road along the creek to Jake Worley's store to sell eggs or buy a sack of coffee, not tripping along downtown to the drug store to suck on a dope and stare back at the boys. By boys, I mean men who acted like boys, and who wouldn't have lasted a day with Papa in the wood lot or the corn rows.

Mama had said to go make a life, and I was doing it, but apparently, making a town life meant subtracting five years off my age and acting like I didn't have good sense.

On Saturday morning, I tagged along with Sissy to her work at the Asheville Development Office. She was taking me to get my hair bobbed that afternoon and figured that I could stand being around the flash and dash—her words—of what was really going on in Asheville, where the bustle had some hustle.

And I have to admit, that office on a Saturday morning was something to behold. It was early March, still with leftover winter on the streets and wind whipping around the corners downtown. But inside the Grove Development Company, it was spring and summer already. I had a feeling it was always spring and summer there.

Sissy's boss was a man named Pentland, who was like a perpetual motion, wind-up doll of a man. Thirty-five, maybe forty, with thinning hair and a permanent smile. When we got there, he was preparing to take an older couple out to view some wonderfully perfect homes that they would absolutely love.

Sissy settled me in a small, inner room where I could make myself useful by stuffing envelopes while I waited on her. What I was stuffing was a letter from the mayor, a man by the improbable name of Gallatin . . . Gallatin Roberts. Each separate sheet had to be folded twice and stuffed into a Grove Development Company envelope, which had to be licked and sealed. I entertained myself for the first hundred or so by trying to get the folds perfect and simultaneously recalling how my mother had pronounced the word as *en-velop*, as though this fancy, business-sized item I was stuffing was meant to *envelop* the mayor's letter. Which, in a way, it was, and I was doing the enveloping.

But I could only distract myself with thoughts of my mother's antique ways of talking for so long, as I could hear just about everything that was going on in the office from where I sat. Flash and Dash Pentland was pitching property to the couple on the other side of a thin wall, and I could see Sissy, the office stenographer, directly through an open doorway, where she mostly answered the telephone. The telephone alone would have been enough to keep me entertained, especially with Sissy working it like crazy, but having her in one ear and her boss in the other was . . . mesmerizing. It was like being on the front row of a carnival show or a vaudeville act, and it was all I could do to keep from licking the letter and folding the envelope rather than the other way 'round.

That morning I learned the lingo jingo of Asheville, North Carolina, on the make . . . *Exactly 2500 feet above sea level, sir, which scientists have proven is the . . . a climate that rests the soul and raises the . . . yes, ma'am, oh yes, ma'am . . . beautiful sunsets made more beautiful by . . . the fastest growing city in . . . organic and physical conditions of life most . . . live longer . . . delightful from each year's end to the other . . . recreation, sports, amusements galore . . . physical satisfaction . . . live longer . . . bracing mountain air . . . peaceful and bountiful . . . the cure for . . . a placid Blue Ridge glen . . . you, sir, yes YOU, are the kind of man who can appreciate . . . pastoral beauty and civic sophistication . . . American royalty choose Asheville, why not . . . charming . . . gentle . . . vigorous . . . lovely nooks full of pastoral . . . all the artistry of nature laid bountifully at your feet . . .*

I wondered vaguely if I could trip over the artistry of nature laid bountifully at my feet and pushed back from the table for a moment to stare at my shoes. Jezebel had begged me to buy new shoes, even though for the life of me I couldn't see what was wrong with the ones I already had. And the word *pastoral* that Sissy and her boss kept throwing around like loose change—I had assumed it meant *pasture*, but it sure as hell didn't sound like they were encouraging people to buy up pastureland. Just the opposite actually. *Gentle nooks* and *placid glens* . . . those were the order of the day. And I had to laugh. The Salters had been farming those gentle nooks and placid glens since . . . well, since 1800 . . . and there weren't many days you'd call either gentle or placid. More like *hell week on cripple creek*, as one of my brothers liked to say.

Neither Sissy nor Pentland was shy about tossing those words around though and dozens more like them. They must have thought words were money because they sure kept them moving. Sissy on the phone and her boss face-to-face.

After a bit, Mr. Pentland himself left with the couple he had in train, and I was left alone in the office with Sissy. As soon as he was gone, she was back on the phone, but this time she was dialing up somebody herself rather than answering a call. Her tone slowed and softened, and I realized that she must be talking to one of her men friends and not about real estate.

Just for fun, while she was occupied, I read one of the letters that I'd been so industriously folding and stuffing for the last hour or so. It didn't all make sense to me, so that I stuck it in my purse to ask Sissy about it later, and as later events unfolded, I was glad I did. The letter, from the mayor to his constituents, says a lot about the fire burning under that time and place.

OFFICE OF THE MAYOR
ASHEVILLE, NORTH CAROLINA
The RIGHT HONOURABLE GALLATIN ROBERTS, esq.

March 1, 1929

Dear Sir or Madame,

I am seeking your support in what will undoubtedly be the most important program in my tenure as your leader. Due to its well-deserved popularity and ongoing growth and prosperity, OUR CITY IS BURSTING AT ITS SEAMS.

We desperately need to act now in order to expand the city limits to include those parts of our lovely domain that are already part of Asheville in everything but name. During the coming year, I plan to pour all of my energy into what we have christened the **GREATER ASHEVILLE** area. We are planning to include the important areas of Kenilworth to the East, Biltmore and Biltmore

Forest to the South, my own home of West Asheville to the West, and the Beaverdam Valley with its iconic Lake View Park to the North as part of the bountiful Asheville experience.

We can no longer hope to continue this era of unparalleled progress and prosperity without expanding the boundaries of our beautiful city, and it would be selfish and unchristian on our part to keep the resources of the city to ourselves. To that end I am devoting the remainder of my term to the creation of **GREATER ASHEVILLE** and will stop at nothing to see our city grow even as it prospers.

I am calling on you now to join me in these efforts and to make the new and **GREATER ASHEVILLE** our legacy to our children and grandchildren! In this way, we can ensure that Asheville will continue to expand in wealth and comfort for generations to come!

I didn't know where Kenilworth was, and I assumed West Asheville had to lie to the west, across the river. I'd heard of Biltmore Forest because I'd heard of the Vanderbilts. To be alive in those days was to live in the shadow of Mrs. Vanderbilt. She and her friends were Asheville royalty. And Lake View Park was where Uncle Frank meant to make himself and the family proud. So I had some sense of what it was all about, but even to me, the letter had an odd sense of urgency, almost desperation, that I didn't understand, not until much later.

10

So, HERE'S THE THING ABOUT hair. My hair, your hair—if you're a woman—that woman's hair over there. It's a goddamn bother and a nuisance, and we are required to spend more time fretting and primping and combing and curling than a choir of angels on a Sunday morning.

But I didn't know all this when I first came to town. I thought hair was just hair. In the country, your hair was an irritation, sure. It was long and hot and got in the way. You had to wash it every few days in the summer if you sweated in the fields. Comb it out at night and maybe braid it for sleep if you weren't dog tired. And then put it up again in the morning, day after livelong day.

Don't get me wrong, country women could be sinfully proud of their hair. If it was Cherokee black or corn silk yellow. Even that rusty red like dogwood leaves in the fall. If it was thick, that was good, because thinning hair meant age. Meant you were getting old, maybe into the changes of life. But then, most country women, once they were past their childbearing and child-rearing prime, had a lot more to worry about than whether they were losing their hair.

And there was some magic in when you first let your hair down in front of a man. Since you only let your hair down at night when you were going to bed, it meant you were likely going there with him. I always imagined that as you took your clothes off, you could hide for a bit behind your hair. Alluring. Mysterious. Coy.

By the time I came to town, I'd had myself several men. But I can't say as I'd ever had the proper time and place to let my hair down. I'd barely had time to get my clothes off, and not all of those.

Nor had I ever had anyone actually do anything to my hair except my mother, who would let it down, comb it out, and cut the bottom three or four inches off every few months with a big pair of sewing shears. After I was twelve or so, I often did hers when she did mine. I remember that the first time I cut hers, I was terrified that I'd somehow slip and scalp her. She also taught me how to wind it up into a bun and pin it to the back of my head, which was exactly what I did for my first week at the bank.

One of my earliest childhood memories is one night when I happened to be in Mama and Papa's bedroom. It was just Mama and me. She pulled the pins out of her hair and let it fall, and I screamed. I was terrified, for I didn't know exactly what had happened because I'd never seen her with hair all down her back. I cried and cried until she let me touch it and reassured me that it was the same thing as on my head.

We laughed about that for years.

Occasionally, if I was sick or distraught over something some idiot boy had said to me—often the idiot boy was one of my brothers—she would take pity on me and sit me down in that same bedroom she shared with Papa. She'd comb my hair out, get the hairbrush that she mostly kept to herself and slowly, luxuriously brush my hair while she cooed to me about how I was not to take what any boy or man of the male persuasion said too seriously. Even Papa.

This was a religious experience for me. I realize I just used the word *luxuriously.* I can't really think of much else in country life you might use that word for, unless it was napping in spring sunshine or stretching like a cat when you first woke up. Whatever it was, it didn't happen often. Just like Mama brushing my hair didn't happen often, which gave it a dreamlike quality in my memory.

And then, of course, I did the same thing for her when she was dying. Brushed out her poor, old, thinning white hair and washed it. Which I did for the last time the morning after she passed, when we were laying her out. And because it was the last time, I let it take forever, my fingers shaking.

So I guess I knew that hair mattered . . . among women . . . and our intimate treatment of one another. But before I came to town, I never imagined that it was such a badge and such a bother. I never imagined that it was at the center of your earthly existence.

White oak leaves in October.

That's the color of my hair. You might just say brown, and it is that, but when the sun hits those brown leaves, they gleam with a reddish tint. Not brazen red like Mable's wig, God no, but something the sun brings out unexpectedly, so that same, tired old brown you didn't notice a moment ago can glimmer a bit, almost wink at you in the light.

I say all this because that Saturday afternoon, I went with Sissy to her beauty parlor on College Street, and a man I'd never seen before, a man named Raymond, cut off my hair. Sissy told Raymond I wanted a Bob, which confused me for a second, for Bob was a man's name, but Raymond knew exactly what she was talking about. It meant he chopped off twelve or fourteen inches all the way around just under my ears, and I won't lie, when I saw the first long fall hit the floor beside that chair, I gasped. I didn't cry out or shed any tears, but my heart skipped a beat or two.

"Sit still, honey," the man said calmly, "or it won't be even."

After that, I sat as though petrified. But all I could think about was whether this was what my mother had meant. "Make a life somewhere else," she'd whispered, almost her last words. "A life that I can't even imagine."

Well, you couldn't have imagined this, I thought. A man in a smock with a half-dozen pairs of scissors lined up on the counter, humming to himself while he trimmed away. Then a device called a Marcel Curling Iron, which he used at Sissy's insistence to turn the edges of what was left of that White Oak hair in against my neck, so that it felt . . . almost like a helmet.

When he was done to Sissy's satisfaction, only then did they let me see it. Raymond swiveled that chair around so that I faced that huge mirror, and to be honest, I didn't recognize the woman in the mirror for a second. She had rather a long, thin neck I'd never noticed before, a firm chin, a strong, brown face, prominent cheekbones, and her hair. Her hair looked like a picture in one of Sissy's magazines. Straight and thick and fitted around her face.

"Damn, Jo," Sissy muttered.

"What's wrong?"

She laughed. "Nothing's wrong. It's beautiful, and I refuse to be jealous of it."

My dreams that night were of flooding green waters and a busted-down bridge. Big Pine Creek was rushing, rushing. My mother was dead. And if Mama was gone, what of Papa?

So it was that on Monday, this strange, new woman that I'd become had my own window in the lobby of the Central Bank and Trust Company. Mable herself shadowed me, but since she had her eye on everything going on around us on the first floor, she was in and out of the back of my cubicle and only occasionally did she perch on the stool beside me, watching me with customers and peering over my shoulder at my clean, new accounting book.

Once or twice she coached me a bit on how I interacted with people. Essentially to be more friendly and less stiff, more smiles and fewer frowns, while I was more interested in making all the numbers dance. But mostly she used the opportunity of supposedly watching me to survey the whole floor in motion around us. She had just slipped out the back door of my cubicle to go deal with an irate customer when the fabled Cameron Scott himself walked up to my window.

When I first looked up from checking the neat columns of figures I'd scribed that morning, he was ten feet away, looking around him as if slightly lost, which made no sense as he seemed to be in and out of Central Bank and Trust almost every day. He saw that there was no one at my window and strolled over.

"Good morning" he said. "I don't think I've ever seen you before."

Well, he had seen me. Several times. But it occurred to me that he'd seen me with my former hair, and maybe standing behind Jezzy. In other words, he'd never noticed me before.

"Good afternoon, sir," I said, for it was almost one o'clock.

He made a big deal of pulling back his sleeve to examine his wristwatch. Later, when things between us were more involved, he would explain that it was an Elgin 19 with white gold around the face. Then, he only held out his wrist to show me the time. "Wow," he said. "You're right. Where has the day gone?"

"How may I help you?" I said, which was what Mable had been nudging me to say all day.

"You can tell me how it is that I'm in and out of here just about every single day of the week, and I've never seen you before." He was wearing a fawn-colored suit, with a light blue shirt and pink bow tie. I was fascinated by the tie, I confess, because it was not a color that I had ever imagined around a man's neck, even dreamy Cammy.

"I'm new," I said. "I just started last week." Suddenly, for no other reason than that pink tie, I was aware of the words coming out of my mouth. Sissy had been on me to talk faster and enunciate more clearly, so I wouldn't sound like a hick.

"What's your name?"

"Josephine Salter."

He brow wrinkled ever so slightly.

"My friends call me Jo."

"Then I shall call you that as well."

Shall?

"I'm Cameron Scott."

"I know who you are."

He smiled. "Of course. My father is a Director of the bank, and he sends me uptown almost every day for one reason or another." And then after a pause. "I'm a graduate of Chapel Hill, did you know that?" This for no apparent reason at all.

I shook my head. "You mean the state university?"

"Just so. I studied history . . . And I'd like to know more about your history."

"I'm not sure that's . . ."

"Appropriate? Of course, it is. My father has a vested interest in Central Bank and Trust, and so do I." He smiled again, that easy, ingratiating smile. "Which means that I have a vested interest in you." He leaned forward, his face almost touching the little, ornate bars of my teller's window.

He was so carefully put together, so immaculately groomed, that up close, the effect was . . . what? Not displeasing. I confess it. I could feel his presence leaning in at me. His face was still thin enough and shaved so close it was almost waxy. His teeth shone. Every single hair on his head was brushed and oiled. And he smelled good.

Is that enough to make a woman respond? For a man to smell good?

Behind me there was a noise like a bullfrog. Mable clearing her throat. “You have business to transact, Mr. Scott?” she asked.

“No, just being friendly with Miss Salter here.” He winked at me. Honest to God . . . winked. And it was then that I realized he had crystal-clear blue eyes. Everything about him—even his eyes—was clean.

He pulled his sleeve up again and glanced at his Elgin. “I’m afraid I better run along,” he said, or something like that.

When he had disappeared through the doors at the back of the lobby, presumably headed up to the second floor, Mable cleared her throat again, again the bullfrog. “You keep away from him,” she said. “He’s got busy hands.”

Even though I was from down in the country, I knew exactly what she meant.

That afternoon at five, when the head cashier, Foster Reynolds, came downstairs to lock the front doors, I carried my account book back to Mable’s room and waited while everyone else dropped theirs off. It wasn’t quite so obvious that I was staying while all the other tellers and cashiers left because poor Mr. Breed was sitting there as well, nervous as a cat.

I asked him how his day had gone and he only gulped and held up his own account book in front of him and mutely shook his head. Out of pure, Christian pity, I asked him if he wanted me to go through it with him. He glanced around nervously for Mable and nodded. I sat down beside him and dug in, pencil and eraser in hand.

Interestingly enough, he seemed to have recorded everything accurately, even account numbers with six or more digits. His handwriting was so large that the numbers overflowed the lines on the page, which hurt my sense of order, but he had captured the essence of his transactions. His problems came whenever he had to add or subtract any number larger than two places, especially when a decimal got in the way, as it most always did, given that we were dealing with dollars and cents. At first glance, his whole page seemed to quiver in front of my eyes, but once I saw the patterns, I helped him redo the math, starting at the top of the first page and working through to his daily totals.

Oddly, he was not a bad student, just a nervous young man who'd stopped listening somewhere along the way, maybe third grade. And when we'd finished his totals for the day, we both looked up and there was Mable, standing in the doorway watching us.

"Checking your book, Mr. Breed?" she asked. She was trying hard not to smile.

"Yes, ma'am," he muttered. "With the help of Miss . . . Miss . . ."

"Jo," I whispered.

"With the help of Miss Jo."

"Good. I suggest you do that every afternoon for a while. At least until you're confident in your sums. Now, go count your cash drawer."

And he was gone. Released and relieved.

"How bad was it?" Mable asked.

"Actually, not that bad, once you see what he's doing. It's subtraction that buffaloes him. Anything too large to use his fingers."

She nodded. "Can you teach him?"

"If you want me to."

She shrugged and sat down, and I wondered if her feet hurt, after roaming the first floor of the bank all day. "It's what we do, you know," she said after a minute. "We correct their mistakes and teach them how to do what they should already know."

"Men?"

She nodded.

"We teach them how to do their jobs?"

She grinned. "Oh, some of them know how to do their jobs,

but they tend to be so busy climbing the ladder . . ." She nodded upward with her head to indicate the three floors above us. "So busy getting themselves up to the second and third floors that they don't have time to make sure the numbers add up, or to take care of the poor little souls that can't do their sums."

"So you do that . . . take care of the lost lambs, I mean?"

"Sure. And I make sure that the first-floor numbers match the cash in the drawers. And . . ." Here she paused. "And I keep an eye out for the wolves in sheep's clothing. The ones who get cute with their books and pocket the spare change at the end of the day or week."

"Why would they do that? It's just money," I asked. I know I sound the fool but keep in mind, I'd never really had any dollars except for egg money kept in a pantry jar.

She looked at me strangely. "You'll learn that some people think money is all there is," she said and shrugged. "And some of them work upstairs and wear the nicest suits and smoke the biggest cigars you ever saw."

I TOOK MY SHOES OFF—WE BOTH did—and helped Mable go through the books that Monday evening. I folded a clean sheet of lined paper into the ruler—what I called it—that I used to mark each line and column and set to work. Those account books that were written big were easier for her to see, and she gave me the others, plus the book produced by Mr. Greene, our creative friend who carefully and consciously hid his miscalculations. And in every instance, I painstakingly showed her what I'd done to check, recheck, and correct the books I audited.

It was close on seven o'clock when we were done, and all the figures were clean and sure, nestled carefully in their rightful columns.

"Jo," she said, when we had finished. "I guess you've figured out by now that I can't see well enough to do this by myself."

"Maybe you need new glasses," I murmured.

She shook her head. "It's worse than that. But here's what's bothering me. I can't pay you to help me, at least not until you've been here a while."

I shrugged. "Why, it's a job needs doing," I said. "You may think I'm a hick, but where I come from, that's enough. Work is work. Plus people help people."

"You sure? It's not always like that here." I gathered that by *here*, she meant here in the bank, in the town.

"I'm sure. Besides, I love the numbers better than anything. Better than the clothes or the shoes or the hair bobs."

"Better than the men?"

"I ain't seen a man worth bothering over since I came to town."

She laughed out loud and her wig slipped a bit.

"You pay me when you can," I said and slid my own worn country shoes back on my feet. "I don't aim to worry about it."

11

There was a telephone at Jake Worley's store on Big Pine that everyone in the valley used to call in and out when there was some sort of emergency. I had seen it any number of times, had even held the receiver up to my ear, jiggled the lever that held the part you listened to, and heard the scratchy, far away voice of the operator. According to Jake, some woman in Marshall named Penny.

But I had never spoken into a telephone before I came to town in '29, and so it took a good deal of coaxing from Sissy to handle the one at the Charlotte Street house that Saturday afternoon. The one on Charlotte Street had a long black object on a cord that you held up to the side of your head. You listened to one end of it and spoke into the other end. The cord was also connected to the base of the phone, which had a little rotary dial on its face, so that if you knew the number, you could dial up your friend without troubling the operator. All the numbers were three digits in those days, and of course the dial was my favorite part. Numbers in a circle rather than a straight line . . . something to think about.

Middle of the afternoon and the damn thing rang in the downstairs hallway. I didn't budge from where I lay reading on my bed, for the ringing telephone was Sissy's territory pure and simple. Sometimes it was for Uncle Frank, but most of the time . . . you can imagine.

After a minute, Sissy yelled my name up the stairs, and told me to get down there. Fast. I flew down those steps, for I thought something had happened to Papa or one of the boys. They had been timbering, so it was easy to imagine death and dismemberment.

When I hit the hallway, there was Sissy with one hand over the mouthpiece of the thing and her eyes as big as saucers. "It's a man," she said, "wants to talk to you."

My chest went hollow. "From up home?"

She shook her head. "Of course not, you ninny. From here . . . in town."

I'm not sure why, but I started shaking my head no, but she thrust the receiver at me anyway. "Talk to him," she ordered. "Find out who it is."

So the first thing I said, the very first thing, was not *hello* or *hey there* but *who is this*. Sounded suspicious as hell, I'm sure.

"Miss Jo, this is Cameron Scott." His voice sounded just as oily as it had face-to-face in the bank, only further away.

"Sissy's standing right here. You want to talk to her?"

"No, I called to speak with you."

I didn't say anything, but after a long pause, it occurred to me that it was my turn. "Go ahead then . . . speak."

Sissy was mouthing the words, "Who . . . is . . . it?" at me.

"I called to ask if you would like to go for a ride this evening. My father has a new motor car, a Packard, and he wishes it to be broken in properly."

"No . . . thank you," I said. And hung up.

"Who . . .?" Sissy all but squealed.

"That Cameron Scott you lust after," I muttered. "Him."

"Good God Almighty, are you sure?"

"He said he was . . ."

"And you used the word *No*! Cammy Scott and you actually said the word *No*?"

"I did. He wanted to go riding in some car . . . New car," I added helpfully.

"Jesus . . . We're calling him back."

We wrestled with the phone for a bit, Sissy actually trying to force the receiver up to my face with my hand still wrapped around it. Me pushing back, and I was farm strong to her city strong so you can imagine how that went.

Then she went to begging. "Please, Jo, for me. Please. I'll dial his number and you talk to him. Ask him if we can both go, and . . ."

"I'm not asking him for . . ." But I paused at that point, remembering despite my stubbornness just how much this all meant to her.

Finally, I agreed, and she dialed: 5-2-9.

He answered, and sad to say, I already recognized his voice. I said who I was, and though I got flustered and called myself Josie, that part went alright. I couldn't bring myself to ask him a favor, meaning Sissy, so I just told him that we would be ready at the appointed hour.

"We?"

"My cousin, Sissy Morgan, and me. We will be ready when you say."

"Okay . . . well, then . . . do you mind if my brother comes along also? Make it a foursome?"

"Nope," I said. "The more the merrier." I'd heard this somewhere and thought myself clever for dredging it up at the appropriate moment.

"Seven, then. We'll come for you at seven this evening."

"Fine," I said. And hung up again. I was getting good at hanging up.

"Well?"

"They're coming at seven, and we're going for a ride in a Packard. A *new* Packard."

"They?"

"Calm down. He has a brother. That's all I know . . . You can have your pick of the litter."

THE 1928 PACKARD ROADSTER WAS a shade of green that has never been seen in nature. With a black top that folded back and a rumble seat. The rumble seat is what matters because when the Scott brothers showed up in this phenomenon, Cameron was determined to drive and he was equally determined that I was going to sit in front with him.

So Sissy, who had taken two hours at least to bathe and dress and fuss with her hair, had to climb in the rumble seat with little brother Benjamin, where they didn't exactly fit except in some intimate fashion they worked out between them. Cameron kept calling them the kids, meaning I guess that we were the adults.

Which he did not drive like an adult, or so it seemed to me.

Once we were off Charlotte Street and turned up the winding roads toward the Grove Park Inn, it seemed to me that I might die a grisly death in the front seat of that damned car. And that was Cameron driving sober. We would deal with Cameron drunk later.

We parked there, pried the kids out of the rumble seat, and went for a stroll inside the lobby of the Inn. I noticed two things as we walked from the car to the massive front door. One was that the hour or so Sissy had spent on her hair—first trying to get the curls out and then trying to get them back in—was wasted, already blown away. The second thing was that the brothers made no secret of passing an odd-shaped metal bottle back and forth between them. *Flask*: the new word I learned that evening.

Cameron took my arm and turned me around for one last loving gaze at the Packard just before entering the lobby. "Doesn't the experience of speed make your blood run hot?" he asked.

I was honest. "Mostly it froze the blood in my veins."

He laughed. "Touché," he said. Another new word.

And in we went. Now, I will tell you straight up. The inside of that lobby is magnificent. Tall, cool, quiet, constructed mostly of boulders so large they made you think God his own self had played a role in the building. Two fireplaces at opposite ends, either of which would hold a tree. Sissy dragged Benjamin, the other brother, straight to one of those fireplaces, and I realized that they must be slightly frozen from the ride in the rumble seat, which had no roof to shelter them.

I went with Cameron to gaze at the sunset, which he showed off to me as if he owned it. And I realized, suddenly as I stood there, that he was dressed accordingly. A dark blue wool suit, in some sort of plaid, with a white shirt, and again that pink tie. And a plaid wool scarf to wrap around his neck while he was driving, the scarf woven also with pink. I kid you not . . . Pink . . . with a capitol *P*. So he looked like the sunset over the Blue Ridge. To this day, I wonder if it was intentional.

Back in the car. Once again, the adults in the front and the kids in back. The flask was empty by this point, and so the brothers decided we needed to visit the Sky Club. Put the Packard through its paces—they talked about it as if it were a horse—going up Beaucatcher Mountain and see what was shakin' up at the Sky.

IT SEEMS STRANGE TO ME now that the first time I ever saw the inside of the Sky Club was with Cameron and Benjy Scott. You could see the club from almost any street in Asheville, nestled up there on the side of the mountain above the town. It wasn't on a grand scale like the Grove Park but rather a solid, rectangular building of three floors. And whereas the Grove Park overwhelmed you, the Sky Club danced with you. It had a sort of mystique all its own. Gray, almost white, stone on the outside, but with a lot of dark corners and dimly lit rooms on the inside. And as you soon as you walked in the front door, where an elegantly dressed Negro man took your coat, you could hear strains of jazz drifting down to you from the second floor.

I was enthralled.

You know by now that I grew up on fiddle tunes from another era, played on the porch of an evening. Always a battered, old guitar, occasionally a banjo. So the music that I first heard that night . . . floating down the wide stairs from the second floor . . . was more than just different.

The first floor was where families came to eat their supper. Older couples alone plus younger couples with children. It seemed safe enough and there was happy laughter. The second floor was where the action was. Music and booze.

Jazz was . . . utterly new to me, like something from another planet. Sweet, loose and . . . dark. Narcotic.

Cameron and Benjy led us up the stairs the way men of their class liked to do in those days. With a firm grip on the woman's arm and broad, sweeping gestures. With a nod to the maître d', and grins and winks for various patrons whom they knew or pretended to know. I wanted to be close to the music—I've always wanted to be close to the music ever since I was a little girl—but that didn't matter. We were seated at a table near the bar, which is what mattered to them.

It was mostly dark in that part of the room. Lights behind the bar, reflected in a large glass mirror and dozens of fancy bottles. Lights on a large open space in front of the band where people were dancing. Sissy was all but dancing in her chair.

Let's just say that if Sissy was disappointed to have been dealt Benjy Scott—the younger, thinner version of Cammy—she sure as hell didn't show it. The minute we sat down, she scooted her chair closer to his and their two hands disappeared under the table. Her eyes barely left his face unless he pointed out something for her to look at or waved at someone across the room.

This was all alien territory to me, and I wasn't sure just how I was supposed to act or what I was supposed to do, plus I was distracted by the music from the beginning. The deep notes of the bass thrummed in my belly, and the trumpet filled the room, or so it seemed to me. I wanted to dance, but I didn't know how. I wanted to hide in a corner and just listen, but I knew I'd never escape the Scott boys. I wanted to float above it all and watch and taste and hear, but that was impossible.

The music somehow cut through the cigarette and cigar smoke that was thick in the air.

Cammy ordered martinis for all of us. Which I tried . . . honestly tried . . . to like. But good God, you couldn't taste the alcohol for the sour. Sissy, on the other hand, gulped hers and asked for another. The boys sipped but with a purpose, a getting drunk purpose. Soon, there was another round, and Cammy poured my first into his glass.

He scooted closer to me and nodded at the band. "Like the music?" he asked, loud enough to be heard over the laughter and the talking, the clinking glasses and the horns. I was focused on the horns.

"What?"

"You like that jungle music?"

If a man's eyes could somehow glitter and be glazed over at the same time, his were, and his face had broken out in tiny drops of sweat.

"Why do you call it that?" From where I sat, it looked like the old guy at the piano was as white as a ghost, thin with a cigarette dangling between his lips, the man on the bass was in shadow, hard to tell. The trombone was maybe white, but the man blowing on the trumpet. Now, he was Black—midnight and summertime, despite the winter outside.

"It's Negro music," Cammy muttered. "New Orleans. Dirty music. Father would say that it isn't what a respectable man of taste listens to." He took a solid mouthful of his martini, or maybe my martini. "But I like it. Stirs the blood."

His chair was even closer to mine now, and I could feel his hand on my knee. Squeezing to emphasize his words . . . stirs . . . blood.

I leaned over close to his neck, which he liked, and said clearly so that only he could hear, "Move your hand."

"What!"

"You heard me. Get your hand out of my lap."

The hand crawled back toward its owner. "If I'm interested in that sort of thing, I'll let you know," I said. Still close so that only he could hear. "But otherwise . . ."

I stood up and shrugged my shoulders to loosen the tension. The room was still there, the music still pulsed in the smoky air, but he'd ruined it for me. I turned toward the bar and asked the barkeep where the bathroom was. He was smiling, always smiling, and he gestured around the far end of the bar, between the bar and the band. "Down the hall, ma'am," he said in a deep, husky whisper. "Careful in the dark." Still smiling.

I smiled back at the barkeep. Jezzy had said he was mythical and didn't speak, but he'd spoken to me. Until I stood, I hadn't noticed how large he was, with thick, sloping shoulders. "I'll be fine, thank you." I leaned toward him and nodded back at the Scott boys and Sissy. "It's them you better worry about."

When I reached the end of the bar and turned toward the hall, I noticed a thin man standing with his back to the wall and his arms crossed. Dressed in dark clothing and standing mostly in the dark, out of the way, but watching the room. I couldn't see his face in the shadows, but I could tell he was watching. As I slipped past, he nodded politely and there was a flash of teeth. I could feel more than see that it was a smile.

While in the washroom, I splashed cold water on my face and ran my fingers through my hair. I still wasn't used to the bob, and it felt strange and a little sinful just to be able to comb it back with only my fingers.

When I edged back down the hall, I met Sissy coming the other way, headed for the ladies' room. She had a Lucky Strike between her fingers, perhaps having forgotten to light it, and she was a little unsteady on her feet. When I asked her if she was alright, she giggled.

"Better than that," she said, overloud. "I'm getting high, and I'm with the Scott brothers, and Benjy . . ." She leaned toward me, meaning to whisper, and almost pinned me to the wall. "Oh my God, Benjy . . . is hilarious."

"Do you need me to help you find the ladies . . .?"

"Don't be silly. Been there . . . before."

I shrugged and let her go. She wasn't as old as me but you had to hope she was old enough to take care of herself. When I reached the end of the bar, I stopped to take in the room again, trying to memorize it all. The barkeep cleared his throat, and when I turned, handed me a glass half full of a light brown liquid.

When I raised my eyebrows, he leaned toward me over the bar. "Boss said you might like that better."

"Better?"

"Than the martinis them boys you're with are soaking up."

"What is it?"

"Apple brandy."

I sipped it and it was sinful good. Dark and smoky and mindful of what my Papa drank to settle his stomach. "It tastes homemade," I said. "It's delicious."

"Strong though," the barkeep said. "Go easy on it." He was well over forty years old, with a long scar on his smiling face. Thick hands and wrists. He wasn't being fresh, I decided. He was just being friendly, protective even.

"My name is Jo," I said to him. "Jo Salter."

He nodded. "I'm Mack."

"Just Mack?"

"Just Mack."

"Who's the boss, Mack? And how did he know . . .?" I held up the glass.

"The boss is Mr. Arrowood." He nodded behind me, toward the corner where I'd seen the thin, watchful man before. But when I looked over my shoulder, the corner was empty. Dark and empty.

"Where did he go?" I asked Mack.

He shrugged. "Hard to say. Everywhere . . ." The band was back, and suddenly, the trumpet blared up its long, sweet note. I could almost feel my hands shake, it went on for so long.

"Thank him for me?" I said to Mack when the note finally died away. "For the brandy."

"Will do," he said and nodded. "The boss knows the score."

12

ALL EVENING, I HAD DREADED the ride back down Beaucatcher Mountain, given how much liquor flask and martini glass I'd seen Cameron pour down his throat. Turns out, the ride wasn't terrifying; it was pathetic. He was so cross-eyed drunk that we crept along, easing down the center of the road, while his head wobbled from side to side. I actually slid over close to him on the seat, just so I could put one hand on the steering wheel to steady it. I didn't particularly want his head to fall off, and I sure as hell didn't want us to fall off the mountain.

I guess you could say that the drive down from the Sky Club was anticlimactic, just like a lot of things with Cameron Scott. But the dream I had that night was not.

It marked me, that dream. I say that because it tore me from sleep with its intensity, its . . . reality. I remembered the texture and feel of it the next morning. I've had a version of that dream several times since, and I can still taste it now, these months later.

I was inside the Sky Club but very late at night. Later, I came to believe that it was the same time in the dream as it was when I woke—3:33 according to the little clock beside my bed. *The club was quiet and very dark except for here and there a glimmer in a far corner or behind the bar. There were people there but not really.* By that I mean *there were ghosts of people, shades of people, dancing and moving about, drinking and laughing but all in a weird, empty darkness and all in complete silence.*

It wasn't gloomy or frightening there but it was dim, murky, mysterious. Haunted by the night's patrons.

The windows were cracked open, I realized, *and cold winter air was streaming through the main room. The smoke was gone, the sweat was gone, the music . . . was dead.*

I needed to find the thin man, with his nod and smile, I needed to tell him something. Warn him . . .

Arrowood.

I chased through the club, into rooms that I hadn't seen but could only imagine. I called out the only name I had for him, Arrowood, *even screamed it once . . . or twice . . . straining my throat, but nothing emerged to break the silence.*

Up on the third floor, I found his private rooms, neat and orderly, so that I knew they were his. I even saw his bed—quiet, empty, perfectly made. All this made me want him more. I had to find him to warn him. Not his room or his clothes . . . him! Arrowood!

And that's what woke me . . . calling out. Naming.

Where was the music . . . what had killed it? Why were the people there, all the people . . . apparitions, specters? Why, oh why, wasn't he there? And what was I trying to tell him? Was I just another voiceless wraith inside a nightmare?

Lying in my bed at the Charlotte Street house, I was convinced that I had to remember. I had to dredge it up so that I could get word to him of the danger. But what danger?

If I could reenter the dream, go back to the Sky Club inside my head, then maybe I could say what it was, speak the warning. But it was too late. I couldn't go back to sleep, couldn't slip down off the ledge of awareness into slumber, so stirred as I was by the vision of the empty club.

Mad at myself, mad at the dream, I got up, cracked my own window open to let in a little of that cold March air that I'd felt on my dream skin. Pulled up the quilt from the foot of my bed and curled up under both city blanket and country quilt. Nestled my head into the down pillow and let myself imagine. Luring sleep and then desire, desire more than sleep. Told myself a story that began inside the haunting of the dream.

I treasured the dream by returning to it. Claiming it for my own. Etching the lineaments of it more deeply inside my head so that it would stay there.

And in my retelling, I searched through the club again. Imagining it, saying it to myself. Letting the music play again and relishing it. Only this time, I did find the thin man . . . in his private rooms. Where *his* bed was. And trust me, I could imagine everything but his voice . . . which he didn't need to do what I wanted done.

I MUST HAVE FALLEN BACK ASLEEP, with a pillow clasped between my legs and a smile on my face. I say must have, because Sissy woke me early the next morning by climbing into bed with me. Warm and sleepy and hungover.

"What are you doing here?" I muttered to her. It was barely light.

"My head hurst . . ." she moaned. Not hurts . . . *hurst.*

"No wonder. Whatever was in those martinis tasted like grandma's medicine."

She made a sound between a moan and a groan. "Don't say that word."

"Martini?"

She nodded. The moan and groan sound again.

"You want me to make you some coffee?" We were both whispering.

"No. Not yet. I want to talk about last night. About Benjamin . . ."

"You mean Benjy?"

"He prefers Benja . . ." She yawned. ". . . jamin."

"Sure he does. You like him?"

"Oh, God yes. He's going to get me and him both in the Rhodo . . ." Another yawn. "Festival. Maybe not king and queen but something . . ."

"I thought you'd both freeze to death in that rumble seat contraption."

Even with her eyes closed, she grinned. "We were forced to keep warm any way we could. Our hands warm anyway."

"Had your hands in his pockets, did you?"

"Worse than that."

"Down his pants?"

"Sort of, but only . . . not . . . Fair is fair. He had his up between my . . . Wait! What about you and Cammy? Where were your hands on the way home?"

"On that damn steering wheel," I said. "I'm the only reason you didn't die with your hands down Benjamin Scott's pants."

IT IS STRANGE THAT A month before, I'd never ridden in an automobile. I'd seen the first one that tried to navigate its way up the Big Pine Road, the driver and passengers dressed like aviators, but I'd never even set my behind down inside one. Until I came to town and discovered that Saturday and Sunday were made for rich folks and their cars. While regular, working people were walking to work and church, they were tooting those crazy little horns and trying not to kill each other while going faster and faster . . . all before a tire blew out and scared all the horses and half the dogs in town.

WHAT I MEAN IS THAT Sunday afternoon, we went for our own family drive, the Morgans and me. Out to Lake View Park where Uncle Frank had bought his lot, the lot that was going to make the whole family proud. Uncle Frank and Aunt Brenda in front, with me jammed between Sissy and Junior in back. Sissy and Junior were excited, even though her excitement was bubbling along under the lid of that martini hangover. I had tried to pour strong, black coffee down her that morning after breakfast, but she wasn't a black coffee kind of girl. Rather moan and groan than take her medicine.

What we learned in the car was that Beaver Lake was the hottest thing around. Uncle Frank kept alternately shouting at us over his shoulder and then twisting back around to focus on the road. Something about the Beaverdam Valley and azure skies, dawn and dusk, the sylvan center of life's reward, the same real estate agent blather that I'd heard at Sissy's office. But what really got Frank going was not the lake, not the golf course, not the club house, but the neighbors.

Turns out that over the past few years, the men that he most wanted to associate himself with had built houses or were building houses in what he kept calling the "Park," Lake View Park, up on the rolling hills that looked down at Beaver Lake.

Some dentist named Sinclair had moved into a stone mansion designed by a Peruvian architect. I had to hide a smile as Uncle Frank shouted this information from the front seat. I'd never been to a dentist at that point, and I sure as hell had never been to Peru. But Dr. Sinclair was one of the original Directors of Central Bank and Trust, and we all knew what that meant.

Sissy's boss's boss, some distinguished soul named Campbell, who masterminded the development of the Grove Park area, had built not just a house. Oh no. He'd constructed a Moorish fantasy villa, with a walled courtyard and a marble fountain. Not only had Sissy never been invited inside, but her boss had only been as far as the back door, where he'd delivered some papers for Campbell's approval. A servant had taken the papers into some inner sanctum and returned them with the great man's signature thirty minutes later.

Uncle Frank drove us by both of these palaces just to impress us with the august surroundings and all they meant to our own elevation in the world. But the place that made him break out in an honest-to-God sweat when he pulled up in the street to show it to us was something called Stratford Towers. I will say it looked like a castle on a hill, as we sat in the idling car staring up at it. It was a gigantic, red brick monstrosity with actual towers and huge chimneys that rose higher than the treetops.

The inside was gorgeous, simply gorgeous, Uncle Frank let us know in a whisper. Now, as a general rule, the word *gorgeous* is not something you'd hear uttered by my Uncle Frank Morgan, or any man of his class, but he said it that day and he said it reverentially. You see, the owner of Stratford Towers was his boss and his idol. President of Central Bank and Trust, Mr. Wallace B. Davis. I'd never even seen Davis at the bank for he worked his magic from the third floor and used a private entrance along with a few choice associates.

If you believed Uncle Frank, Davis and his wife had built Stratford Towers as a living, breathing symbol of what was possible if you just bought into the fairy tale that was Asheville property and invested your own modest riches in his bank. Someday, if we were lucky, Uncle Frank promised us, after we too had moved to Lake View Park, we might all be invited to a soiree at Stratford Towers.

"What's a sor-eh?" I whispered to Sissy.

"Fancy party," she whispered back. "Evening."

We drove another three hundred feet or so further down Stratford Road to West Avon Boulevard in Frank's motor car, less than a quarter mile below Stratford Towers, and then suddenly he pulled up by the curb in front of an acre or so of open, grassy knoll. We all got out and stood and stared.

"This is it," Uncle Frank said quietly.

It occurred to me that it would make good pasture, but I had enough sense not to say so.

"Goforth and Sons Construction are breaking ground this week on a plan devised by a junior partner in Douglas Ellington's firm." There was a quaver in his voice, and it occurred to me that Uncle Frank was close to tears. I glanced at Aunt Brenda and she was already beyond close. She understood what it meant to him, and she was sniffling outright. "Classic Tudor Revival. Eighteen rooms. Four bedrooms and four full bathrooms. Quarry stone exterior on the lower side to set off the wood and plaster. A slate roof." He paused and looked back at us. "Slate!"

"I can see it, Father," Junior said. "It's going to be beautiful."

"Yes, it is," Uncle Frank replied. "You bet your life it's going to be beautiful, and do you know what it means?"

"It means we've arrived?" Sissy said, half-question, half-statement.

"It means that we've more than arrived. Nobody can ever again question the importance of Frank J. Morgan. Nobody can ever again look down on me or on this family."

I glanced back up the hill. Wallace B. Davis can, I thought, but again had sufficient sense not to say.

"West Avon Boulevard is one of the most important addresses in this whole development, hell—in this whole town, and in ten years, when other people are scrambling to find a way into Lake View Park, newcomers with new money, all we have to do is look around us, knowing we were one of the very first. And when they drive by this house, our house . . ." Again, he swept out both arms to rekindle the vision. "When they drive by the Morgan house, they'll stare in awe and ask themselves who the hell is Frank J. Morgan and how did he make his money?"

"This is amazing, Daddy," Sissy said. You could feel the excitement in her voice, and I knew she had visions of music and parties and rich boys dancing in her head. "Can I tell people? Can I tell my friends?"

"Of course, you can. Tell everybody. Tell the world." He pointed down at the ground. "By September, this is going to be our address. Your beaus will have to come here to pick you up for your dates, while Frank Junior and I will be playing golf right over there, aiming down the eighteenth fairway of our own home course, designed by Donald Ross just for the members of the Park."

As we were climbing back in the motor car, I suddenly wondered where I was going to live. After the house on Charlotte Street went on the market, where would I go, for it was obvious Lake View Park was way above my lot in life. All I had to do was open my mouth and the neighbors would laugh out loud. It was almost as if Uncle Frank heard my thoughts because he paused after slamming the back door to the car and before hoisting in himself. He looked past Frank Junior to where I sat in the middle of the back seat. "This will be your address too, Josephine," he said. "There will be a place for you with the Morgan family for as long as you desire."

"Thank you, sir," I said, surprised and genuinely moved. It had never occurred to me that he would want to bring the farm girl to the palace.

"And wouldn't your mother be impressed if she were only alive to see it," Aunt Brenda gushed from the front seat.

13

WHERE DOES ALL THE MONEY come from?"

"What money?" Mable had cracked open a window in her workroom-office and was taking a break with a Chesterfield, blowing the smoke carefully out the window into the winter dark. Monday had been a busy day, and the tellers' account books were full of numbers for us to check.

"The money that the big boys upstairs are spending on lots and houses and cars and what all?"

She grinned through the smoke. "You mean the big boys like your uncle?" It was the first time I'd seen her smoke and the first time she'd shown me that she knew who I was.

"Yeah, like Uncle Frank. He just bought some lot in Lake View Park and he's going on about how he's going to build an estate."

"Like Davis and the others." It was more of a statement than a question.

I nodded. "Surely to God the bank doesn't pay them so much money that they can build castles on the side of mountains."

"Surely to God it does, in one way or another."

"How do you mean, one way or another?"

"What did you do with your first two paychecks?"

"I deposited them in a savings account."

"Right here, in this bank?" She waved the hand holding the Chesterfield around to signify the building. "Your . . . what? Twenty-five dollars is right here in this building?"

"Sure. Right here in the Central B & T."

"What do you think happens to your money when you deposit it? That it goes into a little drawer somewhere with your name on it? And that every so often, somebody like Foster Reynolds comes along, opens that drawer and drops a nickel's worth of interest in to reward you for your faith?"

I had to smile at her. She was into it now and her voice had taken on a deeper strain of irony . . . irony mixed with astonishment that I could be so dense. She lit another Chesterfield straight from the first, crushed the first butt on the sill and threw it out the window.

I reached in my old brown purse and pulled out my official passbook and waved it at her. "Says in this little book that I can get hold of my money anytime I want to. Touch it, count it, fold it, stick in my purse."

"Read the fine print, did you?" She grinned. "Well, you're probably the only adult who ever did."

"What does happen to my money?" I said, suddenly not so sure I would like the answer.

"It goes back into the general fund, what's called the bank's assets." She shrugged. "In your case, it never really left since you just gave the checks right back, probably on the same day . . .?"

I nodded. "Never even walked out the door with them."

She grinned. "The bank uses your money to make more money."

"How in the world do you use money to make money? It's nothing but paper bills and coins. It doesn't reproduce like a cow or a horse or a pig."

She reached up with her free hand to straighten her wig. "Oh, but it does." She stubbed out her second cigarette and edged over to the table to sit down across from me. Even though the door to the hallway was closed, what followed was said in a whisper. A whisper and an occasional growl.

"Oh, come on, Jo. Don't play the country bumpkin. You're not stupid; do the math. What interest rate does that silly little passbook pay you?

"One percent."

"One percent per annum, which means . . .?"

"Per year."

"Thank you. And at what percent does the bank loan out your money?"

I shrugged. "I don't . . ."

"Five to ten percent, depending on how desperate the individual standing in front of the desk begging is."

I whistled. I am a world-class whistler, as that's how I used to call the horses in of an evening. Shake the feed bucket and whistle.

"Starting to make sense to you?"

I nodded. "But what about collateral and . . ."

"The bank does not want the goddamn collateral," she cut me off. "The bank doesn't want your house or your land . . . not unless it's prime Asheville real estate that it can turn over in a week. The bank wants your money, all your money, so it can use it. Move it, sell it."

"So the bank actually sells my money? While I'm not looking? Is that what you're saying?"

"Loan it, sell it. Same thing."

"Isn't that . . . what's the word? Use . . .?"

"Usury? Of course, it is. Come on, Jo . . . do you think the bank exists for your sake?"

"Up until today I did." I said it almost apologetically, for truth be told, I was surprised by what she was saying. At twenty-six years old, I thought nothing could shock me, but there we were. "Foster Reynolds says the bank is for me."

"No, actually, if you listen close, the little cock-sucker is saying something different. He's saying have faith in the bank . . . trust the bank . . . we're going to get rich and you're going to get rich right along with us. Greater Asheville . . . Central B & T. One and the same! That's what he's saying."

"You think he's lying?"

"Foster ain't got enough sense to lie. He believes it. But even Foster knows that you're getting rich at one percent when the bank is getting rich at ten percent. And, here's the fun part, the bank is using your money to get rich on."

"Well, damn."

"Pretty much."

"So the bank can pay the president and the vice presidents and the head cashier money like you and I can't even imagine?"

"Oh, I can imagine it," she muttered. "I've seen their pay stubs. And don't forget the Directors. Your money goes a long way with them too. But more important than their pay is that they can borrow just about any amount they could ever want. They just approve it for each other. Upstairs, they say your paycheck buys your clothes, the bank builds your house."

"But doesn't the bank have to keep some money, real money, laying around somewhere in case . . .?"

"In case what?"

"In case a bunch of folks come in and want to make a withdrawal?"

Mable nodded. "Now, there you're onto something. It's called cash reserves. Law says they have to keep a certain percentage of the deposits on hand as cash reserves . . . case you and me and a thousand other people all need our money on the same day."

I imagined a pile of cash inside the Central B & T vault like corn in a corn crib or hay in a barn. I'd never been in the vault but I'd seen the massive steel door, so it had to be where the money was. "Do they keep back enough cash for a long winter?" I asked Mable.

She shrugged. "Now, that's the question, isn't it, dearie?"

"If I had Papa's varmint gun, I'd be tempted to shoot a few of 'em for messing with my money," I said. "The damn Directors, I mean."

She guffawed. "Fire away. And don't forget your uncle. He's smack in the middle of it. But how about for now, we check these account books so we can go home?"

LAND.

Up home, on Big Pine and places like it—Harmony, Spillcorn, Bluff, Doe Branch, Spring Creek, Runion—the land was where you were born and buried. Where you lived and died. The land was beautiful and harsh and, in its own bittersweet way, the thing that made you. In all seasons and all phases of the moon. It's where you planted and harvested, and it's where you *were* planted and harvested.

But not in town, not in Asheville. Land in town was a commodity—to be bought, sold, and traded. And God help you if you held on to a parcel long enough to like it, let alone love it. Land was meant to be kept moving, just like money, because it was money.

Up home, the land was a lover, even if a rough one at times; in town, land was a whore, bought and sold.

What Mable didn't say that day is that the bank was the one hand and real estate was the other, fingers intertwined. That my money, your money, everyone's money was used to buy and sell lots, parcels, acreage at a dizzying pace. No one owned anything long enough to plant a crop and see it into the barn. And if you did stop long enough to build something—like Uncle Frank in Lake View Park—it was because you'd made your mark and you intended to flaunt it. To say unto the world, I'm faster, smoother, slicker than you are, and here's the proof. My Estate is more Real than yours . . .

By that afternoon when I asked Mable where all the money came from, my own little pittance had no doubt changed hands five times and helped buy or sell three different pieces of land. And I'd never even touched those dollars with my own fingertips.

14

I HADN'T SEEN OR HEARD FROM Mr. Cameron Scott since Saturday night, which caused me to wonder if he'd made it home to Biltmore Forest in one piece. On Tuesday afternoon, however, he showed up at the bank, looking as smooth and well-combed as ever. He saluted me as he went through the lobby and stopped at my window on the way out.

When the customer in front of him had finished up his business, Cameron eased up to the window and leaned forward with his best smile. "I had a wonderful time on Saturday night," he whispered, just loud enough for the teller on either side to hear. "I have a thought or two about this Saturday."

"That's nice," I said.

"They involve you."

I had already thought about what I would say if this happened, and I was ready. But then I wavered, and I swear it was the smell. He smelled like something musky and fruity that I couldn't begin to name, but mostly he just smelled clean.

"I hope your plans include Sissy," I said. That was as good as I could do by way of discouragement, given the smell.

"Oh, Benjamin and Sissy can come along as well," he said. "They won't be in the way." More of the smile and the smell. "Can I call you?"

I nodded. "Apparently you know how."

◇◇◇

AND SO IT WAS THAT on that Saturday night, just my third in town, Sissy and I again ventured out with the Scott boys, Cameron and Benjamin. She convinced me to spend a little more time on my hair and picked out my clothes herself. Why?

Because after dinner—not supper . . . *dinner*—we were going to swing by the house for cocktails. Nothing too formal, as their parents were not going to be at home, but an opportunity to talk, to really get to know each other.

All of this got said over the telephone on Thursday night, mostly to me while Sissy stood by and played the fool. Giggling and sighing over the news that we were going to not just see the mansion but enter into it.

Dinner was at the Battery Park Hotel, another one of Grove's pet projects. It was almost sedate, compared to a lot of what swirled around Cammy and Benjy. They ordered steaks for all of us and not one but two bottles of the most expensive red wine on the menu. If it was intended to impress us girls, it half worked because Sissy grew louder and I grew quieter as the meal progressed.

Sissy pushed and pulled the conversation around to the Rhododendron Festival, now only three months away, and Benjamin—I kept reminding myself to call him that, at least to his face—Benjamin was on the organizing committee. This year there really was to be a parade, just as Sissy had claimed, and a ball at the Club.

"The Club?" I asked.

"The Biltmore Forest Country Club," Cammy explained. "We'll drive by there tonight on the way to the house."

"A parade, and not just a ball . . ." This from Benjamin. "A costume ball! Medieval costumes as in lords and ladies. For that one night, Asheville will be our domain, and we will be its rulers, with all the men and women who support the growth of Asheville there in their proper roles. Dukes and barons, duchesses and . . . baronesses? Bishops and . . . maybe there aren't female bishops."

"And who will you be?" Sissy asked Benjamin.

"I don't know yet. There will be a king but they haven't yet confirmed just who it will be. I might just be a plain old lord."

"You would never be just a plain old anything." Sissy again. "Besides I would be your lady, if you . . ."

She was stuck and I felt for her, but Benjamin, bless his heart, saved her.

"Of course, you could be my escort. I was going to ask you tonight, out at the house."

Cameron raised his glass. "A toast is in order then," he intoned. "To Lord Benjamin and Lady . . ."

"Cecilia," I offered.

"Lord Benjamin and Lady Cecilia. The proud couple. And may I say, you two will be among the handsomest couples at the Ball."

Sissy blushed down to the top of her dress, which meant most of her chest. They drank, I sipped. I wasn't entirely sure just what was happening. Was this some silly game the brothers were playing or did Sissy just have all her dreams come true?

WINE, DESSERT, AND YES, THEY each took a tug on that flask of theirs before climbing in the Packard. Adults in the front, children in the back. Sissy was so excited that I wondered if her panties would make it all the way to Biltmore Forest.

WE DROVE BY THE COUNTRY Club and idled in the parking lot, while Cameron pointed out various attributes, stressing that his father had played an important role in organizing it.

And then the house. No, that's not right. *Mansion* is more accurate. Manor, villa, abode. It would have easily held three or four of the Charlotte Street house or, for that matter, six or eight of our farmhouse on Big Pine. But size wasn't the only thing that reached out and slapped you. It was tall, stately, intimidating. When Cameron pulled up in the driveway in front of the house, you couldn't help but gaze up at it: six white columns in front, massive windows, three stories of brick at least, all of which contained wonders, or so you imagined.

We walked up the steps onto the wide porch. Sissy was glued to Benjamin's arm, and after a moment of wide-eyed staring at the house, I realized that I was holding Cammy's hand. The house had that much of an impact. "My father likes to call it Scott Hall," Cammy whispered for my benefit. "He thinks it needs a name to give it countenance."

"It has a hell of a lot of countenance all on its own," I muttered.

We took a tour of most of the downstairs, although we only peeked into the kitchen. "Not that interesting," Cammy whispered. "It's where the servants work." And my thoughts flashed briefly to Pansy, in the kitchen on Charlotte Street . . . what would she think of all this?

We ended up in what the boys called the library—a big oak-paneled room with mostly dark, heavy furniture. At one end was a massive desk with almost nothing on it except an ornate lamp and a fancy pen set. Dr. Scott's desk, it turns out, for when he was working at home.

Nobody was at home except for us and the two maids, who slept on the third floor. Cammy and Benjamin must have planned what happened next because they fixed us all a drink and invited us to sit . . . just sit and talk. I remembered my midnight forays back at Charlotte Street, when I'd found Uncle Frank's liquor cabinet, so I had enough sense to ask for bourbon. Cammy held up my glass while he was mixing the drink and asked if I wanted a splash. I nodded, not knowing what he meant. It turned out to be a splash of water. And he threw in an ice cube just for fun.

I should have known what was up when I tasted it. The drink was strong, dark and strong. Not much water in that splash, I thought.

The room was warm, there were a few lamps lit here and there, just enough lemon light so that we weren't sitting in the dark. Sissy was all but cuddled against Benjamin in one wide leather chair. She was chattering, or maybe chirping, she was so happy. Cammy and I were on a matching couch, close but not touching except for our hands. I could feel the bourbon on top of the wine from dinner swimming up into my head.

The three of them were talking about the Rhododendron Festival. More of the damn Festival, I thought, a little hazy. What costumes they might wear to the Ball. When Sissy asked Cammy what he planned to wear, he laughed. "Oh, I might black my face and go as a butler," he said, which the three of them thought hilarious.

"Jo, you're not laughing," Benjamin said after a moment.

"I don't think it's funny," I said.

Which sent them off again.

The boys got up to fix us all another drink at the sidebar, and when they strolled back, glasses in hand, Benjamin asked if Sissy would like to see the upstairs. Maybe they'd find some costumes for the Ball in one of the bedrooms. That made no sense, but Sissy was on her feet in a flash—unsteady, sure, but upright.

When the two of them were gone, Cammy dropped back onto the couch beside me again. He'd taken off his tie and unbuttoned the top few buttons of his shirt while mixing the drinks. "I can tell you're bored by the festival," he said, handing me my bourbon. "It's really for the kids." Meaning Benjamin and Sissy. "What would you like to talk about?"

"The bank," I said.

He drew back slightly. "The bank?"

I'd blurted it out, more or less, but I suddenly realized it was true. "Yes, the bank. I want to know how it works."

He suddenly smiled. "Oh, so what you really mean is that you want a promotion."

"Lord no, I've only been there a few weeks. The numbers are fascinating, but what I really want is to understand . . . what role do the Directors play?"

"You mean, like my father?" He was still smiling, and it struck me that he wasn't taking me all that seriously.

"Sure. Like your father."

"We own the bank."

"What . . . you?"

"Well, my father and the other Directors—there are eight of them—they own the bank. But as you can see . . ." He waved his own glass slowly around to signify all of the house and furnishings. "As you can see, when I say we, I mean our family."

"You own one-eighth of the Central Bank and Trust?"

That smile again. "That's why I asked if you want a promotion. If you do . . ." He shrugged as if to say it could be arranged.

I could feel myself struggling to be lucid. "I don't want a promotion, Cammy. I just thought that the Directors ran the bank for the depositors, that they had the *trust* of all the people whose . . ." I suddenly realized that his free hand, the hand without the glass in it, was on my thigh and my skirt was up to the top of my stocking. "What I'm trying to say is that I thought the people owned the bank together, and the Directors ran it for them." There . . . I'd gotten it out.

"What's the difference?" he said. "The people whose money we use to run the bank aren't smart enough to know better, and we can borrow as much of it as we want." He set his own glass on the end table and reached forward to take mine, all with that one hand caressing. Glasses out of the way, he leaned forward and—while I was still thinking about trust and Directors—kissed me. Then he all but breathed into my ear, "That's why I say we own the bank, Cause we can do any damn thing we want with it."

All of him smelled good, even his hair tonic. And now it was mixed with the maple and oak smell of the bourbon on his breath. "Any damn thing at all . . ."

Dear old Cammy Scott. If he'd moved in fast right at that moment, he'd have had me. I'd have spread my legs for him and ridden those bourbon fumes straight into some place dark and wet. Sunk so far down in that rich leather couch that I might have drowned in it.

But he missed his chance. He nibbled my neck and whispered in my ear and took so long to unbutton my blouse that I almost fell asleep. Sissy had made me wear a garter belt, and the garters gave him so much trouble that I started to giggle. Which he didn't particularly like.

Damn if I was going to do it for him, I thought. Even so, I put my mouth on his just to get the taste. To suck up what bourbon was left there on his tongue and teeth. To take the breath out of him. Thinking that might speed him up, might prime his pump. If he was so rich and owned a bank and could do any damn thing he wanted . . .

Turned out he couldn't do just anything. He still only had me half-undressed when his little brother came staggering back into the room and said he needed help with Sissy. She'd fallen down the stairs.

CAMMY STUMBLED TO HIS FEET, and I hastily tucked in my blouse and did up the buttons. I was missing one shoe but after a moment found it under the couch. We followed Benjamin back into the ornate hallway, Cammy cursing under his breath, and there at the foot of the broad stairs sat my Sissy. Laughing and singing to herself.

Together, Benjamin and I hauled her to her feet, and she smiled the sweetest smile at me. "Thank you," she said. "Sorry to interrupt . . ."

I couldn't help grinning back at her. She was, after all . . . Sissy.

It was then I noticed something pink on the stairs behind her and, with one hand still on her arm to steady her, bent over to pick it up. It was her panties, of course, dropped on the way down the stairs. I stuck them in the pocket of my skirt.

"Boys," I said. "I think it's time you took us home."

OUR CONVERSATION THE NEXT MORNING took place in Sissy's room rather than mine. And this time I went in armed with two cups of coffee, fully intending to pour one of them down her throat.

After some moaning and groaning and similar Sissy sound effects, she sat up and began to sip her coffee. "It's black," she muttered.

"After you drink that," I said, "I'll get you some with milk and sugar."

She smiled, a little crookedly, around the cup. "Have fun last night?" she said.

"Not as much as you apparently."

"You mean you didn't do it?"

"If by *it*, you mean get laid by Cammy Scott, no, I didn't. He tried, but . . . let's just say that for some rich boy who claims to own a bank, he ain't the swiftest in the world."

"I guess I beat you to it then." She sipped.

"I imagine you did. I picked your panties up off the stairs for you. You did make it all the way upstairs before taking them off, didn't you?"

"Mr. Benjamin Scott took them off, I'll have you know. First bedroom we came to."

"Looking for costumes?"

"That's right. Looking for costumes for the ball."

"He must have been looking for costumes under your skirt."

"Oh, he . . . found what he was looking for." She was almost purring.

I had to laugh at her and wanted to slap her all at the same time.

"It was . . ."

I interrupted her before she could say heavenly or dreamy or whatever the hell she was going to say. "Sissy!"

"What?"

"You are not that stupid. What if you get pregnant?"

"You can't get pregnant after only one time." She nodded at me primly. Now I really did want to slap her.

"Besides," she whispered. "I love him."

"No, you don't. You don't even know him."

"I'm getting to know him. He comes by the office during the day. If Mr. Pentland is there, he pretends like he came to see him, but if Mr. Pentland is out showing property, he talks to me."

"About what?"

"Everything. He's taking a year off before going to medical school, like his . . ."

"Like his father, I know."

"Exactly. And he wants to come back here and work in the hospital in Biltmore and take over his father's practice someday. And . . ."

"And what?"

"Marry a local girl and settle down and have children. There, I said it." Sissy was sinking into some sort of reverie, dreaming about her Benjamin.

"How many?"

"How many what?"

"Children. A dozen?"

"God no. Two exactly. A boy and a girl."

I thought of my six brothers and what bearing and nursing and raising the seven of us did to my mother. My poor, worn-out mother. "How are you going to limit it to two if you can't even keep your pants on now?" I asked. It was a mean thing to say, but Sissy could be such a child when it came to this sort of thing.

"I don't have to keep anything on." Sissy sat up in bed and leaned toward me, sloshing the rest of her lukewarm coffee on both of us. "And neither do you. Have you ever heard of a cervical cap?" She was whispering.

"Something you wear on your head?"

"No, of course not." It was Sissy and she had to pause to giggle at how stupid I was. "It's a little rubber cap, and you wear it over your cervix."

"What's your . . .?"

"Your cervix is inside your . . ." She nodded down at my lap, and suddenly, I caught her meaning.

"My God. So the man doesn't have to do . . . to wear a rubber?"

"No," she hissed. "He doesn't have to do anything. We're in charge of it."

"I've never even heard of such a thing." Here I had been making fun of Sissy for being a careless idiot, and she was way out in front of me. "Were you wearing one last night?"

She shook her head. "No, not yet. I don't have one. But Benjamin told me about a drug store in West Asheville where doctors send women like us."

I think my mouth must have been hanging open. "Like us?" Thinking maybe she meant prostitutes.

"Modern women like us. You got your hair cut, didn't you? This is like that. Besides, I'm scared to go by myself."

15

WE VISITED THAT DRUG STORE, Sissy and I; although, we had to sneak down an alley and enter through the back door to purchase the items we were looking for. We learned together how to use those items, ignoring the occasional discomfort and telling ourselves we were in charge of our lives.

By June of that year, 1929, three important changes had taken place. No . . . make that four. Four important changes.

One change: By the first of June, Sissy had wrapped herself around Benjamin Scott tighter than a slip knot. And they were well into planning the biggest Rhododendron Festival that anyone in that mountain town could imagine. Somehow it all flowed together like the spot where a flashing mountain creek flows into a strong river—the current of Sissy and her real estate connections merged nicely with Benjamin's country club, soon-to-be doctor life, her daddy's banking world blended into his daddy's need and greed for the biggest and best. And wherever they went and whatever they did was all for the greater good . . . meaning for Greater Asheville. The hospital, the money, the bank, the property values, the festival that would celebrate all these things molded into one thing.

I just said that everywhere they went and everything they did was for the greater good, but that's only half true. Some of where they went was anywhere they could be alone and half naked. She was loving his life—fast and rich—and he was loving her body—

fast and loose. I don't mean this to be ugly, for Sissy was my friend (still is, by the way), but she thought he was going to marry her. She thought that the end of all that spring and summer fun was for her to be a doctor's wife. And I'm not sure she slowed down long enough to ask him what he thought. Or if he would have told her the truth, had she asked.

Which brings us to change number two. I had been carried along on the tide of Sissy's romance with Benjamin such that everyone thought Cammy and I were a couple as well . . . including Cammy. I suspect it was enough to terrify their mother, to think that her darling oldest was "dating" a country girl and might somehow fall prey and end up married to her. But unlike Sissy, I had no illusions. I had no notion that this girl right here—Josephine Robbins Salter—was going to end up in Biltmore Forest. I didn't know where I was going, but I knew it didn't involve hanging on to the arm and the reputation of Cammy Scott while attending receptions at the Club.

What I did intend that spring was to see if the college boy was ready to become a man. To see if in addition to driving that Packard and throwing down a slug or two from his pocket flask, he might also find his way around my body. Truth be told, I like the feel of a man, and Cameron Scott was a good-looking item. I enjoy how some men like Cameron get me all hot and bothered—get me "in a lather," as we used to say up home. And I will say here—seeing as how neither my Mama nor my Papa will ever read this—that I liked the feel of a man's body in need. Hard, insistent need, if you know what I mean.

So in the spring of 1929, I figured what the hell, Cameron Scott was always around, always calling the Charlotte Street house, always offering a ride and dinner and a drink. More than one drink. We were trailing along with Sissy and her Benjamin in search of the best parade route and the finest party location, which bored me to something like madness. So, what the hell, I thought, I should get something out of the Rhododendron Festival as well. Given Sissy's conviction that the magic of the cervical cap would hold certain horrors at bay, I meant to have some fun with Cammy Scott.

I will have more to say on that topic shortly.

Change number three: By the first of June that year, Goforth and Sons had broken ground in Lake View Park on Uncle Frank's dream house. Just down the hill from Wallace B. Davis's castle was to be the Morgan family Tudor mansion. Something Shakespeare might have admired, were he alive to savor the view.

That house represented a big change because the family had to go look at it every Sunday afternoon, rain or shine. It was these Sunday afternoon pilgrimages to Lake View Park that caused me to eventually question whether I was part and parcel of the Morgan family or not. I know that for Sissy, the manse was part of her ticket into the big party that was Benjamin Scott's country club life. For Frank Jr. it was a sign of wealth and achievement. He was already taking golf lessons on the course down by the lake.

For Aunt Brenda, it was . . . what? Some sort of haven. A high place from which you couldn't fall. She had long ago given up her dream of keeping a cow, or even any chickens, in Asheville proper. So maybe the pastoral swales of Lake View Park would give her some slight flavor of the natural world, the world she'd left behind for Frank. Dawn and dusk—spring, summer, fall—but without the sweat and stink of the barn lot.

Uncle Frank? For Uncle Frank, that house, which he took to calling the Morgan Mansion even as it was being built, that house was like dying and going to heaven. It meant that his status was secure. It meant that he'd never have to worry about going back to Yancey County, meant that he could laugh at how far he'd come, a cigar in one hand and a bourbon in the other.

The fourth change. Four is big. I save this one for last because four is the one that mattered most to me—more than Sissy's romance, more than Cammy Scott's ornate gold-plated belt buckle, and more than a mansion in Lake View Park.

Four. Mable was losing her Moxie. It happened fast. More and more often during those months, I was having to be her eyes, and by being her eyes, I was learning her job. I think now that she trusted me so much and so fast because she didn't have a choice; she was desperate. She was trying to hold on to what she knew and what she was good at, even as it slipped like sand between her fingers.

Mable—her last name was Carr—had no family except for three cats and an old maidenish brother that lived with her and cooked for them both. She had no real life—nothing with color and smell and texture—but for that damn bank. And as that spring unfolded, I realized that except for her brother, she didn't have any friends.

Except for me. I became her friend.

Which causes me to reflect that I was no better. Other than Sissy I didn't have any friends.

But for Mable.

What did we have in common? I could add and subtract, I could multiply and divide. I could calculate interest in my head. Numbers spoke to me the way they spoke to her. I needed her to take the lid off that world for me, and she needed me to describe what I saw when we opened Pandora's box.

For you see, it wasn't just her eyes that were fading. It was also her memory. At first, when she taught me something about the bank's accounting process, I learned it out of sheer fascination. I didn't think about it in any larger sense; I just wallowed in it because the fractions and sums and totals were written and spoken in what had always been my own secret language.

$395,395.39. I recall exactly that number from a warm, Friday afternoon in May. What tumblers in the lock of the world gave us that repeated pattern just so that together we could savor it . . . Mable and me, her wig slipping sideways on her head as we laughed.

The books of our Bible, the accounting records of Central B & T, they became a language we shared. Written in our native tongue.

Later, when we became more honest with each other, I began to take notes on things she taught me. Wrote down not the numbers but the words she used to describe the processes by which the money in various accounts moved through the intricate body of the bank. I began to see the whole, not just the daily record of multiple transfusions and transactions.

In secret, she taught me to read and understand the loan documents that governed so much of what Central B & T was doing to feed the real estate explosion that was Asheville . . . and to feed *off* that explosion. By the time we got to the accounting records of the loan department, Mable was almost blind from cataracts. She was working from memory, and I had to read things aloud to her, which she would then interpret for me.

For those months, and for some further into the summer and fall, her tutorials were a secret. Foster Reynolds slowly caught on that I was assisting her, and he stopped by our workroom occasionally after the bank closed to salute Mable and thank me. But as Mable liked to put it, the little cock-sucker didn't understand half of what we did each week.

Here's what I slowly realized while going to school with Mable Carr. As long as it was just the numbers, I was as happy as a hog in slop. Numbers spoke to me, soothed me, sang to me.

Words, on the other hand . . .

When we got to the loan department, everything became more about words than numbers, and the words were as slippery as salamanders. I had bought my dictionary by that point and kept it prominent on the table in Mable's office. What good old Webster's helped me realize is that the kind of words they were using up on the second and third floors could mean a lot of different things. They changed shape and color when you held them in your hand . . . or regarded them closely in your mind.

That spring I learned that the numbers told the truth but the words lied.

16

HERE'S A WORD. *APHRODISIAC.* A word I can recommend as right handy. I cannot now recall where I learned that word in the spring of '29. I'm sure I heard it from Sissy and I'm sure she plucked it out of one of her magazine articles. It's a word she would savor the flavor of, like hard candy in her mouth.

I said that I would have more to tell about sex with Cameron Scott. If I'm honest, the fact that every girl and woman in Asheville wanted to lay claim to the man was not an aphrodisiac. Not for me.

The fact that his daddy was a millionaire from practicing the medical arts and deftly brokering the real estate transactions that created Biltmore Forest was not an aphrodisiac. Sissy was convinced that Dr. Craig Scott was Asheville's number two. Number two in this case meant that leaving aside Mrs. Vanderbilt—who was, after all, a kind of royalty—he had accumulated the most money in our whole end of the state. More than Grove—who was always over-mortgaged—more than Pinkney Starnes, more than the Westall boys combined. Number two meant that he could bathe in money, walk around in money, sprinkle money on his wife and two sons like fairy dust. Pure, naked money.

Not an aphrodisiac.

After I came to town, I met some women—young or old didn't matter—whose panties hit the floor just at the scent of money. But not me.

So how, then, did Mr. Cameron Scott—eldest son and namesake of several governors—get in mine? He took me to the Sky Club occasionally, most often with Benjamin and Sissy. And that was enough. There was something about that place that made me sweat. Made my lips twitch and my hips slip. Made me want to do some of what came after dancing. *Aphrodisiac.*

I don't think he ever did figure it out. Never associated where my thoughts—and later my hands—went after an evening at the Sky Club. All he knew was that I liked to dance.

Say 'em after me: the Black Bottom, the Peabody, the Turkey Trot, and, oh my God, the Charleston. Sissy taught me all of them. During those weeknights after Mable at the bank and her Mr. Pentland turned us loose. It didn't take much to get her to crank up the phonograph in the den on Charlotte Street. She played the man and I played the woman, so she could lead me through them. And Aunt Brenda's conviction—often stated—that the Charleston was "nasty and vulgar" only confirmed what I already suspected.

The night I remember best was a Saturday in early June—the Rhododendron Festival was right around the corner. We had dinner at the club, which in this case meant the Biltmore Forest County Club, with the parents. Six of us dressed like we were going to a funeral, except that in my case I was wearing the black and silver number that Sissy had me buy almost my second day in town. Definitely not a funeral dress as it might make the corpse rise up out of the casket.

It was the first time I'd worn the dress and if you'd seen the look on Mrs. Scott's face when she saw me in it, you'd have said it was a mistake. The woman already distrusted me—hell, despised me—because she thought I was on the make. Had designs on her sweet, unsuspecting son, and I'm sure the dress caused her some palpitations because, as you recall, the dress had a life of its own. It flowed.

Dr. Craig Scott liked it and said so, which didn't help. But then he had a cocktail in hand when he sat down at the table. Scotch.

Benjamin had his eyes on the dress too, which made Sissy smile. After all, she'd helped pick it out.

Cameron pretended he didn't notice the dress for his sainted mother's sake. But you could tell. There was a tremor in the air around him.

All Mother Scott did was watch me like a hawk. Wonder she could even eat because she had eyes mostly on my hands and face, watching my manners like her life depended on it. Sissy had coached me on the cutlery and various courses—which and what and how. I had assigned numbers to everything in my mind. The forks were 1-2-3, the spoons were 4-5, almost like learning a dance. The knife was 6, and I didn't even touch it until I saw Mrs. Scott pick hers up. And when she did, I mimicked how she used it exactly.

I don't recall what we ate. Not a bite. But I do recall what she said to me when the men all got up to go to the bar. Sissy was still at the table, but Mrs. Scott ignored her.

"I believe you are a country woman, Josephine, are you not?" This from the old biddy.

"Yes, ma'am."

"I believe Cameron said someplace like . . . Pinecone?"

"Big Pine Creek in Madison County. Actually, Upper Big Pine."

She didn't care for the fact that I was staring her straight in the eye. "Perhaps you can enlighten me then. Why would an older woman from . . . Pine Creek, seek out a relationship with a college educated man, a man with a future?" I let the *older woman* crack go. What she really wanted to nail me with was *country*.

"I didn't seek out a relationship, ma'am. He's been the one chasing me." Sissy gasped.

"Humppph." It sounded like she needed to spit, and I could guess at who. "Perhaps it has something to do with money? After all, Cameron is the oldest son." She'd lowered her voice for this last bit, hissing just a little.

"Not on my part. I have forty-eight dollars in the bank and another thirty-nine dollars saved back besides."

"You are choosing to be facetious." She was getting some color in her cheeks, like maybe arguing was good for her circulation.

"No, ma'am. I'm choosing to be honest. And truth be told, if I've got eighty-seven dollars in hand, I don't need any man's money." Sissy managed another gasp.

"Well, I'm sure I . . ."

"And another thing." I leaned forward. I could sense the men headed back our way. "Don't you dare hold me and my history against Sissy. I may be a country woman, but she most definitely is not."

"Of course not. Cecilia's father is the vice president of the most important bank in town." She finally broke eye contact long enough to regard Sissy. "A bank my husband is proud to be associated with. And I understand that Mr. Morgan is constructing a proud estate in Lake View Park." She paused to catch her breath and then leaned forward as well. "Just what is it that *your* father does?"

I had it on the tip of my tongue to sass her back. I wanted so to say loud and clear . . . *unlike the rest of them, he actually works for a living.* But Sissy's future was on the table in this little game too. So, I bit my tongue, reined myself in, and managed to just say, "He's a farmer, ma'am," as Scott father and sons sat back down. They all had a Scotch in hand now and were glowing with it.

◇◇◇

As we walked out to the Packard after dinner, Sissy and I lagged behind the boys for a bit. She grabbed my arm and whispered, "Why did you talk back to her? You made her hate you."

I shook my head. "Not hate. That was fear talking. Besides, I just helped her get it out of her craw."

The Sky Club versus the Biltmore Forest Country Club?

No contest.

Biltmore Forest was ornate and quiet and formal, even if you could get an expensive drink over in the corner of the dining room. The light was creamy and cool. Linen table clothes and napkins that you weren't supposed to soil with your lips. Biltmore Forest's 1-2-3 was salad-dinner-dessert, all forks . . . like the one Mrs. Scott wanted to stab me with.

The Sky Club was loud and dark and full of talk and laughter. The bar was right out in the open with Mack's rocky, scarred face behind it. The light was mostly shadows spun through with the blare of a trumpet, the syncopation of the jazz. The napkins ended up on the floor, and you never had to deal with more than one fork. At the Sky Club, 1-2-3 was your feet, your legs, your hips. Say it with me: Black Bottom, Turkey Trot, Charleston.

That night when we sat down and Cammy ordered his round of martinis, Mack came out from behind the bar and brought me my apple brandy in person, which no one had ever seen before, not from Mack. I still had a bitter taste in my mouth named Mrs. Scott, and I bit that apple pretty hard, I can tell you. Washed the taste of that woman's words right out of my mouth.

I didn't need to drink to dance, but Cammy did. I sipped the brandy and vibrated in my chair, giving him time to soak up two martinis and loosen up a bit. That night, there was a new man at the piano. The cadaverous white man was gone, replaced by a young, dark-skinned man in a dapper suit. Still the cigarette dangling from the lips. Maybe you had to smoke to tickle those ivories, I thought and grinned to myself. This man, his hands were fast and the piano was saying something different than it had before. Something more alive and more aggressive.

I could feel a heat starting somewhere down below my waist and slowly rising, the fumes of the music mixed with the smell of brandy. I was glad I was wearing the dress that flowed like water. The river in moonlight.

Finally, I couldn't stand it anymore and just stood up. When Cammy glanced up at me, I jerked my head at him. "Come on, oldest son," I said and nodded at the dance floor. "See what you got."

Aphrodisiac.

All of those dances are meant to go. Cut a dash, fast and loose.

Cammy was a lousy dancer, couldn't let go to what he called the jungle beat. But that's okay. He was just my excuse to be out there. My excuse to rise.

Maybe I wasn't dancing with him anyway. When I first dragged the boy out onto the floor, I noticed Arrowood standing in his accustomed spot, in the shadows beside the bar. His black tuxedo melted into the dark air. But he noticed me and knew me, nodded to me in that secretive way of his. The flash of his teeth.

So maybe I was dancing *with* him, with Arrowood. His eyes and his teeth.

That was enough. There was heat rising.

What I'm about to say will embarrass you. I hadn't worn a brassiere that night because I couldn't make one fit under the top of the water dress. Barely a thin slip. Dancing, I could feel my legs flying and my nipples hardening. I could feel everything rising. Sweat in my hair.

After a first number, filled up with the piano, there was a

second, more bass and that slide trombone. A third, where the trumpet came into its own, and I swear the room got darker and smoother. The air heavier.

Halfway through the third number, the trumpet blaring, I glanced over at the bar, and he had disappeared again. Arrowood there and gone. Where did he come from, where did he go?

I had to do something. I had to take the flaring inside of me somewhere. So I dragged pretty little Cammy out to the Packard in the parking lot and helped him lift my skirt.

How was it? Sex with the second richest, oldest son in Asheville? I promised to tell you and I will. The seats were leather. The windows were dripping. As small as it was, that damn steering wheel kept getting in the way. Cammy Scott was . . . an awkward object to deal with, especially when he'd had that much to drink. To this day, it makes me laugh just to think about it.

It was okay . . . No, that's not true.

All that trouble to get there, and he was finished almost before he began.

17

Like I said, the thing that truly marked my life that spring was the bank. At the bank, I had a purpose that was more than playing dress-up and hanging on to the arm of some rich boy showing off daddy's car. At the bank, I could kick off my shoes late in the day and go to work, doing a job that—increasingly—only I could do.

By the middle of June, I'd been there four months, and I was helping Mable produce each day's summary report of all transactions that took place on the first floor, excepting the loan department. The loan department was its own domain, run exclusively by men. Why they thought a woman couldn't manage to say aye or nay to a loan application or figure the interest due against the outstanding balance, I don't know, but it was all men back there, even in the cubicles.

But here's the thing: even the floor manager of the loan department started bringing their daily summaries across the hall into Mable's "office" at the end of the day, if and when their numbers didn't gee-haw. We all pretended he was bringing it to Mable even though we all knew he was bringing it to me. So maybe two evenings a week, when they couldn't make the totals for all the day's loan transactions match up, here he came. At first, he was apologetic but after a few weeks, he was just friendly, and he'd smoke a Chesterfield with Mable by her open window while I ran my eyes over the report.

My eyes, which I guess really meant my brain, never lost the habit of *seeing* numbers differently. The problem figures in the loan department report quivered on the page from the very first time I saw them, despite the fact that I didn't really know how to read the report. And some didn't just quiver; they glowed that weird rust-brown that meant mistakes compounded *here* and totals corrupted *here*. I got the loan manager to explain the report to me and scrubbed at the numbers until they began to make sense in relation to each other, but I still couldn't tell if they were an accurate reflection of the day's work.

After the second time he brought them in, I asked for the daily account books from the two cashiers—remember, men were cashiers—so I could see where the numbers in the report originated. And after the third time, I sat him down and suggested he reorganize the daily report so that the loans were categorized and summarized by the amount of interest paid (anywhere from 5 percent to 10 percent), not by whether the borrower was Class A, Class B, etc.

"But that's what they want to see upstairs," he explained. "They're mostly interested in who the borrowers are, not . . ."

"Maybe. But that's what is muddling up your numbers. That's why it would take you and me and Mable an hour to untangle one day's transactions. I can make this so simple even . . ."

"Even a man could understand it?" Mable asked, smiling through her smoke by the window.

I had to laugh. "Even a man could understand it."

To his credit, the head loan cashier laughed too. "Alright, show me. But go slow, remember I'm a man."

I did go slow, and I did redesign his report, so that somebody who understood numbers could both create it and read it. Eventually, what he ended up having to do was carry two reports upstairs for each day. One was about the "who" was borrowing money and whether they were current. And the other, my report, was about the numbers. Whether what was coming in was more than what was going out. What sorts of loans were generating a surplus and what sorts were not.

And even then, in the spring of 1929, what was happening in the loan department—at least the parts of it that I was allowed to see—was not making sense. Money was flowing out of Central B & T a hell of a lot faster than it was coming in. It was as if the boys upstairs were pouring liquid dollars from a bucket into a colander. If the daily reports from the loan department were all there was to Central Bank and Trust, it was leaking like a sieve.

Even so, something good came out of Mable and me helping the floor manager for the loan department. On June 1, Mable asked Foster Reynolds, head cashier for the whole outfit, to give me a new title and a raise. He said yes to the title and no to the raise. Doesn't make sense until you recall just how much the bank boys loved their titles. Good old Foster thought I'd salivate over the title and forget about the money, but Mable knew better and pushed him on it. And unexpectedly, when our loan department friend heard what was going on, he had a little come-to-Jesus meeting with Foster as well. One of those door-closed, come-to-Jesus meetings.

The result was that Mable was renamed First Assistant to the Head Cashier, and I became the Second Assistant to the Head Cashier, and . . . hold your breath . . . I got $15.00 per week. Do the calculations quick: $60.00 per month, $3,120.00 in a calendar year. Given everything that's happened since, you may well laugh, but I was walking around on my own little cloud there for a few days. My Papa's nine-hundred-plus acres couldn't generate $3,000 in five years, let alone in one. I thought I was going to get rich. And I did buy two pairs of shoes. Second Assistant shoes, I called them.

In the several weeks that followed, I never told Mr. Cameron Cammy Scott, oldest son, that I got a promotion, and he never brought it up, which reassured me of two things. One, he'd completely forgotten the "my father owns the bank" conversation we had that night on the library couch. And two, he'd had nothing to do with my rise in fame and fortune. I'd plowed that rocky field and hauled in the crop all by myself.

EVEN AFTER THE PROMOTION AND the new shoes, I still spent most of the day as a teller in one of the cubicles. Still smiled and nodded and marked up passbooks and deposit slips. Which was all to the good, because it meant that I didn't miss Uncle Andy Robbins when he came in for his June visit.

He was looking for me this time, was Uncle Andy. Kept bending over to peer through the little barred windows till he found my cubicle. Winked and shot me with his finger, just like he did when I was twelve years old. Jerked his head to say he was headed back to the Loan Department and that we'd visit on his way out. It was the middle of the morning, so I put up the little door we tellers used to close off a cubicle window and locked my cash drawer. I was due a break and as the Second Assistant, I didn't have to ask. The next fifteen to twenty minutes belonged to me.

I met Uncle Andy as he came back through the lobby from the loan cashiers. Same clean and pressed overalls, same white shirt—though truth be told it was faded almost yellow—buttoned to his chin. His old fedora clutched in one hand. Uncle Andy to a T except that he was limping.

"What in the world?" I asked him, nodding at his bum leg.

"Why, I nearly cut my foot off with a double-bitted ax," he said. "Had to tie off a tourney-kit with my bootlace and hobble home from the orchard."

I shook my head, meaning to admonish him. "Working by yourself, what . . .? A half-mile from . . ."

"Hush, girl. What are you doin' from behind them bars? You done your time and they cut you loose?"

"I've got a fifteen-minute break and mean to buy you a cup of coffee."

"I need somebody to buy me a cup. I've done paid every penny to them thieves in the back there."

"Come on. There's a Uneeda Lunch right around the corner of the Jackson Building."

We had apple pie and coffee at the counter. The Greek waitress, a friend of mine from countless lunches, cut Uncle Andy an extra-sized slice when she saw his limp.

"I got something for you from your Papa," he said after a sip of coffee. "Don't let me forget it before I leave."

"How is Papa? Papa and the boys."

"They're all fine. Working like hell, just like the rest of us. But your Papa seems alright. Quiet, which ain't like him, but alright. Your brothers ain't got enough sense to be otherwise." This with a broad wink.

"How's Aunt Mindy?" Aunt Mindy was his wife of 150 years or so.

"She's fine. Full of piss and vinegar. Sends her love like everybody else on the Creek. Although . . ." He leaned forward to whisper. "Between you and me, she's getting pretty damn old."

"And you're not?"

"Hell no. Can still pick up a barrel of cider weighs more than I do."

"Liar. How's ever-body else?" I could feel myself relaxing and slipping into the idiom of home. The language as it's meant to be.

He leaned back at that point, considering whether to take my question seriously or not. He took it. "Ever-body up home is . . . scared. Scared ain't exactly the right word. More like worried. Things is tight, Josie, I don't mind to say it. Tighter than a damn preacher's belt buckle. Normally, we'd borrow against the land, so we could put in an acre or two or three of burley this summer. Come September, we'd pay off the loan and buy something. Coffee and salt for a year if nothin' else."

"Did you try at the bank?" I nodded up the hill toward Central B & T.

"Hell yes. And they just laughed at me. Said to pay what you owe and walk on. So I paid against my boy's note, interest and all. Cash dollars and specie right there on the counter. Thumbed my nose at 'em and walked out." That was the Uncle Andy I knew, servant to no man. Still though, he had aged. It wasn't just the limp. Where he had shaved that morning—probably with a straight razor—he'd missed a patch or two on his neck, and his old, blue eyes were rheumy in a way I hadn't seen before.

"The bank is short of money too," I said. "Everybody's short."

"May be," he said, considering. Sucking up the last sup of his coffee. "May be, but it's shorter up home than anywhere else. Oh, we'll always eat. Cattle and hogs'll see to that. Corn rows to the edge of the woods. But any thought of gettin' ahead died with the winter."

I shivered. "Is Papa . . .?"

"Oh, he's fine. They grow enough food for half the valley. He's just lonesome."

"Did your grandbaby get born, Uncle Andy?"

He grinned and nodded. "Bouncin' baby girl. Looks like her mama instead of my son, thank God."

"What did they name her?"

"Named her Trouble," he said as he pushed himself to his feet. "Count of the season she was born into." You could tell his bad foot hurt him, and I wasn't sure he was joking about his granddaughter's name.

We parted ways in front of the Jackson Building. Before he left, he gave me a parcel wrapped in brown paper from my Papa.

It contained a scarf that had belonged to Mama. Gold and red. Silk perhaps, though silk is hard to imagine. I wrapped it back up in the paper and cradled it against my stomach as I walked back to the bank.

I don't cry, I done already told you. At least not on the street where people can see.

WAS HE RIGHT, UNCLE ANDY? Were the country people hurting more than the blissful, mindless folks in town? And was there a panic spreading up in the coves and valleys and headed our way? Three hard horsemen . . . hunger, fear, and need . . . were they riding into town?

18

THAT FRIDAY NIGHT, CAMMY AND I went to dinner alone. Sissy and Benjamin were tied up with last-minute preparations for their holy Rhododendron Festival, which was to begin the next week with a parade. Sissy had gotten her wish. She and Benjamin weren't king and queen but close on it. I believe they were Duke and Duchess of Merriment or some similar title, and they were to ride together on a floral float sponsored by the Manor, a large Tudoresque hotel at the far end of Charlotte Street.

So Cammy and I were alone downtown. He'd parked the Packard on Pack Square, and we walked to the Battery Park Hotel. This time we sat by the windows that looked west toward the mountains, and I have to admit it was nice. It was early enough so that the dining room wasn't crowded, only a few couples here and there. I was tired from the week and the day, and Cammy was being especially sweet, for Cammy. Asking after Uncle Frank and Aunt Brenda. Offering that he genuinely hoped Benjamin and Sissy would have the time of their lives the following week. That sort of thing.

Since the night I'd lured him out into the parking lot at the Sky Club, I hadn't seen him except for a few minutes here and there at the bank. I decided while we were eating dinner that maybe he liked what had happened in the cramped confines of the Packard that night, steering wheel and all. That maybe he'd been dreaming about it since.

He'd eaten most of a steak and I'd wolfed down some fried chicken, when we paused to consider what for dessert. He was staring at the menu card when I thought it might be fun to tease him.

"I wonder if you liked the dessert you had the other night?" I asked.

He looked up. "What dessert?"

"The dessert you had in the car after we were dancing at the Sky Club. That dessert." I said it with a perfectly straight face.

It actually took him a few seconds to grasp what I meant, and when he did, he blushed to the roots of his nice, smooth hair. "I . . . I think it was the best thing I ever . . . we did."

"Liked it, did you?"

He nodded, still blushing. Then he surprised me. "I'm staying in town tonight," he whispered. "I thought maybe we could . . ."

"Where are you staying?"

"Right here." He was whispering.

I was not. "Here at the Battery Park?"

"I took a room." He was pointing straight up, for most of the rooms were on the floors above. "I thought that maybe . . ."

"I know. I heard that part." He'd caught me off guard. "Let's go for a walk after supper and I'll think about it."

I was already thinking. I had my magical little cap along with the cream that went with it tucked away in my purse. But what I didn't have was a jazz combo hitting any high notes. I didn't have a glass of apple brandy brought by my friend Mack. No Black Bottom, no Charleston to make my hips happy.

And no Arrowood lurking in the shadows to tease my imagination. I think I actually looked around the restaurant there at the Battery Park, hoping to see that attentive shadow, just for a second. But nothing.

All I had was Cammy Scott, staring at me like a sad-eyed, sweet-smelling hound dog licking up a gulp of red wine from his glass. Trying so hard to be sophisticated without really knowing how.

"I'll think about it," I said again. "But just in case, let's have some dessert here."

He was nodding happily. Reached across the table to refill my wine glass. Red wine and chocolate cake, I thought to myself, might be enough to tip things in the direction Cammy wanted them to go.

After the wine *and* the cake, we walked to Pack Square. Strolled, you might say. And Cammy, this new version of Cammy, held my hand. We found his automobile, and he drove us back to the Battery Park. Given the slight, flickering tension between us, I had to smile. We were sitting on daddy's precious leather seats, the memory of which against my bare bottom made me smile ruefully.

"You'll have to take me home afterwhile," I said. "I can't stay out all night, or Aunt Brenda will have a stroke."

"Okay. Jo, I think you're the most . . ."

"Keep your hands on the wheel," I said. "Have you got that flask you like so much?"

"It's in the glove box."

It took me a minute to manage the latch, but sure enough, there it was. As Cammy was pulling up on a side street beside the Battery Park, I unscrewed the top to the flask and took a swallow. Whatever it was, it was raw and strong and burned going down.

"Scotch," he said. "Straight."

"Good," I croaked, and put the flask in my pocketbook.

I had made up my mind by that point, and I didn't intend to feel cheap about it. There was a moment in the elevator, though, when the operator gave me a knowing look, that I doubted myself. But then we were on the fifth floor and after a bit of fumbling, Cammy managed to unlock the door. Number 515.

I kicked off my shoes once we were inside, got out the flask, and took another pull. Fire again, and this time the flame got far enough down to start something warm . . . down where it mattered. I handed Cammy the flask and told him to take off some clothes.

"Which?"

"Any of them," I said. "All of them. I don't care. Start with the silly bow tie."

I excused myself to the bathroom, where I spent quite a few minutes. Taking off some of my own clothes and scrubbing away eight or nine hours of Central Bank and Trust. Inserting the blessed little cap that meant I could stop the dread and the worry before it got started. Surprisingly, I was already moist down there. Maybe I liked hotels after all.

I spent most of the next thirty minutes or so with my eyes closed. I liked Cammy better that way. Not because I didn't like to look at him but because I wasn't sure I liked where I was.

Eyes closed, I hummed to myself and sang in his ear. I scratched his belly and talked just a little bit dirty to him. Farm talk that he'd never heard in his whole, Country Club life before. I rubbed my nose against his skin and in his hair just to soak up as much of that cologne and soap smell as I could get.

And praise the gods above and below, he lasted a little longer this time. Maybe two whole minutes before he rolled over and collapsed beside me.

Better, I thought, than before.

I was still wanting to dance, even after. And when I sat up to look for the flask, the bed springs groaned and popped, which made me laugh. I found the flask underneath my skirt on the washstand, and this time the burn reached down through me in a way that made me feel I wanted something more. More of him . . . more of it, I'm not sure. Just more.

After a few minutes, the boy was snoring. I mean honest-to-God, sergeant in the army, snoring. It was kind of sweet and kind of lonely, all at the same time. I slowly got dressed. Peeked out through the blinds and saw that the sun was setting over the mountains across the river. I was afraid to commune with the flask again, as I was already a little unsteady on my feet.

"Cammy," I said clearly. "Cameron Scott!"

Nothing.

"Cameron, your father is here!"

At that, he sat straight up like a shot had been fired. "Where?"

I smiled at him. "Nowhere. Unless he's got a girlfriend up here doing the same thing we are."

"He would never, not in a thousand years."

"Well, maybe he wouldn't. Maybe he's different from every other man who ever lived. But what I want you to do is get some clothes on and take me home."

Which he did. And that would have been that. Memories of the torn wallpaper in that room, how cold the toilet was when I sat on it. The threadbare carpet and how wonderfully the bed-springs could creak and groan. That would have been that, except that when he pulled up in front of the Charlotte Street house, he said something that knocked everything else out of my head.

"Jo?" he said.

"Hmmmm?"

"I think you're the best thing that's ever happened to me."

Alarm bells should have gone off at that moment but I reckon I was still bemused by the fire from the flask. "That's nice," I muttered, thinking how good my own bed upstairs would feel if he'd be quiet so I could get out of the car.

"I think that we'll have beautiful children together."

That sobered me up. "What children?"

"The ones we'll have someday. Don't you think . . ."

"No, I don't. And don't you think either, not about that."

It was a mean thing to say, I grant you, but nothing compared to what I was thinking.

THAT NIGHT, THAT STRANGE FRIDAY night, stirred up so much inside of me that I tossed and turned before ever going to sleep. What was it? Shame . . . guilt . . . fear? All of that and more. And the very first thing I thought about the next morning was Cammy and his notion of children. Children, for God's sake. Which was the furthest thing from my mind.

I felt dislodged somehow, like I'd drifted into a dream and couldn't recall who I was.

19

I GOT UP THAT SATURDAY MORNING, put on the old clothes that I'd brought with me from home and walked down to the farmers' market on Lexington Avenue. Stores and stalls full of my people. Trucks and even wagons from Haywood and Yancey and Madison Counties, come down out of the mountains into town—even then, even in spring—to trade and sell and socialize. Here and there a team of mules tied off to a hitching post with a bucket of water to share. The men and women swapping lies and livestock, telling tales and making gossip. I so needed a strong tonic, blended up out of the smells and tastes and talk of home, that I went down to Lexington for my relief.

If you never saw it like it was in those days, Lexington Avenue was where the hills and hollows, the mountain steeps and valleys met the asphalt and concrete. It was an oasis of real life that lived on hale and hearty right in the middle of banks and drug stores and insurance agencies. And it contained much of what the mountains were before the banks and drugstores and haberdasheries came to the French Broad River valley.

I could have gone to the train station down on the river and caught the Southern railway special north for thirty miles or so and gotten off to the same sights and sounds, but because of Lexington Avenue, all I had to do was walk a hundred yards north from where Central B & T squatted on Pack Square, and I could hear the voices of home.

The Avenue was a long thoroughfare of pool halls and beaneries, merchandise stores and stalls that all blended into one another like some sort of maze. Every kind of old, beat-up truck was parked halfway on the sidewalk side-by-side with wagons and buggies. There was still an unofficial livery stable at the foot of the street, even though there was a city ordinance against it. Every sort of produce and livestock had been hauled or driven in from the outlying counties and was for sale or barter, mostly for barter.

You could get a shotgun repaired on Lexington or a wagon wheel. You could buy a dose of liquor or a dose of clap in the form of a down-on-her-luck city gal. It had a perfectly horrible reputation uptown in the world that the Scotts and the Morgans traveled in, and I loved it.

When I got down there that Saturday morning, I walked through Hal King's store and spoke to Mr. King himself, who knew me immediately when I allowed I was a Salter from Big Pine. I saw Pinkney Starnes down the street lounging and telling tales. One of the richest men in town, Pink had started out his commercial life on Lexington and had created, or at least discovered, the life insurance business. But like me, I imagine he missed the voices of mountain people.

I bought a couple of June apples off a farmer's wagon and a half-loaf of freshly baked bread. Sat myself down on un upturned bushel basket in front of Mr. King's store. Closed my eyes and savored a bite or two of the little red apples. Bit into the warm bread. Breathed and let my life unspool.

I could smell dry hay by the bale and shelled corn by the bushel. The sharp, frothy smell of cider from a jug being passed round nearby. The earthy tang of manure from the horses and mules tied up and down the street. I'd only seen one pair of oxen but mingled in was the smell of their dusty hides warm in the spring sunshine.

Stories and jokes and sermons walked by me in the street, such that I heard pieces and parts in voices as old to me as my life.

"If her daddy found out what he done, he'd a cut him where it hurts . . ."

"That man does not know God. That man has not a kernel of Christian charity or he would never . . ."

"Honey, you ain't seen what I got to offer. It hangs mostly to my knee even when it's restin quiet . . ."

Two women arguing. *"If I see you makin hot eyes at him again, I'll jerk ever damn hair in your head out to make a rug . . ."*

A poor, old blind man—or mayhap a woman—went tap, tapping by. I opened my own eyes to see and it was a man. Led along by a dog. A very smart dog, it would appear.

"I believe that the New Testament is lord over the Old Testament. That the New Testament preaches a loving God, a Methodist God." An answering voice: *"Well, you can preach that Methodist shit to the women. A man won't have it. A man knows enough to be scared of God."*

A granny woman's voice. *"I'll trade you my husband for that handsome mule you got tied up."* Another, younger woman's voice. *"Naw, grandma. I don't think so. I seen your husband and my mule is better lookin' . . ."*

Farther away, down the street, I could hear the lonesome strains of a fiddle. Some tune from another place and time that spoke to me, tugged at me where I sat. Had I always loved music? I wondered. Ever since I could remember.

"Where did you get those apples, Miss?" A kind voice, a gentle voice almost . . . just beside me. I opened my eyes. Pinkney Starnes was standing beside me, his hands in his pockets. "Seeing you enjoy them so much makes me crave one myself."

I nodded behind me. "Hal King's got 'em inside. I bet he'd give you a handful just for the asking."

"I bet he would," Mr. Starnes allowed. "Where are you from, Miss? I almost recognize you."

"Big Pine Creek in Madison County. Across the river from Barnard."

"Do you know Mr. Nathanial Salter?"

"Quite well. He's my Papa."

"And you are . . .?"

"Josephine."

"Of course. The only daughter and a parcel of brothers."

I smiled. "Lord knows. They're everywhere, Mr. Starnes . . . my brothers."

"Do me a favor and call me Pink. I'm not Mr. Starnes of a Saturday."

"I'll remember that . . . Pink."

"And you work at the Central Bank and Trust. Minding everybody's money."

I laughed. "Call me Jo, Pink. I don't work of a Saturday either."

"Well, Jo, we live in funny times. I've been down here all morning and not fifty dollars has changed hands, not the whole morning."

"What do you mean?"

"I mean a cow was traded for a wagon load of last year's potatoes. I mean a pistol was swapped for two fox pelts and a fur hat. Every sort of swap and trade you can imagine, but aye god, there's no money on the street."

I thought of Uncle Andy. "I've heard that cash is short out in the country."

"You heard right. Everybody wants it, but nobody's got any. I'm concerned, I can tell you. Folks better make a crop this summer or go hungry come winter."

"What does it do to the insurance business then, Mister . . . Pink? Cash being so scarce?"

He smiled. "Funny thing is that life insurance is the one thing that people will buy when they're scared. Fact is, the last time I was on that side of the river, I sold your Papa a policy." He paused to regard me more carefully. "With you as beneficiary."

I swallowed . . . hard. "Is he . . .?"

Pink shrugged. "Oh, he's fine. Just loves his daughter is all, which is a state of mind I can identify with."

WHEN PINK STARNES WENT INSIDE the store, I wandered on down the Avenue. Listening and thinking.

"What did the preacher say to the whore?" This a joke making the rounds with a mason jar of pure white-dog liquor. *"Beats me. What did the preacher say?"* . . . *"Don't fret, honey. God'll forgive you if you get down on your knees in front of me."*

I was drawn to the fiddle I'd heard earlier. By the time I reached the far end of Lexington, near where it turned first to gravel and then to dirt out in the fields beyond town, the fiddle had been joined by a guitar and then by a woman in raggedy overalls with a banjo. It was only the middle of the day, but they were getting to know each other, strumming a bit of this and a verse of that.

After a few songs that would make your eyes sparkle, they paused and called up an old woman named Cassie. "Sing 'My Dearest Dear,' Cas," said the banjo woman, "'fore it rains and runs us all inside." Clapping and whistling from the folks around. They seemed to know her. Then the old granny—the creases in her face lined by snuff juice—lit into 'My Dearest Dear' without hardly a pause for breath. Her voice was a faraway mountain twang, high and sweet and cut through with chimney smoke and wind from some lonely hillside.

My dearest dear, the time grows near
When you and I must part;

And no one knows the inner grieves
Of my poor, aching heart.

My own aching heart jumped in my chest. This old woman was singing for me, and my blood knew it. This old woman *was* me . . . in fifty years.

O my old mother's hard to leave,
My father's on my mind,
But for your sake I'll go with you
And leave them all behind.

I had left and gone, left them all behind. But there was no one I loved like the woman in the song. No one that made all that godawful leaving worthwhile. Not in a Packard automobile nor a threadbare hotel room.

Your name in secret I would write,
Pray believe in what I say,
You are the man that I love best
Unto my dying day.

There was no man that I loved best. There was no man to love that I could see anywhere around, but then my mother had never said to love. Never said that some man or other was the answer to my need.

And in that moment, I recalled her dying voice just as clear as if she'd been standing beside me. "*Make a life somewhere else . . .*" she'd said, "*a life I can't even imagine.*"

As I WALKED HOME TO Charlotte Street that afternoon, my sleeves rolled up and my collar unbuttoned in the June heat, I thought about my life. I held up the spectacle of Sissy's Rhododendron Festival—parades and parties and dances at the club—with the spectacle of Lexington Avenue. Two separate worlds entirely. Put them up against each other in my mind. And I smiled to myself, knowing full well which I loved the best.

20

There was an honest-to-god parade. The high school band playing their hearts out. Floral floats of every description, including one from the Manor Inn—featuring none other than the Duke of Merriment, Mr. Benjamin Scott and his consort, the Duchess Cecilia. I went to the parade on Saturday afternoon with Cammy, who'd driven the Duke up from Biltmore Forest in style.

After the parade, there was a big public spectacle on Pack Square, with the mayor, Mr. Gallatin Roberts, accepting the key to the city from some alderman or other, for his valiant efforts in creating the Greater Asheville that we'd all heard of. I'd never seen the mayor except in passing on the street, once or twice in the bank. Never heard him speak. And I'll be if he didn't launch into a speech about Athens . . . Classical Athens, and what would have happened to the Athenian genius if they hadn't conquered new territory, brought in new citizens, grown and expanded into the Peloponnese so that they became the envy of the ancient world and the inspiration of the modern!

I asked Cammy, didn't Sparta burn Athens to the ground, but for all his Chapel Hill education, he didn't know what I was talking about.

The mayor was impressive though. All that pretend classical learning from two years at Weaver College—where Uncle Frank and Aunt Brenda had gone—along with just enough law school to make him dangerous. And by the way, in case you were wondering, the key to Greater Asheville was at least two feet long and wasn't made to fit in the mayor's pocket or anybody else's.

From there, we went to a Shakespearean pageant on the grounds of the Manor, out at the end of Charlotte Street. Benjamin and Sissy were royalty so they were conveyed via some special chariot, leaving Cammy and me to make our own way. He had the Packard so he drove us out there even though it was only half a mile. He seemed nervous, told me that he wanted to go someplace special for dinner so we could talk.

Cammy wanting to talk, serious talk, was new. He mostly just wanted to drink and play. It caused me to wonder if he was going to break it off with me, whatever "it" was. It had never occurred to me that we would break up in some halfway dramatic fashion just because there didn't seem to be much to break. I figured the day would come when he just wouldn't call the Charlotte Street house anymore, and that would be that. Sissy and Benjamin could go on about their lives, and I could get back to mine.

The thought of pretty boy Cammy taking me someplace special so he could let me down easy made me smile while I watched him search for a parking spot near the Manor. What did he think I was, some sort of china cup and saucer from his mother's collection of precious things? That if he dropped me, I'd shatter. Little did he know, I was more like the old wooden spoon my Mama used for stirring the pot, hand-carved by my Papa from a straight piece of ash—no knots—so that it wouldn't split or crack even if you drove a nail with it.

I was still savoring that thought—precious china cup versus old wooden spoon—when he pulled the Packard up into somebody's yard and just abandoned it there. I jumped out before he came around to open the door for me, just like I always did, and we started up the side street toward the Manor. He'd thought to bring a blanket for us to sit on, so that we could enjoy seeing the panorama of Shakespeare characters, played by the local high school kids, trot across the low stone parapet behind the Manor.

The narrator of the panorama was funny without meaning to be. The students who played the characters wore outlandish outfits borrowed from the high school theater department, I guess. And as each character's name was called out and a short description read, Lady Macbeth with a dagger or old bent-over Lear with a fake beard, the actors would stalk or stagger across the parapet where we could see them. At that point in my life, I had only ever heard of these characters, never really seen them. I'd never been in a theater, not a theater with live actors, and I was fascinated. Juliet, who for sure looked like a child, chased across by her Romeo, who didn't look old enough to be in high school. I love stories, and all this did was make me want all their stories for my own. Read them and, even better, see and hear them.

But Cammy, I could tell, was bored. I'm guessing that he knew all about it from his university days, and this was nothing new. When a Moor named Othello came across in black face, he said something ugly that he thought would make me laugh. But which only made me think of Pansy and her husband, Raymond. I didn't laugh at Cammy but wished instead that Pansy would someday answer the dozens of questions I asked her about . . . her life. Her children, her mother who suffered from the "sugar" in her blood, did she like it when Raymond called her "old woman," how did they get back and forth to work?

But soon, too soon for me, Shakespeare was over, and then the king and queen of the Festival were introduced—in real life, one of the Westall boys and a pretty girl whose first name was Stuart—funny name, I thought, for a girl. I knew that wherever she was standing in back with Benjamin, Sissy had a momentary twinge of envy—wanting to be named Stuart, stepping out as

Queen of the Festival. But then their time came—the Duke and Duchess of Merriment—sashaying across, and I yelled out to her, which I imagine embarrassed Cammy but what could I do? I loved Sissy.

The special place that Cammy had dreamed up for supper—excuse me, dinner—was the Grove Park. Which, I have to say, seemed like an awful lot of trouble and expense just to break it off with me. He could have done that at the Five and Dime or the Uneeda Lunch, I would have understood. I almost said that to him, just to let him off the hook, but by that point, he was so nervous about the whole thing that I let him have his way, and in we went.

A reserved table by the window, looking out toward Mt. Pisgah and the long ridge beside it called the Rat. Sunset orange leaping across the western sky and the mountains fading to a darker and darker blue.

I had the trout and he had a steak, as I recall. He always had steak, as if it was more than his prerogative . . . almost his duty . . . to gnaw on that beef. No flask that night but plenty of wine, which I thought was too expensive. Let him spend the money on the next girl, is what I thought. Maybe she would be named Stuart, and maybe she would have the kind of tastes that would do justice to Cammy's wallet.

No dessert but there was more wine. By that point, I was feeling vaguely guilty because of what it cost for the poor boy to just move on. Evolve. Grow. Be something more akin to his mother's dreams and his father's accomplishments. If I could have figured out how to say what I was thinking, I would have put it right out there. I didn't dislike Cammy at all, and I hated that he felt beholden to me.

"This is awfully hard for me, Jo," he said after the waiter had cleared the plates away. "I'm not good at . . ." He paused, struggling.

"It's alright," I said, and reached across to pat his hand. "I know full well what you're trying to say. I think we've become . . ."

He interrupted me. "You do? You understand, Jo, truly?"

"Sure, I get it. We've had fun. Seen some sights, done some things. And now it's time . . . you know?"

"I do know," he whispered hoarsely. "I do. Thank you for understanding. It is time!"

I nodded at him, encouragingly.

"Josephine, will you marry me?"

I don't know if my jaw hit the table, but it might have.

"What the hell, Cammy?"

"Marry me and become Mrs. Cameron Scott. You'll never have to work again, and you can focus your considerable . . . verve on raising our children."

I wasn't sure just what *verve* he was referring to.

He started in again, lost in his own words. "We can build a fine home out in Biltmore Forest, near my parents . . ."

So your mother can stab me to death with a steak knife, I thought.

"And we can create our own Rhododendron Festival year-round, with you as queen and me as king. I can see it now, I truly can. We'll be the first couple of . . ."

"We'd be the first couple all right. The first couple to commit homicide."

"What?" He said it gently. He was still consumed with his vision, his dream.

"Cammy, we could not be more different, you and me. You come from privilege and money and connections and . . . God knows . . . the power and the glory. I come from the upper end of Big Pine. Not even the lower end, near the river. The upper end, where your big, beautiful Packard can't even navigate the trail nor ford the creek. What in God's name made you think that we were . . . made for each other?"

"But you let me take you to bed. You let me put . . . You liked it when I took you up to my hotel room." He was getting a little loud, which was funny as hell and embarrassing all at the same time.

"I liked it okay," I admitted, almost whispering. Hoping that he'd mimic me and lower his voice. "I liked the bed better than the seat of that damn car. But Cammy, just because a girl lets you play around once in a while doesn't mean that she's in love with you and that you're supposed to fire up the Episcopal Church and schedule the priest."

"You could be pregnant," he said, suddenly.

"I'm not," I shot straight back, a fact of which I was reasonably certain.

"Every woman in this town wants to marry me, by God." This was at least a new tactic, and it had some truth in it. I thought about my friend Jezzy at the bank. She sure as hell would jump over a house to marry Cameron Scott.

"Every woman in this town . . . except one," I said quietly. And it hit me suddenly, out of that beautiful evening sky, that I was the one trying to let him down softly. He was the china cup and saucer. Sweet idea, but I got over it when he started in on me again.

"Do you realize that I am the oldest son of what is probably the second richest family in Asheville? Do you realize that you would come into a life such that you, in your relative ignorance, can't even imagine? Do you realize that, in time, you would become the first lady of Biltmore Forest? That you would absolutely rule the Biltmore Forest Country Club?"

"Don't care," I said. "A cold bed makes for an empty house. Regardless of how big it is."

He drew back then and sneered at me, as if he'd suddenly realized who I was. Somehow, I'd finally managed to insult him just enough to prick his bubble. "You . . . bitch," he finally growled. "You stupid, redneck bitch. My mother was right about you all along. You are simply too ignorant and too backward to have any appreciation for what I'm offering you. You don't deserve it. You . . ." He was turning a bad shade of purple, the veins throbbing in his forehead. "You are little more than a feral cat, screeching in the night."

I thought about that last part, the *feral cat* part, and nodded ruefully. "Something like that," I admitted.

Needless to say, I had to walk home.

PART TWO

FALL 1930

21

IN MAKING A LIFE, WHAT matters and what doesn't?

By the summer of 1930 I'd been in big, bold Asheville for over a year. And as summer turned into fall that year, you might say that the quilt scraps out of which I stitched my life all had to do with work. You'd be wrong; there were some stray bits and pieces hidden away in the pattern that were nighttime dark and mysterious, but mostly, it looked like Jo Salter went to work at the Central Bank & Trust Company. You'd say she was consumed by it.

In July of that year, during a sweaty hot afternoon, Mable had a stroke while climbing the stairs from the first floor to the second. She'd been summoned to explain some items from the previous day's reports and she had them in hand when she stopped, gasped, and fell hard down the stairs. I saw all this because I'd walked into the stairwell with her, whispering the answers to the typical questions into her ear.

I jumped up the stairs and tried to catch her as she rolled down, but even so she fell like a rag doll. The papers flew, her glasses smashed, her dress rode up almost to her hips, and worst of all, her wig flopped down over her face.

I pinned her to the stairs as best I could and yelled for help. And when I say yelled, I mean it. I'm guessing they heard me on the top floor and out in the street. A younger man I'd seen but didn't know came clambering down the stairs from above with Foster Reynolds, the head cashier, right behind him. It didn't seem right to me that these men should see dear Mable with her dress pulled up and her wig off, so as soon as the first man down grabbed her arm to help hold her, I flipped that crazy red wig back over the top of her head, hiding the close-cropped gray hair and revealing her face. Her mouth was gaped open and her lipstick smeared around it.

"Mable," I said to her softly. "Mable, can you hear me?" She groaned and tried to say something but there were only sounds, no words.

Together the three of us slowly propped her up and eased her down to the bottom of the stairs where she could sit with the men on either side. She'd lost a shoe when she fell. I found it and slipped it back on her foot.

Foster sent a cashier down the street for a doctor. I kept trying to talk to her, and after a bit one eye came open and mostly focused. The other stayed half-closed, and that half of her face sagged, it seemed to me, even as she tried to talk back. She could make slurred noises that she seemed to think were words but they were nothing that any of us could understand.

It would be days before I got to where I could understand her, though I visited her once or twice a week, first at the hospital in Biltmore and then later at home. She never came back to work.

The upshot of it all was that after a few weeks of wrangling on the second floor, yours truly became the First Assistant to the Head Cashier. By wrangling, I mean that the boys upstairs didn't want to promote someone so young, with so little experience in banking, and—the real truth—someone they didn't know. Two things swung the tide in my favor. One, Uncle Frank finally took a chance and spoke up for me, guaranteed me as it were. Two, every time they were mystified by the numbers that came up the stairs at the end of the day, they had to call up somebody to explain, and they were stuck calling me. And when they didn't like or understand the news from the Loan Department, the floor manager for loans always took me with him. He and I marched up that same stairwell where Mable had fallen down, and together we'd explain that almost all those with outstanding loans—not just the country people—were struggling to pay. The flow of money was slowing down, day by day, as if some giant hand was cranking closed a faucet. I thought often of Pink Starnes, who'd said quietly to me down on Lexington Avenue the summer before that there was no cash money on the street.

First Assistant meant that officially I worked directly under Mister Foster Reynolds. And yes, I know exactly how that sounds . . . *under* Foster. Apparently, he had some thoughts about what *under* meant as well because the first few times I was upstairs in his office late in the day, bending over the day's reports on his desk, he put his beautifully manicured hand square on my ass. The first time, I was too surprised to say much. The second time, I negotiated, as Mable had liked to call it. "Negotiated" meaning that I explained how he needed to keep his hands to himself or I'd take the fancy fountain pen he displayed on his desk and stab him in the eye with it. I meant what I said.

He got the point, so to speak. Occasionally, he needed a reminder over the months that followed, and he never did stop calling me *Jo honey*, but mostly we got along, and slowly, I taught him how to understand the numbers that were coming up from downstairs. He wasn't an especially quick study, but as summer turned to fall, even he grasped what was happening.

THE MORGAN ESTATE IN LAKE View Park wasn't finished by the previous September, the way Uncle Frank had promised us all the year before, but it was done in early spring. And Classic Tudor Revival it was, which may have contributed to Uncle Frank calling it the Morgan Mansion. And just as he had described it to us, there was a slate roof with two tall, ornate brick chimneys. Eighteen rooms, four of which were bedrooms and four bathrooms.

Think of that. Four bathrooms . . . four!

The farmhouse on Big Pine had an indoor sink with a pump handle, but what you might call the toilet was still a privy hidden away in a pine thicket behind the house. And as far as actually taking a bath, that was something of an ordeal that involved heating water on the wood stove and pouring it into a washtub. In the summer months, Mama and I didn't even bother to heat the water, especially for my brothers. Far cry from four bathrooms inside the house.

Three of the bedrooms at Morgan Mansion and two of the bathrooms were upstairs, where Uncle Frank and Aunt Brenda established themselves, along with Sissy and Frank Junior. I moved into a bedroom in the basement floor, which opened out through a dark hallway into the back yard. There was a rather primitive bathroom—number four—down there off my little hallway, but Lord God, it had a clawfoot bathtub in it, and steaming hot water straight out of the tap.

Aunt Brenda kept apologizing for sticking me way off from the family like that, and the furnace room was pretty much the only room other than storage in the basement. After the fourth or fifth time she offered to make room for me upstairs and I politely refused, I asked her what in the world, and she explained that the room had originally been intended for "servants."

I laughed out right. "You mean like Pansy and Raymond?"

She nodded and blushed. She was still enough of a country woman that she really didn't know what to do or say on the topic.

"Then it's perfect for me," I reassured her. "All it means is that I can get outside and breathe fresh air without having to climb up and down the stairs."

And it was perfect for me. Meaning that I was a working girl and left the house to catch a streetcar into town often before anyone else was up in the morning. Plus I was a woman who liked to dance, who occasionally came in after everyone else, even Sissy, was asleep.

Now, as for Pansy and Raymond. That is a story unto itself. They had walked from their place on Valley Street, down behind Pack Square, to the Charlotte Street house. Early or late, wore their shoe leather out walking to work. But Lake View Park was way too far out for that. They could have ridden the same streetcar as me in the opposite direction—sitting in a special section in the back—but the city took possession of their home at about the same time, and Aunt Brenda convinced them to move out to Lake View Park and live over the garage behind the mansion.

When I say the city took possession of their house, I mean the city took over a wide swath of property on the slope behind the bank and other prominent city buildings that was the traditional colored settlement in Asheville. Eminent Domain, whatever the hell that means. The plain way to say is that the city rooted the colored community out of their own homes as part of some grand plan to remake the downtown area. Where the people who lived there were supposed to go was a mystery, at least to me, and nobody I talked to seemed to even care. So maybe it was okay for Pansy and Raymond to come out to the Park, maybe they were relieved to have work on top of a place to live . . . Maybe.

There's a lot more to say about that, and I intend to say it, but for now, you have a picture of Morgan Mansion in the summer of 1930. And at least, from where I was living in the basement, I got to see a lot more of Pansy and even Raymond than I ever had before. And since I hadn't been brought up in town and hadn't been taught to keep my distance, I talked to them every chance I got. And slowly, they began to say more to me than just "yes, Ma'am" this and "no, Ma'am" that. Don't get me wrong. I was still an outsider to them, just like I was an outsider to the family upstairs, but it was more like I was somewhere in between. I had a place that was neither them nor those.

Which was fine with me. I grew up with all brothers shoving me around, and I've never been afraid to be the only one of something.

For a while after we all settled in out at Morgan Mansion, my only transportation in and out of town was on that old rickety streetcar that ran down by the lake. I'd walk the quarter mile or so down and catch the first car into town and repeat the process in the evening. I grew up walking everywhere, so this was all fine with me, even on one of those summer evenings when it was determined to rain all over my head. I bought a raincoat.

But once I was out there, I was stuck there. No Sky Club for me. No dinner out, no dancing. Worst of all, no music except from Sissy's phonograph.

The good news is that Sissy and Benjamin adopted me. Sissy and I were still good friends, even though she was genuinely horrified that I'd refused to marry Cammy. Not only did she think I'd taken leave of my senses, she also feared that it would endanger her romance with Benjamin. That the Scott family would associate her with me, and she'd be tarred with the same ugly, redneck brush forever. Turns out that Mrs. Scott was relieved that I'd refused Cammy. She told Sissy she was actually grateful that I knew I wasn't good enough for them. That I "didn't belong."

So almost by default, Sissy got Mother Scott's blessing. She and Ben—somewhere along the way he became a Ben—were still together, and now that Cammy had moved on to a Biltmore Forest society girl that his Mama approved of, they could afford to take pity on me one or two nights a week. Pity in the form of supper, drinks, and best of all . . . the Sky Club.

22

I LIKED GOING TO THE CLUB with just Ben and Sissy. For one thing, they let me order for myself and pay for myself. They were young and fun and silly together. I couldn't imagine Ben as a doctor, but he was for sure playing doctor with Sissy every chance he got, and it showed between them. They weren't just steamy for each other, they actually liked each other. Talked to each other. It was enough to make me hope it all worked out somehow. That Sissy could ignore Mrs. Scott's forked tongue and somehow end up at the altar with the second son of the second richest family in Asheville.

The night I remember best we three ate supper at the Battery Park Hotel, always simpler and quieter than the Grove Park or some other fancy place the Scotts favored. At the Battery Park, we could enjoy the view out the dining room windows, eat slowly and actually hear each other when we talked. I was always happy when Ben and Sissy would just forget I was there for five or ten or fifteen minutes, chattering away at each other.

And then the Club. A table near the bar because they knew I liked Mack and Mack liked me. I was still the only person that anyone had ever seen personally served by Mack the bartender. Broad, round shoulders, that rocky face, seldom speaking. He always smiled when he saw me, showing a few gaps in his teeth, and he always brought me a glass tumbler half full of apple brandy, ignoring whoever else was at the table and letting the waitress in her short, black skirt deal with them.

"What is it with you two?" Sissy asked that night. "You and Mack?"

"It's entirely an affair of the heart," I said to tease her. It was a line I'd read in a book and I liked it. "Mack and me."

It was mid-week, late summer—probably the end of August or early September—and the place was only half-full. The whole band wasn't on that night, only the cadaverous white man at the piano, his hands running up and down the keyboard in long, slow melodies that felt like a constant, effortless background to the clinking glasses and casual blather of late summer. And yes, there was a cigarette dangling from the cadaver's lips. Smoke curling around and obscuring his face.

When we sat down, I was careful to sit facing the bar so I could see Mack as he worked, receive and return his occasional smile. But mostly so I could see Arrowood, should he occupy his usual spot—by the bar in the dimly lit hallway. I was determined on that night to play his game, to watch him so closely that I actually saw him come and go, to see where he went when he disappeared.

Everybody said he was wicked, mysterious, violent . . . but nobody said he was a magician. He couldn't just snap his fingers and fade into smoke and shadow.

That night, I actually saw him in action. Saw part of where that reputation came from. To my left, by the dance floor, there was a table full of men who'd been drinking steadily while they ate. The hard stuff . . . whiskey from a bottle bought at the bar. They were loud when we came in and grew louder once they finished eating, pushed their plates to the middle of the table, and began to drink in earnest. Tough guys, you would have said.

If I hadn't been watching so closely, I would have missed much of what followed.

One of the men whistled for the waitress. That in itself wasn't so unusual at the Club. Men whistled at women, then as now.

When she walked over to the table, one of the men put his arm around her waist while they joked with her about their order—which turned out to be nothing more than a fresh bottle. Again, nothing to turn the room upside down. She stepped back to get away from that fat arm, and when she turned, the man slapped her on the ass. They all started laughing.

Like a fool, I'd been distracted by the men playing with the waitress. I'd let my eyes off Arrowood for just that long . . . from the whistle to the slap. So I didn't see him move at all, but then suddenly he was standing beside the table, up close, between two of the seated men. One of the men beside him started to get up for some reason, and Arrowood put his hand on the man's shoulder. Held him in place even though Arrowood himself looked slender as a reed between two solid bricks of mean drunk.

Then Mack was at the table too, delivering the bottle for the waitress. It's hard to describe what happened next because it went fast and mostly all at once. I saw Arrowood reach in his jacket pocket and I saw his arm swing up and quickly down. The bottle in Mack's hand shattered. One of the tough guys was on the floor, one slumped forward with his head on the table. Breaking glasses and broken plates. The stench of spilled liquor mixed in with the cigarette smoke. The other two men got halfway up and then sat all the way down. Mack still held the neck of the broken whiskey bottle casually in his hand. Arrowood was talking, I could tell that, but so softly I couldn't hear what he said.

Then the two tough guys who were still upright half led and half dragged the other two toward the door and the stairs. It didn't take them long to get gone, and they left cash on the table. A minute, maybe two, was all it took. Everyone in the place had fallen silent and turned to stare, while the skeleton at the piano played on throughout, keeping time with the action and never missing a note.

The waitress who'd gotten her ass slapped immediately came over and started cleaning up the mess. And because I felt so strongly a part of the place and because I felt for the waitress, I got up, walked over, and began to help her. The volume of human voices rose up around us again like a tide. Mack was back and forth with a broom and a dustpan for the broken glass; he seemed to accept that I was stacking up dishes and collecting glasses. And Arrowood, of course, was gone into thin air . . . like a specter.

When the table was right again, the harried waitress wiping it down with a rag, I looked straight into Mack's sweet, scarred face and asked. "Where the hell did he go?"

"Who?" he mouthed.

"The boss."

He almost smiled. And with the barest nod and a wink pointed me toward a door in the corner beyond the dance floor, that appeared to lead onto the second-floor balcony, a door I'd never seen anyone use.

I DIDN'T HESITATE AND I DIDN'T knock. I just tugged the door open and stepped through. It didn't lead to the main balcony, where there were tables for people to eat, but to a smaller, second-floor porch walled off from the public eye. You could hear people eating outside around the corner, but this was quieter, more private. One small table and a few chairs. A lit candle on the table.

He was standing at the solid concrete railing with his back to me, apparently staring out over the city below. I let the door close behind me.

"We need to check on those guys in a few minutes," he said. "Make damn sure they're gone." There was something about the way he spoke, something vaguely familiar, but for the life of me, I couldn't place it.

"Alright."

He turned around, a fresh cigar in the corner of his mouth and a lit kitchen match halfway to his face. "You're not Mack," he said softly. Which seemed to be his natural way of speaking, since nobody ever heard a word he said unless he wanted them to.

I smiled. "Nope. Nothing like. Although he's a friend of mine."

He smiled back with half his mouth, the other half still clenched around the cigar. He lifted the match on up and blew it out, apparently meaning to make conversation.

"I'm the woman who likes apple brandy," I said. "At least I started liking it the first time you sent it to me."

He took the cigar out of his mouth. I thought he was going to speak but I was wrong. Instead, he smiled in a way that let me know he remembered me. Me *and* my brandy. I could see his teeth in the yellow candlelight, the smile was not my imagination. His face was all thin, sharp planes of shadow.

"My name, in case you're interested, is Jo Salter. Josephine really, but nobody ever bothered with all that. I know it sounds like a man, but . . ." Jesus, was I that nervous? "So, it's . . . just Jo."

Another nod and he stuck the cigar back in his mouth. Was it possible that he was nervous too? Me having tracked him into his lair . . . trapped the wild creature?

"What's your name?" I asked him, as gently as I could. "What goes with Arrowood?"

He paused for the longest time, as if we had all the time on the ticking clock, before taking the cigar out of his mouth yet again. "Where you from, Jo? You're no city girl, despite the company you keep." And that was it.

That . . . was . . . it. Everything. His voice was as country as mine. His voice was like hearing one of my brothers sitting on the porch after a long, hard day, letting the work sweat dry under his shirt. Exactly like, except gentler, softer. Easier on the ear than one of my brothers.

"Big Pine," I whispered. "Madison County." I felt something like tears forming in my eyes. As if I was confessing to a long-held secret of my own.

This time it was more of a grin than a smile. "I know where it is," he said, and oh, the singing in that voice. "Upper part of the valley or lower?"

"Upper."

"You know Jake Worley's store?"

"Jesus, God," I said. "Who are you?"

"Arrowood from Spring Creek," he replied. "Across the mountain from you." And then after a moment. "I been to Worley's Store is all. More than once before I left out from home."

"What in the wide world is your name?"

I could swear he was about to answer. Reveal the secret. But before he could speak, the door opened behind me and Mack looked in on us.

"Them bastards gone?" Arrowood asked.

"They're gone, boss. One of the boys watched them drive out of the parking lot."

Arrowood nodded. "They leave enough dough to cover the second bottle?"

"More than enough for everything they ate, drank, or busted." Mack hesitated, cleared his throat, and then handed me a glass. "You left your drink, Jo. I didn't want it to vaporate."

I smiled my best smile at him. To know Mack was to love him. "It looks like you freshened it for me."

"Them apples get stale if you leave 'em alone too long." He grinned and pulled the door closed behind him.

I sipped, watching Arrowood over the rim of the glass. It

burned nicely going down, and I wondered if it was what his cigar smoke tasted like, in liquid form. On impulse, I handed the tumbler to the mystery man from Spring Creek. "Want a taste, Arrowood?" I asked.

"Levi," he said quietly, "to my friends." He took a swallow of the brandy, sighed, and handed the glass back to me. "My uncle made this last fall. It ain't his best, but it'll put a crease in your pants."

"I'm not wearing pants," I said to Levi. And immediately blushed. "Not so you'd notice."

It was the first time I ever heard him laugh.

23

WAS IT THE STOCK MARKET collapse from the previous October? I thought not. After all, the stock market was in Manhattan, New York City, a hell of a long way from Asheville, North Carolina. Was it the pressure of having to do justice to Morgan Mansion? Living the high life in a home that was as big as a small hotel? Again, I thought not. Was it watching Frank Junior do little else with his life than play golf and hang around the drugstore with his friends? Doubtful.

Something was bothering Uncle Frank, though, that autumn of 1930. He was distracted, worried. And a couple of times, he actually invited me into his study after dinner. Which never happened. Not with Sissy or Junior. Not even with Aunt Brenda. And once we settled in and he offered me a glass of something sweet he called sherry wine, he quizzed me about the numbers. The bank numbers.

I explained to him what the daily reports showed. People still trusted the bank, still brought their money there to deposit. The dailies from the tellers up front weren't strikingly different than they were a year ago, except that the amount of money being deposited versus the amount withdrawn had slowly, day by day, decreased.

"Not disastrously," I reassured him. "Incrementally." And then added, "bit by bit."

He nodded, sipping his bourbon whiskey, which, if I'd been

a man, he would have offered me rather than that liquid candy in its little crystal glass.

"What about the loan department?"

I stared at him for a moment before I answered. He wouldn't quite meet my eyes. "Uncle Frank, don't you see the reports we generate every day?"

He looked up and shook his head. "They go over those down on the second floor. You know, Foster, and the men who work at that level. Then, once a week, on Friday, they present the summary for that week to us."

"Who's us?" I wasn't trying to interrogate the poor man. I was genuinely curious. I had only picked up bits and pieces of what went on up on the second and third floors from things Foster and others had said in passing, always assuming I was too stupid to understand. At that point, I'd only been as far as Foster's office and never even dreamed of rising up to the holy of holies on the third floor.

"Us?" Uncle Frank seemed puzzled. Maybe the bourbon was getting to him.

"You said *us* . . . up on the third floor."

"The vice presidents and the men at that level. The men who operate the bank day to day . . . We report to the president and the Directors."

I hated to tell him but they didn't operate the bank day by day; that happened on the ground. "You report once a year?" I asked him. "To the Directors I mean."

"Oh, no. Once a quarter." He looked vaguely troubled for a moment and then recalled how we'd started down this rabbit hole. "What about the loan department?"

"Well, there you have a problem. From what I can tell—and all I see are the dailies from the loan cashiers—the vast majority of your outstanding loans are struggling to pay. Maybe they can make interest but not much toward the principal. Everything is slowing . . ."

"It's those goddamn rednecks from out in the country! Slouching in here in their overalls and busted boots. Offering a bushel of potatoes or a hunting dog against cash. Like we're running a produce stand instead of a bank!" I'd never seen him quite like this. He was sputtering, and a dark blue vein was throbbing in his neck.

"Actually, Uncle Frank. That's not it. That's not your problem. Sure, the country people are slow to pay what you and the boys upstairs call your Class C loans, but those are typically small amounts at high interest. It just doesn't amount to that much money. Where you're bleeding is the big real estate loans, the Class A loans. When one of the fat cats . . ."

"What do you mean, the *boys upstairs*?"

"Excuse me. The *men* upstairs."

He nodded. Tried to take a drink out of an already empty glass.

"What I'm trying to tell you is that the country people owe you fifty or a hundred bucks plus interest in a year. Crop money. Acreage money. What you need to figure out is how to get payment out of the big loans. Town loans . . . houses, hotels, churches, development and construction money." I could not believe that I was having to explain this to him, me an ignorant country girl and him the Vice President of Something or Other.

"Real estate?"

I nodded at him. "You once told me that the whole point was to keep the money moving. Always moving, faster and faster, so everybody would prosper. Well, if the money is slowing down—and it is, day by day—then the big money matters more than the little money."

"Will you pour me some more bourbon, Jo? Just a tot . . . I need to think."

⁂

WE HAD SEVERAL CONVERSATIONS LIKE that, and occasionally I thought something might be wrong with his memory—you know, like he was a lot older than his sixty-something years—because I felt like I was repeating myself. It was as if I was trying to drive an idea into his head and his head was fighting it. And yet, he kept asking. I used to ask Mable where the money came from, and now it seemed like he was asking me where had the money gone.

Plus he was losing weight, which for a man like him, is not a good sign. Aunt Brenda was fussing because his clothes didn't fit him, and she had to send his pants out to be taken in because he wouldn't allow her to do it herself. And at dinner—for it was called dinner once we moved to the Mansion—he wasn't himself. He was quiet for long stretches, so Sissy and Junior tried to pick up the slack and talked a lot more than usual. Sissy about Ben and Junior about his new golf clubs.

Then, one Monday afternoon in early fall, he came all the way down to the first floor of the bank and asked me to go with him to a big rally in the city auditorium where the mayor, Mr. Gallatin Roberts himself, was going to introduce the new and Greater Asheville. "Will I be back by five o'clock?" I asked him "So I'll have time to audit the accounting books and produce the dailies?"

"Of course, of course. Plenty of time."

You have to take into account how unusual this was. I'd never gone anywhere with Uncle Frank during the week, and a big event at the Auditorium with the mayor strutting his stuff was for the boys on the third floor, not first floor girls like me.

Uncle Frank drove the two of us the four or five blocks over to the Auditorium, which was up on the hill close to the Battery Park Hotel. He was subdued while driving, but he did take the time to explain more about what was going on. And the explanation would have sobered up a rummy.

The city was in financial trouble, he explained. Big financial trouble because every year the city fathers floated bonds to cover expenses while they waited for the tax revenue to come in at the end of the year.

"You mean like a farmer who borrows to put in his crop against the hope that the weather will hold, and he can pay off at the end of the growing season?"

He took his eyes off the street in front of us just long enough to glance over at me. "Exactly like that," he said, "although I never thought about it that way . . . Only in this case we're talking about hundreds of thousands of dollars, not . . ."

"Fifty or a hundred." I finished his thought for him.

He nodded. "And slowly, year by year, the city has been falling further behind . . . like your farmer."

"Where's the city's money?" I was afraid of the answer.

"Central B & T."

"Shit." I said it without thinking, but boy, did I ever mean it.

He nodded again. "Yeah, that."

"So, why are we pitching a big party over this Greater Asheville campaign? Sounds a little hollow to me."

He had just pulled into a parking space on Haywood Street, a block from the Auditorium. He set the brake and turned off the car engine, which wheezed, knocked a few times, and died. He twisted slightly on the seat to look at me, and I was struck again by how his face had aged in the last year. Losing weight hadn't helped, and there were lines and wrinkles etched into his cheeks that hadn't existed when I first came to town.

"The mayor fought like a madman for the past eighteen months to expand the city limits to include places like Lake View Park, North Asheville, Kenilworth, Biltmore Forest, East Asheville. That's his Greater Asheville. Can you guess why?"

I didn't know Kenilworth or East Asheville, but I sure as hell knew Lake View and Biltmore, and I guessed that North Asheville was the part of town Sissy and her bosses were busy peddling for Grove Estates. "Money," I said simply.

"That's right. He wasn't after the poor parts of the county. Who cares about them? He was after the tax base represented by the wealthy sections, and he went all the way to the legislature in Raleigh to get it. He won't say it, and nobody else will either, outside the top floors of the bank or the inside offices at City Hall, but the whole Greater Asheville movement was a last-ditch effort to pull the city out of what could have been a disaster."

"You said *was*, as in *was* a last-ditch effort. I hope you mean he succeeded."

He sighed and actually smiled. "I think so. He's got to make it to the end of the year, so he can collect the taxes from all those new sections, and he has to hope Biltmore Forest doesn't win their lawsuit against the city. But I do believe we're going to make it."

So we went on into the Auditorium and found seats near the front. And we jumped up and applauded just like everybody else when the mayor prayed his prayer of thanksgiving and waved his arms in the air. Greater Asheville was ours, and all would be fireworks and parades from now on. It was only later that night that I thought about the last thing Uncle Frank had said that day. *He's got to make it to the end of the year,* and then—even more worrisome—*I do believe we're going to make it.* Just who did that *we* include, I wondered as I was trying to fall asleep? The town? The family? . . . Jesus, the bank?

24

HOW TO DESCRIBE LEVI ARROWOOD?

I can't really compare him to someone else. Truth is, he isn't really like anyone you know. Or I know, for that matter.

He's not a big man. Just short of six feet and thin. In light or shadow, his face is all angles, a sharp jaw and high cheekbones. His cheekbones and his brown eyes would cause you to think there's a Cherokee branch in the Arrowood family tree, and I suspect you'd be right.

Sandy hair. You know what I mean when I say sandy? Halfway between blond and brown. For the longest time, I thought he had almost black hair because I only ever saw him at night in the Club. It took daylight to tell me something different. Eventually, I came to know that his hair turned lighter in the summer and darker in the winter. But that was later, as the seasons unfurled.

In my dreams—which was all I had of him for several weeks after learning his name—he took on several forms. Maybe it was the mystery of him, his reputation for wickedness—what real woman can resist that? Maybe it was his knack for disappearing before I could really see him, watch him, understand him. I had a thousand questions, and only a handful of answers. Spring Creek . . . Jake Worley's store . . . his first name . . . out of the Bible no less. And his voice. I could hear his voice in my dreams, and the things that voice suggested left me hugging my pillow between my thighs and chewing on my sheet.

Can a voice be erotic?

It can be if it's slow and soft. If there's a trumpet's blare of jazz behind it like a match being struck. If everything about it is masculine. And . . . if its every syllable reminds you of who you are. If each sentence flies your body home.

About all I had of Levi Arrowood up to that point was his voice. But in the middle of the night, that was enough.

I NAGGED SISSY FOR HER AND Ben to take me back to the Sky Club. They were out together three or four nights a week; surely, they could take their third wheel along for the ride occasionally. Sissy knew that the Club was some kind of home for me. She'd watched me help Mack and the waitress clean up the mess after the short but bloody brawl last time we were there. Even with Ben hanging all over her, she'd noticed that I had disappeared for ten minutes or so after that. But even Sissy couldn't quite believe that I'd spent those minutes alone with the legendary Arrowood.

When I told her about it, all she kept asking was whether I was sure it was him.

"It was him alright."

"Sure it wasn't a ghost? Some sort of jazz spirit?" She was teasing me.

"No," I admitted after a long pause. "Actually, I'm not sure about that part."

A week later—end of September—we went. Saturday night. Ben picked us up later than usual, after we'd eaten dinner at the Mansion. I wore the black dress that flowed like it had been poured over me. As Sissy and I were walking out to the car, Ben took his eyes off Sissy long enough to notice the dress and whistle. "Jo's loaded for bear," he whispered to Sissy, just loud enough for me to hear.

I just smiled at the two of them and climbed into the rumble seat.

◇◇◇

The joint that night was alive. The whole band was up front, the bass, the trombone, the blaring trumpet, and the young Black man at the piano, making the notes ring out. They were all dressed alike—black suit, white shirts. Clothes like their skin: black white black white black.

We couldn't even get close to the dance floor. At first, we all three sat at the bar, waiting for a table to open. Sissy and Ben had turned around on their barstools, sipping martinis and watching the action. I nursed my brandy and talked to Mack whenever he stopped mixing drinks long enough to even glance my way. At one point, I noticed a big stick leaning in the corner behind the bar. When I asked Mack what it was, he only said, "Louisville Slugger, Jo. Thirty-two inches."

I liked the number. "Playing baseball tonight?"

He shook his head. "It's a peacemaker. For when things get really rough. I like to have it handy of a Saturday night."

I smiled at him. I could feel the brandy burning in my cheeks, and I was as happy as I knew how to be. Right then, right there. The bass and the trombone were pushing some sound. I spun on my stool to look around. The piano man was lighting another cigarette from the first cigarette. The trumpet was mopping his face with a towel, which he then tossed on top of the piano.

I could see Levi Arrowood standing behind the piano with an unlit cigar clenched in that sharp jaw of his. Light the damn match, Levi, I thought, join the fun. But as dark as it was beyond the piano, I could see he was watching something. I tracked his eyes past the band to a table: four guys and two gals seated smack beside the dance floor. The men were wearing expensive clothes but looked hard. The women looked . . . soft in the head and hard in the body. Their stockings were rolled provocatively down below the knee, which sent a message. There was a little food on the table and a lot of liquor. The women were smoking and sipping something sweet. The men were just drinking.

At that moment, the trumpet joined and the piano followed him into the fray. I slipped off my barstool and set my glass on the bar. I knew Mack would keep it for me. My hips were already moving. I turned and pulled Sissy's Ben off his stool. "Come on, little brother, I can't sit still." Sissy nodded, and I dragged Benjamin Scott out onto the floor. Who knows exactly what they were playing, other than their hearts, but I was doing the strong Black Bottom, and Ben kept up as best he could.

Black and silver. That is all you know and all you need to know about that number.

My dress was reflecting the nighttime light of the sun, and Ben was grinning and mostly watching. People were laughing and the room was spinning. The river of my dress runs into the sea, flowing in the silver moonlight.

My God says they play jazz in heaven.

And on earth . . . right up until Ben and I bumped into another couple, and the woman fell down. We grinned and gasped a little bit and said we were sorry. Ben tried to help her up, but she'd broken a strap on her shoe and couldn't quite make it. The man pushed Ben . . . harder than he needed to.

It was only then that I realized they were from the table Levi had been watching. Tough guys and hard gals.

"Keep your hands off her, junior," the guy said, "before your pansy ass gets hurt." He was older than any of us. Fifty maybe.

"Excuse me, sir," said Sissy's Ben, "I was only trying to be of assistance."

Laughter from the table where the rest of them were sitting. "Say it again, pretty boy," from the other woman.

The place got quiet. Even the band fell silent, which seldom ever happened. "I offered my apologies, sir . . ." Ben began again, but the old guy cut him off.

"You apologizing for being a fairy or for your girlfriend being a slut?"

In all my years of fighting with my brothers, I don't think I'd ever been called a slut . . . not to my face. I stepped in closer, beside Ben, who was stammering.

"Buster," I said low and quiet straight at the man's ill-shaved face, "it was your pinhead girlfriend ran into us. I think you ought to apologize for her."

You could tell he didn't like that. The people at his table were laughing at him. He turned to stare me down. "Where are you from, sister?" That was about all he could manage. "Sounds like someplace to hell and gone out in the boondocks."

I could feel Mack and Levi closing in. Mack on the other side of Ben, and Levi on the other side of their table, where no one had really noticed him yet.

"Where I'm from the men don't act like you," I said. I reached slowly over and pushed Ben back a step or two. I figured I'd gotten him into this, and Sissy'd never forgive me if something happened to him. There was sweat in my eyes and trickling down the hollow of my back.

"It's time to ease it on down, Mr. Jameson." This was Levi. Somehow, he'd slipped all the way around the table and was standing beside me. I could tell he was trying to get between me and the old guy. "The boy apologized. Your girlfriend's okay. Everybody just needs to relax."

"Shut up, Arrowood. I'm having a conversation with her . . . the country slut."

"You shouldn't say that, Mr. Jameson. I'll have to ask you and your friends to leave."

"I'm not ashamed of where I'm from," I said.

"You ought to be." The old guy was looking straight at me with sagging, bloodshot eyes. "Where *you're* from, the women use corncobs for Kotex."

Levi let go of my arm and hit the old man so hard on the nose that his face exploded. He went down like a hog that's been hit in the head with a sledgehammer. The other three men at the table were up now. One hefted his chair as if he meant to use it, and Mack stepped in that direction. Showed him the Louisville Slugger. "Don't," Mack said to him. "It wouldn't be any fun."

Everything was still, except for the old guy groaning on the floor. The seconds stretched out. The dust motes floated quietly in the air. Finally, the guy with the chair slammed it back down to the floor, showing us how tough he was, even though he had no intention of mixing it up with Mack.

Levi nodded. "Thank you," he said the to the chair guy. "Smart move. I will help you and your friends get Mr. Jameson out to your car. I have a feeling he'd appreciate it if you stopped by a doctor's office on the way home. His nose is broken."

"Go to hell, Arrowood."

I could tell out of the corner of my eye that Levi was smiling.

"Sure," he said, "why not? But first, let's get the district attorney out to the parking lot. He's bleeding all over the dance floor."

25

THE DISTRICT ATTORNEY! YOU SLUGGED the district attorney?"

It was almost one in the morning, and Levi was behind the bar.

Sissy and Ben had left at ten after I promised her I'd get a ride home. Even Mack had gone upstairs to his rooms at midnight after they locked the first-floor doors and windows.

At some point in the evening, Levi had lost his tie and his shirt was loose at the collar. He was mixing something up in two glasses. Something with bourbon in it and a cherry. After stirring each drink, he handed one glass to me and held the other for himself. "I believe I did . . . slug him, I mean."

"Won't you go to jail?"

He sipped and shook his head. "No. He can't afford to let it get out that he was here. Oh, he'll find ways to make trouble for us, but . . ." He sipped on the drink in his glass. "You like it? It's an . . ."

"If he'll make trouble, then why did you break his nose?"

". . . an Old Fashioned. It's how I like to end the day."

I sipped. It was sweet and hard. Tasted like . . . something else I'd been thinking about. "But then why?"

Levi looked down, staring into his glass, wondering how much to say. "Shit on him. Shit on Jameson. He's a mean bastard. And besides . . ."

"Besides what?" I realized I was whispering. It was so quiet in the room. After the party was over, the music only a memory, even the echoes had died away.

He sighed. "Because I'm damned if I was going to let him talk to you like that."

I smiled and sipped the Old Fashioned. "Levi Arrowood, my knight in shining armor."

"Hell no." He shook his head.

"I say yes."

"No."

"Oh yes."

He grinned ruefully. "Maybe. I wanted to hit him with the blackjack I carry in my jacket. Maybe I was ready to kill him."

I glanced at my hair in the mirror behind the bar. It looked like I'd stuck my head in a fan. I sat my glass down and tried to comb it with my fingers.

He walked around the bar, sat his glass down beside mine, and slowly began to comb out my hair with his own fingers. One hand resting on my shoulder, one hand moving through my hair. I turned on the bar stool so that I could face him.

Put my hands on his waist inside his jacket and closed my eyes. I was just like that old dog who needed petting so damn bad that my tongue lolled out and my eyes rolled back. I hadn't had anything resembling true human touch in so long that it felt the most luxurious thing I'd ever known.

"I'm going to kiss you," he said. "Though I hate to do it."

"Don't care. Do it."

His lips were dry. Or were they wet?

Maybe dry and then wet . . . from my tongue. One of his hands still rested on my shoulder, inside the collar of the dress. One was in my hair, still stroking me like I was his dog. My eyes closed to keep the tears in. And I thrust my tongue shamelessly into his mouth.

He tasted like bourbon and yesterday's cigar. He tasted like summer sunlight along the river. He tasted like burley tobacco curing in the log barn. He tasted like everything I ever wanted to feel in my mouth.

His hand stopped stroking and clenched in my hair, pulling my face into his. And his tongue was against my teeth, and deeper, sweeter and harder. His tongue was Old Fashioned in my mouth, and I wanted to drink his spit and suck him down my throat.

The length of his whole body was between my legs and pressed against me. I was pulling him into me as if I were starving for it. As if I might live if I got it.

And then, by God, he pulled away.

Pushed back from me and sank down on the floor. It felt like he was peeling my skin off. Turning me inside out of myself.

"We need to talk," he said hoarsely. "Just . . . talk."

So we sat on the floor and talked. Sipped the drinks he'd made for us and talked. Till four in the morning.

I AIN'T NEVER HAD NOTHING . . . EXCUSE *me . . . start again. I never had very much when I was a boy. My mother died when I was eleven, thereabouts, and eventually my daddy married her sister just to keep up with us kids and help run the place.*

The farm was on Spring Creek. A hundred acres give or take, a half a mile off the creek. Up a pretty little cove you'd mistake for heaven if you didn't have to hoe corn all summer or cut timber all winter.

I was my mother's third child and the second son.

It meant I wasn't set to inherit nothing . . . anything. Meant that I could work till my arms pulled out of my shoulder sockets and the eyes sweated out of my head, and my older brother, Gordon, would still inherit the land.

I liked Gordon well enough. We never fought it out with our fists . . . if that's what you mean. But as long as he was alive, I was the lesser son, and I had to make my own way.

And if that wasn't enough, when Dad married Aunt Tildy, she turned out to be meaner than a striped snake. I was maybe thirteen or so when they went to church, and she moved in. She brought a razor strop she'd kept from her first husband, and she thought the way of the world was for her to whip us with it if we didn't do just as she preferred. She'd whip Gordon and me for the least infraction, and that was enough to keep the girls in line. They wouldn't fight her the way we boys did, although they did like to spit in her coffee cup before filling it up.

That went on for a year or so, till one evening, Gordon and me . . . Gordon and I . . . had a conference out in the far barn, where even Dad wasn't likely to overhear. I was fourteen by then and meant to go. I'd had enough of my new mother and told Gordon that I'd put that strop beside her head the next time she threatened me with it. Ever the peacemaker, Gordon said to wait it out, but I said I couldn't do that. Not another day. So he stayed on—in part, I believe, cause he stood to inherit—and I went. That very night.

Where did I go? Not so far. Five miles further up the creek to my uncle's house. Uncle Nathan. And that's where I made my start in life. He had a wife and three daughters but no son to help him, so I fit in there. It turns out I had some talents that nobody, including myself, had ever guessed at. And what I could do seconded what Nathan could do.

He makes the finest corn liquor in that part of the world. And I mean the very finest. You'd think you were drinking spring water right up till your head fell off. He makes apple brandy too, that brown liquor you claim to love. But the brandy is mostly a sideline, something to bribe the sheriff with. The corn is where his true artistry lives.

Where did I fit in? Well, I hate to plow. I discovered that. Hated to plow almost as much as I hated my stepmother. I guess I don't have much use for corn in the field at all, not until it's safe in the crib and you can begin to manufacture something useful out of it.

But studying under Nathan, I got to be a pretty fair distiller. If I practiced for another twenty years, I could probably produce a jar as clean and clear and strong as his. Probably make a name for myself. But that's not where my talents lie. My talent is movement. Here to there and back again. I know all of Madison County, part of Haywood, and most of Buncombe like the back of my hand. Let go of my hand, Jo, and I'll show you.

And I can move through that whole territory like . . . well, like a ghost. I can move a load of liquor from Spring Creek to Weaverville to Clyde, and nobody would know a thing except maybe an unexpected breeze ruffled the window curtain or a floorboard creaked in the dark of the night.

When I told you I'd been to Jake Worley's store, I didn't say I'd been there at high noon. I was there when only Jake was around to receive the goods, and you were sound asleep in your daddy's house. I've been places during the day these last few years that I didn't recognize at first because I'd only ever seen them when it was pitch-black dark—with maybe a glimmer of lantern light or the flare of a match.

So ten years of running, riding, driving. If the war had lasted longer, I'd have joined the army, but it was over before I had a chance. Five years of delivering here . . . to this place where we're sitting. Then the manager here decided to keel over from a heart attack. You might say I applied for this job, tongue in cheek. There wasn't any paperwork involved.

Caught? No, I was never caught, though I was shot once and stabbed twice. Marshall's a tough town. Lexington Avenue.

Have I ever killed anybody? Why would you ask that?

I've been mostly alone, as far as women are concerned. Here and there the occasional . . . did you say romp? That wasn't the word I had in mind, but it will do. I can't afford to be tied up. Woman, don't tie me down—that's what I've always thought. The best I can do for a home is three rooms upstairs, and I eat in the kitchen back there. I don't have . . .

Yes, I'll show you the rooms sometime but not tonight . . . No, not tonight.

Because you scare me to death.

You scare me because I like you. I think you're funny and smart. I watch your eyes is how I know you're smart. Watch how you talk to Mack, who thinks you hung the moon. And there's something else.

It's how you move. Not just when you're dancing, although, damn, there is that. The way you walk and sit and turn and nod. You are a distraction, a hindrance, an obstruction. Yes, you. Most nights I hope you won't show up here so I can do my job in peace, and most nights I end up watching the damn door hoping you'll . . .

Your dress? What do I think of it? I think, goddamn your dress is what I think of it because all I want to do is get you out of it. No, not now. It's late, Jo . . . I done said you scare . . . you scare me worse than any woman I ever laid eyes on. You terrify me.

What's scary? Your hands. Your voice. I just want to listen to your voice say anything. Tell a story. Tell all the stories . . . You're falling asleep, Jo, and I'm driving you home. Hand me your glass before you drop it.

I'm taking you home, Jo Salter.

26

NUMBERS DON'T LIE. MISS GENTRY taught me that at Dorland Bell School in Hot Springs, North Carolina, during the four years Mama and Papa boarded me there. I've never had a reason to believe otherwise. You can trust a number to be what it says it is.

But then, along came Levi Arrowood to cloud my judgment. Maybe there was more than one kind of truth telling. A nighttime truth versus a daytime truth. My daytime truth was still the bank. And the heart of the bank, at least for me, was still numerical. You can only ignore the numbers but for so long.

The daily life of the bank continued undisturbed. There was the occasional fuss back at the cashiers' stations in the loan department—an angry farmer or real estate broker or businessman protesting, yelling even, at the cashier's demand for money. Now and then a lawyer hollering like lawyers like to do, but mostly the lawyers did their pleading and squawking up on the second and third floors.

Because I was on the move a lot more now—from cubicle to cubicle all over the first floor plus in and out of Mable's old office, now mine—I saw a lot more of what was going on. From the back hallway, I could just see the door to the private elevator, where I saw Gallatin Roberts go in and out more than once. The famous E. W. Grove had dropped dead a few years before at the Battery Park Hotel, but his son-in-law Seely was in and out of the bank. Men I knew to be Directors—including several I'd seen at the

Sky Club—were showing up more often. And of course, good old Cameron Scott walked past me three or four times a week acting like we'd never met.

The back of the bank, along with the stairs and elevator, used to be quiet, and the men who did pass through, easy going and pleasant. But something was changing, day by day. The week after Levi and I sat up all night talking at the Club, a strange and ominous thing happened.

I got invited up to the third floor.

It was on Friday morning when my boss, Mister Foster Reynolds, he of the plastered hair and the occasional hand on my ass, invited me—no, ordered me—to go with him to the afternoon meeting with the bank officers. Apparently, the week before, things had gotten a little heated when the three vice presidents, including Uncle Frank, didn't like the numbers they were seeing and turned on Foster and the manager of the Loan Department. Foster's Dapper Dan hair treatment must have melted under pressure because he was making the unprecedented move of inviting me, a first-floor do girl, to the Friday afternoon meeting so I could explain the what and why behind the report.

Like I said, you can only ignore the numbers for so long. And they don't always translate into words you want to hear.

I spent the morning going over the weekly summary that made up the reports that Foster and my friend, the loan manager, actually carried upstairs. Unbelievably, at least to me, the weekly summary wasn't an accurate representation of the dailies that I'd painstakingly produced the first four days of that week along with the Friday before. Foster had somehow managed to tangle up the process of merging five days into one week. And yes, the errors on the page still flickered and glowed in front of my eyes when I studied the draft report—just like they had when I first audited an accounting book for Mable. In an hour, I had the figures right, and during that hour, I realized that Foster was probably more honest and less capable than I thought. His mistakes were careless, sure, but too random to be dishonest. It made me wonder if I was the only person in the whole building who could add and subtract without a machine.

Friday afternoon. The third floor of the bank was all offices opening off a wide central hallway. As Foster and I walked from the stairwell to the conference room, I stared around in naked wonder at the plush setting. Some of the office doors were open, some closed, and all featured leaded glass panels with names and positions painted on in block letters. Vice President of Development. Vice President of Government Relations. Legal Counsel. I didn't recognize the names associated with these titles, but then there was Frank J. Morgan, Vice President of Finance. Uncle Frank. I didn't know what the "J" stood for. Where the doors were open, you could see thick carpeting, heavy oak furniture, floor lamps, and windows that looked out over Pack Square—hell, over most of the city.

I wondered where the president's office was, and then I remembered hearing Mable say it was on the fourth floor, where even she had never ventured.

In the conference room, there was a wide oak table with matching chairs. A pitcher of ice water in the center of the table on a tray with matching glasses for the men. One wall also featured large, elegant windows looking to the north, toward Charlotte Street, but beyond that, to the mountains. The mountains of home, and I was struck by the irony of where I was.

Somewhere out there, on a high ridgetop, my mother was buried, her lonely stone burnished by the rain, snow, wind, and sun. She'd instructed me to make a life, a life she couldn't imagine, and here I was. Three floors up in the most important bank in the region—or so the constant chatter of public relations would tell you. At that very moment, I had a sudden, deep desire to visit home. To sit and talk with Papa and visit Mama's grave. I wanted to sink into the place from whence I came.

Then the room started to fill up . . . with the men who bossed the money.

Here's how they arranged themselves.

The room and the table within it were rectangular. Four solid chairs along each long side, plus one at the head and one at the foot. Foster had been clear that I was not to sit at the table but in one of the smaller chairs along the wall facing the windows. Plus, I was not to speak unless spoken to. He actually said I should be seen and not heard, like a child. And then added that I should try not to even be seen unless he needed me to explain something.

As the room filled up, I stood with my back to the wall beside my chair, and when the men started to sit down, I sat as well. For a brief moment, I thought of Levi Arrowood, my Levi, and how he watched the club like a hawk without letting himself be seen. I thanked him silently because that was exactly how I wanted to watch this meeting. I realized that I didn't mind Foster's instructions, for being invisible was the best way to see and hear. The bosses would speak more freely if they managed not to notice me.

Foster and my friend Paul, the first-floor loan manager, sat side-by-side in front of me, along one long side of the table. I knew them already, of course, and I figured out who everyone else was during the next hour, based on the conversation. On the other long side of the table, in front of the windows, sat down the three vice presidents: Uncle Frank, who came in chatty and joking; somebody named McCoy, who turned out to be the VP of Development; and somebody named Coxe, VP of Government Relations. The three of them looked to have been cut from the same bolt of expensive cloth. Large, portly men—even though

Uncle Frank had been shrinking of late—dressed in fine suits with gold cuff links and tie clips. When they came in, the odor of good cigars and high-priced cologne wafted in through the door with them.

In looking at the three of them, I suddenly realized what the words *Fat Cat* actually meant. They were so pleased with themselves they might have had whiskers.

But then something strange happened, something that dampened the mood considerably.

Three more men came in through the door. One was just as expensively dressed, if anything his shoes shone more brightly, but he was not smiling, not joking. He walked the length of the room, passing just in front of me, and sat down at the head of the table. I knew immediately from his photographs who he was . . . Wallace B. Davis, the president of the bank. And did his presence ever sober up the VPs . . .

Behind Davis came a thin, middle-aged man dressed in a nice but not so expensive suit along with scuffed shoes. He sat down against the wall like me, a couple of chairs down. He actually nodded to me when he sat, the first time anybody had acknowledged I was there. Turned out to be Joe Boxer from the mayor's office.

I said there were three in this second group, and there were. The last man in, who closed the door behind him, was Dr. Craig Scott, Cameron and Ben's father. Director. Like Uncle Frank, he showed no sign that he recognized me.

It occurred to me that if some anarchist type set off a bomb in the room that very moment, cash dollars would float in the air for hours, and the big, Packard engine that was Asheville would stutter to a standstill. Here was power, maybe not naked power, but power swathed in three-piece suits and shiny shoe leather.

The meeting started off simply enough. Foster Reynolds, with an able assist from Paul the Loan Manager, presented the week's summary to the three VPs, with Davis and Scott watching silently. While these preliminaries were going on, Boxer from the mayor's office actually got out his pocketknife and began to trim his fingernails, just like one of my brothers trying to get the dirt out from under his nails after a day in the fields.

Uncle Frank was leading the way at that point, jovial even in the face of his boss, Davis. His questions to Foster and Paul were nice, big softballs, such that even they could answer. I could see sweat on the back of their necks—Foster and Paul that is—but everything was still easy and friendly.

Suddenly, Davis spoke out. His voice was higher than I expected, not girlish but surprising, nonetheless. "Hell with that," he said. "What do the long-term trends show? My understanding is that last week, we got into the previous several months, and things didn't go so well."

Uncle Frank's face was glowing now, but Coxe cut in smoothly, taking the reins from him. "Things didn't go well. Mr. Reynolds couldn't exactly give us a cogent summary of July, August, and September. I expect they are prepared to sum things up more effectively today."

Davis glanced from Coxe on one side of the table to Foster and Paul on the other. "Well?"

Be damned if good old Foster didn't twist around in his chair and look straight at me. "To that end, sir, we have brought along my assistant, Miss Josephine Salter, to provide a coherent look inside the numbers."

You might have warned me, I thought, but then again, he had, or I wouldn't be there. Every eye in the room was on me, including Craig Scott's. There was some blinking and throat clearing, as if they were all surprised to discover a woman in their midst. Maybe they'd thought I was a man up till then.

I stood up, in order to see Coxe and McCoy clearly, and then I did what I assumed Foster and Paul had been doing for weeks. I asked everyone present to open the folder in front of them and look at the two-page summary of the past week. Joe Boxer scooted forward to look over Paul's shoulder.

I took them straight through the numbers and then provided them with as succinct a summary as I could. Deposits were down over 11 percent during the last week, compared to the previous week; 19 percent over the last month, compared to August. Withdrawals were creeping up as deposits were slowly creeping down—consistently over the last six to eight months.

WALLACE DAVIS: Tell me about loans, Miss . . .

ME: Salter.

DAVIS: Miss Salter. Talk about loans. I want to know if we're making any money.

ME: We aren't. Over the last six months, all payments against outstanding loans have begun to dry up. What was once called Class C loans—small amounts of capital, high interest rates, typically given to people outside the city limits—have slowed considerably. But that's not the problem. What you have typically referred to as Class A loans—real estate investment, major building projects, downtown development—large amounts of money at low interest . . . payments against principal on those loans have all but ceased.

DR. CRAIG SCOTT: For how long, Jo? (Nobody even paused to wonder how he knew my name.)

ME: Since the first of this year, sir, at least.

VICE PRESIDENT COXE: But wait just a minute, Miss Salter. You can't document your answers with what you've given us in this folder. This is one week's returns, not figures on six months. Christ, you're making this up.

ME: No, sir. Give me a week, and I can show you in detail where you're bleeding. Since the first of the year, like I said.

COXE: I don't believe that . . .

DAVIS: Shut up, Phil. You know she's right. Foster was just too scared to say it. (Turning to me) What did you say your title is, Miss?

FOSTER REYNOLDS: She's my first assistant, sir.

DAVIS: Didn't ask you. Asked her. What did you say, Josephine?

ME: I didn't say, sir. No one did. I'm the First Assistant to the Head Cashier.

DAVIS: Can you come back next week and show us in detail what you're talking about? Demonstrate what you're saying about the past six months? No, better put together the whole year . . . since January first.

REYNOLDS: I'm not sure Miss Salter . . .

DAVIS: Shut up, Foster, and you too, Coxe. I didn't ask either one of you to show up next week. I asked Miss Salter . . . Miss Salter?

ME: Of course, sir. I work for you.

DAVIS: Boxer, can the mayor be here next Friday afternoon?

JOE BOXER: I'll check his schedule.

DAVIS: Check it twice. This is more important than cutting the ribbon on some damn flower show. Craig, do you have any questions?

(I sat down at this point, assuming I was done.)

DR. CRAIG SCOTT: (looking straight at Uncle Frank) Mr. Morgan, what is the exact amount of cash the bank currently holds in reserve?

FRANK: I don't have a precise number, sir. But I'm sure . . .

SCOTT: No, you're not. You're not sure of a damn thing. (turning to me) Jo, can you see if you can find out the answer to that question and bring it with you to the meeting next week?

ME: I'll do my best, sir.

SCOTT: Good luck. We need to know that number against the amount of money deposited . . . what, over the past year?

DAVIS: Two years. This has been coming since the winter of '26.

SCOTT: And Jo?

ME: Sir?

SCOTT: Of the total amount in reserve, what percentage are funds belonging to the city and county?

ME: Yes, sir.

SCOTT: Goddamn it, Wallace!

DAVIS: I know. You need to see if you can't scuttle the lawsuit Biltmore Forest is threatening to file against the city.

SCOTT: I can do that . . . I can do that a hell of a lot easier than you can call in all those loans.

There was a long, somber pause. It was as if nobody could think of anything else to say. I was already working out in my mind how I could find out what Davis and Scott wanted to know. It was a math problem, and a gloriously huge math problem at that.

Then, suddenly, the men were standing up. Davis was asking Uncle Frank and the other two VPs to stay after the meeting to conference with him. I followed the rest of the men out through the doorway into the hall. I left the room last and shut the door behind me. Foster was leaning against the wall, sweating. Paul was gulping down water at the water fountain.

Then Craig Scott turned around before getting on the elevator just to speak to me.

"Jo," he whispered, "I'm sorry my idiot son couldn't convince you to marry him."

"Sir?"

"You would have been good for him. God knows."

"But would he have been good for me, sir?"

The good doctor smiled and shook his head before turning back to the elevator.

27

Two things that Friday night, the night after the tumultuous meeting on the third floor. The first happened at the Mansion, just when Aunt Brenda called up and down the stairs that it was dinner time. The second happened in my dreams. Both raised up the hair on the back of my neck.

Sissy had just walked in from work. Junior was somewhere, upstairs probably, recovering from the rigors of a round of golf. I was in the kitchen, perched on a stool and talking to Pansy while she put the final touches on pork chops, creamed corn, and biscuits. I was going to jump down and help her carry everything out to the table and she was going to try to prevent me—the same game we played every evening. Me getting in her way and her playfully shoving me out of it.

The same game we played that evening, as Aunt Brenda came in and sat down. Sissy and Junior. Movement, talk, laughter. And no Uncle Frank. The family sat down, except for me. Pansy was still in and out of the kitchen, asking if she should fix Mr. Morgan's plate. I stood by my chair, feeling my stomach flip silently over. The car was in the driveway, we all knew he was in the house.

I hadn't said anything to anybody about the meeting that afternoon, how it felt like thunderclouds gathering. After all, what was there to say that wouldn't betray Uncle Frank's distress to his family. I wondered if he'd bring it up at dinner since both he and I had been there.

Aunt Brenda spoke up. "Oh, fix his plate, Pansy. He said something about checking on the furnace."

"I'll go look," I said quickly. "I'm already up."

When I ran down the back stairs to the basement hallway, I found him in the furnace room, sitting in an old wooden chair that had been discarded down there. He was staring, just staring at the open door of the furnace, watching the coal burn. Blue and orange flames, red shadows inside the cavern of the furnace.

I spoke to him, but he didn't answer. Couldn't answer. When I spoke again, he raised his head slowly in my direction, and suddenly I knew what he would look like when he was an old man. Ancient, shrunken, tired to death.

I said before that maybe there's a nighttime truth as well as a daytime truth. A truth that flows out of you rather than a truth that crashes in on you. Levi Arrowood felt like a truth that was slowly blossoming inside me, rather than a truth that was attacking me. That's how I knew it wasn't him in my dream that night.

I was being chased down dark hallways. In and out of rooms where the only light was shadowy lamplight or moonlight glancing in through the windows. A man in a suit was chasing me, hunting me down to hurt me somehow. I hid under a desk and tried to hold my breath so he wouldn't find me, and I could hear him searching for me, limping on broken feet and grunting like some kind of animal.

Under the desk is when I realized I was trapped in the bank.

Central B & T, somewhere on the second or third floor where I wasn't supposed to go. Something I was never supposed to see. Lurking there was a big, doughy white man who was going to hurt me. Parchment skin and midnight black hair. His expensive suit, numbers scrawled in chalk all over the fabric. Maybe he was going to kill me.

No . . . he was going to rape me.

If I saw the numbers. If I broke the code.

I crawled out from under the desk and sprinted barefoot out into the hallway. My skirt was bunching up around my waist and I kept pushing it down as I ran. Ran from the man with the numbers. He knew who I was, knew me in some horrible way and meant to hurt me.

Finally, the stairwell, and I was leaping, jumping down . . . but oh, in such slow, painful motion. My skirt flying up, and I could hear him grunting as he flew down on top of me and his cold touch . . .

. . . jerked me awake. Alone in my bed. Alone in the basement room at Morgan Mansion. I was sweating, gasping. Because I could remember the man with the numbers written all over him. And how, by God, real he was.

The only antidote I could think of to the nightmare of numbers, the grind and threat of the bank, was my other sanctuary, my other truth. I needed to go to the Sky Club to erase the memory of the dream. I wanted to hear music. I wanted to dance. I wanted to forget.

I needed to see him. I had to know if he was real and not just another dream . . . Levi.

That evening, Sissy and Ben dropped me off on the way to some soiree in Biltmore Forest. "I'm assuming you'll get a ride home," she said when I climbed out of the rumble seat in the Club parking lot.

"Where's home?" I said spontaneously, standing there on the gravel. It was the first few days of October, and you could feel autumn in each breath. The air felt like change coming. But then when Sissy began to look worried, I nodded to reassure her. "Of course, I'll get a ride. Go on and have a good time."

I was there early enough that I ate supper by myself out on the second-floor terrace. Fish plus a handful of little potatoes, and a glass of white wine that Mack sent out to me when the waitress told him what I'd ordered. I was ravenous, and the fish was maybe the best meal I'd had in months. I'm not sure it was the food so much as evening falling over the city, the chill in the air that reminded me of home, my real home on Big Pine, and the luxury of sitting there alone.

The waitress—her name was Barbara Jean—brought me a second glass when she saw that I'd drained the first. It was chilled and felt like the cool evening air in my mouth and throat. Chardonnay, she called it.

And then, as I sat with that second glass, the collar of my coat pulled up around my neck, he came out and sat with me for a few minutes, Levi. I offered him a taste of the wine, and he sipped and smiled. "Tastes like the fall air," he said quietly, and I marveled at him.

"Good God," I said.

"What?"

"You just said what I was thinking a few minutes ago. Almost exactly what I was thinking." I know it was a silly, girlish thing to say, but sometimes in life you just say what you think.

He smiled. "Well, we're country people. Have a lot in common . . . You recall what I told you the other night. You were awfully sleepy."

"Of course, I recall. Despite Uncle Nathan's brandy . . ."

He smiled. There was enough light left in the sky plus the flickering gas lamps on the terrace, that I could see his hair clearly, and thought *sandy* for the first time. "I remember the Old Fashioned you gave me for dessert," I whispered. For some reason, my voice was husky.

"What did it taste like?"

"Sex."

He blushed and glanced down at the tabletop. "That's the wine talking," he muttered.

I laughed at him, though truth to tell, I was blushing too. "No, that's me talking, I'm afraid."

"I like you talking. It eases me to listen to you."

And I just breathed. Sat there in the cool, dusky air. Night falling down the mountainside and enveloping the city. When I took another sip of my wine, it tasted better since his lips had been on the glass.

"I have to go to work," he said after a bit and stood up.

"Will I see you later?"

"I sure as hell hope so."

I nodded and, though it might have been too dark for him to see, smiled.

It was a strange night, with time skipping forward, folded over itself. I know the band was good that night because I can recall snippets, threads of jazz, sometimes cool and sometimes hot. I danced a few times with men who asked. But mostly I sat at the bar and talked to Mack, if you can call nodding and smiling and pointing a kind of talking.

I slipped outside and stood on the side porch a few times, the small, upstairs porch where I'd first talked to Arrowood and he'd finally confessed his name was Levi. It was dark out there, and cold, on that October night. And it was there I decided that I loved the name Levi. Said it over a few times, savored the shape of it on my tongue and teeth. Liked it in my mouth.

I must have seen him a few times that evening, lurking and watching. Nodding and smiling at the guests. Solving a problem or two without even speaking. But I don't recall it now. Just the sense that he was there.

Later, after the crowd had slowly disappeared, I helped Barbara Jean and the other girls clear the tables and carry dishes back into the kitchen. Nobody seemed especially surprised that I was helping. Nobody asked me "what the hell?" and Mack smiled at me in passing.

Then the girls were gone down the stairs, shrugging on their coats. Mack saying good night and disappearing toward the stairway up to his own quarters on the top floor.

Where was he? I wandered back into the kitchen again, and it was there I found him. Washing dishes of all things. His jacket off, sleeves rolled up. I walked up behind him, intending to pick up the dishtowel and help with the drying. His sleeves up above his elbows but still getting soapy wet. When I reached around him for the towel, I brushed up against his back and felt that slight contact sizzle down into my belly. "Tell me again why you left Spring Creek," I murmured against his neck.

"Wasn't going to inherit," he whispered slowly. "I told you that much already. Nothing to gain by staying, even though I do love that valley . . . Besides, I figured out that there wasn't no future for me walking behind a mule."

"You said you didn't like to plow."

"No." I could hear the grin in his voice, feel it through his back. "I hate to plow."

I put my arms around him and ran my hands down his forearms into the hot, soapy water. Pressed myself into him. Well, you can plow me, I thought to myself, with that mule of yours. Thought but had barely enough sense not to say.

He paused in the dish washing, to take my hands in his, washing them and holding them. "What are you thinking, Jo Salter?" he said after a long moment.

"That I admire a man who knows how to get his hands wet."

28

Daytime truth lives in the bank. The bank is the church of numbers, the high, holy place of dollars and cents, if you believe what they tell you. Slowly, I was starting to wonder where all their numbers came from. And at the end of the day, what did they mean?

On Sunday afternoon, out at the Mansion, I got a phone call, the first one in weeks. Sissy had to come running downstairs to the basement to wake me up out of a beautiful, long, relaxed nap. It was worth it, though, because it was Levi. He'd dropped me off so late the night before, that it was early. Before dawn but not by much.

He wanted to check on me, he wanted to thank me, he wanted to see me, he wanted to be sure, he wanted . . . all of those things. And in the struggle to say them over the crackly phone line, he mushed them altogether into one thing.

"Me too," I said finally, to put him out of his misery.

"What?"

"I feel the same way."

"You're not just . . ."

"Playing with you? No, I'm not."

"Then . . ."

"Yes . . . But Levi, you have to do something for me. You have to."

"Alright. Name it."

"Take me home."

"I thought I already . . ."

"No. My real home. Next Sunday, I want you to drive me up to Big Pine. Or at least as far as that roadster of yours will go. We can walk the rest of the way."

There was a pause, and it felt like the static on the line increased for a long moment. "Will you do it?" I asked.

"Are you going to stay?"

"No, just to visit for the day. Will you . . .?"

"Of course, Jo. I'll take you. I might have to make one or two stops along the way."

"That's fine. You can pick up liquor, you can drop off liquor, you can throw liquor out the window. I don't care. I just need to see my Papa and walk around the farm. Maybe visit the cemetery."

He didn't ask why, didn't need to. He was hill born like me. Home was always tucked away in the mountains, just behind that dark horizon, beyond where the city folks know to go. Instead, all he asked was what time did I want to leave.

"The crack of dawn," I said. "The first rooster crow . . ."

So I HAD SOMETHING TO look forward to. I had something to salve my heart as my mind spent the week digging down into the finances of Central Bank & Trust.

On that Monday, October 20, I made a deal with Foster Reynolds to use an empty conference room on the second floor, where I could spread out the records I thought I needed. Then I went around and begged for the reports, all the reports starting January 1, 1929. Almost two years of weekly summaries going all the way back to just before I came to the bank as a lowly teller, making $12.50 per week.

But after I spread all of those out on the conference room table—and you need to understand there were ninety-four of them—I realized that they would tell me part of the story, but a hazy one at best, as Foster wasn't the most dependable accountant in the world. After studying them for most of that day, I realized what I really needed was the quarterly reports that the VPs had created out of these weeklies so that I could see the cash reserve at the beginning of the previous year and then how it had grown. Or more likely shrunk.

Given that Uncle Frank was one of those VPs and already aging before my very eyes, I stopped, locked the door of the conference room and went downstairs to work on my own daily summary from the teller windows.

What if what I came up with didn't match the quarterlies? What if things were much worse than I imagined? Whose head would roll?

Tuesday, I argued with Foster and lost. Went downstairs and dragged Paul the Loan Department supervisor back up to the second floor with me, so we could both argue with Foster. Finally, I convinced him he had to go up to the third floor and request the quarterlies if he wanted me to help save his job. Still, he hesitated; he was terrified of the third floor. I nagged. He went.

On Wednesday, a secretary to Coxe, one of the VPs, brought down the quarterlies for 1929 and the first three for 1930. Seven summary reports in all, delivered by the three VPs to Davis and the Directors. They confirmed what I'd already begun to suspect from the weeklies. The quarterlies were a more-or-less faithful summary of the financial history of the bank for the previous twenty-one months.

On Thursday, I stayed at the bank till almost 10:00 at night. All day redoing the seven quarterlies to my satisfaction and then slowly reducing them to two pages. From the two pages I wrote out my summary, rewrote it, and rewrote it again. To make three points.

On Friday morning, I remembered one more question and sent Foster upstairs to ask Uncle Frank. The answer . . . 4.6 million. Or as I wrote it my notes = $4,632,412. That's how much the city of Asheville had deposited in Central B & T. Buncombe County had slightly less than three million, and the city school system nearly $400,000. At that point, even I began to round off to the nearest hundred thousand. Those three numbers became the fourth point in my report.

I didn't have time to think about what it all meant. Not really. Only that most of what I'd learned was frightening. Up until that very day, I'd never consciously realized that numbers could be a threat.

This time, two more Directors were in the third-floor conference room. And the mayor. Let us not forget the mayor. And this time, I was seated at the table with Foster, while Paul got to retreat to the chairs by the wall.

The bank president, Wallace B. Davis, again sat at the head of the table, where he had before. This time, the mayor, Gallatin Roberts, sat at the foot of the table, near the door, with his assistant, Boxer behind him. On the long side of the table opposite Foster and me, sat Doctor Craig Scott and two other men, and as circumstances unfolded, it became obvious that they were also Directors. The odd thing was I'd seen them both at the Sky Club more than once. If I had them pegged correctly, one liked to eat dinner there with his wife and the other liked to sit at end of the bar and drink . . . hard. He didn't eat, he didn't flirt with the waitress, he just hoisted the glass and grimaced at the taste.

The vice presidents—McCoy, Coxe, and Uncle Frank—weren't in the room. At first, I thought this odd, but by the end of the meeting, I realized why.

Davis didn't bother with personal introductions; he cut straight to the chase. The purpose of the meeting was to drill down into the financial health of the bank and to share that information with the mayor and the most important of the Directors. The only person in the room he introduced was me, and then he summarized nicely what he'd asked me to do.

When Foster tried to speak first for some reason, perhaps thinking he needed to take credit for me or for the work, the glare that Davis gave him would have made a stone statue sweat. Foster got the message and leaned back in his chair. Oddly enough, though Foster beside me was flustered and hot, I felt cool, almost cold, as if there was a window open behind me.

ME: Gentlemen, if you will, please open the folder in front of you and examine the first two pages. They are a brief financial history of Central B & T starting on January first of last year up through the end of September this year. The bottom line, so to speak, shows the cash reserve of the bank—as well as I've been able to recreate it—at the end of each month during that period, ending with the last.

DR. CRAIG SCOTT: I was afraid of this, Wallace. Goddamn it.

MAYOR GALLATIN ROBERTS: There's no call for that kind of language, Dr. Scott. And in front of a lady . . .

SCOTT: Sure there is. Can't you read? Besides, Jo's from the country, she's heard worse. (Looks up and winks at me)

ME: I've *said* worse. Mr. Mayor, do you understand what you've seen so far?

ROBERTS: I can see that the cash reserve has been steadily shrinking since the beginning of last year.

ME: Yes, sir. It was declining slowly but steadily through last October, and then it became worse month by month.

DAVIS: In other words, after the stock market crashed. Can you explain to these gentlemen what happened here . . . at Central B & T?

ME: I'm not sure I understand what happened. All I can do is read the numbers and reach something like a series of educated guesses.

DAVIS: Go on.

ME: There's a third sheet in the folder. Because I know numbers, not words, I've tried to explain the patterns I see in the simplest possible terms. One, the money that the bank now has on hand—what Mr. Davis and the others call the cash reserves—is significantly less than the recorded customer deposits.

ROBERTS: What does that mean?

ME: It means that if everyone who has an account at the bank walked in the door tomorrow and asked for their money, the bank could not produce half of it. If any one of the largest depositors walked in . . .

ROBERTS: What the hell!

SCOTT: See what I mean.

DAVIS: Go on, Miss Salter.

ME: Two, the reason that the bank's liability is far greater than its assets is that over this same period, it has continued to loan out large sums of money even as the cash reserve has shrunk.

DIRECTOR (FAVORS DINNER WITH HIS WIFE): Why in God's name would you allow this to happen, Wallace? Damn it, we're all at risk here! . . . Sorry, Mayor.

DAVIS: I have a feeling you're about to find out. Miss Salter . . .

ME: Three, during the past year, the bank has continued to provide new loans in large amounts to customers that already had outstanding debt. A few individuals but mostly builders and developers, corporations.

SCOTT: Have you been keeping everybody afloat, Wallace?

DAVIS: I believe it would be more accurate to say that *we* have been keeping everybody afloat. The people in this room, I mean.

If we'd called in all those original loans from 1926 and '27, building in this city would have ground to a halt. There would be no streets or public buildings or hotels. There would be no business at all. This place would be a ghost town. (Shrugs) Up to now, we've been the only thing that saved this city.

(Silence)

DAVIS: Is there a point number four, Miss Salter?
ME: Yes, sir. One more and that's it . . . Dr. Scott asked what percentage of the bank's cash reserves are on deposit from the city and the county. (I pause, not sure if Davis wants me to continue.)
SCOTT: And . . .?

(Davis nods.)

ME: Somewhere around 80 percent. With more time, I could give you a precise number.

(Silence)

ROBERTS: My Lord Jesus. The city is the only thing propping up Central Bank & Trust.
ME: More accurately, sir, the city and county together.
ROBERTS: Good Lord. Wallace, what . . . what have you done.
DAVIS: You mean, what have *we* done? (Shrugs) You're half right, Mayor. The city is holding up the bank, and the bank is holding up the city. If one fails, the other fails.
ROBERTS: What if I withdraw the city's funds and place them in the safekeeping of another institution? (Turns to look at Boxer, who shrugs and nods at Davis.)

DAVIS: Sure Gallatin, shop the city's money around. The other banks in the region would love to have it, but they are just as exposed as we are. And if you pull out, we fail, and they'll all fall like dominos.

SCOTT: You . . . I mean *we* (glances at the other Directors) can't afford for either one to fail, either the city or Central Bank & Trust. Wallace, what do you propose?

DAVIS: Foster, I think it's time for you and Mr. Boxer to take a cigarette break.

FOSTER REYNOLDS: I don't smoke.

DAVIS: You do now. You can wait in your office on the second floor. We'll send for the two of you if we need you.

REYNOLDS: But what about . . .

DAVIS: Miss Salter? She stays. We may need her . . . (After Boxer and Foster Reynolds leave.) Here's what I propose. It's almost November, Mayor. It's time to step up the tax collections all over your Greater Asheville. You need to bring in as much money as possible as fast as possible and you need to bring it here . . .

ROBERTS: But that doesn't solve all your problems . . .

DAVIS: No, but it gives us time for the winds to shift, and money to start moving again. Craig, you need to see what you can do to scuttle the lawsuit that your pretty little Biltmore Forest keeps threatening the mayor with.

SCOTT: I can do that. The neighbors won't like it, but they can afford to pay their taxes. What about the bank?

DAVIS: We are going to call in every outstanding loan on the books. Starting on Monday. Quietly though. Quietly. There can't be any sense of panic . . . Anything I'm missing, Miss Salter?

ME: It's the big ones that matter. Don't waste your time squeezing a farmer for five hundred dollars when the developer owes you half a million.

DAVIS: (Smiling) I know what you mean. Put the pressure on our friends. (Glancing at the Directors while speaking to me) Is that what you're saying?
ME: Yes sir. That's what I'm saying.
DAVIS: Last thing then. Everybody in this room—and that includes you most of all, Mr. Mayor—has to go out and reassure the public. The city is on the rise and the bank is as solid as a rock. Say it tomorrow, say it on Sunday, and keep on saying it. Loud and clear. Nobody can share what we talked about today. And I mean nobody. (Glances at me)

"I'm about as nobody as it gets," I said to him in return.

29

I DIDN'T GO HOME THAT NIGHT. By that I mean I didn't go back to the Mansion after I finally finished up around 6:00. Instead, I used the telephone in Foster Reynolds' office to call Sissy at work and tell her I had a date.

Date was code for I was starting out the evening somewhere else and wouldn't be home before breakfast. Sissy, bless her, used it far more than I did, to signal that she had plans that didn't include coming home to the family dinner table and might involve slipping into the house through the basement door in the wee hours.

On that Friday night, I knew I couldn't face Uncle Frank, knowing what I knew. I would have to tell him everything that I'd told Davis and the Directors if he so much as hinted that he wanted to know. After all, he was family. And if you want to know the truth, the prospect of telling Uncle Frank the four conclusions I'd arrived at scared me . . . down to the pit of my stomach. He was already drifting, seemed to me, and after all, he was the Vice President of Finance. I wasn't even sure I understood everything I knew, and I didn't know everything.

So I went to earth. That's what a fox does when the dogs are on its trail, and they're running so close that their teeth gnash and their breath stinks. The fox goes to earth, meaning to its den. The place where no one or nothing can dig it out and chew its head off. I went to earth at the Sky Club, which may sound crazy, I admit—a speakeasy and jazz club high on the side of a mountain—but it felt safe. It felt like the foxes' den to me, the place where nothing could harm me.

I didn't mean to avoid Uncle Frank forever, but I needed to think. I needed a night's sleep—or at least a night's feeling and dreaming with a little sleep mixed in—before I tried to explain to Frank what I knew. Even before I could face him over the supper table. It was the first time I went to Mack and Levi, seeking shelter at the Club, but it wouldn't be the last.

I kept a pair of comfortable shoes at the bank. I wore them back and forth to work every day, given the quarter-mile walk from the new house in Lake View Park to the streetcar stop. That day, that Friday, I was glad to have them because I could slip into them at six o'clock and walk to the Sky Club. It was maybe a mile and most of that uphill, but I didn't care. I just needed to be outside, away from the numbers.

All my long, sweet life, when the inside of something has driven me crazy, I have stepped outside. Breathed the same free air as any bird.

As I walked, I cast about for something pleasant to think about—something that would push that afternoon meeting out of my mind, at least for the time being. It was then I remembered the trip up home that was coming in two days. All day with Levi, escaping from the hard pavements of town and into the swirling depths of home. Real home. And so I let myself imagine what it would be like . . . to walk up into the yard and surprise Papa and the brothers. To laugh and cry, to feed some corn husks to the old mare in the field. Sit at the table and eat real food, food that came straight from our own pastures and fields. To walk up to the cemetery and visit with Mama.

Introduce Levi to Mama . . .

What did I mean by *that*? Introduce Levi . . . Was he that

special? Was he the answer to some unasked question? A question I wouldn't let myself even think?

I knew that I couldn't get him out of my mind. I thought that once the mystery of him was solved, he'd lose the luster, fade into the shadows, fall silent. Once I could name him, then I could identify him, classify him, and move on. I wouldn't have to think about him, worry about him, yearn for him.

Shit . . . did I really just think that? *Yearn* for him. I stopped in my tracks, trudging along College Street, halfway up Beaucatcher Mountain on the way to the Club. What did that even mean? *Yearn* . . . I didn't yearn for anything, except perhaps for my Papa's hearth. The sound of his voice and the smell of his pipe. The taste of bacon and beans cooked on that old stove. I yearned day and night for my dead mother. Those are things I yearned for. Not for some man.

Hell . . . no!

Except that maybe I did. Here I was, standing stock-still on the side of the street, as first one and then several cars motored past me, one honking its horn. Why, when things got hard—mean and tight—at the bank, didn't I just go home to the Mansion? Or even go all the way back to Big Pine with my tail between my legs? Those places were some sort of home. Why did I—without even bothering to think overmuch about it—just start walking up this damn mountain, heading for . . . him?

I yearned for him. Admission, confession. I needed to tell him what had happened, even though he might not fret for one single moment about Central B & T. I needed him to listen to me and act like he cared. I needed him to tell me everything would work out. I needed him to console me.

Another automobile went by and honked at me to get out of the road. I shook my fist at it as it motored on up the hill.

Standing there, I realized that I had just started walking

because from the very beginning of the meeting that afternoon, when I stood up to speak and started in on Point Number One, I wished he was in the room. Fading into the shadows in the corner if that's the way he needed it to be, lurking where only I could see him, but I wanted him there in case I stuttered or stumbled. Hell, in case I fell flat on my face. But he was only there in my mind.

And now . . . now I wanted to feel his arms around me.

Which was . . . pathetic!

Yes, pathetic. I thought about turning myself around and marching myself back down to the streetcar stop and going home to the Mansion to deal with Uncle Frank. I should be propping him up rather than looking for some man to prop me up.

"The hell with him. I don't need him even if his name is Levi."

That part I said out loud, and I mean *loud* out loud. I know because I looked around to see if anybody heard me. Sadly, somebody did.

Himself.

The reason the passing automobiles had kept honking was because his roadster—the liquor car, I called it in my mind—was pulled over on the side of the road opposite me, the engine idling. He was sitting behind the wheel, leaning partway out the driver's window, watching me. He was smiling. No, that's not right, he was grinning. That sandy hair I told you about, the sharp planes of his face, the white teeth. And every bit of it was grinning.

"Jo . . ."

"What!"

"Just get in the car."

"Hell no. I'm walking."

"No, you're not. You're standing. Just get in the car."

"To go where?"

"Just one stop. The back of the Manor out on Charlotte

Street. Well, two stops. The butcher. The cook needs steaks. Then I'll take you up to the Club."

I stood there, staring at his foolish, grinning face. I could feel my own face, smiling at him without permission. "The hell with you, Levi Arrowood," I said before I walked around and got in the car. I'd never been in his car when it wasn't four in the morning. It was rather nice.

"What are you mad at me for?" he asked.

"For not being worthless," was all I could think to say.

AT THE KITCHEN DOOR OF the Manor, he carried in two cardboard boxes from the trunk of the roadster. When I asked what was in the boxes, he grinned again. "Jars, Jo. Eight of them," was all he said. Twenty steaks from the butcher on Merrimon Avenue. Two sacks of potatoes at an unscheduled, third stop. Minus eight plus twenty plus two. With him jumping in and out of the car, me mostly just curled up on my side of the seat with my shoes off. Laughing at these numbers and at him.

And then we were back up the mountain, parking beside the kitchen door at the back of the Club, where I helped him unload the steaks and potatoes. It felt like I'd slipped into the moving picture of his life for a few minutes, an unknown actress for sure, and probably playing a minor role, but still I was in the frame, and it was an easy place to be.

I ate supper again, back at my favorite table out on the veranda. Steak this time and red wine. Barbara Jean brought both without my asking, only saying that the boss had suggested the steak and Mack the wine to go with it.

I was so tired from the week at the bank that I could barely chew. It took most of an hour for me to maul each bite, with each followed by a sip of wine. Deep, red, delicious. It was cooler on the porch than it had been the week before; the sun set sooner and darkness gathered more quickly. Even so, I was yawning at the early dusk.

Levi came out to light the candles on the tables, including mine. When he did, he paused for a long moment with his hand on my shoulder. "You're tired, aren't you?"

I nodded, stifling another yawn.

He lit the rest of the candles on the porch, nodding to a few guests at their tables, and then sat down with me.

"Why don't you take a nap? Go up to my room and crawl between the covers. I'll check on you later."

"I need to tell you something first," I said quietly. "Just you and nobody else."

I could feel him sit up straighter, his attention sharpening, as if he was going from my Levi to the infamous Arrowood in the space of a breath. He didn't speak, only waited.

"If you have any money in the bank or if the Club has any money in the bank, you need to withdraw it."

"Which bank? Yours?"

I stared at the silhouette of his face, flickering in the candlelight. "Probably doesn't matter which one. But mine for sure. Central B & T."

"Soon?"

"Monday morning."

He nodded and reached across the table in the shadows to rest his hand on mine. "You've had a hell of a week, haven't you, Jo Salter?"

"You have no idea."

"You can tell me on Sunday. All of it . . . or at least as much as you want to tell." He was Levi again, fully with me.

"All of it," I said simply. "I'll tell you all of it."

He nodded, and I think, smiled.

"Why don't you go upstairs and take a nap. Slip between the sheets and let it all go."

"Your sheets?"

He grinned; I could feel it through his warm palm and fingers. "Better not crawl between anybody else's."

"Are you sure?" I whispered. "You don't mind me up there by myself."

He squeezed my shoulder. "Sure. Take a bath if you want. You're barely upright as it is."

I DID TAKE A BATH, AND let the tension of the long day drain out of me.

And when I was done, scrubbing myself dry with one of his pitifully thin towels, I leaned toward that bed like a tree falling in high wind. But what in God's name to wear. Obviously, I'd taken off all my clothes to bathe, so it meant putting some pieces of something back on, but I was so tired that I couldn't think which and what. So, cover your eyes if you don't want to know, I did something sinful. I got into his bed stark naked. Only my skin as my answer to the world.

I was warm from the bath, and his sheets against me felt cool and stiff. I turned the pillow over and its underside was as if chilled just for me. I could smell him on his pillow. Cigar and soap—some sort of harsh soap. Apples, I thought, fallen into the tall grass, woodsmoke, an old quilt on the bed. Nothing comparable that I've ever smelled before or since. Other than him.

I was so close to sleep, my mind slipping its gears, when I started near to wake. What if I dreamed? That nasty, doughy man in his suit of numbers who chased me, hunted me, would rape me. Me naked and the numbers man could force . . . But then the long, easy thought seeped into my mind that he couldn't find me there.

High on the mountain . . . in the sky almost. I was safe within the walls of the Club. He was barred from me. He snuffled and snarled below, on harsh pavement and cold brick. Sucking soot and sweat from the faltering lives that roamed the streets.

Were I to dream in that bed, it would be of my Mama. Mary Freeman Salter. Or my Papa. Lewis Salter. They would circle round me here. They too could come beside where I lay, and sit in peaceful conference, with the quiet skein of time unspooling. I was . . .

. . . safe.

I dove deep and slept in silent wonder. Listening to the two of them, Mama and Papa, whispering, humming, singing, chatting with each other. Two people making chorus. I dreamed only of their voices.

Till his footsteps in the room waked me.

I knew at once that it was very late. Midnight or after. The floors and the walls were silent and settling themselves to rest. Though it was the middle of October, he opened the curtains and cracked a window. So very quietly, meaning not to disturb me.

Foolish man. I was always disturbed in his presence . . . in the deepest way imaginable.

I watched through slitted eyes as he took off his dress shirt before the window and then stripped his sleeveless undershirt off over his head. Threw them both to the floor and let the air flow in through the window over his naked belly and chest. I was jealous of that air.

He walked into his bathroom, and I could hear water running in the sink. A spit bath, Mama would call it. Freshening himself . . . for sleep. For me. When he came back out, I could half sense, half see him in the windowed moonlight. He stripped off his dress trousers and stepped toward the bed in his shorts. His skivvies, he called them.

"God no," I whispered.

"Hmmm?"

"Them off . . ."

He knew what I meant. After a moment, he pulled his shorts over the half-hard front of him and then down over his man's legs. His thighs were as tight as a bow string, my Mama says, and the lobes of his ass hard and round as two gleaming creek rocks in the staunch moonlight.

I threw the covers back and closed my eyes completely because I wanted to feel him without the bother of sight. The bed groaned and he was beside me—hard like ivory and supple as leather—pulling my face up to him with that hand. He is kneeling astride me—rigid against my aching tits—rubbing his stones over my straining belly. He is everywhere between my thighs—his tongue stiff and heavy in my sex.

I ask for it. *Please God* . . . not in words. Not in any language ever spoken by a civilized being. But in the wild before words. The singing of one blooded beast into the ear of another.

Do me

Be me

Name me

Take me

Swear me

Live in me without border . . . blending skin.

And stay there please, yourself whole and stiff inside me long after the dawn and through the blistering days to come.

Be as ancient as the flood within me!

YOU COUNTRY CLUB LADIES OUT there in the big world may dream of your Jesus hymns and symphonies, but by God, Levi Arrowood could make me sing.

30

IS IT A SIN TO want to get rich?"

This from Uncle Frank. It was Saturday afternoon, and I'd followed him into his study, both of us knowing that we needed to talk. Mostly, that he needed me to talk and I needed him to listen.

I gave him the very same three pages that I'd given Davis and the Directors the day before. And as he seemed so distracted, I explained the four conclusions I'd reached. One, two, three, four: the city is propping up the bank and the bank is propping up the city.

"What's he going to do?"

"He?"

He nodded in the general direction of Stratford Towers, the palace just up the hill. "Davis. What's he going to do?"

It was odd the way he said it, as if Davis was now the bank, and he, Frank Morgan, had stepped away.

"Well, Uncle Frank, the mayor is going to spread good will and wring all the tax money he can out of the newly annexed parts of the city, and the bank is going to call in all the outstanding loans it can."

Frank laughed with a strange bitterness. "Is he going to call in his own mortgage?" Again, he nodded up the hill at Stratford Towers. "Is he going to call in mine?"

I had absolutely no idea how to respond. "Uncle Frank, I don't . . ."

And that's when he said it. *Is it a sin to want to get rich, Jo?*

I knew what Papa would say. He would say, the higher you ride, the further you fall. But that didn't sound like something that would console Frank.

"It's all I ever wanted," he went on. "I grew up poor, Jo. I mean my own father worked all of us on that place like we were his bond servants, and there still wasn't enough to eat. Boys in the fields and girls in the house and barn. Six days a week. On Sunday, we were allowed to rest, but we couldn't leave the place because he was afraid we'd run off."

"Mama did run off from her family."

He nodded. "First chance she got. When she was sixteen, she somehow got to know your papa on the sly, and on the day she left, the two of them had enough sense to get themselves legally married in Marshall before our father caught up with them." He smiled. "It was the smartest thing she ever did. Took me two more years before I escaped, and when I did, I swore on the Bible that I would never again be hungry and that I would never be poor . . . Never."

"You're not poor now, Uncle Frank. Just look around you." I had a sudden flash back to the day he'd driven us all out to look at Lake View Park. "It's beautiful. You're here, you've arrived. Think how amazed Mama would be if she could see you in this house."

He nodded. "Yes, but can we keep it . . .? Let me ask you something, Jo. You've made your way at the bank. You've done far better than anyone, including me, thought you could. You read numbers like I read the newspaper." He paused, as if he was afraid to ask the question. "Can Central Bank and Trust survive?"

Lie, I thought to myself. It's that simple. Just lie to the man.

The truth was in the three pages I'd given him, and he didn't want to see it.

He was still staring at me, and in the end, I half-lied. I didn't say *yes it can* or *no it can't*, but stopped with, "I don't know."

He smiled at me, though very faintly. "Oh, I think you know," he muttered. "You're just too kind to say it."

I DIDN'T DREAM ANY SORT OF story that night because I didn't sleep much. I swam in and out of dreams that were all muddled up together, half-awake and half-asleep. People who were alive talking to people who were dead as if they knew them well enough to love or hate. And the last flickering scenes in that moving picture show were of Frank and Brenda, Frank Junior and Sissy in the family automobile driving and driving in the dark, lost on the road.

HAVE YOU EVER SEEN A woman in pants?

In those days, you wouldn't see such in the country. Women wore dresses morning, noon, and night—to the fields, to the barn, to the store. Maybe a different dress if you were walking into town to shop at the General than the dress you wore to work around the farm but still. Even to ride a horse or a mule when such was required.

But by 1930, women would ever so often be seen in pants. It brought stares on the street no doubt. And speculation about whether they were trying to pass for a man or play the part of a man with some other woman. People will think or say anything.

What I'm working around to is this. If I've shocked you once or twice in these pages, there's a big one coming around the corner now. *I owned a pair of pants.* Wool trousers. That I'd bought with my own money at the Bon Marche downtown. Sissy was decidedly not along on that little shopping trip because she would no more have allowed pants than she would have put up with me buying a fedora and penciling a mustache on my lip.

But here's the thing. It was cold that October, and every sign from wooly worms to corn husks said it was going to be a bitter winter. The winter wind lives in the streets of Asheville, then as now, burrowing through the alleys and howling around corners like some icy creature from the poles. Women teetering in their shoes and using both hands to push down their skirts.

And I was sick and tired of my legs freezing all the way up to . . . well, you know. While I watched men marching by me in wool socks and wool pants and wool everything else.

Besides, my trousers were stylish. Fitted. Sleek. I liked how they felt, and I liked how they looked.

And I was determined to wear them that Sunday when Levi Arrowood drove me up home. No doubt my Papa would shake his head and my brothers would fall down laughing, but I didn't care.

When Levi picked me up at the Mansion that morning, he came to the front door, rang the bell, and stood in the entrance hallway, chatting with Aunt Brenda and Sissy. Sissy had hauled herself out of bed unnaturally early just to see what he looked like in the light of day.

He looked fine to me. For one thing, he wasn't wearing black. He had on corduroy trousers and a denim coat. The coat wasn't new nor was it old, and it fitted him. By that I mean, it fitted his personality on that day. One foot in the country and one foot in town. He had a gray wool cap in his hand I'd never seen before, and he seemed relaxed, smiling and flirting just a bit with Aunt Brenda. I'd never seen the man flirt in his life, and here he was of a Sunday morning, telling Brenda he was sorry he couldn't stay for breakfast but he'd be pleased to come to supper some night and couldn't wait to taste her cooking. I half wanted to drag him back to the kitchen and show him off to Pansy, but I figured that wasn't in the cards.

My pants? Aunt Brenda shook her head sadly, Sissy made bug eyes at me behind everybody's back, and when Junior walked through on the way to the dining room, he took one look and asked, "Why are you dressed up like a man?"

Walking from the door to the car, I asked Levi what he thought. He stopped halfway down the sidewalk and told me to keep walking. I did. And when he caught up with me to open the car door, he was smiling.

"Were you looking at my backside?" I whispered, assuming Brenda and Sissy were still peeking out the blinds.

Bigger smile. "Could be," he said. And then, "Boy's a fool. Last thing on earth you look like is a man."

IT TOOK US TWO HOURS to drive from the Mansion on out the Weaverville Road to the Marshall Highway; then along the River Road through downtown Marshall and so to Walnut; and then down the winding, gravel road to Barnard where we could cross the river on the old bridge there. We stopped for gasoline in Marshall, and I asked Levi if he needed to pick up or drop off anything.

He grinned. "It's Sunday morning, Jo. Not a lot of business to be done on Sunday morning . . . Now, if we'd come through last night . . ."

The road on the other side of the Barnard Bridge got to be less and less friendly as we went. It crossed the creek a half-dozen times before we reached Jake Worley's store, and when I say crossed, what I really mean is it went straight through the creek at certain wide, shallow spots, which I named each in turn for Levi: Noel's Ford followed by Randall's Ford followed by Earl's Ford and so on. We left the car at Jake Worley's store halfway up the valley because, as Levi put it, he'd prefer not to tear the bottom out of the chassis over the next ten rocks we came to.

Which was fine. I wanted to walk.

I wanted to go slow and smell the air. I wanted to stop to speak with a dog or two that I hadn't visited with in a year. I wanted to wave across the creek to Aunt Maude and swap a tale or two with Cousin Earl, who lived in the Robbins cabin that was rumored to be the oldest building on the creek. I wanted to feel my way home, letting the place that made me flow through me. To mind and remind me of who I was.

Never tell him I said so, but I grew to love Levi a little bit that day, for he moved right along with me—if anything, slower and more measured. He knew how to lean on a fence and talk corn and wheat, sheep and chickens, cattle and hogs. Was it time yet for hog killing? It wasn't, all agreed. Though cold, they were waiting on Thanksgiving to come and go. The first lick of real winter.

Dogs.

Dogs are a separate category of mountain talk. And always the best of that talk, at least among the men. For dogs do most everything on a mountain farm. They herd and guard and sing and hunt. They raise up the children and keep the old men company beside the fire. Alpha and Omega.

Most of all, they hunt. Now, a woman may get her hands on the runt of the litter and turn it into a house pet to lay by the stove, but the final question over the most heroic of dogs is whether they will hunt. And if they hunt, will they sing. I have known dogs—Plott hounds and Blueticks and Redbones—named Hercules and Sally, Caesar and Caesar's Ghost, Cleopatra and Bone. Oh, the list goes on and on of the great ones, the dogs of myth and legend. I found out that day, as we worked our way up Big Pine, that Levi had raised up a pup of his own while living on his uncle's place, name of Bodie. Bodie was killed by a bear that he chased hard into a laurel slick—which broke Levi's heart and contributed to his decision to move to town.

And in this fashion, we walked and talked our way up the Big Pine Valley—me pointing out one landmark after another, the two of us easing into our native speech. This un and that un. We'uns and you'uns. Over thar. We went and took and raised up a ruckus.

Words matter. More than you or I know how to say.

He might just have loved me a little bit too. On that day. Though he would never admit it in a thousand years. For we could breathe with each other then. Be silent with each other while listening to the creek run. Hear a faraway rooster that wouldn't hush up though dawn was long past.

When we came up the road opposite the house, I could see a lonesome old man coming along from the barn. He was limping a bit and used a walking stick. His hat was pulled low over his face to shield it. I paused with Levi at the swinging bridge that would carry us over the creek and into the yard.

"Who's that?" Levi asked. I shook my head and shrugged.

The bridge swung with our weight and jounced us a bit. For the first time that lovely day, I felt out of rhythm with Levi, as if he didn't quite know me yet nor I him. The old man must have heard us for he looked up at the creaking sound the bridge made under us. He used his hand to shade his eyes against the high sun, and I believe he recognized us before I recognized him. He dropped his hand and leaned into his stick as if the sight of us staggered him. Then he flung his long arm into the air and hailed us, called out to me by name. Oh, my saints . . .

It was my Papa.

31

I RAN UP THROUGH THE YARD grass, long and shaggy and riven with fallen leaves. He tossed away his stick and threw his arms wide to gather me in. His overalls were dirty and patched, but soft from long wear. His lean face—oh, his dear face—was clean shaven except for his mustache, which somehow had turned gray and bristled against my cheek like a stiff brush. His smell was all pipe tobacco and barn work.

"Why are you crying, Josie? Are you sad to . . .?"

"I'm not crying . . . My eyes are watering against the cold."

He chuckled . . . and brought an ancient linen handkerchief out of his bib pocket. Gently, gently, he swiped at my face, which caused me to giggle like I was ten years old again.

"Who's that man you've got dragging behind you? Is he a stray from down the road?"

Levi took that as his cue and walked up as well, a tentative smile on his face. Oddly, just at that moment, I noticed a strange similarity between those two faces, though different in age by thirty-plus years. Both lean, sharp and watchful, both shaped by weather. Both regarding the other with friendly curiosity.

"Papa, this is Levi Arrowood, from over Spring Creek way. He lives in Asheville now. Levi, this is Lewis Salter, my Papa."

Papa smiled that sly smile of his and stuck out one brown, calloused hand. Which Levi grasped and held, the two of them locked into some knowing that I couldn't penetrate. Some recognition beyond me.

"Sir, I'm pleased to finally meet you. Jo talks about you like you made the earth and rested on the seventh day."

That got a nod and wink out of Papa. "She might just be right about that, except for the seventh day part. You got to get the ox out of the ditch, boy, even on a Sunday."

FROM THERE, IT BECAME A quiet day. Of my six brothers, four were out of the house now, living on their own up and down the valley—married and unmarried, babies and whatnot—and Papa had given the youngest two the day to roam and run. Hunting one thing or another, chasing after girls at church if not deer in the high meadows.

I made up a hot dinner out of what I could find in Mama's pantry. Cut up and fried some potatoes in butter, with a pinch of salt and more pepper. As the potatoes sizzled, I chopped up an onion and threw that in as well. There was a pot of beans on the stove that I let warm as I worked. I found a slab of bacon that seemed fresh enough and put strips of that to fry in a separate skillet. Sent Levi to the spring house, and he came back with fresh eggs and a jar of milk. So there was corn bread.

It wasn't much, nothing resembling a homecoming feast, but eventually there was a hot meal for the three of us, and everything I touched reminded me of Mama.

After dinner, I walked Levi up to the cemetery. Papa came partway, as far as the gate to the upper pasture, and as his bad leg was hurting him, waited there for us to return.

I had visited home the previous Christmas but hadn't made it all the way up to Crooked Ridge. Thus, I hadn't been there since the day we laid Mama to rest twenty months before. The last quarter mile left us both breathless, and as we climbed into the saddle of the mountain where the cemetery lay, it felt to me as if we had walked back in time. The afternoon air was cool and sharp, the autumn trees a wild throw of color as if some giant hand had found an ancient quilt on the foot of the bed and flung it over the ridge—covering the trees in rust red, yellow, and orange, and filling the thick, high grass with a barrage of leaves.

Both of us a little dizzy from the climb and you felt it could have been any autumn day in the past hundred years, as quiet as your heartbeat except for the wind that scuffed and scurried through the gap. The chatter of a squirrel and the muted call of a thrush.

When we reached the sagging, rusty wire fence that surrounded the graves, Levi paused at the gate, to give me time alone if I wanted it. But that didn't feel right, and I grabbed his hand to pull him along with me. We seemed to float. Later, when I thought back, it felt as if we floated past any number of graves—Salter, Robbins, Worley, Buckner, Randall—till we came by the tuft of ground where she lay.

Mary Freeman Salter
1871-1929
Gone Home

Over the months, I'd forgotten the words she'd picked out. Nothing about the Light of Jesus or the Lord is my Shepherd. *Gone Home* where? How?

"What was she like?" Levi asked quietly. I still had hold of his hand as if it were an anchor.

"Quiet, mostly. Though full of unexpected things. Little jokes . . . sayings . . . some of them off color. She was strong-willed but never against Papa or anybody else really. Strong-willed to work, to make do, survive, I guess . . . She's the reason I came to town."

"How so?"

"A few days before she died, when it was just the two of us in the house, she called me in close to tell me to leave. *Get the hell out of here*, is actually what she said. *Make a life somewhere else . . . a life that I can't even imagine.*"

"A life she couldn't imagine . . . that's what she said?"

"Her exact words."

"Have you done it? Made a life?"

"I'm working on it."

The wind picked up for a moment and tossed the leaves around us. I shivered, and Levi stepped closer, pried his hand loose so he could put his arm around my shoulders against the chill.

We stood like that for a moment, me remembering the gash my brothers' shovels had made here in the cold ground.

"Levi," I whispered. "I'd like you to meet Mary Freeman Salter, my mother . . . Mama, I'd like you to meet Levi Arrowood, from over on Spring Creek. I do not know his middle name because he is too proud to say. Nor do I know his Mama nor Daddy's names because he forgot to tell me that too."

I paused to let the wind talk for a bit. As the wind is wont to do.

"That's true. You would think he'd be a little more forthcoming. He has a brother named Gordon and an Uncle Nathan if that rings a bell. I believe his Mama is over your way." Gone home.

The wind, chatting, ferrying a thousand leaves down around us.

"I don't know much about him, I confess. To be doing what I'm doing. What we're doing." I leaned forward to whisper. "He does it . . . pretty damn well, Mama, I have to say."

A question in the breeze. Cold against my cheek.

"Well, he's a bootlegger. And he runs a nightclub . . . you know, a blind pig . . . a dance hall."

"Speakeasy," Levi offered.

"A speakeasy. Where they play jazz that makes your feet go crazy."

A current of even colder air down through the trees. Ruffles the bob hair on my head.

"Not just your feet . . . makes all of you go crazy. All of me anyway."

The bittersweet of autumn wind. The smell of rain and wet leaves.

"No, he doesn't sound like he will. Not yet anyway."

Enough of winter in the air to make my eyes water.

"I know. But I can't help myself."

A breathless pause in that high place followed by something like a chuckle . . . a bucket full of laughter tossed high in the air. Fading though . . . fading. Make a life it whispered as it went. Make a life I can't . . .

"Can you hear her voice?" Levi murmured after a moment.

"In the wind, I can."

"What does she say?"

"She says you don't sound like the marrying kind. Says you'll like as not get yourself killed."

He nodded. I could feel him nodding even with my eyes closed, he was holding me that tight. "I can understand that, but I have no notion of getting killed, Jo. Neither knife nor gun."

And grinning. I could feel his foolish grin through the strength and warmth of his arm. I felt safe there, and after a bit, turned into him, wrapped my own arms around his waist.

He let the fall breeze dance around us for a bit longer before he said decisively, "Edgar."

I stepped back to look at him. Study his face. "Who?"

"My middle name is Edgar."

◇◇◇

Before we left that afternoon, we warmed by the fireplace for an hour or so, and Levi told Papa about his life up till then. He offered Papa one of his cigars from the denim coat pocket, and Papa took him up on the offer. They each lit up with a blazing twig from the fireplace, and how they didn't set their hair afire I can't say. I just leaned back in Mama's rocking chair and listened, let their twin voices flow into me like smoke.

Crops and dogs and politics—damn that Hoover to let things fall to pieces—and what was life like in town for a country boy, a boy from Spring Creek. They talked about me some little bit, as if I wasn't there, and it was the most pleasant thing in the world to have myself passed back and forth between them.

I dozed a bit, I do believe. It had been such a long, goddamned week . . . and a country woman's rocking chair is the calmest thing there is on earth, and the laziest, Lord knows, and then place it beside a fire in an old stone fireplace. The Roman Legions would take a nap.

With my eyes closed, their voices sounded like one voice after all. In harmony with the crackling fire.

When I pried my eyes open after a bit—no telling how long in minutes—they had a fruit jar they were passing between them. Not companionable drinking, which you might have expected, but more of a calm, business-like consideration.

"The bead is just right, now ain't it?" I think that was Papa.

Levi considering. "Hell, Lewis, I believe it is."

"And smooth?"

"Smooth as smoke and ash."

"Well, could you sell it?"

What the hell, I was thinking, are they about?

"Who made it? You?"

"My next to youngest boy, Michael . . . I grew the corn."

"What would Jo say? She care?"

"Josie? I don't know . . ."

"Why don't you ask me?" That would be me, of course, opening my eyes.

"You care if we sell your brother's product in town? In Asheville?"

"By we, you mean . . .?"

"You and me. We. You care if we sell your brother . . . Michael's liquor in town?"

Hell with Michael. Levi had said *we* and by it he meant him and me, he and I . . . the two of us.

"Don't do it just for me," I said, eyes wide open now. "Do it because it's good, as good as your Uncle Nathan's or at least close enough to make it worth our while." I threw that *our* in out of pure happiness.

Levi smiled at me. I confess, even half asleep, I got a little thrill in my chest when he smiled at me. "It's damn good, Jo. Your brother isn't Uncle Nathan yet, but Lord God, for a man in his twenties, he cut this just right."

I didn't tell him that I thought Michael was slow, not in front of Papa. "How does it work then?" I asked.

Levi turned back to Papa. They'd both smoked their cigars near down to a nub by then. "Tell Michael I'll pay him five dollars cash for every quart he can make. Sooner rather than later. In a month if he can manage it. And again a month later."

He turned back to me. "We'll sell it in town, Jo. People out of work got money for two things only. Food and booze. You with me?"

I looked at Papa. "Is five dollars a quart fair, Papa? Will it make things better for Michael? For you?"

He nodded and tossed his cigar butt into the fire. "It's more than fair, Jo. In fact, Levi is probably cheating himself." He smiled an ironic smile and then winked at me. "Doing it for your sake, I suppose."

Levi was shaking his head. "Doesn't matter, Lewis. Jo and I can sell it for top dollar, and . . . besides, we all need to stick together. Winter's going to be cold this year. Likely last for a long time."

They both turned to look at me.

"Thanksgiving," I said to the two of them. "I want to come home for Thanksgiving. Month from now, give or take. Tell Michael to get his lazy ass to work and still as much liquor as he can without sacrificing the quality. We'll pick it up then . . . Levi and me."

"And again at Christmas?" Papa looked back and forth from me to Levi.

"Again at Christmas," Levi said. "Maybe Michael could recruit one or two of your other sons to help him."

Then a strange thing happened. We shook hands on it, but not like you'd expect—one at a time. Rather, my right hand in Levi's left, his right in my Papa's left, and Papa's right in my left. It was a long time before we let go of each other, a circle unbroken before a fire still burning.

32

IT WAS DARK BY THE time we got back to town and pulled up on a side street near Uncle Frank's Morgan Mansion. Somehow, in all our driving and walking and visiting, we had left the bank till the very end. For me, that world, the world of dollars and cents, didn't fit with those backroads, especially not up at the homeplace.

When Levi parked his roadster around the corner and under some trees, I knew it was time. Time for me to be as honest with him as he was learning to be with me.

"Levi Edgar," I said. "I need to tell you what happened on Friday."

"Scoot over this way first." He reached across and pulled me toward him. "Or we'll freeze."

I was glad to scoot. The last week in October, and it was dark and cold. Some moonlight sifting silver down through the trees but that was all.

"On Friday afternoon, we had a big meeting up on the third floor of the bank. The president, several Directors, and the mayor."

"Good Lord, the mayor?"

I nodded against his shoulder, the soft denim of his coat. "And I reported the figures since the first of last year . . ."

"Why you? Don't take this the wrong way, but I thought you were the Assistant to Someone who . . ."

"I'm the Assistant Head Cashier, but that's not why me. Why

me is because I . . . I do numbers. I see numbers, I think numbers. You're cuddled up in the car seat with a woman who dreams in numbers."

"So, they need you?"

"Turns out they do. But they didn't like it very much when I showed them the numbers and explained what they meant. They didn't like it at all."

"Did they turn on you?"

"No, but they turned on each other."

I explained to him about the last two years and the four points. Central B & T overextended, loans out everywhere, the city and bank propping each other up. He got it. You could tell he grasped what I was saying.

"The whole thing's going to collapse, isn't it?"

Oddly enough, it was almost the exact same question Uncle Frank had asked me just the day before, and I'd been afraid to answer. With Levi, though, I wasn't afraid. "I don't know for sure. Maybe they can call in a percentage of the outstanding debt and the mayor can squeeze enough money out of the taxpayers, but I don't see how . . ."

"How they can make it through the end of the year?"

Again, I nodded into that soft, worn denim. I liked the way my face felt there.

"Is that why you want me to withdraw everything?"

"I have almost seven hundred fifty dollars in Central B & T. I'm going to take it out tomorrow afternoon right at five o'clock, just as the bank's closing so as to not draw attention. But I don't know what to do with the cash." If I'd been a little sleepy before, I was wide awake now. The thought of cash money will do that to you.

"There's a safe at the Club. In the back office behind the bar.

You're welcome to put your money in there for safekeeping. I've been thinking about it since you said something on Friday. That's what I'm going to do."

"Will you keep my money separate for me? I know it's not much, but . . ."

He sat up straighter for a moment. "Of course, Jo. What do you think, I'd try to steal from you? It goes into a separate box or envelope."

"I didn't mean . . . You know what I mean."

He relaxed again, nodded against the top of my head.

"Levi, who owns the club?"

He considered for a moment, a long moment. "Alright, Jo, you were honest with me about the bank. And I suspect I'm not supposed to breathe a word of it to anybody else, right?"

I nodded. "You can't. You'll get me fired."

"I understand. Well, I'm about to return the favor. I'll tell you about the Club, but you can't even think about it out loud if there's anybody else in the room."

"I'll get you fired?"

"More likely thrown in jail. You trusted me, so . . ."

I waited.

"I run the Club for a group of local men, who don't want their names associated with it because of their . . . social standing. They own the building, but I always meet their representative downtown to protect their reputation."

"Okay."

"And I want to buy it from the group. I want to own it. Land, building, business, everything." He was whispering, this last part. As if the words were rising up out of his very gut. "I want something of my own, and it seems like the Club is the best chance I'll ever have."

"I'll help you," I whispered. And I meant it. After all, he was offering to buy liquor from Michael, which was the same as buying it from Papa.

"How?"

"I don't know. I can do the books for you. I can make all the numbers sing for you."

"I'd be happy if you just made them talk to me occasionally."

"Where's your money now?"

"Wachovia. I chose it because Fred Seely uses it. Grove used to bank there."

"Grove used to bank anywhere that would loan him money."

"I know." He paused. "I have almost eight thousand dollars saved up, Jo. It's taken me years, and I can't bear . . ."

"To lose it, I know. But if Central B & T fails, I'm afraid the rest will go down too. I think you have to take it out. At least for now. But try not to draw attention to it. Maybe a few thousand at a time . . ."

He nodded against the top of my head again, and this time his jaw felt hard, clenched. "This week? Do it this week?"

"Yes, and put it in the safe, like you said . . . I feel silly crying on your shoulder about my little bit when you're worried about thousands."

Slowly, we both relaxed. Breathed. Sank against each other.

"Levi . . ."

"Hmmm?"

"You want to come in? We can sneak in the basement door down where my room is."

I could tell he was thinking about it. Hesitating. But then . . . "I don't think so. Not tonight. But bring your money up to the Club after work tomorrow. We're not open for business, but we can make something to eat, and I'll bring you home after."

I slipped out of the car and walked around to the driver's side window. "I'm not sure how to say this in just plain old words," I whispered to him, "but it means a lot to me that you took me up home today."

He leaned out the window. "Oh, I think you took me home, Jo. I was just the driver." I leaned forward and kissed him hard on the mouth. And whatever that kiss said, I meant it.

We were hard and soft together, but then, once I was inside and in bed . . .

Came the nightmare.

I was somewhere running in the dark. Inside a building again, and at first, I couldn't tell what or where. Then I realized . . . *the bank at night. He was dogging me again, chasing me, and in the next instant, I was thrown on the floor and he was on me.*

I was on the hard, cold floor, and he was between my legs, and his prick was inside me. I was trying to push him off me, but it was too late, and he was pounding me. The man with the numbers chalked on his clothes, his pants down around his knees.

I screamed for Levi, but he was on the outside somewhere and couldn't get to me.

The numbers man was jerking his whole body so hard to impale me, that his hair—black hair—was flying forward and back on his head each time he hammered into me.

Forcing my legs apart and deep into my gut and deeper, tearing me.

I could feel myself screaming but couldn't hear a thing except his grunting. And the worst part of all was that . . . the helplessness, the utter and complete humiliation.

I could not see his face.

I had to see his face. I had to know who he was. Punching into me like I was dirt, meaning to hurt me.

And it didn't end. He didn't shoot, he didn't stop, just kept . . . till I jerked awake.

And I still couldn't see his face.

◇◇◇

The next morning, Monday, I passed Pansy in my little downstairs hallway, as I was going out and she was coming in.

"What happened to you?" she asked. She reached out to grasp my shoulders and pulled me over into the light from the little basement windows. "You look like . . ."

"Like what?"

"Like you done been rode by a witch. All damn night." Like I said, we'd progressed to the point we could actually touch each other and talk to each other.

"I was rode by a witch," I said, and I described the nightmare to her. "Like being punched between my legs by an animal," I said.

She reached up and touched my face. Let her hand actually rest against my cheek for a brief moment before she recalled who we were. "Was it a white man?" she asked. "Forced you?"

I nodded. "White as a ghost," I said, "but I couldn't see his face."

"You forget about that," she said. "Paint your own face up a little more 'fore you go to the bank, so you won't scare nobody with that look. And you let that dream go on. Best you forget it."

"I don't think I can forget it," I said. "I'm sore down there . . . just from what he did to me in a dream."

She nodded. "I know. I know. For some of us, Jo, that stuff you're talkin' about, it ain't no dream."

33

COLD.

November 1930 was bitter cold and windy. You could not imagine there ever being another springtime and no summer. The wind in the streets howled around corners and blasted you down the sidewalks.

Except for the few dollars in my purse, all my money, $763, was tucked away in a cigar box in the safe at the Sky Club. Levi's money, $8,239, rested in several shoe boxes in the same safe. I know because he asked me to count it and to keep track as dollars came and went. It was not the first time he trusted me, but this trust between us went deep. How deep?

24-7-12.

The combination of the lock is how deep. He said that combination was his will and testament. If he disappeared or died, I was to take the money, all the money, and go far.

"What do you mean, disappear or die?" I nagged at him to know.

NOVEMBER 13, A THURSDAY, PINKNEY Starnes came to see me at the bank. Just before lunchtime, he slipped in through the front door, quietly and unobtrusively, as was his way. He asked after me and eventually found me in back, watching over the shoulder of one of the loan cashiers, as he took payment from Julia Wolfe, a local real estate investor. Supposedly she was related to the Westalls, and Lord knows, she pursed her lips and stared vacantly over her spectacles just like they did.

When Mrs. Wolfe snapped shut her purse and stomped on off, Pink asked could he take me to lunch, and I agreed that he could. We walked through the wind across Pack Square and down a side street to the Greek Diner, far enough away from the main business doings that we could take a booth in the back and say whatever we liked.

I remember we both had chili, him with crackers and me with corn bread. I had coffee—it was that kind of day—but he had tea. Hot tea. "Blood pressure," he said with a wink. "You ever heard of such a thing? Blood pressure?"

"That's why you drink tea?"

He nodded and half-smiled. "Yep, my blood pressure is twice what yours is, I imagine. And when it takes a notion, it can knock me flat down in the street."

"But you're a young man," I protested.

"So they say. But my heart doesn't always share that opinion."

I started to ask him if he had a life insurance policy, but surely to God. He sold the things.

"Why did you ask me to lunch, Mr. . . . Pink?"

The waitress brought the chili and smiled a special smile at Pink. Seems she knew him, cared for him in some way. When she left, he took a bite and nodded. "Not bad," he muttered, "but mostly I come here because it's quiet."

I tried the chili and waited. Tried the corn bread and waited some more.

"I asked you to lunch for two reasons," he said. One is more neighborly than the other, so I'll start with the plain question first." Another bite.

"Go ahead, Pink. You can ask me anything you like."

He nodded and smiled that quiet, ironic smile. "That bank of yours . . . is it going to survive?"

"You know I can't tell you that," I said. And in saying it, told him everything he needed to know.

"What are you going to do after?"

"You mean . . . for a job?"

The steam from his tea was fogging up his eyeglasses. He took them off and nodded . . . encouragingly.

"I don't know. I haven't thought . . ."

"Well, I need you."

"What?"

"You know I'm the main person behind the Imperial Life Insurance Company, don't you?"

I stared at him. The whole world knew that.

"There are several involved, but I'm the one started it and I'm the one worries it along day by day."

"Are you offering . . ."

"You a job? Well, yes, I suppose I am. You like numbers, don't you? Everything I hear says that you love numbers more than the fat man loves molasses."

I had to laugh at him. "That's right," I admitted. "I am a friend to numbers. Mathematics."

"My youngest boy is like that as well, though not to the extent you are. But he's in college now, and I mean for him to stay there. At least through the next few years, while everything goes to hell."

"Is it? Going to hell?"

He smiled. "Of course, it is. And I expect we'll find out just how low the basement floor of hell might be."

"You want me . . ."

"To come to work at Imperial. If and when your bank, in that tall, fancy building, fails to open its doors and people start throwing rocks, then I want you to come to me. I need you. And I'll pay you."

"Why me, Pink? There's got to be more qualified men or women . . . hell, dogs or cats."

He closed his eyes and shook his head. I hoped he wasn't in pain. After a moment, he opened them again.

"That reminds me of the second thing I meant to speak with you about. What they call the depression in the national newspapers is coming. It's out there. Started in the country and then got a stranglehold on the stock market and all those New York high rollers, dragged them under. It's coming our way, and when it lights here, country people have to stick together. People like you and me and your friend Arrowood. People who came into town to make a life, we have to stick together, or they'll plow us under. You know that?"

I nodded. "I can imagine they will. So this is you being neighborly, giving the poor country girl a sheltering place when the winds start to howl?"

"Oh, I'd do it for your Papa's sake . . . sure. Lewis and I have known each other for a long time. But even so, I'd seek you out because you have a talent. God taught you to add, subtract, multiply, and divide—not some Presbyterian mission schoolteacher. And truth be told, I need you whether the bank holds or not. Whatever they pay you . . ."

"A hundred dollars per week." I figured that would bring him up short.

"I can double that. And you help me steer Imperial through the next few years."

"You can't afford to pay me that," I said bluntly, "not with times the way they are."

"You'd be surprised by what I can do," he said, "just like many have been surprised by you."

◇◇◇

SIX DAYS LATER, NOVEMBER 19.

The bank lobby was jammed full of people all day. People of every kind and sort, depositing and withdrawing, leaving and taking. One giant lumberjack of a man, fresh in from a logging camp in Haywood County, stood straddle-legged in the middle of the marble floor in his flannel shirt and work boots, waving his previous month's pay over his head and demanding to open an account. He, by God, believed in the president, in the bank, and in the good old U.S. of A. I steered him to Jezzy, who flirted shamelessly despite the rank logging camp smell and took his money.

I ran from one spot to the next all day long as the whole place was in a kind of frenzy. Things went so hard and so fast that more than one of the tellers was in tears by lunchtime. At first, I thought the transactions would break even, but by early afternoon it was clear, to me at least, that a tide had turned and the withdrawals, small and large, were running hard against the deposits. Money was flowing out the door in a stream and only coming back in a trickle.

Around two o'clock that afternoon, I ran upstairs to Foster's office and made him come back down with me to the first floor. When he caught on to what was happening, the two of us went from teller to teller, instructing them to limit all withdrawals, no matter who, to fifty dollars. Then the two of us stood out in the lobby, telling those customers who were demanding more that the vault was closed for the day and to come back tomorrow. We were just trying to survive till five o'clock, and both of us knew it.

Foster watched while I went over the account books and did the daily summaries that evening, urging me to hurry, but I didn't rush despite the growing sense of urgency. We had totaled more transactions in that one day than we normally did in a week, and the whole process took longer and was harder to check. The loan department did almost nothing, but for the tellers out front, it had been an eight-hour sprint.

When I finished and handed him the report, he took one look at the bottom line and cursed at me. "Damn you, Jo. This is it? This is the best you've got for me!" I thought he might cry.

"The numbers are what they are," I said to him. "I didn't make them up."

The Directors met that night. Uncle Frank did not come home to the Mansion till just before breakfast the next morning. The next day, we never even unlocked the doors at the Central Bank & Trust Company.

34

NOVEMBER 20, 1930. THE DARK of the moon. One of the coldest days yet in that dying year.

At nine o'clock, Foster and I stood by the front door out of habit, even though we'd been ordered not to open it, and in fact, Foster had given up his keys the night before to Frank and the other VPs. We could see through the window blinds that there was a small crowd waiting, looking at their watches and stamping their feet in the cold.

Nine-fifteen and the crowd was growing, and we could hear several strong voices yelling at us to open up.

Nine-thirty and I retreated back to the rear of the room and gathered the tellers plus the loan cashiers in my office. The crowd in the square was already growing.

Ten o'clock and McCoy, one of the VPs, came down to tell all the tellers and cashiers to go home. When they said they were afraid of the crowd outside, he informed them that the Asheville City Police were stationed in the alley behind the bank where the employee entrance was and would soon be guarding the front door as well.

Ten-thirty and I was the only person left on the first floor besides Paul the Loan Manager. Foster had retreated upstairs. There was a flickering glare through the front windows. Someone had built up a bonfire made of slats from park benches in front of the bank on the sidewalk. People were yelling and throwing rocks at the front door despite the police.

Eleven o'clock and I slipped up to the front to glance out through the window blinds closest to the door. Shouldn't have. The broad sidewalk in front of the bank was so crowded with people that many were standing in the street. Milling about and shouting. The lumberjack from the day before saw me peek out through the blinds and stepped between two policemen to start pounding on the front door—not knocking—pounding. I retreated back to my office. Paul was nowhere to be seen, had apparently scurried upstairs.

Noon and the crowd outside had begun to disperse. From the second-floor conference room, Paul and I could watch the square below without attracting too much attention. The bonfire from that morning, built more to keep people warm than to cause trouble, had burned down to ashes on the sidewalk, and the wind was already swirling the ashes away into the bleak air.

Two o'clock and those of us who were left in the building from the first and second floor . . .

Foster Reynolds, Head Cashier

Paul Reynolds, Chief Loan Officer

Josephine Salter, Assistant to the Head Cashier (me)

James Fletcher, Second Loan Officer

. . . were all called up to the third floor to meet with the VPs.

As we walked from the stairwell to the conference room, I could see the secretaries throwing on coats and scarves, grabbing pocketbooks and heading for the stairs. Obviously, they'd been ordered home, and most of them looked glad to go.

Uncle Frank and Coxe were seated at the conference room table, side by side with a telephone in the middle of the table and papers scattered over the surface. I recognized much of the paper as my own work, the reports I'd generated.

The third VP, McCoy, was pacing in front of the window, occasionally glancing down at the square below. Once the four of us minions were in the room, McCoy nodded at the door, and

Paul closed it. Why, I wondered, if there was nobody else left to hear what was said? And what McCoy had to say was no surprise.

The bank would not reopen that week, and unless a massive influx of cash could be identified, it would not reopen at all. *Ever?* Foster asked in a hangdog sort of way, and McCoy ignored him. It was Thursday, and the four of us would be paid for that week's work at some yet-to-be-determined point in the future. The tellers and cashiers who worked for us might be paid for three days' work that week (in other words, through the day before), again at some vague point in the future. Should they contact us, we were not to promise them anything.

As of end-of-day Friday—the next day—our services would no longer be required. Any personal resources that we had secured in Central B & T would not be available to us for some time and perhaps ever. *Are you saying that I can't even withdraw my own money?* asked Paul coldly. *That's exactly what he is saying.* Uncle Frank looked up from the table. *You fool, the bank is closed. Broken. There is no money.*

We were free to go while the alley behind the bank was still secure. We were to return the following day on our regular schedule, in case we were needed. We should make arrangements to clean out our desks and take our personal belongings with us on Friday afternoon.

That was all, we were told.

Except that as we filed out of that third-floor conference room, the room I'd only visited three times in my life to that point, Coxe looked up and asked me to stay. The three men I'd come in with glanced back at me, Paul angry and Foster pale as a ghost. Uncle Frank told me to shut the door, Jo, and I did. And to sit down, which I did also. Even though there were lamps burning, the room felt cold and dark. I wondered vaguely if somebody had turned off the heat.

McCoy still stood by the window, but at least he'd stopped pacing. With no preliminaries or explanations, Coxe began. "Miss Salter, the state bank examiners from Raleigh will be here in the morning. It is their job to determine if the bank's charter is to be revoked, and more importantly, who, if anyone, is responsible for the failure of Central Bank & Trust. They will also determine if any charges will be brought by the state. They will want to examine our financial records for the past several years, and quite frankly, we feel that you are the best person to present those records and to answer their questions."

"Am I in any trouble?"

Uncle Frank, who had not met my eyes to this point, looked up suddenly and shook his head. "No, no." His face was that ancient face I'd seen staring into the open furnace some weeks before.

Coxe again: "No, quite frankly, you are not in trouble. We are. We're not asking you to lie or misrepresent, indeed, not even to obfuscate in any way."

I didn't know what *obfuscate* meant but I could guess.

Coxe went on. "Explain it to them the way you explained it to the Directors a few weeks ago. That's all we ask."

McCoy spoke while still staring out the window. "Try not to make us look like fools, Jo, if you can."

"I'll do my best," I said.

And that was it. No one had anything else to say, and after a moment, I got up and went out, closing the door behind me. I went downstairs and used the phone in my office to call the Sky Club. Levi himself answered.

"Can I come up and sit for a while?" I asked him.

"I'll come pick you up," he said. "I don't want you out on the streets by yourself."

"Please," I said. And after a moment. "Be careful."

◇◇◇

NOVEMBER 20, 1930. THE DARK of the moon. On that cold day, Central Bank & Trust, along with seven other banks in Buncombe County, failed to open their doors. That night, my boss, Foster Reynolds, went home and tried to cut his own throat. As with so many things, he failed at that too and only managed to sever his vocal cords.

As dark and cold as that day became, it was nothing compared to what followed after.

PART THREE

WINTER 1931

35

IN MAKING A LIFE, WHAT matters most?

Or in making a death?

Have you ever noticed how clothing, no matter how fancy, eventually falls to pieces? Doesn't matter if it's my Papa's old overalls or Uncle Frank's $100 silk suit. First the cuffs fray, a stray thread or two comes loose when you yank on it, the cloth at the knees and elbows grows thin and shiny. Papa's overalls, which maybe cost $2 at the General rather than $100 at Bon Marche, gets torn and ragged, despite Mama's constant mending and patching. Uncle Frank's suit goes back and forth to the cleaners and the seamstress, but eventually, no matter what, the cloth itself—whether denim or silk—starts to go. The threads themselves tear and separate. I suspect it's the same with a shroud as it is with a suit. Eventually . . .

And when the clothing falls away, what is left but the naked, shivering bones?

In the weeks following the crash of the banks, things began to unravel—at first slowly and then very quickly.

On Friday the 21, I was at the bank for ten hours, working in the third-floor conference room with the three bank examiners from Raleigh, who'd driven through the night to get there. John Mitchell, the Chief State Bank Examiner, spent most of the day in and out of the room, meeting with Davis and interviewing the three VPs. I got the boys who made their living crunching numbers like me—

one named Darden and the other named Roberts. At first, they couldn't believe how bad things had become. Then, when I helped them drill down into the records that I had used a month before to prepare my own reports to the Directors, they were appalled—that's the word Darden used—at how sloppy the record keeping had been once you got above the first floor. Finally, by mid-afternoon, the mood shifted yet again, almost to one of resignation.

Their boss, Mitchell, came in the room with my boss, Wallace Davis. Darden and Roberts had their jackets off and their sleeves rolled up, as they were hard at it. Mitchell and Davis looked like they were fresh as daisies—shaved, bathed, and dressed. Davis had to have been up all night, but he still looked surprisingly spry. Neither sat down, but Mitchell leaned forward on his hands over the table where we were working while Davis stood behind him with his arms crossed.

"Gentlemen," Mitchell began.

I took this as my cue and stood up to go, but Davis gave me a slight shake of the head, and I sat back down.

"Gentlemen," Mitchell again. "Mr. Davis and I have come to an understanding. We've agreed on the language we're going to use, at least for the time being. Central Bank and Trust has suspended operations pending a reorganization. Right, Wallace?"

Davis stepped forward. And in his surprisingly high voice: "Exactly, John. The collapse of the real estate market in Asheville followed by depressed business conditions in the country generally over the past two years have created extremely difficult conditions for a public-minded institution such as ours. We have fought long and hard to support the Asheville community in every way possible. We are confident that a fair appraisal of the assets of the bank . . ." He paused to give Darden, Roberts, and me a long stare. ". . . based on the sound value of the securities behind the same, will show the bank to be solvent."

Mitchell nodded throughout this performance and then picked up the thread again. "Wallace is going to meet with reporters out in front of the bank at three o'clock, so that we can get the word out. Should make the morning papers here and in Raleigh. Any questions?"

I had a hundred questions, but I wasn't one of the gentlemen, so I kept my mouth shut. Darden and Roberts must have known better too, so they just nodded.

When Mitchell and Davis went out again, Darden and Roberts looked at me.

"What the hell?" I whispered.

"They're going to try to save it," Darden whispered back.

And Roberts: "They're afraid if they don't, half the private banks in the state will fold."

"What securities are they talking about?" Darden whispered. "Are there any stocks or bonds hidden away somewhere? Safe deposit box?"

I shrugged. "How would I know?"

"Maybe they mean real estate. Collateral on the loans."

"If they do, they're screwed," I said. "The margins on all the outstanding loans are long gone. The real estate in Asheville isn't worth a tenth of what it was two years ago."

We sat silent for a moment. "Well hell," one of them finally said.

"What are we supposed to do?" I asked. "You can see the numbers."

"Finish up our report and pass it on to Mitchell," the other one replied. "And then we all go home and keep our mouths shut."

"What about me?" I asked.

"Sister, you better find a job somewhere not in a bank."

I LONGED TO SET UP CAMP at the Sky Club, where I could be close to Levi, but I also knew that for a few days at least, I needed to stick close to home at Morgan Mansion. I had no idea how Uncle Frank would respond to the whirlwind, plus there was Aunt Brenda and Sissy to worry about. I felt like I'd been assigned guardian angel to the whole family except for Junior, who was oblivious to anything beyond the golf course and the drugstore.

I spent most of the day on Saturday with Darden and Roberts, and the three of us made an honest report to Mitchell, who must have ignored it because the *Asheville Citizen* on both Saturday and Sunday went full bore with the story that he and Davis had cobbled together between them. Central Bank & Trust was in the middle of strategic reorganization, even though I knew full well that we'd all been given the pink slip and not to expect that last week's pay anytime soon.

Uncle Frank came down to dinner on Saturday evening with the family and was subdued but not distraught. He was going to take a few months off, he explained to everyone. Rest and recover from the stress of the last year or so. Then, in the new year, seek a position with another local bank. American National, perhaps, which had survived a similar run on its reserves at the end of the week and emerged with a good reputation. Life would return to normal in the new year. I could see the relief in the rest of the family.

Sunday, Levi came to see me at Morgan Mansion, and I slipped away just long enough for the two of us to walk down to the lake together and walk slowly around the shore a couple of times. "How can they print this?" I kept asking him, waving the newspaper he'd brought me. "The mayor says everything is fine and not to rock the boat. Fred Seely says everything is safe and sound, so our *duty* is not to panic. Our duty, for God's sake. Duty to who? Duty to the Country Club?"

"Easy, Jo. You know what they're doing." He took the newspaper that I'd rolled up and tossed it into a handy trash bin. Took hold of my hand, and we kept walking. "Breathe a little," he said to me with a smile.

"But truly, Levi, they're spreading this . . ."

"Horseshit?"

"Yes. That. But how can people like Roberts, the mayor, and Seely tell people it's their duty not to want their money. Their own money!"

"Come on, Jo, they're just trying to prevent an even worse run on the banks that are left. They're trying to stop the bleeding come Monday morning."

"So they don't believe what they're saying? Roberts and Seely and all these damn bank presidents who the newspaper holds up for heroes?"

He shook his head. "Lord, no. How could they after what happened? They're just trying to save their own hides."

We walked, holding hands like any country couple, and after a bit, I began to marvel. Marvel at the fact that we were there together, easing along the lake shore as if the world was a safe and sane place. A beautiful place on that Sunday afternoon, at peace with itself after a week of turmoil and loss.

"I'm grateful that you warned me," Levi said after a few minutes had passed. "Grateful that I'm not trying to swallow an eight-thousand-dollar loss . . . Might try to drown myself." We were just passing the little cove in one corner that had been walled off from the rest of the lake into a swimming pool, and he nodded at the diving board. "Jump right in."

"Can you swim?" I asked him.

He shook his head.

"Me either. Who learns to swim in the country?"

"Is it so bad?" I finally said after a pause. "So bad that all these big wigs have to lie?"

"Sure seems like it. Seems like wintertime is here for real. Freezing time. Cold and dark time."

"Is our money safe?"

"Safe in the safe?" He snorted. "Yes, I believe it is. I had the lock replaced in August, and we're the only two people in the world who know the combination."

We walked on. I marveled some more. That he and I both had survived. That we were there together, and he didn't seem ferocious or wicked or dangerous, except when he needed to be. Just Levi. Soft spoken and kind to me. What man bred in the country could ever be gentle? But he was, at least with me.

When we rounded the lake a second time and started up through Lake View Park to the Mansion, I finally broke the spell. "Thursday is Thanksgiving," I said quietly. "Can we still go up to Big Pine, you and me?"

"Of course, we can," he offered, in that quiet way of his. "But Jo, here's the thing. We're going to be hauling your brother's liquor on the way back. And a lot of it, or so I hope. We'll be breaking a few laws. If you're in the car with me, you'll be breaking the law right along of me. You ready for that?"

I had to smile at the earnestness in his voice. In his face. I squeezed his hand. "I just spent two days head-to-head with the state bank examiners," I said. "I'd much rather get arrested with you for hauling shine than by them for cooking the books."

"You sure?"

"As sure as I've ever been of anything."

36

THIS TIME ROUND, THE MIDDAY meal at Papa's house was a feast. Homecoming and celebrating. One of the married brothers had shot a turkey in the upper pasture, and his wife had roasted it. Another had cooked a beef roast from early morning, such that it was tender and juicy. Another had fried a fat chicken. Corn and potatoes and pies of all kinds. I didn't bring a thing except for myself and Levi. Levi brought two jars of apple brandy—his uncle's best—one that got opened on the porch and drunk up by anyone and everyone as the day progressed. And the other put back special for Papa, no one else to touch it.

I say I didn't bring anything but as soon as Levi and I crossed the swinging bridge, he got swept away by the brothers, and I crowded into Mama's little kitchen space with three sisters-in-law. I threw my coat in the old rocker, rolled up my sleeves, and pulled Mama's apron off the back of the pantry door. And began, laughing and chatting with them as we worked to put the vegetables and bread on the table and keep everything else hot. Women together in a warm kitchen, and the sharp November air outside.

The smells alone were delicious. Oak burning in the stove, the drippings from the roast beef and turkey, the fried chicken warming, the gravy simmering in a pot, salt and pepper and the old walls around us. Just to be in that kitchen again with the stove at full throttle made my stomach growl and grumble with gratitude and hunger.

I'd worn a dress that day instead of my trousers, meaning to fit in with the family. The best of my old country dresses, and so I did look the part except for my hair, but even so, I was struck at how different I felt after almost two years away. I was a little awkward around the wood stove and burned myself at one point. I spilled and spattered more than was quite right, and the girls noticed but were too kind to mention it.

Sixteen people crowded into that old stone farmhouse that day. Papa made one, Levi and I two more, six brothers and four with wives, plus three of the next generation. Papa's grandchildren, ranging in age from six years down to six months.

When the serious eating commenced, after a blessing pronounced by oldest brother, Will, we were spread out all over, some around the big table in the living room, some in the kitchen and some on the porch. The two children who could sit upright and hold a spoon ate sitting on the stairs.

I got to sit beside Papa because I was the prodigal returned. This despite the fact that I was a woman, as women would normally eat in the kitchen. And Levi got to sit beside me despite the fact that he was an outsider. Once we made it clear that he was from Spring Creek and not from town, that made sense and he was allowed to stay by me.

When the dessert came round, I did go into the kitchen and chattered away with my sisters-in-law. Brought in a tot of the brandy in one of Papa's old, chipped mugs for them to taste. Which they all did except one, the youngest, who patted her belly to let me know she was bearing and didn't feel quite up to it.

After dinner, we all lay about as if struck down, napping on any available chair or bench. Even Levi nodded off sitting on the edge of the hearth beside Papa's old rocker. I watched it all, feeling it like a dream. A dream of what home was once and might never be again.

When I wandered back into the kitchen, the youngest sister-in-law was rocking slowly in Mama's rocking chair, and when she heard me, opened her eyes. "How far along?" I whispered to her.

She shrugged. "Two months maybe. I haven't told anyone yet except Alan."

"Why?"

She sighed. "I'm afraid, I guess."

"Afraid you'll lose it?"

She nodded. "That and I'm afraid for her. Afraid of what this mean, old world will do to her."

I smiled. "Is it a girl, then?"

She nodded. "I think so. I don't wish it, but I think so."

"I understand."

"Are you?" she whispered, nodding at my own belly.

I shook my head. "No, not yet. I think I'm afraid too."

Later, after everyone but Michael and the other baby brother had left for home, we loaded twenty-four quart jars of Michael's best into tow sacks and slung them carefully over the backs of two mules. I counted $120 out of Levi's leather wallet and gave it to Papa to hold for Michael. Then the hard part—I said goodbye to Papa . . . but only till Christmas. "Only till Christmas, I promise," I whispered into his ear. Then Michael and Levi led the two mules down the road to Jacob Worley's store, where we loaded the jars into the trunk of the roadster, padded carefully in place with the tow sacks and blankets that Levi kept there for that very purpose.

IT WAS MOST DARK BY the time we reached the Sky Club that night. I helped Levi unload the liquor into a special room in the basement of the Club, where it could be locked up safe and sound. I hadn't promised to be home at the Mansion till the following morning, so we had time to go slow after that.

The Club was closed for Thanksgiving Day, and we had the place entirely to ourselves. Even Mack was gone to Charlotte to see his daughter. We made a supper out of leftovers brought back from the dinner at Big Pine and ate it alone together on the second-floor terrace looking out over the city.

"What are you going to do now?" Levi asked me at one point.

"You mean now, tonight?"

"No." He smiled at me in the light of the three or four candles we had lit. "No, I'm hoping you'll stay with me tonight. I mean what are you going to do now that the bank has closed up?"

I told him about Pink Starnes and the Imperial Life Insurance Company.

"Will you take him up on his offer?"

I nodded. "I think so. It's a steady salary, more money than I ever really imagined, before or after coming to town."

"It's funny, isn't it. In the middle of the great panic, no money to be had, and people will still buy life insurance."

"Life insurance and liquor."

He grinned. "Thank God for that. For the liquor part, I mean."

There was a long, comfortable pause. Both of us nibbling more than eating, still full from dinner. "The big question for me," I murmured after a bit, "is where I'm going to live."

"What do you mean?"

"I mean, what if Uncle Frank loses that house, then what? Besides, I'm twenty-eight years old, Levi. I think it's time for me to get out from under their roof and find my own place."

Another long pause, this one not so comfortable. We were both a little afraid to say whatever might come next. What? That I might need or want him. That he might need me. That there might be something like love involved; although, God knows, just the word itself made us both skittish.

"You could live here," he said. And then after a moment. "I would like that."

"No, you wouldn't," I said. "Not yet anyway. I don't think you're ready for . . ."

"For what?"

"A full-time woman in your . . . hair."

"My hair?" He reached up and ran his fingers through it.

I had to laugh at him. "Your house, your home, your kitchen, your . . . bedroom. Where would I put my clothes?"

"Well, we have these old, beat-up chifforobes. Two I can think of."

"That's sweet, but . . ." I couldn't bring myself to say the word marriage or anything even vaguely associated with it, and yet, suddenly, I could feel myself wanting it. Wanting to say out loud that if we were going to live together, I needed that. Or something like it. What the hell did people do in town about getting married anyway? "Not yet," is finally what I said to him. "Maybe just . . . not yet."

He nodded and then said a funny thing. "I'm here, Jo. You know I'm here if you need me."

I need you tonight, is what I thought. And then said it out loud.

37

WHILE CELEBRATING THANKSGIVING, I MANAGED to forget that city and county deposits made up 85 percent of the funds that were lost when Central B & T collapsed. What none of us knew, me included, was that the city was up to the roof of its gorgeous new City Hall in debt. When Gallatin Roberts and others pushed through the Greater Asheville strategy to make the city solvent again, they didn't count on property values plummeting the way they had since 1926. Sure, by the winter of 1930, Asheville was *greater* in size but poorer by far in value.

Between Thanksgiving and Christmas, the City of Asheville, along with Buncombe County, defaulted first on the interest payment of their vast outstanding loans and bonds and then on the maturing principal. They didn't close and lock the doors on City Hall like we had at the bank, but they should have.

People were outraged.

Christmas came and went. It was a sad and somber one in the Morgan household; although, Uncle Frank did seem to be bearing up. There was an occasional smile for Sissy and Junior, a hug for Aunt Brenda. But he was distant all the same, as if living in a separate world from the rest of us. And that year on Christmas Eve, there wasn't the usual pile of presents under the Morgan family tree.

Levi and I went back up to Big Pine on Christmas Day, with a warm wool sweater for Papa and store-bought toys for his grandchildren. In addition to another load of Michael's liquor—bought and paid for—we came home to the Sky Club with a gift from Papa. Of all things in this world, a puppy. A tiny mixed breed of a thing made up of beagle and redbone blood, that rode happily home in my lap. "What," Levi asked, "should we call him?" And even as he spoke, I remembered the dog he'd lost as a boy. What was that pup's name, I asked him? "Bodie," he replied. And Bodie became our dog's name.

New Years and I went to work for Pink Starnes at the Imperial Life Insurance Company. There will be much more to say about that presently.

Shortly thereafter, though, a grand jury met and returned indictments against those thought to be responsible for crippling the city. The Buncombe County Superior Court convened an extraordinary six-week session based on the indictments of city officials and bank officers. These indictments included many of the actors in this story, including the mayor, Gallatin Roberts, and the president of the bank, Wallace B. Davis. My uncle, Frank J. Morgan, was also one of the twenty-seven men charged with sundry violations of state banking laws, conspiracy, and fraud.

A few weeks later, on Tuesday, February 17, he shot himself.

I'm not sure why, but I came home from Imperial at lunchtime that day. I had this itchy feeling that things weren't quite right, and at breakfast, Pansy never once stopped shaking her head. When I asked her in the kitchen what was wrong, she pointed to her stomach and her head and claimed there was a booger in the house. A ghost. A witch. I would have laughed at her, but I could feel it too.

So I caught the midday car home from town to have lunch with the family. At first, Uncle Frank, Aunt Brenda, Junior, and I were all at the table together. Eating vegetable soup with saltines. Uncle Frank didn't say much of anything, so I set in telling about the Insurance Agency. How Pink had started it up on Lexington Avenue almost from scratch, how nobody believed in him or in life insurance at all to begin with, and how he became one of the most successful men in Asheville. You can imagine me going on and on, covering up a total lack of conversation from anyone else at the table, except from Aunt Brenda, who encouraged me.

Along toward the end of the meal, Uncle Frank suddenly stood up and said it was cold in the house and that he needed to go check on the furnace. Right then, when I heard that word—*furnace*—I should have known something was wrong, but I was telling about the various people who worked at Imperial and the funny questions people asked about life insurance, so I didn't pay Frank any mind. After all, the furnace had become an obsession of his since he no longer went to the bank every day.

He left the room, and we could hear him clumping down the stairs to the basement. Junior got up too about that time and, without a word, left the dining room to go upstairs. No "excuse me" or "thank you very much," just got up and walked out as was his wont.

Brenda and I were left alone at the table, Pansy in the kitchen. And since we were alone, I asked her about Uncle Frank. I'll never forget what she said. She said, "I think he's going to be alright. Once this legal business is over and it's clear he did nothing wrong, I think he'll be able to move on and find another bank. Oh Jo, I think he's going to be alright."

That's when we heard the shot. It seemed to me that it was impossibly loud, like cannon fire. I pushed back and jumped up. "You stay," I said to Aunt Brenda. "Stay!" And when I started for the hall, I yelled to Pansy to come into the dining room and sit with Brenda.

Down the stairs first, the way I'd gone hundreds of times by then. Nothing in the furnace room itself, though the door to the firebox was open, red flames from within coloring the cement walls. I shut the firebox door and was back in the hallway, when I noticed that the door to the backyard was standing wide open. Why . . . why open?

I ran out, thinking I don't know what . . . That I would find him? That I would save him?

Not far from that basement door, the door I used to come and go, especially late at night, was a set of stone stair steps that led to the upper part of the backyard. Uncle Frank was sprawled on his back beside those steps, his legs and arms flung out at crazy angles. An ancient pistol—later the police would say that it was a .38 caliber Iver Johnson revolver from well before the war—was still in his right fist. Still smoking.

How could it still be smoking?

He'd blown the whole side of his head off. His ear was gone, his right eye was gone, his nose blasted sideways. His mouth was slung open and full of pooling blood. His brains were everywhere on the grass, mixed with shards of bone.

I could feel myself screaming, though I could hear nothing.

Nothing except the echoes of the gunshot. Pansy's Raymond came running around the corner of the house, and I begged him to get something to cover Frank's face. A blanket, anything at all, before Aunt Brenda could see it.

The police, I thought, the ambulance. Doctors, hospital.

And they did come. All of them. The police along with Frank's personal doctor, although there was nothing the doctor could do for Frank. The ambulance, which only served to take him to the funeral home. The hospital being of no use whatsoever.

I told my part of it first to the police officer and then to the detective. How did I recognize the body if there was no face? First by the clothes, I said, and the shoes. His favorite pair of brown leather shoes, the laces neatly tied. Could it be anyone else? And

I said no. No, it couldn't. Frank had a crooked finger on his left hand that he'd broken as a child. And there was the finger.

There were no rings. He'd taken off all his rings, including his wedding ring, but there was the crooked finger. The suit pants, recently taken up because he'd lost so much weight. And the white shirt, the top half now stained with blood and brains. A stain that would never come out, a shirt that would have to be burned.

Brenda collapsed as they were loading him into the ambulance, so there was something for the doctor to do after all. Junior sat beside his mother as she lay on the couch, holding her hand and staring vacantly at the wall. Like a little boy again, in shock.

So it was left to me to call Sissy at the real estate office and tell her to come home. Come home now, for her father was dead. At the first word, she was moaning. Moaning and then screaming as she slammed down the receiver.

After I called her, I called Levi. I had to tell somebody that was mine. Somebody for me. And I didn't know anybody else to call.

He came. God love him, even though he was no friend to the police nor they to him, he came. And sat with me and Sissy till long after dark, greeting the people who came to pay their respects. Explaining that Aunt Brenda wasn't up to seeing anyone, not then, not yet. Sissy crying on the phone to her Ben, who did not come, though she begged him.

How strange we must have seemed—Levi and I—to the rich and worthy people who pulled up in their expensive automobiles and rang the front doorbell, bringing flowers and food. I kept explaining that I was the niece and that Levi was a family friend, but you could tell they thought we were imposters. Servants maybe. In the house that was already fading away and lost, the first house in that town to be flung down from the heights.

38

THE FUNERAL WAS TWO DAYS later in the middle of the afternoon at home. Even though Frank and Brenda were members of Trinity Episcopal downtown and full-fledged members of the Biltmore Forest Country Club, either of which would have served, Brenda chose to hold the service at home, in the large dining room at Morgan Mansion. I suppose it was her first act of rebellion, now that Frank was gone. She knew he loved the house, and she herself—country woman to the core—had little use for the rarified atmosphere of the Episcopal church or the country club.

Some group called the Knights of Pythias—Uncle Frank had apparently been a high-ranking member—took over the arrangements and coordinated with the Episcopal priest, so that Brenda didn't have to think about it all. I went with Sissy to the funeral home to pick out a casket and, without going into the details, convinced her that it had to be closed throughout. On the day of the funeral itself, the Knights of Pythias arranged for a sword to be prominently displayed on top of the closed casket. The priest meant that along with the sword, there was an equally large cross on display. Both, oddly enough, together.

Here's the strange thing. Frank would have loved his funeral. In fact, it's a shame that he missed it. Asheville's elite turned out in full force, and they were dressed immaculately. The cars that lined Stratford Road and West Avon Parkway were the richest and finest machines on four wheels. It was a sunny afternoon, and the funeral home attendants set out rows of chairs in the front yard of the Mansion, so that the overflow crowd from the house could sit at their leisure to watch and listen.

Frank's pallbearers included two bank presidents, two former mayors, the District Attorney, and Dr. Craig Scott, the patron saint of Biltmore Forest. The District Attorney, Jameson, was the man who'd insulted me at the Sky Club right before Levi broke his nose. He didn't recognize me under these sober circumstances. Wallace B. Davis was one of the two bank presidents, and one of the few people who spoke to me.

After the expensive casket was loaded into the hearse and we all made the trip out to Riverside Cemetery, there was a reception of sorts, again back at the house. Although my role at the funeral had been a little ambiguous—I was part of the family but not the front-row part, the grieving part—my role at the reception felt more obvious and more natural. I helped serve.

Pansy was going full bore in the kitchen, and I was in and out, back and forth, carrying trays of little sandwiches and cakes out to the dining room and into the library, where those hordes of beautifully dressed people were milling about. On one trip, I was carrying a huge pitcher of punch out to the crystal bowl in the library, when I ran head on into Cameron Scott and the girl he'd replaced me with.

He introduced us—I think her name was Eustacia or something like—which was awkward because I didn't have a free hand to gesture or shake with. And just to report, she was perfect. By perfect, I mean she was the perfect height, the perfect shape, she was dressed in a slim black number that emphasized the shape, and she had tiny feet. She was perfectly made-up, and her hair looked like it had been created by an artist and set on top of her head. It wasn't a bob but something much more elaborate. And as you might imagine, it was a creamy blond.

I sidled around Cammy and Eustacia, smiling as I went, and toted the pitcher of punch on into the library, ever so grateful that she was living her life instead of me.

Wallace Davis had nodded to me earlier, at the service, and he made a point of speaking to me when I paused in my rounds just long enough to stand in the hall and gulp down a cup of the punch. "Still working, I see," he said. "Always working."

"It's what I'm good at," I admitted. "Sometimes, I think it's all I'm good at."

"Not the socializing?" He gestured at all the people around us, buzzing and talking.

I shook my head. "Not really."

"Me either," he said. "Not after something like this." And with that, he wandered on out the front door and walked across the lawn toward his own mansion up on the hill.

He's also under indictment, I thought, just like Frank.

The other person who spoke to me—other than to ask me for a napkin or where to put an empty plate—was Craig Scott. As things were winding down, and people were starting to slip out to their autos or, in many instances, to walk home because they lived nearby in Lake Park, I grabbed a few minutes in a chair set back against the dining room wall. I was near the kitchen door, so I could hear Pansy if she called to me, and I was off my feet for a few minutes.

Sitting there, feeling the tension begin to seep out of my shoulders and neck, and who should appear but Dr. Scott, who pulled up a matching chair beside mine and sat down. He looked as tired as I felt.

"How are you holding up?" he asked.

"I'm alright," I said. "It's Aunt Brenda and Sissy I worry about."

"Why do you think he did it?" It was a genuine question, there was wonder stirred up with concern in his voice.

I shrugged. "He was afraid he was going to lose it all. The house, the car, the . . ."

"The reputation?"

"Sure. He told me once that he meant never to be poor again. Never. And now he won't be."

"What about you?"

"Me?"

"Will you be poor again?"

"Rich or poor doesn't matter so much to me," I said, without thinking very much about it. "I never wanted to be Frank and Brenda. To have all of this . . ."

He sighed. "That's funny, Jo. Everybody else in town wanted it. I wanted it. Hell, still want it."

Sissy came into the dining room dragging Ben Scott by the hand. I'd seen them together off and on during the reception, even though he hadn't been part of the family group and hadn't stood by with Sissy at the cemetery. She was crying, weeping really, and Ben was attempting to comfort her. By an odd twist, here I sat with Ben's father, the two of us watching them from across the room.

"Do you think they'll make it, those two?" His question, but I could have asked it just as easily.

"She's going to be poor now," I said, suddenly sad. Maybe for the first time in that long, harsh day, so incredibly sad.

He nodded. "Yes, she is."

"And he'll have to fight your wife if he wants to keep her. Is he up to it?"

"Maybe . . . She grew up poor, you know, my wife. McDowell County farm girl. That's why she's . . . the way she is."

"Well, the hell with her."

He smiled. The smile turned into a grin. And then he laughed. Not quietly either. He stood up, still laughing, and looked down at me. "I'll tell her you send your regards," he offered before slipping away. Still laughing.

Isn't that what we do at funerals? We cry, certainly, wail away like Sissy, sounding like a firehouse siren. Or we laugh. At the sheer absurdity of it all. The striving, the ambition, the scratching and clawing. To make money, to make a mark. Making a life suddenly becomes making a death. A good life . . . a good death? *Make a life I can't even imagine.* Make a death that no one could ever anticipate.

I could feel myself starting to laugh too. It was crawling up out of my gut and threatening to overwhelm me. God help me, and Sissy staring at me from across the room. Ben had followed his father out, and there was just the two of us left in the room, Sissy and me. The way we'd started so many months before.

I took her upstairs, undressed her, and put her to bed. All the while her saying something to me about Ben. He hates me, he left me, he loves me, he wants me, can't abide me. Abide, I thought. Abide? I made her take the tranquilizer that the doctor had left for her, along with a splash of whiskey. Rubbed her shoulders and sang to her. Still trying not to laugh. When she finally began to snore, I crept back down the stairs. The kitchen was quiet, Pansy gone.

Down the back stairs to the basement. Not really knowing where I was going except to my room. My simple room.

When I got there, my simple man was waiting for me. Levi Edgar Arrowood. He was reading a book and sipping from a flask. An ancient, battered metal flask that looked like it had survived a war or two. He was wearing his old corduroy pants and a work shirt I'd never seen before.

When he saw me, he hauled up off the bed and put his arms around me. Lord God Almighty, he smelled like liquor and smoke and a red oak tree felled by lightning.

He felt hard and soft, like I needed him to feel.

I was crying and laughing by then. Or is it laughing and crying? He put his arms around me. Did I say that already, about the arms?

"Want to go for a ride somewhere, sister?" he asked, his voice muffled by my hair. "Get away from all this?"

"Who in hell is running the Club?" I sobbed.

"Mack is calling the shots up there," his sweet voice still muffled.

"Take me to Mack please." More sobbing but quieter than before. Easier by a degree or two. "I want to go home."

39

MAKE AN OLD FASHIONED, NEXT chance you get. Make it the way Levi makes it once the crowd thins out and he slips behind the bar. Sweet and strong, I tell you . . . with a brandied cherry. Tastes like sex in a thunderstorm.

After the club was dark and quiet, he made us both a drink. And when the glasses were empty except for the cherry stems, he led me upstairs, and we made love while I cried.

What is the difference, you ask, between making love and having sex? I can tell you the answer if you care to know it. After that night plus others that followed during the winter, I have intimate knowledge of it.

One is most often slow and the other fast.

One involves having as much of your skin in contact with the skin of your lover as is physically possible, while the other really only involves a few inches of your skin and his.

One feels like wanting to enter his body and remain, safe there, while he enters you to remain as well, one yoked creature that endures. While the other is in and out fast, like a safecracker.

One leaves your emotions sated, the other hungry.

One is giving and giving as much as you have, the other taking as much as you can get.

One is complex, the other simple.

One is multiplication (1 x 1) and the other childish addition (1 + 1) or . . . if you're a woman, perhaps it's even subtraction (1 – 1).

One is the stirring together of your two emotions and two minds and your . . . whatever is more than emotion and mind, while the other is the frenzied mating of your two animal bodies. Sounds like one of Sissy's magazines, I know. Still, true though.

One makes it almost impossible to leave, the other makes you restless to go.

I think that until I met Levi, I had only ever had sex. Which—don't get me wrong—was not so bad. I don't regret it and sometimes now don't really even remember it. It was skimming, not diving.

But that year, the year of the crash, Levi and I learned to make it. We didn't know how to say the *word*, but we did learn to make the word. Truth be told, we were like a rather fine engine together.

You may still be curious about that night. The night after Uncle Frank's funeral? That night we began with me in tears and ended with him in tears.

40

Oh, I hated it even as I did it. I dreaded leaving, but even so, I made the man get up and take me back to Morgan Mansion early the next morning. I won't say *I made him take me home* because I'd begun to think of the Sky Club as home, and the Mansion as my duty.

But it was the day after the funeral, and I knew that Sissy would need me front and center. Perhaps Brenda as well, although she would be overrun with well-meaning visitors that day. Church ladies and country club ladies, neighbor ladies and all kinds of ladies. Enough to make me glad I wasn't one.

Junior? Who knew what to expect out of Junior? He'd probably play golf, then drink beer till his eyes crossed, and in so doing, play away his sorrow.

Still, though, I thought I should be there when Sissy woke up. She'd want to tell it all about her and her Benjamin. Plus she'd want to find some way to breathe air again, stomach food again, get dressed and go to work again. She had to get up out of the bed regardless, and I meant to help lift her if I could.

I was there when Sissy woke up. It was like the old days, the year before, when I brought her a large mug of strong, black coffee and then sat on the edge of her bed while she sipped. I was tired to death, and I'm sure I looked it. But I had Levi in my dreams, a silly smile that kept creeping onto my face, and the knowledge that if the walls around us splintered and the ceiling fell, I could find my way back to him, even if I had to walk every step of the way up Beaucatcher Mountain.

What did Sissy have . . . to sustain her?

Why doesn't he just marry me, goddamn him anyway? That was the first thing she said, after a half-dozen sips of coffee, the first of which burned her tongue.

"Ben?"

Benjamin Caswell Scott, she said and took a sip. *It's hot, Jo. Coffee hot and he's Scott. Why the hell doesn't he just marry me—goddamn him—anyway?*

Afraid of his mother? Of course, he's afraid of his mother. I'm afraid of his mother. She's a hothouse bitch. You *are the only person I've ever seen who isn't afraid of her.*

But what if it all falls to pieces? What if there's no money and we lose the house? What if I have to take care of mother while she slowly . . . slowly declines? What if there's money but my damn brother gets everything?

What, breathe? You're telling me to breathe? And drink . . . Okay. I'm okay. No, I'm not. What if he throws me aside? What if the whole thing falls to pieces because there's not money enough? And I can't make the money move anymore with my tits? Or my ass? What if . . .

What if he loves me, truly loves me? For my mind and my jokes and my silly little ways. What if he truly loves me and wants me, but can't abide me because the damn bank failed and Daddy . . . Daddy did what he did?

Then he's a sorry . . . what? A sorry excuse for a man? Is that what you said? Man? He's not a man, never pretended to be a man. He's a boy. A beautiful, beautiful boy. With medical school and everything, he's the answer to my prayers since I was old enough to go to school. The boy who will save me . . .

What's he want? He wants to know if our family will still be . . . still be . . . prominent . . . when all this is over. That's what he wants.

He wanted me to take the pills when I was pregnant . . . Madame Drunette's Lunar Pills, and I took his damn pills and wasn't pregnant anymore. Now he wants me to be . . . prominent. Prominent but not pregnant.

Daddy ruined it all. He did this to me. He destroyed all my . . . Daddy always was selfish, he could only think of . . .

Ouch! What did you do that for! That hurt, Jo.

The hell with him anyway, Ben I mean, not Daddy . . . I love Ben. I love his shoes and his shirts and his monogrammed pajamas. I love his socks, oh my God, his socks. And I love the money he throws around when we go out. I want that, Jo. That's all I want . . . for it to be easy every day. And every night. Just fucking easy . . . and rich. Don't you want to be rich, Jo?

She knew I'd turned Cammy down. Refused him and hard. She had to have some hint of who I really was. My own woman making up life as I went. But she was tired that morning, and grieving, and she didn't know how to go slow. She didn't know how to give her Benjamin Caswell Scott time to grow up. Say no to his mother and say yes to her. Sissy was always in a hurry.

I tried to explain to her what Craig Scott had said to me. Tried to make her understand that Ben had to stand and fight. I even said—now, listen to this—that being poor with the man you loved was a hell of a lot better than being rich with a man you despised.

She laughed right out at me. No, that's not quite right. She howled. Said I was some country mouse bitch come to town and still had manure on my shoes. Actually, she said some things a good deal less kind than that, but I forgave her even as the words flew out of her mouth. She was desperate and sad. She had lost her father suddenly, violently, and now she was afraid there was no man to take his place.

She'd been raised to need a man. Not just any man, but a man with money. Money flowing in and out, back and forth, monogrammed pajamas and a brand-new automobile. God help her. I tried. First, I tried to tell her she didn't need Ben to make a life, and when that didn't work, I tried to tell her that maybe Ben was about to become a man. Right then and there, he was going to rise up and show his mother the back of his hand. He was going to come for her, and it would be everything she ever wished for. But she had to be ready for him the next time he pulled up in the driveway!

That last bit helped. I'm pretty sure it was a lie, but it helped her get out of bed and get dressed. It helped her eat some of Pansy's hotcakes. It helped her help her mother in turn. Coffee and hotcakes turned the tide.

I WENT TO WORK THAT DAY. Friday, February 20. I felt like I had to get out of that house, so I caught the streetcar into town and made my way to the new Imperial Life Insurance Building on College Street. They didn't expect me, but as always, they were glad to see me.

I worked in a back office on the second floor. I was a few doors down from Pink Starnes' office, which was on the corner, overlooking the intersection. He didn't use his office much. He was restless and he liked to be out on the street. Down on Lexington, talking and trading, or uptown on the square, taking the pulse of things, he called it. Getting a feel for what the people were saying. He usually checked in on me once or twice a day when he was in town. And often would call in from the road when he was out with one or another of the agents, selling or servicing policies.

The strange thing about Imperial was that from the very beginning, I was in charge of the books. When I'd started at the bank, I was the lowest person on that totem pole. Everything and everyone were above me, and only Mable saw what I could do. Who I might become. The numbers were the key to it all, the sanctity of columns and figures.

But when Pink found me and plucked me out of the wreckage over on Pack Square, he already knew. Somehow in his constant roving and chatting, roaming and talking, he'd found out there was some rough country gal over at Central B & T who made the accounts all fall into place. A human adding machine, that's what he'd heard about me, or so he said, and he knew immediately he had to have me. He was only one generation removed from the Toe River Valley over beyond Burnsville, and he loved talent from out of the hills better than he loved hot bread with butter. His words, not mine.

So when he brought me into Imperial the first week in January, he didn't start me off in the basement and make me earn my way upstairs. He slipped me straight into the slot where I could do him the most good. Head Accountant. Head of what, I'm not sure because I was Imperial's Accounting Department, all of it. Oh, there were a few agents working the first floor, for those lost and lonely souls who wandered in off the street wanting to insure their lives, but there were no other accountants. Mostly the policies flowed in from all over Western North Carolina onto the desk of Mr. Bertram, Head of Sales, who entered the numbers in pencil on a spreadsheet and passed each day's spreadsheet to me.

All I really had to deal with was the math.

I could close my door almost anytime I wanted, and the people out there in the world disappeared. It was just me and the glorious tables of figures. During those harsh days after Frank died, my little office was a haven. It smelled faintly of ink and paper, maybe fresh paint, but all that only made a safe and happy scent for me.

All that office had in it was an Imperial Life Insurance calendar for the year 1931 and the solace of number.

The essence of life insurance in those days was this: people paid you nickels and dimes and were paid back in dollars. Sometimes lots of dollars. Doesn't make sense as a business model, does it? Until you add in the variable of time. Time is at the heart of it. In the interim between when they started to pay you and the sad day on which you paid them, the nickels and dimes added up into far more cash than the payments that went out. At least often enough so that the sum total of all our efforts was, in time, an extraordinary amount of money. Which money was on deposit at the Wachovia Bank. Why? Because, Pink explained to me, Wachovia was different from Central B & T. It was a branch bank, made up of many locations, and should it run short in one location, there would always be more cash on the way from the home office in Charlotte or one of the other branches—imagine an armored car climbing up the mountain in the middle of the night.

Even so, despite the whole branch bank idea, there was a safe in the basement at Imperial just like there was a safe at the Sky Club, and Pink, along with a few other senior officials, kept a significant supply of their own cash on hand, in addition to a handy reserve of the agency's cash. Just in case.

As close as I could tell, Pink Starnes still owned just over 50 percent of the entire business, and as it grew, his personal wealth grew. Quietly, slowly, but then again, that was just the way he liked it. He and his wife still lived in the same house in West Asheville they'd bought when they married, having added on a room here and a room there as children came along. It was a ramshackle, crazy sort of place with a shed or two in back plus a chicken lot. Once, when I asked him when he was going to move to Lake View Park along with all the other rich folks in town, he laughed out loud. Laughed so hard that he coughed and had to open the window to spit.

"Lord, Jo," he said. "I fought off Grove when he was alive. He had a lot to sell me in Grove Park that was the finest there was. I fought off Craig Scott and Biltmore Forest, when Biltmore Forest was everything a man could ever wish for. And I very politely told your old boss Wallace Davis to go to hell when he tried to drag me out to Lake View Park."

"Why? You've got the money. If you don't believe it, I can show you."

He stared at me for a long moment. "I'll tell you why. Just because I think you're one of the handful of people I know who might understand. I put most of my money back into the business. Do you know what a mistress is, Jo?"

I smiled at him. "I know what a mistress is, Pink. I might even be one."

"Well, Levi Arrowood is . . . a lucky man. This is my mistress." He was standing in front of my desk, and he waved his arm around to signify the whole place, the building, the business. Imperial is my mistress, and don't you think for one minute that my wife isn't jealous as hell of her. Imperial is my creation. Some men . . . or women write books or paint pictures. Some create vast estates or buildings, like Seely at the Grove Park, but I'm making something nobody else can.

"Imperial came out of my body, my blood and spit. A hard time getting born, but it's by-God here now, and I don't intend for any bank crash or great depression to kill it. I intend to grow it into something so rich and so strange that nothing in this world can kill it . . . You asked me about Lake View Park. Well, the hell with Lake View Park and Grove Park and all the Parks. My money goes right here, to feed Imperial. My mistress and my baby." He was smiling as he said all of this, as if he knew it sounded more than a little crazy.

"And I need you to help me," he added quietly after a moment. "When I get tired and sick, will you help me?"

"I already am," I said. "And when I need help. Me and Levi . . . will you help us?"

He smiled. "Hell yes, I'll help you. Hill born. If you're ever in trouble, don't you trust these Park people, these country club people. They'd plow us all under to save their mansions. You and your Levi ever need help, you come to me.

41

As YOU CAN IMAGINE, ONE of the very first questions I asked when I returned to Imperial the day after Uncle Frank's funeral was whether or not the company had insured his life. Sadly, it had not.

Neither had it insured the life of Edward Gallatin Roberts, the esteemed former mayor of Asheville.

One week after Frank had blasted the side of his head off in the backyard at Morgan Mansion, Gallatin Roberts—who was also under indictment and who bore the brunt of the public outrage over the massive loss of public monies—did something eerily similar. Roberts had already been dismissed as mayor and was awaiting trial when he went into the public toilet on the fourth floor of the Legal Building, where his private law office was, held a pistol up to the side of his head, and fired a round all the way through his skull and into the stall door.

As with Frank, the details were horrifying.

First of all, you need to know that the Legal Building was the very same edifice that had housed Central Bank and Trust right up to the day that we failed to open three months before. The bank occupied the first two floors and part of the third. Roberts' office, along with those of many other prominent attorneys, was on the fourth.

On that day, February 24, in the early afternoon, he apparently took a .38 caliber revolver out of his desk drawer, walked down the hall and into the toilet, sat down on the commode, and killed himself. The shot must have reverberated throughout the whole building, echoing in the empty offices and marble lobby of the ghostly bank below as well as up and down the halls of the distinguished and the worthy on the top floors.

According to the newspaper, the shot was heard most immediately by a blind attorney named B. B. Worsham, whose office was just beside the toilet. Worsham actually heard the sound of the collapsing body striking the floor and stumbled into the hall yelling for help. The newspaper doesn't say who answered the call, which means that it was somebody the editors didn't think worth mentioning, probably a secretary or maybe a colored man or woman who was cleaning the offices.

As always, it's the high and mighty who find the ugliest way to destroy themselves and the servants who walk in on them and have to clean up the mess.

What the newspaper does say is that "some 20 minutes elapsed before the body was identified as that of the former mayor. Identification was delayed because of the semi-darkness of the small room, and the distorted features of the deceased."

Standing on the street corner the next day, I bought the morning paper from a local boy hawking the **BODY OF ROBERTS TO LIE IN STATE IN CITY HALL**. How could I not think of Uncle Frank? Of course, they couldn't identify the body. When you take a pistol to your head, you wipe out your entire being, as if you'd never existed. The only way that I'd been able to identify Frank was his clothes and his shoes, that and the pitiful, crooked finger on his left hand.

But then maybe that was the point. To disappear entirely off the face of the earth and take all the pain and embarrassment with you. There's a hundred ways to end it, and you pick the one that destroys your entire existence, erases your name off the books. And then no one can criticize you, blame you, indict you, censure you. Your reputation survives intact and all the guilt is shot away.

That had to be part of Gallatin Roberts' last thoughts. Maybe he took the idea from Uncle Frank. He wasn't at the funeral, but you know he read the newspapers and saw how sympathetic the articles were to Frank Morgan, civic leader, outstanding citizen, and regional expert in credit banking. Uncle Frank would never stand trial, never have all his weaknesses and frailties exposed to the world. Now, Roberts would never stand trial either. He would never be found guilty. He'd be innocent through eternity.

And yet . . . the guilt must have been there. The day after his death, a long letter from Roberts to the community appeared on the front page of the Asheville paper.

My soul is sensitive, and it has been wounded unto death. I know exactly who the men are who were instrumental in trying to destroy me, but now, I forgive them.

For twenty years, I was in public life, and I never did a dishonest act during all these years and yet, I have been shamefully charged with committing a felony. God knows I did no wrong during my term in office. My hands are clean and my conscience is clear, and I want to say further that Mr. Bartlett and Mr. Rogers are both clean good men, and have done no wrong.

I have given my life for my city, but I am content. I did what I thought was right. I trust the people of Asheville will cease to wrangle, and all pull together for the common good. Why do you hate each other? Don't you know that life is just like a fleeting shadow, and that you will soon pass to the great beyond? I do not hate a soul on this earth. Won't you people highly resolve to cease your bickering and strife? I want you to do this.

I worked hard for a larger and better city. I knew that it was imperative. Every act of my life during my term of office was for that which I thought was for the best interest of the community . . .

When I went into office nearly four years ago I found millions of dollars of the people's money in the Central Bank, and I tried with all my soul to protect it, and did protect it for nearly four years.

What would you have done? Would you have closed the bank and lost it, or would you have made an honest effort to save it?

Farewell and adieu,

Gallatin Roberts

That letter terrified me. Not because Gallatin Roberts felt he'd been wronged. If he truly thought that, he'd have been happy to stand trial in order to be exonerated. No, what terrified me was that he was in up to his neck with Wallace Davis and the others, the Directors and the Officers, using the city's money to prop up what he called the Central Bank. And using the Central Bank to cover up the fact that the city was so far in debt, it couldn't pull up its own pants.

Sometimes if you're downtown at night, you would see the bums out and about, drinking straight from a bottle of jake leg liquor and dropping their pants to piss on the wall of a big, beautiful building constructed a few years before out of Tennessee marble. Sometimes, you'd see two of those rotten, stinking drunks staggering down the street with their arms flung around each other's shoulders, headed God knows where, barely holding each other up and barely putting one quivering foot in front of the other. If either one let go for a second, they'd both fall flat on the concrete sidewalk.

That was the Municipality of Asheville and Central Bank & Trust. Two rot-gut drunks staggering along together, barely upright and barely moving. Until their grip on each other slipped, just for a moment, just long enough. Then one fell on his face and the other on his ass.

Even more terrifying was that Uncle Frank must have been part of it all, and he must have understood what was going on. His grip had begun to slip months before, when he began to stare into the open firebox of the furnace, when his waistline began to shrink and his face to age. He must have known. And despite the knowing, he clung to the slight hope that Gallatin Roberts would promote Greater Asheville into some kind of savior. Funny that he saw it unraveling even before Roberts. He got out sooner and, oddly enough, with his reputation intact.

The thing about Roberts is that, unlike Uncle Frank, he didn't want to be rich. He wanted to be good.

Country boy from Flat Creek, baseball player, sometime law student, hard worker, married his schoolhouse sweetheart. Elder in the Presbyterian Church and teacher of the men's Bible class. Walked to church from his modest home on Brevard Road in West Asheville. The man worked so hard to be reliable, earnest, generous. He wanted so badly to be a true pillar of the community that when the walls of Jericho came tumbling down around him and he saw his reputation spit on in the street, he couldn't stand it. He didn't lose money when Central B & T went under, he lost face.

They say he must have been planning his suicide for days.

Frank, on the other hand, went down on instinct and went down hard. He didn't leave behind any money for Brenda and Sissy and Junior, but ironically, he left behind a world of sympathy. He wasn't a victim of circumstance until he died, but then people began to mourn.

I said Roberts' letter was terrifying, and it was. For me. He and Davis and the others—the officers and the Directors—had let people like me work away in good faith, without ever bothering to warn us. Uncle Frank had never once told me to get out, or even to get my money out, even when he saw the ship driven on the reef. Davis and Roberts had let us all lean into the grindstone that was that bank right up until the day they locked the door and told us not to expect a last paycheck.

Terrifying? Hell yes, when you think that I could have been indicted too, but for some reason I was not, probably the shadow of poor Foster Reynolds hanging over me. The prosecutors must have assumed that Foster would have known and conspired but not me. He was the head cashier and I was his assistant. He must have been guilty, but I couldn't have been. Why? Because I am a woman.

When Foster tried to cut his throat with that straight razor the night after the bank closed, he must have finally figured out what was coming, even though he was far too stupid to have anticipated it or done anything about it. It was enough to make me feel sorry for him, even if he did have trouble keeping his hand off my ass.

Was I glad to be a woman, once I realized it shielded me from suspicion?

Well, I was always glad to be a woman. Every day I pulled up my panties and rolled my garters into the tops of my stockings. I might have been especially glad on the day when I realized that if the world was fair, if it treated me same as a man, I might have been indicted by the grand jury. Sometimes the loaded dice bang off the curb and come up in your favor.

Foster took a straight razor to his own neck. Uncle Frank drifted out into the backyard with a one-shot pistol clutched in his hand. Gallatin Roberts chose a fourth-floor public toilet in which to pull the trigger.

Me, I walked up the hill to the Sky Club and curled up in the arms of Levi Arrowood. That's how I survived the month of February 1931.

42

So what was Levi to me anyway? What was I to him?

If you listened to Pink Starnes, you'd assume we were involved and that other people knew us as a couple. My Papa had given the two of us a puppy, not to one or the other but to both of us. Hell, if you just listened to me, when I occasionally let slip something about "Levi and me," you might think that something named "Levi and me" existed.

So if you're wondering what we were, what to call us, it's no more than I was doing myself.

I was twenty-eight years old by the winter of 1931. He was only twenty-seven but about to turn. Too old to say that he was my boyfriend. That's what Sissy called Ben . . . her boyfriend. And Lord knows, "boy" was the right word in that case.

But boyfriend and girlfriend doesn't quite work for a bootlegger and nightclub operator side-by-side with an accountant who loves to dance and has a passion for numbers. An accountant, by the way, who was falling increasingly in love with wearing trousers. I was up to three pair and had introduced them to Imperial Life, where they drew stares from the men and outright laughter from some of the women.

Levi called us partners from time to time, with Papa or someone at the Club. But he mostly did that in private conversation. I liked partners, except that everyone assumed I was in the liquor business or at least keeping his books for him. And by February of that year, I was keeping his books for him. Trust me when I say that they were a mess before I took a pencil to them.

Pink Starnes had used the word mistress in passing, and almost without thinking, I'd admitted such. After Pink left my little office that day, I hauled my Webster's out of the desk drawer and looked it up. Definition #4: *Woman loved & courted by a man; woman illicitly occupying place of wife or having habitual illicit intercourse with man.*

Fair enough. Levi could be downright courtly from time to time. I did occupy a place inside the Sky Club that looked more and more like a part-time wife. Mack and the others had long ago accepted me as such. And Lord knows the intercourse was illicit and habitual. As habitual as we could manage with the world falling to pieces around us. But there was that word *loved.*

Maybe. Just so long as neither of us ever had to say it. If we said it, it might jinx us. We could talk to each other about almost anything and did. Anything but that.

FOR EXAMPLE . . .

Tits.

I figured I could *write* the damn dictionary definition for that word myself. See also *chest, mammas, boobs, knockers, melons, bubbies.* Surely to God bubbies only applies to little girls. See *breasts,* although nobody actually says breasts except for doctors. Nurses only when there's a doctor in the room.

Mammaries. One of the first things Sissy ever said to me was to complain about hers.

Tits was the country word. As in *that there's about as worthless as tits on a boar hog.*

Or *he's been suckin on the hind tit his whole life.* Which made me think of Levi, the way he was raised.

Or *it's as cold as a witch's tit.* Which is about how cold it was that February.

I said we could talk about almost anything. So there he was, lying beside me one Sunday afternoon, half asleep after some truly fine illicit and habitual intercourse. I was still a little breathless and he was half in a coma. I liked that I could knock him out with my body.

"What do you really and truly think," I asked him, "about my tits?"

He opened one eye. "Can't you tell?" He yawned.

I shook my head. "I think you like them fine in the heat of the moment, but I want your honest opinion." I scooted up on the couch in his office where we were lying, in order to present my tits more fully for his examination. Reached over and pried his other eyelid open with my thumb. "You're a man of the world. Aren't they just too damn small? Don't lie."

"Well, hell, Jo. Let me see." He licked lazily on one nipple, which responded shamefully, and then sucked on it a bit. "Tastes fine . . . No, better than that. They are . . . succulent." He was proud of himself for *succulent.*

"That's all because of you," I said. "What you do to them. What I want to know is whether they're big enough for you."

He tried not to smile. "In case you ain't heard, Jo, anything more than a mouthful is a waste. And in this case . . . I love them right along with the rest of you."

"Did you just say . . .?"

"I did not. I did not say love. And if I did, it's your tits I love, not the rest of you."

"That's not what you said. You said: *the rest of me.*"

Now, a smile sort of flickered on his lips, like a tiny flame trying to catch. He was trying to keep the grin off his face. "Well, okay. But I was referring to your body. Not your heart and soul. Not eternal romance. I can't get enough of your *body*."

"Fine. So my tits *are* big enough for you?"

"Must be." He closed his eyes again, slipping back into that coma I mentioned earlier. "I do dream about 'em," he said quietly.

So, BY HIS DIRECT TESTIMONY, he loved my body. Which over time, was causing me to like it as well. Sort of how the moon reflects the light of the sun. But did he love the rest of me? The heart of me?

If I could have said what the heart of me was, maybe I could have answered that question. I was busy making a life, but I couldn't yet see the ultimate shape of it. The heart of it.

Did I want him to marry me?

What a strange question. I'm not sure of the answer. Certainly, marriage didn't seem to be part of the bargain when my Mama had charged me with making a life she couldn't imagine. She'd gotten herself married at sixteen and borne seven children—which wore her body down to a fraction. So maybe it was because of her that I was leery of marriage. Leery of the bondage that marriage seemed to mean.

I wanted the man. Mid-winter, I even needed him.

And I confess that I wanted him to want me.

So call me harlot, concubine, mistress, I don't care . . . I was his lover.

43

LATE WINTER, EARLY SPRING, AND the great houses began to fall, one by one.

The first to go was the gorgeous home of Dr. Sinclair, the dentist, who was a relatively silent member of the Central B & T Board of Directors. You will recall the large, stone mansion designed by the Peruvian architect. The bank examiners overseeing the wreckage of Central B & T called in the mortgage, and suddenly Dr. Sinclair was out on the street looking for a place to live. I reckon the Peruvian architect didn't feel the tremors, unless of course, he hadn't been paid. Sinclair's wife felt the quake, however. Word was that she left him right along with the house.

Then went the Mediterranean dream palace—remember the walled garden and the marble fountain—of Mr. Campbell, the boss of Sissy's boss. That mortgage got called in as well, and even Seely and the Grove Park Development couldn't save Campbell, who moved into the Manor Apartments on Charlotte Street, but without Mrs. Campbell, who might have cared more for the palace than she did for the prince.

The great houses fell and when they did, marriages were crushed beneath.

At least Wallace B. Davis fought for his financial life; although, he eventually lost. Of all the city and bank officials indicted by the grand jury, he was the only one finally convicted.

He was sentenced to a term of five to seven years in the state penitentiary for violating banking laws.

He didn't blow his brains out. His wife didn't leave him. She signed over Stratford Towers to an investor that Davis owed money to, moved into a small, modest place on a backstreet, and settled down to wait for him. He didn't publish a pitiful plea for mercy and understanding in the Asheville paper. Rather, he went off to serve his time with a shrug of his shoulders. And somehow, you suspected he'd be back.

There are certain things that when thrown down shatter. The china cup, the crystal goblet, the expensive vase. All of those things are city things. Then there are certain things that when thrown down, even on pavement, never break. The corn cob, the chunk of firewood, the plow point. All those things are country things, hard things and tough. Truth be told, they are used to being thrown down; it's in their nature.

Then there are things that actually bounce. The harder they are thrown down, the higher they return to play. The hard rubber ball. Wallace B. Davis was a rubber ball. At his trial, he all but dared the judge to throw him down.

What was I? Not a china cup, that's for damn sure.

But like all the families of Asheville's rich and famous, the Morgans had to find out what they were made of—wood or crystal. Uncle Frank owed almost half a million dollars on the house when he died, a figure that once again threw Aunt Brenda into a state of shock. By mid-March, the bank examiners called in the mortgage and the family broke into its separate pieces.

Aunt Brenda moved into a small house across the river in West Asheville and began to cast about for work. Frank Junior took on a job at the country club where he'd spent countless hours playing golf. He began life over again living in a tiny suite of rooms at the club, earning his way by teaching lessons and pouring illegal hooch into the flasks of prominent members on the sly. You had to wonder if the hooch wouldn't eventually get him into trouble. Sissy's job at the Asheville Development Company somehow survived the crash, so she had some income of her own and found rooms to rent at the Manor—one floor above her former boss's boss, Mr. Campbell, the ex-prince of the marble fountain. It tickled her—and me—that her apartment was above and slightly larger than his.

She wanted me to go in with her, to share the rooms, and split expenses. And it was tempting. But there was something about that winter, the winter of '31, that told me it was time to bounce. Time to make my own way. I honestly thought it was only a matter of time before Sissy used those mammaries of hers to change Ben Scott's mind about marriage. Then where would I be?

I had money in the bank. Well, actually no, I didn't have money in the bank, thank God. I had money in the safe at the Sky Club.

So I decided to find myself a place to live on my own, while Levi and I figured out just what our partnership consisted of. I took a slow afternoon off from work at Imperial and visited three boarding houses, all within easy walking distance of downtown. They were all run by women in their fifties or sixties. Widows mostly, whose husbands were dead or otherwise mysteriously missing. All the houses were cold—remember the winter wind in Asheville—and the rooms were sad and somehow lonely, as if the drapes had just been thrown open after months of dusty darkness. Plus they all smelled of worn-out varnish and coal oil.

The last place I went to was the Old Kentucky Home, a house on Spruce Street about a block off of Pack Square, owned by a woman named Julia Wolfe, the mother of the writer. You will recall Mrs. Wolfe from her appearance at the bank back before the crash. She was arguing with the tellers in the Loan Department as to why she should be required to pay against the principal of her several loans. She of the pursed lips and occasional vacant stare.

Rumor was, despite being related to the Westalls, she'd lost almost all of her real estate holdings over the past eighteen months and had retreated into the house on Spruce Street, licking her wounds. I figured that if she did have rooms for rent, they'd be cheap, given her reduced circumstances.

The rooms were cheap, that's for sure. Also dark, cold, empty. There were only two other boarders staying in the house, a traveling shoe salesman from Ohio and a down-on-her-luck middle-aged woman who asked me on the sly if I knew any eligible men, married or not didn't matter.

Mrs. Wolfe herself was dressed all in black, with her hair pulled severely back, her eyes wavering behind thick, wire-rimmed spectacles. "The one thing I will not allow in my house," she chirped at me, "is alcohol. My dead husband was a rounder when it came to the bottle, and now that he is gone, I will have nothing to do with it. So . . ." She paused to actually wave a bony finger in my face. "There will be no drinking in this house, not in the parlor, not in your room, and not even on the porch."

"What about men?" I asked her. "Can I entertain men in the parlor or on the porch?"

"No, ma'am. I don't take in no lungers and I don't take in no . . . busy women. No, ma'am. Now, if you was to take an interest in one of my sons, that would be different."

I left soon after. I could not imagine what one of her sons would be like. The famous one, Thomas, who had written the tell-all book about Asheville, had gotten the hell out of his mother's house as soon as he could and settled in New York or some such place. As for his brothers . . . stammering, stuttering, laughing maniacally . . . the thought was more chilling than the air inside her strange, old house. Who wouldn't take up steady drinking if they were forced to live there?

I decided after my three strikes in the boarding house line, that I'd treat myself to supper at the Sky Club. After that afternoon, I desperately needed something hot to eat and a friendly face. A table in the corner, one of those steaks sizzling from the kitchen, and Mack himself bringing me the perfect glass of wine from the bar. I even took a taxi up the mountain, as the winter dark was already creeping down from the hills and the gas streetlights were sputtering to life.

I got my table in the corner, and I ordered that steak. The only surprise was that instead of the ribeye I asked for, Barbara Jean brought out a filet that was so thick and juicy it made my mouth water just to see it steaming on the plate. Mack himself brought me a glass of dark, dark red wine—Cabernet he called it—and told me to take a sip with each bite. "Savor it," he said with a wink. And then, before he returned to the bar, he leaned over and half-whispered, "the boss has a surprise for you."

"Do you know what it is?"

He nodded and smiled mysteriously.

"Well . . .?"

"Not saying," he replied. "He wants to show you himself."

The club was surprisingly busy for the middle of the week in the middle of the winter, and there were only a few stray peas and a bite of mashed potatoes left on my plate by the time Levi himself stole a few minutes to sit with me. The young Negro man was at the piano, so things were a little more lively than normal. Levi was wearing his dark and mysterious face that night, with his hair wet combed back flat over his head. You almost wouldn't recognize the Levi I spent time with in the daylight, easy with a laugh and a shy smile.

"And how are you this evening, Miss Salter?" he asked when he sat down at my table, using his professional man of mystery voice.

"I'm better now that I've eaten and enjoyed a glass of this . . . Cabernet."

"One glass?"

"Well, Mr. Arrowood, this is the second glass. You caught me."

He smiled his secret smile.

"The steak might be the best I've ever had. How did I rate a filet rather than what I ordered?"

He shrugged. "The cook insisted. She claims you're a friend of hers."

I wrinkled my brow. "Do I know . . .?"

"The old place is full of surprises tonight," he said.

"When do I get to see some of them?"

He glanced around the room, his perpetual watchfulness. The piano was alive, but there was only one middle-aged couple dancing slowly, wound up in each other. Mostly, it was people eating, talking, the clash of fork and knife on plate, here and there a splash of laughter.

"Bring your glass, Miss Salter. In fact, have Mack fill it up before we begin our little tour. I'm going to show you a few things that will amaze you."

Again, I raised my eyebrows. "Amaze, is it?"

He nodded. "Probably an understatement."

Mack had a silly grin on his battered, scarred face, when he topped off my wine glass, pouring out of a bottle I'd never noticed before. "What in the world?" I whispered to him. He just nodded me toward the boss. I was to follow and be astonished.

First stop was the kitchen. You will recall the kitchen, where months before I'd found Levi at midnight, up to his elbows in soapy water, scrubbing the evening's dishes. That was nothing compared to this, however. I almost dropped my precious wine glass when I found Pansy hard at work over the big stove, a cloth wrapped around her head, minding a couple of skillets and as many boiling pots all at once.

I managed to set the glass down so she and I could dance around and laugh at each other. A hug, a real hug, not the half-hugs we'd managed for ourselves back at Morgan Mansion, where she was servant and I was . . . nobody quite knew what. Something was different at the Club, freer, more open. More honest. I think I actually squealed, I was so happy to see her there. She just laughed at me.

She smelled like the kitchen, hot stove and sweat and skillet grease plus the treatment on her hair and the Vicks she loved to rub on her chest in winter. In other words, she smelled wonderful, and I teared up right there on the spot. I began to roll up my sleeves. "I'm going to pitch in and help right now," I said to the two of them, Pansy and Levi.

"No, you ain't," she said back, just like she always did to me. "I got this all under control . . . You go on with Mr. Arrowood. He got something else to show you."

"I'll come back later," I whispered.

She nodded. "Come back down later and sit by the stove. Talk to me while I'm working." She glanced at Levi. "That alright with you, boss?"

Levi smiled at Pansy. "She can sit anywhere she wants. Just don't let her cook anything."

I was still blinking hard to stifle the tears when I walked out into the back hall with Levi.

"What's wrong?" he asked.

"I love Pansy Walker," I said.

"Well, then, why are you crying? She's safe. She's here."

"You are a fool, Levi Edgar . . . whatever your other name is. Haven't you ever heard of crying because you're happy?"

We were standing in the back hallway, which led from the kitchen out into the main dining room and the dance floor. But it was dark there and we were mostly alone.

"I never heard of . . ." He started to say something, but I cut him off.

"Well, you cry when you're happy or when you're sad. I mean, I don't because I don't cry. But if I did, I'd cry when the man I . . . fooled around with . . . found a way to help someone who . . . Why did she come here of all places?"

"Because she needed a job and she said that she was your friend. That and she didn't have any other place to go for work."

"What happened to Raymond, her husband? I guess he's her husband."

"She'll tell you. Not my place . . ."

"Levi . . ."

"What?"

I leaned forward and kissed his neck. I didn't get all up against him because he was still working and we were in a spot where someone headed to one of the restrooms could have seen us.

"Thank you," I said into his collar.

"That's only part of the surprise. That's not even the best part."

"Show me." I was working like crazy to keep my hands off of him. To distract myself, I ducked back into the kitchen, winked at Pansy, and reclaimed my wine glass.

He grasped my free hand and led me up the back stairs to the third floor. I was still half stunned by finding Pansy there. Working away like she owned the kitchen, as I'm sure she would in short order. When we reached the third floor, the top floor, he led me down the central hallway to the end of the building opposite his own rooms.

There, he opened the door off the hallway that mirrored his own doorway down the hall. Inside was a small sitting room with a larger bedroom off of it. A bathroom with a clawfoot tub. The bedroom had a double bed in it and a chifforobe in the corner. Hooks on the wall for more clothes. And windows, a whole wall of windows above the bed that looked out into the woods behind the club.

"What's all this?" I asked. "Isn't this where Mack lives?"

"Mack moved down to the basement, where the liquor is stored. Somebody tried to break in last week and was hammering away at the lock on the liquor closet when we ran them off. He volunteered that one of us—him or me—had better sleep down there from now on, and he seemed to think he was the better man."

"He is the better man."

"I reckon. So, during the last few days, he relocated all his stuff down into the basement and left these rooms wide open. One of the waitresses who does our cleaning went through and . . ."

"Levi, why are you showing me this?"

"Well, Mack thought that . . ."

"What did you think? Don't put it off on somebody else. What did *you* think?"

"I thought you'd better come live here. Damn it, Jo . . . I thought you'd be safe here, not in some rented room or boarding house. The city's coming apart at the seams, and I don't like the thought of you down there at night."

"So you're going to rent me these rooms? Is that what you're saying?"

"You don't need to pay. You can just . . ."

"I'm going to pay rent, Levi. Room and board."

"Well, alright, but . . ."

"I'm not a kept woman, Levi."

"What's a kept . . ."

"A woman who screws her way into a warm bed and a hot meal."

"Good God, Jo. That's not what . . ."

"Levi, you need to come up with a price. From what I learned this afternoon, a dollar a day gets you a room and two meals. No dinner. Breakfast and supper. Does a dollar a day suit you?"

"Jo, are you not the least bit . . ."

"A dollar a day?"

"Goddamn it, Jo, Will you let me finish a sentence? One sentence, that's all I ask."

I had my hands on my hips, standing there beside the bed. Trying not to cry and trying not to smile at the same time. "Go ahead."

He paused for the longest time, and I thought I was going to get the hiccups, trying not to cry or laugh.

"Are you not the least bit surprised? This was supposed the be the real surprise, and I thought . . ."

"Levi . . ."

"Let me finish, goddamn it. I thought you'd be happy. Are you not the least bit . . .?"

I waited. I truly did. But it seemed he was done.

"Levi, I'm so surprised that I don't know what to say. After this afternoon . . . I don't know what to say. But I am . . . saying yes."

"Are you . . . Why are you crying?"

"I'm not. But if I was, it would be because it's perfect. You don't know how cold and dark it is out there in those godawful boarding houses." I was hiccupping. "I'm just relieved, Levi. Can I stay tonight? I'll get my all my clothes and trunk tomorrow, but can I stay?"

"Of course, you can. But what will you sleep in?"

I thought of a dozen things I could say, none of which were particularly ladylike.

44

WHAT HAPPENED TO RAYMOND?"

I was sitting on a stool in the kitchen, watching Pansy finish up for the evening. All the dinner guests had been served. There were pieces of apple cake and dishes of peach cobbler sitting on the side table for a waitress to grab just in case somebody wanted dessert. Pansy was scrubbing the three large skillets and the countless pots and pans that she'd put to the test that night, so I grabbed a dish towel and started to dry.

He's gone. Since Mr. Frank blown his brains out, he left out for South Carolina, where his sister's at.

I don't know if he's coming back, and I don't care. If he don't come back, I intend to buy me a divorce from him anyway. He had him a girlfriend all along. You didn't know that, did you? Didn't suspect, did you?

He's a man, ain't he? Ain't that reason enough? But he was worse than most. He's was after that jellyroll anyway he could get his hands in it, and this gal all but wave it in his face.

That's why he didn't want to move out there to the Lake to live behind Mr. Frank and Mrs. Brenda. He had that half-breed piece on the side worked cleaning houses down around the Grove Park. Once we came out to the Lake, he had to get his skinny ass on the car and ride all the way into town just get his pecker pumped by that bitch.

Sorry, I know you ain't used to such language, but . . .

Claim you know what a pecker is. I suspect you do. But the problem about Raymond is he couldn't keep his stuck down his pants where it belonged. So when Mr. Frank shot his own head off and everything started coming to pieces, I told Raymond to go on. Grown ass woman don't need a man to pay her way no how. He didn't like that, not one damn bit, but it's true.

Where am I staying? I'm staying down on Valley Street in our old house, his and mine except I don't call it ours no more. I call it mine now, and since the banks closed, the city ain't trying to take it no more. My sister's in there with me. She done lost her job in one of the big houses, but she'll find another. Her cooking makes mine look slapdash.

I walk. That's how I get back and forth. What do you think God give a woman feet for? It's raining, sometimes I catch a ride, but mostly I walk.

No, you ain't worrying about me walking at night. I got Raymond's old straight razor in my purse. Sharp enough to shave hair.

But listen here, Jo, there's something I got to tell you. Something that ain't nice, but this is the season for telling it. That old gospel truth. You know, once I said to you that dream you had—bout that man forcing you—told you that stuff happened. Once we got out to the Lake, that Junior, he come up to our little rooms over the garage when Raymond was gone and he was harder to fight off than . . .

That's sweet, but I don't need you to kill him, unless you happen to have a chance. What I need is for you to keep him away from me.

Last time he came up those garage stairs, he hit me so hard in the face that he knocked me flat on the floor and while my wits was swimming around, he forced my legs wide . . . well, you know what he done. You dreamed it yourself.

No, don't you say that. Just keep him away from me. That's all I'm asking. You and Mr. Arrowood just keep him away cause he'll follow me up here sure as there's a God in heaven. Once a boy like that gets a taste, he . . .

"If he shows his face up here, Pansy, he won't live long enough to regret being born, the little prick."

She nodded. "I just thought you should know. That's all. I ain't doing that white boy no more nor none like him."

AFTER SHE LEFT FOR HOME, I sat at the bar for a while, thinking. Mack poured out a small tot of brandy, and I sipped it slow, for I was burning on the inside.

When the place cleared out, Mack said good night and left to go downstairs. After a bit, Levi came and took his place. Took his jacket off, folded it carefully and laid it across the bar where it was dry and clean. As he started to make us both an Old Fashioned, I cleared my throat.

"Levi?"

"Hmmm?"

"There's somebody I need to kill."

He looked up at me then and stopped mixing the sugar syrup he was going to add to the bourbon. "Anybody I know?"

"Frank Morgan . . . Junior."

"Your cousin? The skinny kid?"

I nodded. "He attacked Pansy."

Levi stared at me for a long moment, his face still and silent. "By attack, you mean . . .?"

"He knocked her down with his fist and forced her."

Levi nodded. "Shit on him then," he said and went back to mixing the ingredients. "But you better let me do it. Would you be satisfied if we just beat him half to death?"

"So long as neither Pansy nor I ever have to look at him again," I said. "That might be enough."

THAT NIGHT, I SAVED MY leftover brandy, which sat on the bar while I savored the Old Fashioned Levi made for me. I saved it in the glass Mack had poured for me and carried it upstairs when I went. I thought I'd dip my tongue in it a time or two while I got used to my new rooms. Washed up in my new sink. Bounced up and down on my new bed. All of which I did . . . washed and bounced and ran my tongue around the inside of the glass. I was still in my slip when I eased out into the hall and drifted down toward Levi's room.

To do what, I wasn't sure. But the rub of the slip on my naked skin raised up a spark. My nipples were hard as buttons.

I didn't knock.

He'd left his door cracked open, which seemed to me sign enough. Sign that he hadn't forgotten about me. When I pushed back that door and stepped in, he was lying on his bed, naked as far as I could tell. He was lying on his back with the sheet and quilt pulled up to his waist. His eyes were closed and he was pretending sleep. Or maybe he was asleep, I didn't care.

I tiptoed over to his bed, hiked my slip up around my waist, and climbed on top of him. One leg to either side, I sat his hips like a saddle.

His lips twitched. He pretended to snore.

Ever so slowly, I poured a tablespoon or so of the brandy on his chest and belly. That popped his eyes good and wide.

"Lord, Jo Belle," he said. "Don't waste good brandy."

"Don't intend to," I said, my voice husky in my throat. Leaned over and began to lick it off him. All of him.

45

THE NEXT MONDAY EVENING, WHEN the Club was closed, Levi and I decided to have supper down at the Asheville Country Club, so that Levi could have a look at Junior, be certain he recognized him. And perhaps, should the opportunity present itself, reason with him about how he treated Pansy.

Reason with him meant that I was thinking of stabbing and shooting.

We drove down in Levi's Plymouth, and because of a stop Levi needed to make, rode through downtown. Even though it was just after five o'clock and still daylight, the town was almost deserted. There was nothing going on at the drugstore, where normally there would have been a crowd of young men and women—fancy boys and flappers—milling around inside and out. The streets were full of wind, moaning around corners and whipping over the pavement. Only a few, lonely people were about. And those you did see were hurrying along clutching their skirts or with a hat brim pulled low over their faces.

When we drove through the square, here and there were small groups of men huddled together on a corner. The first two floors of the Legal Building, where Central Bank & Trust had lived and died, now had placards and posters glued to its walls, and the windows were completely boarded up. The building itself looked like a corpse. Standing in front were two men—young, white men in their twenties—hatless in the wind, holding homemade signs in front of their bodies.

MUST HAVE WORK
OR STARVE
PLEASE!

And . . .

LAST CHANCE
WILL DO ANYTHING
FOR WORK

They looked like brothers, or at least friends. The same hand had lettered both signs.

In front of Finkelstein's Pawn Shop, catty-cornered across the square from the Legal Building, there was a crowd of men, plus more than a few women, standing in line to sell their valuables. A lone policeman stood watching, presumably there to keep them from robbing the pawn shop or each other.

"What will they do when they run out of things to sell?" I asked Levi, who only shook his head.

"How can it have happened that fast?" he muttered. "One day, the city is exploding with money and jobs. There's a new building going up on every street corner, and then . . . then this."

"It was rotten at the core," I said. "Pink Starnes saw it in the country people on Lexington Avenue two years ago. Everybody tried to ignore it, as if we just talked loud enough and moved the money fast enough, then it couldn't catch up with us. We'd just keep building and selling forever. Until we died."

"Well, those people standing out in front of Finkelstein's Pawn weren't selling and building."

"Some were," I said. "I recognized a couple of people from Lake View Park and such. Customers from the bank who were drunk on the thought of it . . . But you're right. It was all built on the backs of poor people, black and white . . . Country people."

WHEN WE PULLED INTO THE parking lot of the Asheville Country Club, nestled in the midst of Lake View Park, it was as if we'd left behind one world for another. You'd never have thought there were pawn shops or bread lines three miles away in town. You couldn't see the soup kitchens on Broadway or people begging for work.

You could believe the world consisted of eighteen well-manicured holes.

The parking lot at the Country Club was only half full, but Levi parked well back from the front door and in the shadow of several trees that were left near the caddy shack. "In case we end up sharing a few words with your cousin," was all he said.

When we walked in the front door, there was a lot of thick carpet and heavy furniture, golf trophies on display in glass cases. It wasn't Biltmore Forest fancy—the Biltmore Forest Country Club was more refined and more polished—but it was shiny and new. You felt like you had to whisper at Biltmore Forest, but there was raucous laughter coming from a side room here.

We strolled down the hall till we saw a sign pointing us toward the restaurant, **Members and Guests Only**. When the hostess asked for our names and if we were members, I explained that Frank Morgan was my cousin and we were his guests. It was half a lie, of course, but a reasonable one. She seated us at a small table not far from the kitchen door, which must have meant that Cousin Frank was a Junior at the Club as well as in life.

We were served water and then ordered food. No alcohol was in evidence, which, according to Levi, meant that they were obeying the law out front and the boys were doing their drinking in the back, somewhere not so public. I ordered tea with my broiled fish, and Levi ordered coffee with his chicken.

While we were waiting on the food, a tough-looking, middle-aged man wearing a worn suit came over and without any introduction, asked Levi if he could join us for a few minutes. For a second, I thought he'd come to throw us out.

"Of course, Sheriff. Have a seat," Levi said. You might not have noticed the tension, but I knew Levi well enough to hear it in his voice.

"Not no more," the man said. "I went out of office at the end of the year. Going back to work for the railroad. Who's your friend?"

"This is Miss Josephine Salter. Jo, this is Jesse James Bailey, the only man to have been sheriff of both Madison and Buncombe Counties."

"At the same time?" Wonder in my voice.

"Lord no," Bailey said. "Either one is bad enough as 'tis. Are you a Madison County Salter?" He was smiling and his voice was friendly. I could feel Levi relaxing.

"Yes, sir. Big Pine Creek."

He nodded. "Know it well. I grew up on the railroad tracks down that way. Still love the railroad to this day . . . Miss Salter, I need to swap a few words with Mr. Arrowood here. Would you mind . . .?" He shrugged.

"You want me to powder my nose?"

Bailey smiled. "Might be better if . . ."

"It's alright, Sheriff," Levi said quietly. "Jo can hear anything you might have to say. She knows my business."

"If you say so," he said. He paused as the waitress brought out food. Used one of the napkins from our table to polish his spectacles while he waited on her to set down the plates. "You want anything, Sheriff?" she asked him, and he shook his head. "I'm gonna rejoin my friends over there in a minute. Just need to share a thought or two with Mr. Arrowood first."

"Share away," Levi said, after the waitress pushed through the kitchen door. He didn't pick up his fork to begin eating, so I waited as well.

"Brother Arrowood," Bailey said. "I've followed your career right along. I know where your booze comes from up on Spring Creek. Your uncle if I'm not mistaken."

"Leave him out of this," Levi said quietly.

"Just listen," Bailey said. His voice low now as well. "Your path and mine have run along more or less side-by-side over the years, but I've never had a direct reason to get involved with you. I know how much liquor you sell up at that Sky Club now, but it's inside the city limits, so I always felt that you belonged to the Police Department. Outside my jurisdiction, so to speak. Every time I've been working over here, you've been working over there, or vicey-versey. Which is just fine by me. I hate to put a young man with a future in jail."

"You think you could . . . catch Levi? Put him in jail?" I imagine I was supposed to keep my mouth shut and let the men talk, but it was a scary thought.

Bailey smiled. "Miss Salter, I could catch the Old Scratch himself if he was running liquor in my territory. But I ain't here to spread discord and dismay. I'm here with a friendly word." He turned back to Levi. "You know our friend Jameson, right?"

"The District Attorney? That Jameson?"

Bailey nodded. "The very one. He has it in for you. Hates your guts as a matter of fact."

"I broke his nose for him," Levi admitted with a shrug.

"After he insulted me," I added, since both of them seemed not to mind me joining in.

Bailey nodded. "I heard about the nose. And laughed out loud when I did. Now that I know why you did it, I understand even better." He smiled and nodded to me. "But Brother, the man is the D.A. and he is as crooked as Satan's walking stick. The power in the city has kept him away from you thus far, but now that things are so . . . uncertain, I suspect he'll come after you."

"Raid the club?"

Bailey nodded. "Expect him on a Saturday night right in the thick of things. He'll sit out in the parking lot and send in the police. He won't bother the guests—he knows better—but he'll confiscate every drop of drinking juice in the place and he'll arrest you on the Volstead Act. You and a few choice employees. Bartender and such."

"Why are you warning us, Mr. Bailey?" I was genuinely curious. "Aren't you the law?"

"Two reasons, Miss Salter. Maybe three. I was an officer of the court right up till the first of the year, but not no more. Two, I never did like Jameson. He's crude and he's mean. And then there's number three."

"Number three?"

"We're all from the same part of the world. You, me, and Brother Arrowood here. All from down in Madison, grew up poor." He stood up to go and smiled down at the two of us. "But for the grace of God, I might be the bootlegger and Arrowood here might be the sheriff. What do you think of that?"

He walked away as we started in on our dinner. Either the fish or the chicken would have made Pansy blush for shame. The chicken was fancied up but tough as shoe leather. The fish was . . . hard to describe. Slimy maybe.

Bad food and nothing to drink. Caused you to wonder what kept them in business . . . Golf?

"Could he have caught you?" I whispered to Levi at one point, while we labored away at the food. "Sheriff Bailey, I mean."

Levi grinned. "Jesse James Bailey could catch smoke and hold it in his hand," he said, not caring who heard him. "Man dynamited more stills and confiscated more cars in these two counties than you could ever imagine."

"Then it's a good thing he isn't after you."

"Sure, and it's an even better thing that he warned us. In the old days, Jameson would have left us alone, but . . ."

AFTER WRESTLING WITH THE CHICKEN and fish, we decided that we'd find something at home for dessert. Home was the Sky Club, where we could play with little Bodie while we sipped some dessert.

When lo and behold, Junior himself came in through the terrace doors and walked over to our table. "Cousin Jo," he warbled. "They told me that you were here with a guest, and I was happy to hear it." He sat himself down without an invitation. "And who might this young man be?" he asked, grinning like a moron at Levi, who was at least five years older. As far as I knew, he'd seen Levi twice before, but it was just like him to be so self-involved as not to recall.

"Frank Morgan . . . Junior, I'd like to introduce Mr. Levi Arrowood. He manages the Sky Club up on the mountain. Levi, this is my cousin, Frank."

Levi nodded and almost smiled. "Pleased to meet you," he said in barely more than a whisper, reminding me how quiet he got around trouble.

"Why, howdy-do to you too, Larry. Any friend of Cousin Jo's is . . . you know how it goes. And I'm happier than a hole-in-one to meet you. I've always heard about the Sky Club from some of the swells down here, my friends of course, and I've longed to check it out. What say I return the favor and come up as your guest . . . now that you've supped at my table?"

It was extraordinary. He seemed a different boy, man, whatever he was. The Asheville Country Club was his native element, and here he was, cracking jokes as if he owned the place. Brash, confident, talking away at Levi, all the while calling him by the wrong name, as Levi was coiling inside himself.

"Junior," I said, for that's what I'd always called him. "Did you know Pansy had taken a job up at the Sky Club?"

"No," he laughed. "But I'm glad to know where that gal ran off to. I never much cared for Raymond, but I did like me some Pansy, even if she couldn't cook."

Levi leaned over and took hold of my arm . . . before I could reach for Junior's neck.

"Why don't you walk out to the car with us, Frank?" Levi asked, even more quietly. "I'll give you my business card, and we can be in touch. Talk about you coming up to the Club."

"Absolutely. Absolutely. And maybe you'd like some golf lessons one of these days. I can turn you into a pro overnight, Larry. I have the gift."

He chattered away at us as walked out to the Plymouth. I had to smile at Levi's bootlegger sense in parking in an isolated spot, because by the time we reached the car, we were in the dark. I was walking side-by-side with Junior, with Levi a few steps behind us.

When we were several feet from the Plymouth, Junior asked me if I knew where Pansy was living now as he sure would like to pay her a visit. It was eerie timing because just at that moment, Levi stepped forward, grabbed one of Junior's wrists and yanked his arm up behind his back. Before I could even speak, he slammed Junior face down on the hood of the car so hard that I was afraid he'd leave a dent—in the car, not Junior.

"Jo wants to explain a few things to you, Frank," Levi

muttered as he felt around for the back of Junior's head with his free hand. When he found it, he jerked Junior's head back till his neck popped.

"Huh . . .? Wha?"

"You heard me, boy." Levi was in Junior's ear. "Jo's going to explain the facts of life."

I leaned forward over the hood so that my face was only a foot or so away from Junior's. I hissed more than spoke. "Pansy told me what you did to her, you little shit. I wanted to castrate you with a pair of scissors and then stab you in the face, do you . . ."

"But I didn't . . ."

Levi whanged his face hard into the hood and yanked his head back again. "Pay attention," he muttered.

"But I'm bleeding!"

Face to hood again, harder.

I reached over and twisted his ear. It was slick with blood. "Listen, Junior. If you show your face at the Sky Club, I'll rip it off. If you bother Pansy again at work or at home or on a street corner in broad daylight, I'll come after you. Do you . . ."

"But she's a nig . . . Jo. Don't you . . .? She belongs . . ." He was having trouble talking, spitting out blood.

"Have you got your knife?" I asked Levi.

"In my pocket. Use the long blade."

I reached into his pants pocket and came out with his German pocketknife. "Got it," I whispered. Opened it and held it where Junior could see it.

"I understand. I understand." Junior was blubbering. "Don't cut on me. Please, Jo. I didn't mean . . ."

"Can I cut him?" I asked Levi. "Just a little?"

"Nah. Not tonight. I think he got the message."

Levi raised him up off the hood, frog walked him to the edge of the pavement and set him down roughly in the weeds. He leaned over and whispered something to Junior and then kicked him hard in the ribs for good measure. Walked back and opened my car door for me.

As we were driving back up the mountain . . . home . . . I asked what was the last thing he'd said? He looked over at me and smiled.

"I told him that if there was a next time, I'd let you do whatever you wanted to him."

"Doubt there'll be a next time," I said. "We'll probably never see him again. But if we do, we'll hold him and let Pansy cut him."

46

I'VE SAID IT WAS A cold winter, and it was. Not as much snow and ice as in other winters, but somehow everything felt colder. The waitresses and musicians at the Club told countless stories of hobo camps along the railroad tracks that were full of hundreds of men and some women, who traded their bodies for any scrap of food or a piece of a blanket.

Pansy described how Black families were huddling together under one tilted roof for warmth and support and because many had no place else to go.

Everybody everywhere seemed to grow thinner and more desperate right before your eyes as if a plague was secretly ravaging their bodies and their minds. Everywhere the litany was the same, the crying out for work and food, food and work. Please . . . please. Most men would do almost any kind of physical labor for a quarter an hour, including men who'd owned businesses and worked with their brains prior to the crash. Most women were forced to work just to help feed their families. And sometimes the work they did happened in the dark, whether they lived in the hobo camps or not.

And as is so often the case when the panic strikes, the poor were the least affected because they didn't have far to fall. They already kept a flock of chickens, they already put in a garden, they already ate squirrel and rabbit, fished the creeks and rivers. They were close enough to their food that no dollars came between the lots, the fields, the rivers and the cookpot. Pluck it, skin it, gut it, eat it.

There were hilarious stories of the used-to-be-rich rich men or women who begged their maids and chauffeurs to teach them how to pluck a chicken or skin a rabbit. And if that's what the critter looked like naked, how in the world do you cook it?

When Levi and I visited up home in March—once to his Uncle's on Spring Creek and once to see Papa on Big Pine—we found that up in the coves, winter had begun to ease off. The tendrils of spring could be seen in the fields and along the ridges. The sun was returning to the earth. And when you talked to country people who farmed, as most of them did, they shrugged their shoulders at the Great Depression of the newspapers. Nobody had any money, they admitted that, but they fully expected to work just like they always did, in the barns and fields, and they expected they'd eat just like they always had. "If you grow what you eat, ain't no money changes hands." We heard that time and again.

At the Sky Club, we fell into a rhythm of our own in late winter. Like me, you probably recall the quilt that your mother or your grandmother stitched together out of the leftover scraps of the family's clothes and other bits of cloth. A beautiful pattern wrought from the makings of many lives. And if you lived back in the mountains, that quilt didn't hang on the wall or rest folded on a rack. It was wrapped around you for warmth, covered you while you slept. It held you and sustained you. It was as if our little family—Levi, Mack, Pansy, me—were stitching a quilt of sorts, intended to sustain us, no matter what the world offered by way of cold and violence.

Little Bodie, the scrawny hound pup, grew by the day and took to following Levi or me everywhere around the place but particularly outside. Pansy and I planned a large garden for the abandoned patch of ground beyond the far end of the parking lot. We found a man on the edge of town with a mule, who came and plowed it under for us, and we laid out rows for corn, beans, and squash. We meant for us to eat, Pansy and me, even if the Club closed down.

But strangely, it didn't. We had to cut back to four nights a week, Wednesday through Saturday, and put more time and energy into moving and selling the liquor than we did dinner and jazz. But during those four nights, there were crowds of people who came to escape. And to escape, they threw themselves around the dance floor till they could hardly walk—and drank straight shots of corn liquor to burn away the blues. Sometimes jazz is primitive—like a narcotic—a whoop and yell, something rambunctious on its hind legs. And that winter, as the debris from the crash settled into people's lives, they became desperate for any kind of escape. Especially the kind that throbbed in the pulse like a war drum.

THEN TWO THINGS HAPPENED TO us in late March that threatened all the tenuous peace we had quilted together, stitch by careful stitch. Because the rumors persisted that Levi Arrowood was hoarding money up on the mountain, two men came in the middle of the night to rob us. And because Levi and I could not leave each other alone, I missed my monthly period.

Normally, sometime around the twentieth or thereabouts, I start feeling headachy, a few days later my stomach starts to feel bloated, then sometime toward the end of the month the cramps start right before the bleeding. Usually, I turn pale and wan, tempers get a little short, but I don't turn into an outright witch like my Aunt Maude. She once broke a broom handle over her husband's head when he asked what was for supper. Mostly, I just want to sleep for a day or two.

But that month, March of '31 . . . nothing. No headache, no stomachache, no cramps down where it hurts. No blood. Normally, I was as regular as the clock on the mantel, so by the last few days the month, I began first to wonder and then to worry.

Here's the thing of it. Almost every woman I've ever known has been through this. It's not who you tell . . . it's whether you tell *him* or not. The father. Now, if you're safely married and stowed away at the end of a quiet street with a two-year-old already learning to walk, sure, tell the man and let him strut around like cock-o-the-walk for a few days. Crow a little bit. But if you're not married and not rich, then what?

It helped that I liked Levi and trusted him. Maybe even loved him, but at this point, it's more important that I liked him. Could sit quietly after supper on a Sunday night and not talk at all, just pet Bodie and hand a glass of bourbon back and forth. Oddly enough for a country boy, he loved to read, and we liked to read to each other . . . by the woodstove that winter. When a subject arose, I could talk to him about anything.

Or at least I thought I could until I was five days overdue, ten days overdue. Then my throat closed up, and I began to stammer.

IN THE MEANTIME, WHILE I was waking up every morning hoping for blood on the sheets, we had taken steps to foil Jameson, the District Attorney. Mack had found an old coal chute in the basement, which we boarded over with a sliding contraption like a barn door but with the rail and the wheels hidden in the ceiling. It looked like a solid oak wall, which it was, but a solid oak wall that could be pushed aside if you knew where the hidden latch was. Once Mack and Levi built in shelves, we could store all the corn liquor and apple brandy in there, along with anything else of value—black market wine or bottled whiskey—with the idea that if we were raided, the police could only confiscate what they could find. Every night we were open for business, we only brought out what we anticipated needing and left the rest hidden away. In time, the coal chute would serve us well. But for now, it was just part of the story of those days, along with breaking ground for a garden, teaching a puppy the difference between inside and outside, getting into a rhythm with Mack and Pansy and the folks who worked four nights a week at the Club.

We were finding that rhythm, the jazz that we orchestrated together, day by day. It was my body that was out of sync and falling further behind. And when the second week in April rolled around, I figured it was time to grow up and talk to Levi. But before I did, I wanted to have an out, an escape. If I was going to turn into a problem, I wanted to at least have an answer.

I tried him on a Monday night, after a day's hard work inside and outside. He was feeling good, it seemed to me, relaxed for him, and maybe even happy. You could sense that spring might be coming along, as it had in all the years past. It was warm enough that after supper we sat out on the terrace, just the two of us. Pansy had stayed home that day, and Mack had gone into town.

I asked him to make us an Old Fashioned, which he loved to do. It was the one cocktail that he could manufacture better than Mack. We carried the drinks out onto the terrace, both of us bundled up against a stout evening breeze. Bodie trotted onto the terrace with us and curled up on an old blanket we kept there for him. Levi had brought a book along, thinking we might read a bit, but before he had a chance to get started, I told him I had something important to tell him.

We were sitting side-by-side, looking out over Asheville at the far-flung sunset. It was beautiful, a study in orange and blue, and I felt that I was about to spoil it. He regarded my face, closely, carefully, in that way of his. Eventually, he asked, "You're not about to leave, are you . . .? Leave me, I mean."

"Lord no," I said, and smiled ruefully. "Not that."

"Then what?"

I swallowed. "I think I'm going to have a baby."

Time slowed then. I had a feeling that the old railroad clock over the bar stopped. Of if not, the second hand itself creeped at best. He didn't say anything . . . why the hell wouldn't he speak?

He raised his hand up to shade his eyes against the long rays of the setting sun, all the better to study my face.

"Are you going to say something?" I asked. My voice, I could tell, was hoarse.

"I don't know what to say." His voice was worse than mine. Sounded like he had sand in his throat.

"Are you . . . happy? Mad? Scared?"

"Who would I be mad at . . . myself?"

"Mad at me for letting it happen?"

"I think I was there when it happened . . . Or at least I hope I was."

"Just the two of us. Whenever it happened, it was just you and me."

He nodded. And then he did that damn thing he could do where he lapsed into silence. And the poor old second hand on the clock must have given up entirely. My heart stopped ticking, at any rate.

"I been thinking about what to do," I said. Coughed . . . and then went on. "I don't aim to saddle you with this. Nor me either. When this happened to Sissy, she swallowed a couple of Madame Drunette's Lunar Pills and that took care of the problem. Near about turned her inside out, but it . . . ended it."

"What the hell? Madame Drunette's what?"

"Lunar Pills. You can get them at the same drug store where I got my . . . cervical cap. You know . . ."

He shook his head, gently at first and then almost violently. I was afraid he was trying to shake the very thought of me out of his brain. "You will do no such thing," he said, low in his throat.

"But it would solve . . ."

"My child. No, no, that's not right. *Our* child is not a problem. Will never be a problem. Don't call him a problem."

"Levi, it might not be a *him*. You know that, don't you? Might be a bull-headed girl like me."

"Don't care. You can't do this. Lose this child, I mean. I won't have it."

"What the hell you mean, you won't have it. You can't tell me . . ."

"It's my child too, Jo."

It's a good thing that the Club was set off by itself and there was nobody else around. We were both yelling like crazy people.

"It's more mine than yours, damn it. It's in my body."

"It's not an *it*, Jo. It's . . ."

"Whatever she is, he is . . . is inside me. I have to carry it . . . sorry . . . her. Carry her, bear her, nurse her. You just get to . . . stand around and watch!"

"That's not fair. You act like I don't love you."

"You don't. If you did, you'd let me decide this for myself, not try to order me around like you owned me. *I won't have it.* That's what you said: *I won't have it!* Like you just get to decide for the both of us and I'm supposed to follow along with my tail between my legs. Do what I'm told. Well, the hell with that, Levi Arrowood. I get a vote in this too. Did it ever occur to you that maybe, just maybe, I don't want this baby!"

"Don't you?" I think that's what he said. While I was jumping up so hard my chair slammed back into the wall and nearly hit little Bodie on his blanket, I think he said, "Don't you?"

While I was flinging through the door into the restaurant, stomping up the stairs, and slamming the door to my room behind me.

47

Oh, my Lord God above me in heaven . . . He wants the baby. What am I supposed to do now? He . . . wants . . . the . . . baby.

That meant he wanted me. Or no, maybe he didn't want me. He just wanted a son. Damn him anyway—Levi, not the baby.

No, wait, think. Did he say that? No, he didn't say it had to be a boy baby. Just a baby. Why in the wide world would Levi Arrowood want a child? It was inconceivable.

Did I want the baby?

That's where we ended up, wasn't it? That really is what he was saying when I pitched a fit and stormed up to my room.

Did I?

Did I want to be a mother? Did my mother want me to be a mother? Did I even have the faintest notion how to be a mother? Pansy had children. Two grown children. Maybe she could teach me.

But why on God's green earth would Levi Arrowood want to be a father? He was a bootlegger and nightclub operator, not a father. He'd make a terrible father.

Or would he?

But still, why would he want a child?

I lay down on the bed that night, running all of these thoughts over and over through my mind. Just when I was finally starting to relax, starting to drift just a bit in my thoughts, I realized something. When Levi was a child, his stepmother hadn't wanted him. His father had tried but his stepmother had wanted nothing to do with him or his brother except with that razor strop.

Meaning that he wanted children to be wanted? My God, that had to be it. He wanted children to be loved. And he wanted to give what he'd never been given. I sniffed just a little when I came up with that. But maybe it was true. It had all the deep bass notes of the truth.

And didn't he also say that he loved me. I drifted closer to sleep, curled on my side in bed. Happy thought. But no, that's not exactly what he said. What he said was . . . *you act like I don't love you*. And then I bit his head off. Well, hell yes, that meant he loved me. He basically said he loved me . . . in his own way. Didn't he?

And I liked his way just fine. It suited us. Him and me.

Further, closer. Sleep was softly over me like a blanket and in me like a melody. Bringing dreams. I held both my hands over my flat stomach while I dreamed.

WHAT WOKE ME WAS THE sound of Bodie howling. The loneliest, most heart-rending sound from deep in his throat. I got up and pulled on the old bathrobe that I wore sometimes up on the third floor.

I crept down the hall. The door to Levi's room was open and his bed had been slept in, but he was gone. Bodie's howling was far below and sounded like outside.

Down the stairs to the second floor and I could hear voices back in the office. Low mean voices. Hissing almost. I eased my shoes off and slipped barefoot into the bar. Mack's Louisville Slugger was in its usual place on the bottom shelf. It felt hard and heavy in my hands, but by God, I was from Big Pine and I knew I could swing it.

Around the corner by the piano and then along the hall that led to the office. Everything dark in the restaurant but the office door was ajar and the light on within. The hissing voice was louder now, saying something I could almost make out. Levi's cold, calm reply . . . *that* I could hear. He was refusing to do what the hissing said.

As I eased down the hall, I almost tripped over something big. Oh Jesus, it was Mack. Sprawled on the floor, groaning but unconscious. When I reached down to him, ran my hand up his arm to his shoulder, he twitched, but his neck was slick with blood. *Leave* . . . he seemed to mutter . . . *leave* . . .

He was trying to say Levi, I was sure of that. Trying to call out. I stepped over him, careful not to slip in his blood. Bodie was still howling, his pup's throat hoarse now.

Through the open door, I could see that there were two of them. Not big, not hard, not especially tough to look at, but the one with his back to me held a policeman's nightstick in one hand and a hunting knife in the other. He was wearing a red flannel shirt with a tear in the back that had been badly mended and one of his shoes was untied. It's what I would always remember about him, the shirt and the shoe. I could smell the body stink of him from where I stood.

I couldn't see through him and I couldn't swing the bat from where I stood in the hall, so I eased in through the door and to my left. There was our old black railroad safe against the wall, with all our future locked up in it. There was Levi standing in front of the safe with his head bowed stubbornly and his arms crossed over his chest. In the moment's flash, I noticed that all he had on was his undershirt and his work pants pulled hastily up and belted.

The second man was beyond Levi by the window, and he had the gun. He was gesturing with it, pointing now at the safe, now at Levi, waving, urging Levi forward. He was trying to make tough talk, but he was so nervous that it came out in squeaks and whispers. All he wanted Levi to do, over and over, was open the damn safe. Just open it and they'd let him go. Leave and never come back. *We're starving, mister*, he croaked. I remember he said that right before he looked up and saw me.

Me in my underwear and bathrobe, feet bare and eyes wide.

"Who the hell are you?" he said incredulously.

Nothing for it but to swing. I twisted around and swung the slugger as hard as I could with both hands. Aimed at the head of the torn-shirt man and missed low. Missed his head but caught him hard on the back of his shoulder. Loud crack, and for a split second, I thought I'd broken the bat. But he was down on the floor screaming in pain and the bat was whole in my hands.

Levi dove on the floor after torn shirt's knife, which had skittered from his hand. For lack of something better, I stepped over torn shirt and went for the starving man. "Come on," I said to him, or something like that. Bodie was howling, torn shirt was screaming, Levi was yelling my name, and I was hot for it all.

I went forward fast and it took starving man too long to remember his gun and when he did, he threw it at me. I ducked while Levi stabbed him in the thigh. Hard. Buried the hunting knife to the hilt. Now starving man was screaming and hopping past me toward the door, tears streaming down his gaunt face. He yelled at torn shirt as he went by, and torn shirt lumbered to his feet and stumbled after him.

I could hear the one crash into the door frame on the way out, the other trip over Mack and fall. But within a few seconds they were gone, falling down the stairs. Escaping from . . . us, me and Levi.

My vision was blurry. Why was I gasping for breath? I felt like I'd been punched in the stomach but couldn't remember when . . . or who?

Levi was on his feet and straight to me. Pried the bat out of my hands. *Jo.* He was saying my name over and over. *You're bleeding! Oh shit, Jo, where . . . are you shot . . . Jo!*

I looked down and my bathrobe was hanging wide open. I *was* bleeding. My panties were soaked and it was running down the inside of my legs.

And so my menstrual blood finally began to flow, in the middle of the melee that was all that night and, indeed, all that season.

48

IT TOOK OUR LITTLE FAMILY some days to get over the robbery.

When the two desperados had broken in the back door, good dog Bodie had been right there barking and growling, all twenty pounds of him. They just picked the pup up and tossed him outside and closed the door behind them. Never dreaming he had a voice like Caruso. A young Caruso anyway.

Bodie woke Mack, who was asleep in the basement. Mack caught up with the two of them in the hallway headed into the office, where after some slamming around, they beat him down with the nightstick. Then they came face-to-face with the safe, which must have brought them up short.

Which is where Levi came in. Bodie's howls woke him up out of a light sleep. We'd just had our first big fight—not our last—and he was mostly tossing and turning instead of sleeping. When he went downstairs to check on Bodie, he saw the light on in the office.

He walked in on them with a pool cue in one hand and his blackjack in the other. Which was all fine and good, but he hadn't counted on the gun. As he told me later, most of the guns he'd come upon in his life were loaded. Turns out this one wasn't, but he didn't know that, so he gave up the cue and jack to stand his ground before the safe. Damned if he was going to open it. He figured if they shot him, at least I knew the combination and could calculate a future. Oh, and if I heard a gunshot, surely to

God I'd have enough sense to stay away. Maybe even call the police.

Later, we would agree that I was sadly lacking in that kind of sense.

That's more or less where I came sneaking in, half naked and carrying a baseball bat.

Who was the hero of that night? We all—Mack, Levi, me—decided that Bodie was the hero. When Pansy showed up the next day, she cooked up a mess of scrambled eggs and bacon. We got the eggs and Bodie got the bacon.

MACK'S HEAD WOULD HEAL . . . ONE more scar to add to the rest. But did I heal? Did Levi? My bleeding was gone in a few days, my body limber again. But it took Levi and me longer than that to get over the fight, if that's even what it was. We were tender with each other but also scared. In particular we were scared of sex. I think we were both afraid of trapping the other somehow. He was afraid of trapping me into something I didn't want, and maybe I was afraid of trapping him into something he didn't really understand.

As affectionate as we were toward each other, neither of us wanted to make that first move toward . . . intimacy. I desperately needed the formula to define us, but I couldn't do the math. Do you realize how hard it is for me to admit that? I could not add it all up. For the life of me, I could not balance the equation that was Levi Arrowood and Josephine Salter.

And so to cover it up, the tenderness and the dismay, we dove back into our lives. That we could do for each other. I went to work every day at Imperial and studied their books just like I had the bank's back in the beginning, as if they were the textbooks and I was the student. And then, after I felt like I'd followed every equation and considered every numeral, I began to recreate how

Imperial kept records on the thousands of policies, so that I could report by region or by salesman or by amount or by type. I didn't need to talk to anyone really, except for Pink and his daughter, who stood someday to take over his role. I just wanted the numbers. After the bank, it was a relief just to refresh and revise and reshape the numbers. Not to change them, you understand, but to tame them. Clarify them.

On the weekends, I dug into what Levi called his books, his accounts, and I tried not to laugh out loud at how ridiculous they were. He had lists of goods and columns of numbers written on newsprint, on brown paper pokes, on scraps of paper. Some were stuffed in desk drawers in the office, some were folded neatly and stuck into the inner pockets of his suit coats, some were thrown down carelessly onto the top of his dresser at the end of a long night. Slowly, we began to collect all of Levi's random jottings and notes to himself, and even more slowly, I trained him to keep some record of each transaction, even those involving the illegal purchases and sales of hooch. I created out of all this a coherent record.

I was never trained in double-entry bookkeeping but inherited a form of it at the bank. I brought that with me to the Sky Club where I developed our own set of double-entry records, week by week. I used a set of brand-new ledger books that were thrown out when the bank collapsed. In these books, I created a record of each week in *two columns*, with debit balances penciled in the left-hand column and credit balances in the right-hand column, so that it was easy enough to total and compare both columns at the end of each week, which I did on Sunday afternoon.

Once I got the record keeping under control, I could account for the amount of money in what I started calling the Sky Club account, which in reality was the amount of cash in Levi's shoe boxes inside the safe. This included, I might add, the seven dollars rent I paid into those shoe boxes each Sunday from my own cigar box in the same safe. My box was slowly growing in size from my pay at Imperial but at nothing like the rate we were accumulating cash in the shoe boxes. I had $983 and the Club had $10,294 on the first Monday in April. But as you will see, it wasn't enough.

WE ALSO DUG IN THE garden, we hid the cases of liquor and brandy, we repainted the first-floor restaurant, we bought the best meat and produce we could find. In other words, we were slowly building a business. And when I described what we were doing to Pink Starnes, he nodded and winked. "The Sky Club is your child," he said. "Yours and Arrowood's together." He paused and then added, "You're lucky to have each other."

Which made me sad again along with the happy. Pink didn't know that we'd flirted with the possibility of a real baby. He didn't know that it had spooked the two of us—Levi and me—such that we'd pulled back from each other ever so slightly. Pulled back from each other in our nighttime selves.

Until the following Saturday night when somehow things shook loose again.

Jazz. All you know sometimes, and all you need to know.

There was the faintest scent of spring in the air all day. While Pansy and I were outside, I told her about missing my period and how for a week, I thought I was pregnant. And that ever since I'd been afraid to get in bed with Levi, afraid of . . . And before I could even finish, she interrupted me to say, "Jo, honey, when you get throwed off the mule, the best thing is to get back on quick. Longer you wait, the worse it gets."

"Mule?"

"Don't act stupid. You know what I mean. His mule. Once things get rolling tonight, you go wash up and put on that dress, the silver and black number looks like it was painted on. And you get you a strong drink and circulate. Hear me, circulate. Dance with any man you like or no man at all and let Mr. Levi Arrowood lick his lips for a while as he's making his rounds. And for God's sake, quit thinkin' so much."

So I did it, just what she said. I hadn't had on my river of moonlight dress in forever, seemed like, since back in the fall before the world fell apart. Once the club was full, I crept upstairs and took a quick bath, washing every inch of skin like it might come under scrutiny. Panties and a thin slip under . . . the moonlight.

When I came back down to the second floor, I went first through the kitchen to pass inspection. Pansy had her hair up in a rag by that point and was making that stove sing and dance. She took one look at me and laughed out, shaking a ladle at me, and yelling. "You on fire, Jo Salter. Now, go set the whole, damn place with the blaze."

As cold and heartless as that winter was proving to be, there were nights at the club when all the various jazz musicians in town would just show up. Some we were paying and some we just fed drinks, and they all played. They played because they loved it, because they needed it, because they wanted the sound and what it did to their souls.

ONE FINE, NEGRO MAN I'D never seen before got out front with a steel guitar at one point in the evening and played a song called "Dark was the Night and Cold was the Ground." Such a song and the perfect match for that awful winter. It was a hard, harsh blues song that for five minutes gave the whole proceeding a somber sound, but then the band jumped back in behind him, and the joint began to swing again.

The musicians who traveled the circuit—New Orleans, Chicago, New York—liked to tell me that a woman who could really move was called a torso tosser or a hip-flipper. Well, I freely admit I didn't have much torso to toss, but I could flip a hip with the best of them.

I made my way round the room, with my tumbler of apple brandy in hand. I danced with two or three and I danced by myself. I kept in smiling touch with Mack, but every time I got close to Levi, I eased away from him into the flow of the crowd. At one point, I came across my cousin Sissy seated at a table with three men. Three men and no Benjamin Scott.

Sissy got up and joined me at the bar. She had hit the sauce pretty hard, it seemed to me, and there was an undertone of sadness to her whole person. We whispered together long enough for her to tell me that Ben had dropped her like a hot potato. "Like a goddamn hot potato," she kept saying. Who were the men, I asked her, the men she was with? Fast boys in the real estate boom, she said, including her old boss's boss, Will Campbell.

"There isn't any boom anymore, Sis," I said to her.

"Oh hell, I know," she said. "I know. But Campbell's wife went back to South Carolina, and he's the best thing I can get my hands on right this minute. Best thing I got going."

The music was flowing and flaming around us, and she was all but dancing on her barstool. "Oh, Sis, I'm sorry about Benjy," I yelled in her ear. "I know you wanted him."

"The hell with him," she said. "He never loved me for myself. He just loved to fuck me."

And with that, she was gone, weaving back toward the table where her real estate boys were waiting. Used to be rich, used to be fine, used to be . . .

For a long moment, the music having died down to just the piano, I longed to save her. Throw her a lifeline and pull her out of her life. Drag her up the mountain and settle her in . . . where?

In the basement with Mack. Just the thought of Sissy with Mack made me laugh, and I was on the move again.

Oh, that night was all jazz. And I showed them the Turkey Trot like they'd never seen a turkey trot. Wild turkey in the springtime. And the Charleston? Lord, yes.

But as the evening waned, I gravitated more and more toward Levi. Like a planet around a sun, I suppose. My feet, my legs, my hips carried me closer and closer to him. And when we finally locked up the doors and windows downstairs, he led up to the third floor with a silly grin on his face. "Been drinking?" he asked me, with his arm around my waist.

"Hell no," I said. "Been dancing." But I think I might have slurred the words.

"Can I show you to your room?"

"Only . . ." I stopped stock-still at the top of the third-floor stairs. "Only if you come inside."

"Inside your room?"

"Inside me," I muttered.

"Are you sure?" He was so serious. Wanting not to hurt me. Not to take advantage of me.

"It's one of the few things I am sure of in my whole life," I said. "And Levi . . .?"

"Hmmm?" By now he was steering me down the hall toward my room.

"Have you got some protection?" I was still drunk on the music, and that might have been my last coherent thought of the evening. The last, long cast of a wave crashing on the beach.

"In my pocket," he said.

"Thank you," I whispered into his ear.

SUNDAY MORNING. CAME LONG AND slow. First one and then the other, rose quietly and went to the bathroom for a few minutes. Returned to bed and curled again. The light slowly flowed into the room as if even the sun had all the time in the world to make itself manifest.

Eventually, I offered to go down and make a pot of coffee. Bring two cups back to us, there, in the sun-filtered bed.

"I would like that," he said lazily. "Coffee in bed. And once we've sipped our coffee, I think we need to talk some business."

"What business?" I was standing barefoot, tying my robe around my waist. My waist that was covered up with the scent of him, the touch of him, the juice of him. I liked him all over me, dried on my skin.

"Our business. Yours and mine, fifty-fifty. I think it's time we came to an understanding."

49

YOU'RE MORE THAN A LITTLE crazy if you take me on as your partner. You have ten thousand dollars in the safe, and I have not quite a thousand. I should get . . ."

"Can't do it without you," he said.

"But it's ten to . . ."

"Not everything is about the money, Jo. If you'll stop long enough to catch your breath, you'll realize that."

I stopped long enough to catch my breath.

As we both sat up in bed, the covers pulled up to our waists. The coffee was hot and strong. The day slowly emerging, the rays of light from my windows shifting shapes around the room.

"Are you sure? Really sure . . . I mean this, Levi . . . that I'm worth it?"

"Jesus, Jo. I can't do it without you, and you can't do it without me. Last night, I asked you if you were sure about something else, and here we are. This morning, you're asking me if I'm sure, and I'm giving you the same answer."

"What did I say last night?" I was smiling at him.

"It's one of the few things I'm sure of in my whole life. And that's what I'm saying this morning. In the light of day."

I sighed. Big, this felt big. But hadn't Pansy told me to quit thinking so much? "Okay," I said eventually. "Should we shake hands on it?"

Which we did. Which we finished our coffee. Which we

then slipped back down under the covers and spent the morning in bed.

Celebrating our partnership. 50-50.

AND SO WE WERE READY when the time came to negotiate the purchase of the Sky Club. From the group of silent investors who owned the building, the land, and the business. Turns out there were three of them but until the day we actually sat down in the same room, Levi had only known the one, the man he called his contact.

The contact was more-or-less a nobody as it turned out. Nice guy but not a heavy hitter. It was Boxer, the attorney who'd worked in the mayor's office before Gallatin Roberts got thrown out on his ear. Eventually, we found out that he might have held 10 percent of the ownership, not more. They only kept him around to collect the regular payments from Levi and deliver messages if they had something to say.

At Levi's request, Boxer arranged the meeting. Two o'clock in the afternoon in the first-floor room of the Sky Club, the Family Room we called it, since alcohol was never served there. That's where the surprises began. Boxer arrived first, and when Levi introduced me as his partner, Boxer and I smiled at the memory of our last meeting at the bank. Two passengers watching the officers of the Titanic argue with each other right before it slipped beneath the waves.

"Remember, Arrowood. No names for the other two. They prefer it that way. I'll do the talking for them, okay?"

Levi and I both shrugged at the same time. Why not?

After a little bit of chatter with Boxer, we could hear an automobile crunching the gravel in the parking lot and the two principal owners came in. I had to cover my mouth with my hand to hide the fact that I was all but laughing. First in the door was W. R. Campbell, the real estate salesmen and investor who'd just lost his Mediterranean mansion and was living in a tiny apartment in the Manor. I couldn't quite bring myself to call him Sissy's Campbell, even though, by her own admission, she'd attached herself to him and was waiting for him to rise again.

And, oh Lord, the third owner was my old friend, Dr. Craig Scott. When he saw me, he raised his eyebrows in mock surprise. The man was everywhere, had his hand in everything. Including, apparently, a supper club that fronted for a jazz and booze joint.

We all sat down at one of the large, round tables in the middle of the family room. There was nothing on the table but a pitcher of ice water and a tray of glasses. No paper in evidence, nobody was taking notes. If there were details to be discussed, apparently, we all trusted our own memories.

Boxer had just set about performing his preliminary introductions, which he thought weren't real introductions, the other two being silent partners, when Dr. Scott interrupted him. "What are you doing here, Josephine?"

I grinned at him. "Mr. Arrowood and I are partners."

"Full partners? Fifty-fifty?"

Levi nodded but didn't speak.

So, I said it. "Full partners, yes sir."

Dr. Scott grinned. "Well, that changes everything."

"What do you mean?" Campbell was nervous all of a sudden. Something I hadn't expected.

BOXER: Should we leave?

SCOTT: Oh, hell no. On the contrary. What it means, Will, is that this is serious. Means that if Jo here is the business and Mr. Arrowood is the . . . supplier, then they can make this place profitable. You'll be working for them someday.

BOXER: I'm not sure we should use . . .

SCOTT: Names? (pauses to laugh, apparently delighted) Oh, give it a break, Boxer. Jo knows everybody here, even if Mr. Arrowood doesn't. She's even been in my house, I suspect, thanks to my no-good son.

Mental note: explain that crack to Levi later, even if he doesn't ask.

CAMPBELL: Why are we here then? (incredulously) You two want to buy the Sky Club?
LEVI: The land, the building, and the business.
SCOTT: (whistles) This is serious. What's your offer?
LEVI: What will you take?
CAMPBELL: $100,000.
ME: Sir, with all due respect, I believe that's the price of three years ago. Before the crash.
SCOTT: Like I said, what's your offer?
LEVI: $15,000.
CAMPBELL: $50,000 . . . cash.

Thought: if he just dropped his price by half, he must be desperate for money.

SCOTT: (looking at me) What do you think, Jo?
ME: Between 15 and 50? Both numbers have a five in them.
SCOTT: (smiles) Yes, they do . . . Split the difference? $32,500?

(Levi and me both shaking our heads)

LEVI: $17,500.
CAMPBELL: That's ridiculous.

Thought: the man is sweating. Cool afternoon, and there's sweat beading in his hair. Stray thought: is Sissy screwing . . . he's old enough to be . . .

ME: (to Campbell) Sorry, sir. As Papa would say, you're all hoof and no horse. You need the money and we have it.

SCOTT: What say, Will? I don't need the money but you sure as hell do.

CAMPBELL: $20,000. Cash. Not a check.

SCOTT: (grinning) Sure. Mr. Arrowood?

LEVI: (glances at me and I nod) $20,000. One month from today.

BOXER: Can I say something?"

SCOTT AND CAMPBELL: No!

BOXER: Names . . . secret.

SCOTT: What my friend, Boxer here, is trying to say is that neither Will nor I can afford to have our names associated with the club. At least not with the ownership and sale thereof . . . So, the sale itself is entirely dependent on it not being a public transaction. Of course, we'll file the necessary legal papers, but after it goes through, we need to know that we can depend on your discretion. That rumors won't begin to circulate that we were backing a booze parlor and jazz joint on the sly. Can we count on you two to keep the whole thing a secret? Previous owners unknown . . . or at least undisclosed.

ME: Of course, you can count on us.

CAMPBELL: But we don't know . . .

SCOTT: I trust her judgment more than I trust yours, Will. Let it go. Boxer, you draw up the papers. Dated one month from today. And use both their names. (nodding at Levi and me). By the way, it's none of my business but are you two . . .?

ME: A couple . . .? You're right, it's none of your business.

LEVI: Yes, we are. And proud of it.

SCOTT: Congratulations, Mr. Arrowood. (grinning) My advice . . . let Jo run the business.

AFTER THEY WERE GONE, IT was just Levi and me standing on the front porch of the club, both of us a little in shock at how fast it had all happened. Eventually, Levi got a cigar out of his suit coat pocket, unwrapped it and lit up. "Need I point out, partner, that we don't have twenty-thousand dollars?" he asked.

"Not yet," I admitted. "But we have a month. And we have friends."

He nodded and grinned through the smoke. "And about that visit you made to the Scott's big, fancy mansion in Biltmore Forest? With that shit Cameron Scott, I would imagine . . .?"

"Are you jealous, Levi Edgar Arrowood? Seriously . . .?"

"Hell yes . . . I'm jealous. What were you doing there?"

"I was looking for you," I said. "I just didn't know it yet."

50

The meeting with the owners took place on a Tuesday afternoon. By the weekend we were up to almost $17,000 with the assurance of a $5,000 loan from the Imperial Life Insurance Company. When Pink Starnes had suggested we come to him when we were in need, he meant it, and he responded. Unfortunately, that was all he could do as he was beset from all directions by mountain people who knew and trusted him, mountain people who'd been hurting for years now.

Our problem was that there was no money to be had anywhere on the street. The regional banks were still in shock from what had happened in November, and every other institution that might be a source of capital was either shut down or equally gun shy. And those individuals who had money were holding on to it more fiercely than ever before. Pink was right about that too. Those club people, as he called them—meaning the country clubs—would plow us all under if that's what it took for them to keep their maids and chauffeurs on salary.

We still had three weeks to raise the money, but it didn't look promising. Even back in its heyday, the Sky Club had never generated a $1,000 clear profit in a single week. No matter how many times I did the math, I couldn't see us with $20,000 in hand by the transaction date. I thought of going up home and asking Papa for a loan, but it seemed to me so unlikely that he would have the kind of money we needed that I put the idea out of my head, saving it as a last-ditch strategy, something for the last few days before the deadline.

THEN, ON THE NEXT SATURDAY night, disaster struck.

Nine o'clock at night. The Family Room downstairs had mostly emptied out except for a few married couples lingering over dessert. The second floor was humming, just getting started into something rich and dangerous. The young Negro artist on the piano, with the trumpet and trombone trading blasts, the bass throbbing underneath. We'd been careful with how much booze we brought out, but still there was a collection of bottles and jars at the bar, and Mack was doing his Saturday night best.

The place was full of noise: glasses and plates and bottles. Waves of conversation and laughter. Now and then a couple on the dance floor.

The only crazy thing was that on that one night, this one night in particular, Dr. Craig Scott of all the people in Asheville, was in the house. He was even seated at the bar, trading war stories with Mack and—it looked like to me—admiring the women who were scattered through the crowd. A suit but no tie and something brown and strong in his glass. When I stopped by for a few minutes just to check in with him, he winked at me.

"What are you doing here?" I all but yelled, over the blare of the band. "Thought you couldn't be seen . . ."

"Wife's out of town," he shouted back. "Bored at home, so I figured I'd take a look at what really went on here. It's amazing, isn't it?"

I recalled what Cam had said about his father. "The music isn't exactly what a gentleman should listen to, is it?"

He shook his head. "Of course not. New Orleans style. Hot and sweaty."

I nodded and smiled. "Well, be careful, Doctor, you just might get to like it."

He smiled. Everything seemed to pause for a moment, the musicians frozen in mid-note. "So, Jo, just how close are you and Arrowood really? Inseparable?"

It took me a second, but then I knew what he meant. He was asking for himself. Daddy Scott, the second richest son-of-a-bitch in the mountains.

I smiled tightly. Nodded emphatically. "Inseparable," I shouted.

"I thought so. Shame though. At least for me . . ."

And at that very moment, there were pounding feet on the staircase. Running and pounding feet, emphasized by the blasts of whistles.

I made my way toward the stairs. *What the . . . whistles?* I thought, may have even said out loud when I saw Levi on the move from over by the dance floor.

Then it all made sense. There were uniformed coppers everywhere. Jesse James Bailey's prediction had finally come true.

We were being raided.

Here's how it went. They herded all of the customers left on the second floor over to one side of the room and let them sit quietly by themselves, even let some of them take their drinks with them. A handsome, young officer assured them that *they* were not in any trouble, that *they* had wandered innocently into this den of iniquity, that *they* would be allowed to leave as soon as his fellow officers had searched the premises for illegal spirits, and so on.

The employees—Levi, Mack, the waitresses, even the musicians—were all herded over to the other side of the room. What made not one bit of sense was that they separated white from black: Levi, Mack, the two white waitresses, the bass, and the trombone from the colored waitresses, the piano, and the trumpet. Didn't make sense in our world except that these were the police and they didn't know any other way.

What they did know was who Levi was. He got a lot of pushing and shoving just meant for him. He was careful to keep his hands up in the air where they were in plain view and keep his mouth shut, but you could tell they were trying to provoke him. Made him strip his suit jacket off while they searched him, and of course they found the blackjack he carried in his pocket.

When the herding and separating started, I got shoved over into the group of patrons, but as soon as I saw what was happening, I brushed past the smiling cop and started across the floor. "Ma'am . . ." He grabbed my arm. "You can't leave. Not until . . ."

"I'm not leaving," I growled at him. "I work here." And kept right on going across the floor to join the employees. I started for Levi, meaning to get between him and the cops, but he motioned me away ever so slightly with his head and eyes, so I joined Mack and the waitresses instead.

By this point, you could hear Bodie getting wound up. He was shut up in Levi's room upstairs, where he was mostly happy and quiet on work nights because he was allowed on Levi's bed and liked to dig himself a nest in Levi's pillows. But the damn whistles had stirred him from his dreams, and the howling had begun.

Soon he'd be furiously scratching at the door to get out.

A squad of cops was tearing the bar apart, packing anything that looked or smelled vaguely like alcohol into cardboard boxes for evidence. A hard case lieutenant, who looked like maybe he'd grown up down along the tracks and been beaten with one of his own nightsticks, was standing in the middle of the room directing operations. After a few minutes of Bodie screaming, he turned to one of the cops standing over the employees and shouted at him to go "shut up that damn dog."

I started forward, hell if they were going to hurt Bodie, but at that very moment, the howling stopped. I turned back to look at Levi, the question written all over my face, and he mouthed the word *Pansy.* I glanced around the room, and sure enough, she wasn't there. And knowing her, she had found a safe place upstairs for her and Bodie to hide. I could imagine the two of them in the dark, with her hand wrapped around his muzzle.

Dangerous and stupid, that's what she'd always said about beat cops, stupid and dangerous.

It took them maybe thirty minutes to satisfy themselves that they'd found all the liquor there was to find on the second floor. The lieutenant finally nodded. On the way out, they smashed bottles and threw glasses into the fireplace just for the hell of it, dropped plates and even busted up a chair or two. And then as they were leaving, the thing I dreaded most happened. The lieutenant nodded over at our group.

"Slick there is going with us. Cuff him and bring him."

Of course, he meant Levi, and they dragged him toward the stairs as they went.

The minute their backs were turned, I went straight across the busted-up room to Craig Scott. He was sitting toward the back of the crowd of customers, calmly finishing his drink.

I was gasping, more from anger than anything else. You could hear them all but throwing Levi down the stairs. "It's the goddamn District Attorney, Dr. Scott, that ass Jameson. Go down and reason with him. You're the big man in this town. You can . . ."

"Call me Craig," he was eyeing me calmly, and even paused to suck the last sip of scotch out of his glass. "I can what?"

"You can reason with him . . . Craig. You don't have to tell him you own the place. You can just . . . do what you do. Threaten him with something. His job if nothing else. Do it as a favor to me."

He stood up and handed me his glass. "Jameson is an ass, I

grant you that. And I suspect you need Mr. Arrowood on the street, if we're to finish up our little business proposition."

I nodded frantically. "Hell yes. I can't do it without him. Go, please. Before they haul him off."

He smiled resignedly. "Like I said, Arrowood is a lucky man. Let's see if his luck holds tonight."

I WENT DOWN TO STAND BY the front door to wait. After a bit, Pansy and Mack joined me, so we could worry together. Thirty minutes later, Levi limped slowly up the front steps. His shirt was all but torn off his back, one eye was already swelling shut, and his lips were swollen and bleeding. Even so, he was trying to smile.

"That lieutenant," he muttered painfully through the blood, "is sure a hard-fisted son-of-a-bitch."

51

ANOTHER WEEK PASSED AS LEVI began to heal. His black eye faded, his swollen lips assumed something like their normal shape. His wrenched shoulder came around, and he could pick up full crates of liquor again. We were back in business by the following weekend, meaning that the band was blowing hot to a stream of food, booze, and dancing. He could kiss me again without grimacing.

$17,532.

No matter how many times I counted up the cash in the shoe boxes and the cigar box—everything we had—we were still $2,468 short of the money we needed with one week to go.

That Sunday, I brought up the idea of asking Papa for a loan. I could tell Levi wasn't happy with the idea. He brought up yet again all the places we could try to get money. He even suggested asking Craig Scott to help us finance the place, and I told him how Scott had propositioned me the night we got raided. Which only tipped him over into a furious rant about dirty old men and caused him to go stomping out of the club for a walk with Bodie. In all my dreams about the mysterious Mr. Arrowood, I had never, ever imagined him as the jealous type. And yet, here he was. It made me smile.

We were both so on edge because we wanted it so badly. Monday came and went. I tried again, and on Monday night, he agreed. Maybe it was our last chance to come up with the money.

Tuesday, he'd take me up to see Papa, and we'd ask him together. The two of us as partners.

The nights were still cold when we went up home that spring. We left Bodie at the club with Mack. I wore my favorite trousers and an old sweater, and Levi his denim jacket. It felt like the first time we'd ever driven up into Madison County together.

Two hours to drive from the Sky Club on out the Weaverville Road to the Old Marshall Highway; then along the River Road through downtown Marshall and so to Walnut; and then down that winding, gravel road to Barnard where we could cross the river on the one-lane, wooden bridge there.

When we reached the tiny hamlet at Barnard, we parked and got out to visit a little. Levi swapped outrageous lies with the old boys clustered on the porch at Gudger's Store. I meandered out onto the bridge, breathing deep the cool air rising off the river. I walked halfway across and let my mind float free for a few minutes. Stared downriver toward Stackhouse and Runion. It was the first week of April and the trees were budding out, especially down low in the river gorge where the weather wasn't so severe.

Here were a thousand shades of green. Each tree its own barometer of green, varying even from low branches to high as spring rose up out of the earth and flowed upward into the heart and sap of the trees. It was dazzling to my eyes. Each tree, each leaf almost, was its own emerald. You'd never know the human part of the world was torn apart and suffering for the natural world had returned. Whatever thoughtless force rose from the river and painted the hills with vibrant spring, she was here. She was on the move, and even as humanity fell into pit of its own making, nature was as fierce sure as ever.

The water below me, rushing away to Tennessee, was gray and green, torn by the rocks and shoals, but singing, flying, nonetheless.

What were the pitifully small concerns of vagrant humanity when the river was eternal? There before and there after . . .

After a bit, Levi walked out to join me. Leaned with me against the bridge railing and put his arm around my waist. "What are you thinking, Jo Belle?" Jo Belle was his pet name for me, what he called me when the world wasn't listening. "You look a thousand miles away."

"I'm thinking that whatever happens the next few weeks, whether we raise the money or not, whether we can buy the club or not, that whatever happens, we'll be alright. We'll still eat. We'll still make a roof over our heads. The sun will rise."

". . . and the river will run away into the sea."

I turned to smile at him. "You might make a poet, you keep that up."

He shook his head. "Naw, you started it. And you're right. I been thinking the same. Whatever hand gets dealt, we'll play it."

"Partners?" I felt like I was almost finishing his sentence for him . . . and immediately regretted it, for I never, ever pushed him.

A smile played over his lips, over his whole mouth really. Then he nodded. "I've had that thought," he admitted. "Though I have no idea what you might want to say about it."

WE PARKED AT JAKE WORLEY'S store as we always did. Did our howdy-dos with everyone there and walked on up the valley toward the farm. Paused to visit here and there, with this one and that one. "Papa was alone at the house," one hump-backed granny told us. The young-uns, by which she meant my two little brothers, were gone over to Hot Springs to see about some girls they liked at the Dorland-Bell School, but they should be back in a few days.

It was just the kind of story that got told up and down the valley, where everyone's business was handed about until it was worn smooth by many fingers. Levi and I smiled at the news because it meant that we could talk about money with Papa alone. It was going to be hard enough to bring up our needs without having others sitting in on the conversation of it.

As we came along the road opposite the homeplace, I noticed that there was not the usual feather of smoke at the chimney. I wasn't alarmed for the day had turned off warm, and I imagined Papa would be satisfied with a cold dinner. Leftover biscuits and apple butter maybe. When we walked down the trail to the swinging bridge, the two hound dogs Papa kept about the place raced from under the porch to meet us.

They wouldn't hazard the bridge but barked and growled as they splashed through the creek. They wanted nothing but to leap and lick all over me and sniff and nibble at Levi 'til we were both tickled to laughter. Their names were Corn and Pone, so that Papa could yell at them to his heart's content, all the while sounding like he was calling them in to eat.

So we crossed the bridge laughing, my feet and legs springing to the rhythm of the old ropes and planks from memory. The bridge a kind of dance that I knew from childhood, while Levi stuttered and stumbled as he always did. Which gave us more laughter still.

As we started up from the creek toward the house, I took Levi's arm, for somehow, the sharpness in the air, the sunlight glittering off the rushing creek, the new grass in the yard . . . all said again that we were who we were, that life would not be brooked nor bound. That there was possibility in each new turning.

Just at the last corner in the path before it rose to the porch, I saw the first dark sign. At the chopping block beside the house, where Papa and the boys busted up sections of logs into firewood, the ax and go-devil were thrown carelessly down. Splits of wood were left where they'd fallen.

At that moment, my eyes went wide and the breath caught harsh in my throat.

In the seventy something years of his life—summer, winter, spring, fall—Papa had never once left tools on the ground. Never once left an ax or even a knife where the weather could get to it.

"Lee," I said to the man beside me. I couldn't quite gasp out both syllables. "Lee, run to the barn and see if . . . if he's there . . ."

He knew, my Levi knew. He glanced at my face and at the chopping block and took off without waiting to ask.

My chest was tight. I tried to grab at my breath as I climbed up the last pitch of the path, but it was gone from me. The front door off the porch was closed, seldom used, and never locked. It was nothing for my numb arms and feverish hands to shove open. I called out as I went in, called out though somehow, I knew. My stomach knew.

He'd made it in the back door and almost to his rocking chair by the hearth.

He was sprawled on the ancient, scarred oak floor, one leg drug out behind him and one hand flung forward against the rocker of his chair. Reaching . . . his fingers curled in agony.

And his grizzled face, his neck, his lovely old hands were cold . . . colder than anything God ever intended.

I screamed out then, to call him back. Through all the long folds and skeins of time I called to that man who'd made me, the man who'd named and taught me. The one man who'd cherished me before any other.

It was not possible that he should be gone.

For the world could not be so bereft.

PART FOUR

SUMMER 1931

52

WHAT MATTERS AND WHAT DOESN'T . . . in the binding of two lives together?

There was so much to feel on the day we found Papa and so much to be done. Levi and I carried the body, stiff and cold, to the bed he'd shared with Mama. I sat with Papa while Levi ran down to Worley's Store to start the news in its various rounds. In less than an hour, neighbors had gathered, men and women alike. The men stayed mostly out in the yard with Levi, while the women came inside.

Various young boys were sent out on the run to bring my brothers. Jake Worley was to call down to Hot Springs and get the message out, so that the youngest two could start the sad journey home.

The women undressed Papa while I sat and watched, unable to move. They massaged his frozen limbs with hot rags and slowly, slowly, rearranged his legs and arms to something more normal. When it came to his face and head, I stood and claimed my place. I would shave him, I told the women, and I would wash his hair. It was what was expected of me, his daughter, and it was what I expected of myself.

And so we worked, we women, quietly and with slow patience, to refresh and anoint his body. When we were done, we placed two silver coins on his eyelids to hold them closed over the lifeless, gray orbs. We tied a spare piece of ribbon from Mama's sewing basket under his jaw over the top of his head to hold his mouth closed until his jaw set. My fingers can yet recall the lineaments of Papa's face from what we did that day.

When first one and then another of us was overcome with grief, she would go out to the front porch to the rocking chairs set there for that purpose. And rocking, she would wail. Weep. Cry out. For these were Papa's cousins, nieces, sisters. His neighbor women through every season.

The men had retreated farther from the house, afraid of us women and the harsh, stinging emotions that came with death. When the first of my brothers arrived, having run to Papa's place from where he was plowing in his own fields, he came inside long enough to take one long look at Papa's wasted form, naked except for a towel thrown over his waist, and returned to the yard, where he did what we have always done. He recruited several of the best carpenters to go out with him to the barn, there to select some of the finest planks laid up in the rafters and begin to cut and fit a casket.

Things happened so very slowly and quickly after that. We found Papa's body on a Tuesday afternoon and figured he'd lain dead in the floor since at least the night before. We didn't embalm upcountry in those days, so it meant that we'd hold some sort of service on Wednesday morning and carry him up to Crooked Ridge that afternoon. Slow and fast, as I said.

There had to be a doctor, for the county's certification of death, and there had to be a preacher to speak some words. Since Levi's car was already parked at Worley's, we sent him to Marshall to notify the doctor, a man improbably named Duck, as in Dr. Duck, who made his way across the river and up to the Rock House on horseback that evening, Tuesday evening, so that he could agree that Papa was dead of natural causes. His language was different from ours—*cerebral thrombosis* as the result of *cerebral arterio-sclerosis*—but the meaning was the same however you named it. One side of Papa's sweet face looked stiff and frozen while the other relaxed more normally into what might have been sleep. I held my lips to both sides of his face, meaning to cherish and remember it all.

Papa had not been a church man, accompanying Mama to services only at Easter and Christmas, and only after some arm-twisting on her part. I recall once that a young preacher made his way up the valley to the farm, intending to bring the fear of Jesus to Mrs. Salter's husband and so drag him into church. Papa did not even come to the house but rather met him in the barn lot for this theological arm wrestling. The preacher, young and earnest, had asked Papa where he expected to spend eternity, and Papa asked him how many growing seasons was eternity? The preacher came up with a "hundred million thousand" or some such ridiculous number, and Papa grinned at him. "Where will *you* be all that time?" Papa asked. "Why, in heaven with the saints," cried the preacher. "Then I believe I'll try the other way," Papa said, "for I've had enough of you."

So, you see, we had a problem. We meant to have a short service at home, on the porch and in the yard, but what preacher could we call on, who wouldn't start in on heaven and hell, even on a pretty April morning? But then we women solved the problem. We would ask our own Tony, one of my middle brothers, to lead the service. He was no real preacher, meaning he hadn't taken the correspondence course and he didn't brag about being called out of the fields by God. But he was easily the sweetest man we any of us knew, and he thought and felt with his Bible in mind. He and his wife were so nice that she barely spoke above a whisper, and he never spoke without a smile.

Will and I talked to him that night on the porch, Will being the oldest and I being the daughter, and after a few minutes he agreed. He'd do it for Papa. "Do you need to prepare?" I asked him, as we three sat in the near dark. "Work up a scripture or something?" I couldn't see his quiet smile, but I could imagine it. "Why no, Josie, I don't. It feels like I've been expecting this ever since Mama died. I even spoke with Papa about it back in the winter, and he comforted me rather than the other way around."

So we had the doctor's certificate and we had a preacher who was very unlike a preacher. The box was finished and ready for the next morning. All the brothers would go up to Crooked Ridge at dawn and together break open the ground, pick and shovel, tearing into the ground beside Mama's grave. Levi volunteered to go with them, and they agreed that one more hand with a shovel would be welcome.

After a supper served up in the yard from all the pots and pans and bowls brought by neighbors, we women laid out Papa's body in the front room of the house and let folks come in a half dozen or so at time to sit with him. As they came and went, I soon grew hoarse from answering the same questions over and over, from receiving the same blessings and hearing the same platitudes, while saying thank you over and over again. I finally slipped outside and walked with Levi up into the orchard. He spread out his denim jacket so I could sit down dry in the tall tufts of grass, and then dropped down beside me despite the damp.

We sat quietly for a while, just being together, gazing upward as the platoons of stars began to emerge in the darkening sky.

We'd barely spoken since we'd found Papa's body that morning, in part because we hadn't been alone together, and the entire day had flown by us in a rush. It felt then as if we were silently rediscovering each other, remembering who we were after having been tossed in the whirlwind all the long day.

We were both leaning back on our hands so we could watch as the night came on from over the ridge behind us. After a bit,

Levi reached over and placed his rough palm over mine, his hand warm and reassuring. "I can't tell you how sorry I am," he said quietly. "I know full well how much you treasured your Papa. And to be the one to find him . . ."

"It was better that way," I said and meant it. "Truly it was. Better that we found him than someone else and we got the message over the telephone from thirty miles away. That would have broken my heart."

I could feel him nodding, and he squeezed my hand tight for a long moment. "It causes me to think that we should go see my own father," he said.

I twisted my face toward his. "What? All this time, and I just assumed he was dead . . . You never . . ."

"Talk about him? I know. Once he married that wife of his, and she turned out to be such a red devil, it was as if I parted ways with him. I never meant to. It just fell out that way, week to week and month to month. Every time I said now is the time to visit and rejoin with him, I let it slip away. But that's not what we've in front of us. It's your Papa . . . that we've lost. It's you I'm worried about."

"Promise me," I murmured. "Promise me that when this is all over, you'll take me up to Spring Creek to meet your father. Good Lord, Levi, I'm sorry. Here, I've been going on and . . ."

"Jo, listen to me. I just want . . ."

"Promise me that we'll go before you start with your *listen to me*. Levi . . ." I leaned over then, almost as if I was collapsing from the inside out. I was collapsing from the inside out, falling over so that my head was in his lap. "You promise me that . . ."

"Well, we'll go then. In a few weeks, maybe when the flowers are blooming in the woods . . . we'll make a trip up Spring Creek."

I nodded hard against his leg. "Yes, please . . . Your father is the only one who's left."

"How do you mean?"

"Of the four of them, our parents—mother and father for either of us—your Papa is the only one. The only one we have left to steer by. To tell us what for . . ."

"He's a poor man, Jo. He has no money, and he's got a witch for a wife."

I giggled, I confess it, especially since my head was in his lap. "What kind of a wife?"

"A demon witch that rides him like a broomstick."

"Is that what your stepmother does?"

"God yes. What I was trying to say is that she sucks up all the life and any of the money that might come along in my father's life."

I nodded against his leg again. Imagine how that felt . . . against his corduroy pants pulled tight over his thigh. There was nothing sexual about it, but oh my Lord, was it warm and comforting. I thought of Mama: his thighs was as taut as a bowstring.

"Your father," I murmured, "is the only one we've got left. We need to go save him from the witch."

He chuckled. I think that's the best word for it. Chuckled . . . quietly, and it struck me as how maybe I was the only one who'd ever heard him chuckle, quietly and in the dark.

Time passed as the stars and planets wheeled in the dark blue sky above. "What do you want me to do tomorrow?" Levi asked eventually. "Stand back and let you be?"

"God no," I said. The intensity in my stomach boiling up. "I want you to stand right by my side, all along."

"I don't have to stand in that place, Jo, and it might embarrass you . . ."

"Embarrass me how?"

"To have a bootlegger for a . . . a bootlegger to be courting you."

"You have never embarrassed me, Levi. Not for one, single second, here or in town. I need you to stay with me tomorrow."

"As if we were married?"

"As if we were more than married. Connected. Tied. Bound up."

"I can do that," he said after a bit. "I've got to go with your brothers early up to the cemetery to dig the grave. I promised them that. After, I can stay close." And then after a bit. "Where do you want me tonight? I can go down to Worley's and sleep in the car."

I shook my head, fiercely now against his leg. Scratching, almost bruising, my face. Not knowing the answer but not wanting him away from me either. "Let's just sit up with Papa," I said. "After a long while, nobody else will stay the watch. Michael and Bob will find their own rooms. After midnight, one or two in the morning, it might just be you and me till dawn." I paused, struggling for the right words. "It's the last I'll ever see of his face, and that memory will have to last me."

Levi leaned over then and wrapped his arms around me, as I lay with my head nestled in his lap. "It will last you," he said. "For as long as you live." And then. "I've got you safe and sound," he murmured to me, as if singing to a child. "The dark will never hurt you." Over and over, he sang to me, as the stars spun silently round above us.

Within us.

53

HERE ARE MY BROTHERS ALONG with their women, their names and ages as of that April day in 1931.

William or Will, age 37, married with children. Stolid. His wife, Margaret.

David or Dave, age 35, happily married with no offspring. Big and rough enough for the life given him. His wife, Claudia.

Alan, age 32, quick with a grin and a wink. A solid family man even so. One daughter and a pregnant wife. His wife, Carolyn.

Tony, age 30, seemingly the happiest marriage. Quiet smiles. Would pray over anything, once for a dead mule. His wife, Julia.

Just here is where I fit in the lineup, though I am no brother.

Michael or Mike, age 22. Still at home trying to farm and making liquor. Rather vacant otherwise. Favors a Briggs girl name of Lynn.

And Robert or Bob, aged 19, going on 30. Wished only to escape to the town, first chance. Mayhap taking his girl name of Patty or leaving her behind.

Six sons and six brothers. All hungry for land, excepting Mike and Bob. The first four, starving for an inheritance, for bottom land, and for stock.

TONY DID US PROUD IN the morning. Read to us and then spoke quietly about the many mansions above. Beyond even the mountain peaks. Told us about a famous reunion on the other side, between our Mama and Papa, her chiding him for being so slow to arrive. Slow to join her in that bright land.

The brothers, with Levi helping in the steepest places, carried the casket on their shoulders up to Crooked Ridge, with the rest of the family and the neighbors trailing behind. It is high and lonesome up there. You could hear the raven's croak. The air so thin that all of us gasped for breath.

Once there, beside the grave, Tony spoke of ashes and dust. Of joining a far larger family of bodies perfected. Light such that no human eye could regard. A blazing sunrise.

And that was all, no shouting or screaming. No recriminations or guilt. We sang "Amazing Grace," suddenly and spontaneously, following the lead of some slip of a girl, a distant cousin who broke into song.

I sat on a tombstone, one of the Ramseys, and watched while my brothers plus Levi shoveled the dirt back into the open maw of the grave. It was a brazen shock when the first clods struck the casket lid, but then easier and easier with each shovel full. Even sitting there, in the gap of the mountain, close by my father and mother's graves, I could again sense spring rising up though the ground and into the trees. Despite the gut-deep sense of loss, it felt to me as if the light were returning.

THAT AFTERNOON, AS WAS THE custom, the seven of us children met in the front room of Papa and Mama's house to read his will and speak together about patrimony.

In the Big Pine valley, as in other far-back communities in the mountains, it was not the custom for women to sit with men when they discussed what they called business. Papa had not held with that notion, however, and when he was alive, had insisted that I sit in on family decisions, overriding the vehement protests of several brothers. I won't say which brothers except that they were the most old-fashioned as well as the loudest.

So, on that day, it was us seven alone to read the will and say whatever else there was to say. I brought up my four sisters-in-law, since three were already mothers, and they all legally involved, but that was too much for William, who was hog-tied by tradition, and Dave, who sputtered and pounded on the arm of his chair. "No damn place for a woman . . . You're bad enough as it is." Meaning me. Tony explaining in his kind way, "you're only here because you got no one to represent you." Meaning Levi, because we weren't married.

So I gave up that fight, figuring that I couldn't bring city ways into my mountain family all in an afternoon. Or bring women's wisdom into this male proceeding. Except for my wisdom, such as it was.

The will was straightforward enough, except that there were some surprises. Some cards that Papa had held so close to his vest that even Will, the oldest son, didn't expect them. All told, there was almost a thousand acres of land that was equally distributed among my six brothers. One hundred sixty acres apiece except for Michael, give or take an acre or two as the land rose and fell. Those that were already farming and timbering, meaning those that were already married, received plots adjacent to or at least not far from where they already lived, as if the men and their families were stakes driven into the ground. Their choices made and their lives considered settled.

Michael got a smaller piece but it was the fifty acres around the Rock House, including the house itself. Which meant that he would not have to leave and have his own fragile understanding and pattern of life bursted open. I glanced at Tony when this was read out, as I'm sure both of us were wondering who would care for Michael. See that his clothes were washed and that his food was cooked. Bob, we knew, would sell his portion and hit the road, first chance he got.

As for cash, there was little, roughly $3,500 split seven ways. Meaning I was one of the seven. Whereas the land—which held the most value—had been divided by a factor of six, leaving me nothing, the cash was to be divided by a factor of seven, meaning that within a few weeks, William would write checks to all of us. I was tired and distracted by all that had happened and by all that was being said, but not so tired that I wasn't aware of having been cut out of the land. Was sensitive of the loss and ready to resent it.

Still, though, it was the custom. Men were first when it came to land. And in our family, if you left the confines of the Big Pine Valley, truly left, then you didn't inherit from what you'd abandoned.

Also, I wasn't so tired that as things moved along, the brothers beginning to argue about their parcels of bottom land versus steep, pasture versus forest, it also occurred to me that my $500 wouldn't give Levi and me what we needed to buy the Sky Club. Had he lived, Papa might have loaned us the money . . . maybe . . . but my slender inheritance wasn't enough. All our planning and all our preparation were for naught.

My face grew hot with that thought. I could feel tears of frustration beginning to form, but damned if I was going to cry in front of them. Give them the satisfaction of seeing a woman lose control of her emotions during a family meeting.

Will spoke my name, first softly and then more assertively to override the complaining and trading that had blazed up among the others. When I looked up, he stood, took a few steps across the room and handed me an envelope featuring my name written prominently in pencil by my father's hand. I took the envelope from Will but didn't, at first, open it. I expected it was a note or letter of some kind, and I knew I couldn't read it without tears.

But when Will sat back down, he nodded at me, almost formally, so I slit open the envelope with my fingernail and unfolded the sheets within. At first, I couldn't make sense of it because it was too familiar and didn't belong there in the front room of the Rock House. The document was printed on the embossed letterhead of the Imperial Life Insurance Company, where I worked, similar in likeness and language to documents I handled every day.

Then the loops and lines inside my head came together and I remembered what Pink Starnes had told me. It was Papa's life insurance policy. On the line left blank for the beneficiary, my name—Josephine Salter—was printed in neat block letters that I knew to be Pink's own careful penmanship. Papa had signed it. Only he would pen the Salter "S" that way, with a wide, sweeping tail. The amount to be paid out upon the death of the insured was $5,000.

I folded up the policy and carefully reinserted it into the envelope. My hands were shaking.

"What was that?" Alan asked lightly, easily, though he was quick enough to see that the envelope was important.

"Something for me," I said. "Equal portion to the land." I figured that was enough for them to know. Enough for now at least. My heart was thudding, I admit, for it was plain to me that he had loved me as he loved them, even though I was a woman and had left the valley.

It was a strangely private moment too because they were all arguing back and forth about land versus money. Too much land and not enough money. "$500 each . . ." got said, got shouted and growled, along with "goddamn it" and "what are we going to do?"

It struck me that the four older brothers were expecting this, expecting Papa to pass and leave them something . . . money, not land. Why hadn't I seen this coming? Why didn't I see him slipping? And what had I expected anyway . . . that he should live forever just because I needed him to.

"Wait!" I cried. "Just wait a minute."

They simmered down a bit. Not quiet but bearable.

"Why is land so bad?"

"It's not worth anything," brother Dave growled. "With this panic and depression we got goin', it ain't worth the paper the deed is wrote on. All it's good for is to work, and even then, we can't grow nothing to sell."

"Don't take it the wrong way, Josie . . ." This was Tony. "The money matters. Five hundred dollars in this day and time is valuable. Hold us together for a few years more, but then what? You can't sell corn nor eggs except for pennies. We can breed cattle and hogs, and sell some of the meat down at Barnard, but you come home with barely a pound of coffee and a sack of salt."

"We need money, cash money, Josie." This was Alan. "You don't understand. We love the land. Well, at least some of us do. And we can eat what we grow and what we butcher, but good Lord, we were hoping for cash. Soon we'll have to leave and go north. Find factory work."

"Is there no cash crop?"

"Nothing. We can plant burley in the creek bottoms, but the steep land's not fit for it. And times are so desperate that tobacco is the only thing that'll sell."

"What if we found a way for you to sell your corn?"

"We can grow goddamn corn by the acre. Up to ridgeline and back again on any piece of land that's not standing on its head." One of them said this, I'm not sure which.

"But an ear of corn's not worth a penny. Ten cents a bushel shelled. What the hell you mean, Josie, sell our corn?" This was Will, the solid one. Even he had some heat in his old voice.

"Levi and I can sell your corn," I said simply.

"Hell no, you can't." Dave, certain of himself as always. "Not here and not there."

"I need Levi to help explain this," I said. "Let him come in."

"Are you married to him?" Alan. "Legal, I mean. Courthouse legal. If so, bring him on, as he can . . ."

"He can what!"

"He can do business," Will said. "No offense, Josie, but you are a girl . . . woman. And if you was married to Levi, then we could vote to have him in here. Though there ain't a man jack of us believes that either one of you can sell worthless corn."

"No, we are not married. Not by the courthouse anyway, Mr. Alan Salter. But I need him to help me explain."

"How to turn mountain acres into cash money . . .?" Will said, disbelieving.

I nodded. "That's exactly what I'm talking about. Cash to fold up in the bib of your overalls."

The quiet brother . . . Tony. "Let him come as far as the window. Throw open the shutters there, Dave, and let a little air in. Mr. Arrowood can come up on the porch and stand by the window."

"Is that regularly done, Tony?" asked Will. "Anybody? Can an outsider parlay through the window and not break with the . . . rules?"

"He's an advisor, Will, that's all." Alan was grinning as he said it, enjoying the show. "Let him come as far as the window, and Dave here won't have to resort to violence."

Dave was clenching and unclenching his huge fists, but he didn't offer a rebuttal.

"Very well," Will decreed. "Dave will open the window, and Josie can go out on the porch and hallo for Levi. He can come up as far as that so we can consider this crazy plan."

"But he can't lean in the window, can he?" Alan again, enjoying himself.

"Hell no," muttered Dave. "Too much. That's too damn much."

We all nodded except for Michael, who didn't care. By the window but not in the window.

Which was how it all came to pass. I summoned Levi from the yard, where he'd been skipping rocks at the creek. He stood stiffly on the porch at the open window, but not leaning in through the window, God forbid. I stood inside the window, so I could pass a stray word back and forth, translate as it were, while we negotiated.

I began. "Levi and I can sell your corn by the quart. Not by the bushel. We will pay you five dollars per quart jar of corn liquor . . ."

"As long as it's made by Mike over there." Levi interrupted me. "He's the craftsman."

"What did he say?" Will asked. Will was a little hard of hearing.

"He said that Michael has to still the liquor. Only Michael."

We all regarded Michael.

"That boy can't write his name in the dirt with a stick," Alan offered. "Why him?"

"He has the gift," Levi said, leaning perilously close to the window. "Doesn't matter if he can write his name. In a few years, he'll be making the best liquor in the mountains."

"He has a gift," I repeated.

"For unto everyone that hath shall be given, and he shall have abundance," said Tony.

"What the hell does that mean?" Dave asked.

"Means that our brother Michael has been given a special talent. Book of Matthew, chapter 25."

We all paused to consider. Seems we were biblical.

"That's right," Levi said after a moment's reflection. He'll need help though. You, Bobby, or one of the others. He can't sit by the kettle twenty-four hours of the day. The rest of you just need to grow it. Corn by the acre, by the hundreds of acres. All you can grow. Could even run two stills."

Most were nodding, even Bobby, the youngest.

"Where you gonna put up a distillery like that?" Will asked. "We got a thing called a sheriff down here in Madison County. Most of us voted for him, but that don't mean he won't come sniffing."

Another long pause, and it seemed to me everything was teetering, about to collapse due to the law. The damn law.

Until Alan cleared his throat. "Gentleman . . . you too, Josie . . . I happen to have a cave on my land. Up high but with a bold spring nearby. Only person who's ever seen the inside of it is me and Carolyn."

"What was you doing inside of it?" One of the brothers.

"We were exploring," Alan said, solemn as a judge.

"I'll bet you was. Exploring that cave between her . . ."

"Excuse me!"

"Sorry, Josie. Forgot you was here."

"If the cave is big enough, secret enough, and there's fresh water by, we can cook liquor in there for years." This from my Levi, bringing us back to the point.

"Then it's settled. Michael can make the liquor, with one or another as his helper. We'll use Alan's cave for the distillery. The rest of you can sell your corn crop at five dollars on the quart."

"My land is not good for corn. At least not more than my cattle and my family can consume in a year. Where do I fit in the scheme?" This was the quietest voice of all . . . Tony.

"It's not a scheme," I offered. "It's a business. But as for . . ."

"Apples," my Levi said through the window. "You told me last night, Tony, that you might have the best orchard in Big Pine. You grow any Jonathans up in that orchard?"

Tony nodded slowly and then smiled. "I have twenty Jonathan trees at least. Do Jonathans make good cider? Is that what you're saying?"

"Not cider but brandy. Jonathans do just fine. Ever hear of an apple name of Parmar or Parmer? From Virginia . . ."

Tony shook his head. "No, but we can graft them in if we can get the stock."

"We can sell the brandy for more than the corn," Levi offered. "Your part is to grow the best brandy apples in the county."

Tony nodded. "I believe that too is in the Bible," he said.

"Surely not that apple in the garden of Eden," I cried out. "Although, for brandy making . . ."

"No, no." Tony was shaking his head and smiling. "Song of Solomon, Jo. Those apples are the ones we want."

Thus, it was born on that very day, the day of Papa's funeral. Bob was to help with transportation, which would get him into town from time to time. Michael was to cook the liquor with helping hands. Each and all were to reap the earth's bounty, namely in the form of certain varieties of corn and apples.

Each and every brother to have his part . . . in the business that became known far and wide as Salter Brothers Produce. But then as now, and every day in between, that public name was a front for what we were truly about.

What brother Tony called bringing the spirit to the people.

54

THE SECOND MEETING WITH THE group of "secret" investors who owned the Sky Club was a lot faster and a lot friendlier than the first. We sat at the same table downstairs in the family room. This time only Boxer and Campbell were there, which surprised me. Where was Craig Scott?

Turns out that it didn't matter. When Boxer produced the paperwork, the good doctor had already signed the bill of sale and the deed, and none of us were going to challenge the signature. Levi and I handed over an Imperial Life Insurance envelope with exactly $20,000 in cash in it, and yes, I had counted it myself with shaking hands . . . three times. The new paperwork had both our names on it: Levi Edgar Arrowood and Josephine Robbins Salter. Just like that, with the single word "and" between Arrowood and Josephine. Levi's name was first, but I didn't care. At least with my life insurance money and the loan I'd negotiated with Pink Starnes, I felt like our investment was close to equal.

AFTER FIFTEEN MINUTES OF MULTIPLE copies, involving the signatures of all four of us—Boxer, Campbell, Arrowood, Salter—we were done, according to attorney Boxer. I asked that he count the money and give us a signed receipt for it. Which he did, with a nod and wink.

Sitting right there at the table, Campbell demanded that

Boxer count out Campbell's $9,000 from the envelope, which he immediately secreted away in a leather wallet and stored it securely in an inside coat pocket. With that, Campbell was up and gone, with barely a nod and nothing like a "thank you" or "nice doing business with you" for Levi and me.

"What's his problem?" Levi asked Boxer, who shrugged. "Other than being an asshole? . . . Sorry, Miss Salter. His problem is he isn't rich anymore. He's been like that ever since the crash. Lost the house, lost the wife, his children don't know him. Doesn't trust anybody now."

But I had a different question, a math question. "How come he walked away with $9,000, Boxer? What's your share?" The second the words were out of my mouth, I realized it was none of my business.

Again, he just shrugged. "I'm not a partner. I get my ten percent for being the face of this happy, little group. Now, I'll deliver nine thousand dollars to the good doctor, and then I'll get the deed registered in your names at the courthouse without anybody being the wiser. I'll even drop off a copy of the new deed for the two of you next week."

"We owe you anything?"

"Nah." He handed me a copy of the executed Bill of Sale, placed the rest of the paperwork in his brief case and stood up. "I like you two. Glad to do it, plus it keeps everything out of the public eye, if you know what I mean."

"Thanks, Joe," Levi said.

Boxer ratcheted his fedora firmly onto his head, nodded, and winked again. "If you ever need a lawyer . . ." He left the sentence unfinished and slipped out the door.

"You trust him?" Levi asked.

"Oddly enough, I do." And I did, far more than Sissy's Campbell.

◇◇◇

NOW . . . IMAGINE THIS. WE SECRETLY had over $2,000 left in the bank, which is to say, upstairs in the safe. Only now, that money, the business account, as I called it, was in one shoe box. Our shoe box, and yes, I'd written the words "Sky Club, Business" on the lid of the box in black ink. A week later, we added the deed to the Sky Club to our little hoard, still amazed that the two of us owned it outright.

We'd given up trying to keep his cash separate from my cash at that point. In the spring of 1931, that kind of money was unheard of, so we told no one, and barely even spoke of it ourselves. Since I kept the books for the Club, I was aware of when, where, and how cash flowed into the shoe box and flowed out again, and as you can imagine, I was absolutely determined that what I'd watched happen at Central Bank & Trust on Pack Square would never happen at the Sky Club on Beaucatcher Mountain.

The only money rub we really had between the two of us—Levi and me—was that I'd told him in no uncertain terms that while I planned to put most of my weekly salary from Imperial Life into the Business Box, I intended to keep back $50 for myself. That didn't bother him a bit. In fact, he encouraged me to keep more. But then I told him that out of the $50, I intended to keep paying my own rent for my own room, down the hall from his. At this, he mostly just shook his head and muttered something under his breath to the dog, something to do with me and *stubborn*.

I tried to explain to him that I was an independent woman, I liked being an independent woman, and I meant to continue being an independent woman. We were having supper one night when the club was closed, sitting over the remains of a fried chicken Pansy had left for us in the fridge. He just stared at me quizzically. I even launched again into the story about how my mother, on her dying bed, had begged me to make a different kind of life, a life she couldn't even begin to imagine. Which for me, meant . . .

"Jo Belle," he interrupted me. "Do you think she could have imagined this?" He waved his arm to indicate the dance floor, the bar, the piano. "Could she have imagined any of this? The Sky Club for God's sake?"

"No." I had to laugh at him. "No, not this, not at all . . . On the other hand, I think she could have imagined you." I grinned at him, sitting there in his work shirt, his sandy hair tousled. "She once told that if you had to sneak around, that the best place to do it was in a church."

"What?"

"In a church, you know, in between the pews, with . . ."

"You're making that up! I refuse to . . ."

"Actually, I think she said it to me in a dream, but still, it makes sense." I waved my fork at him.

"It makes absolutely no sense. On the floor, Jo? This is your mother we're talking . . ."

"You use your clothes for padding. That's what she advised. Acted like she knew what she was talking about."

"So what you're telling me, Jo Salter, is that you want to get me into some church at night and take advantage of me between the damn pews. All that and you still insist on paying me rent."

"That's right." Then a delicious thought occurred to me. "Maybe what I'm really paying you for is your sexual favors . . ."

I believe he was blushing. Which I always considered an accomplishment. "Free," he gasped. "My favors, as you call them, are . . ."

"I don't think it has to be night, Levi."

"What?"

"The church. You said I wanted to get you in amongst the

pews at night. Aren't churches empty during the day?" His lips, when I leaned over the table to kiss him, were greasy from the chicken. Which is a fine thing.

WE NEVER DID AGREE ABOUT the rent I paid, especially after we bought the club, but what we did agree on, after I suggested it, was that we needed a gun. We'd been robbed once, you will recall, and stood around battling the robbers with nothing more than a Louisville Slugger.

As a general rule, I didn't feel much one way or another about guns, but the number of scars on Levi's body—mostly where he'd been cut or beaten but once where he'd been shot—made me tremble. And by that summer—the summer of '31—people were getting desperate. For money, food, shelter, but especially for money. When we were down on Big Pine for what had turned into Papa's funeral, his varmint gun, an old .410 shotgun, was hanging handy on its pegs over the back door, and that had got me to thinking.

So two weeks after we bought the Sky Club, Levi met me in front of Imperial Life after work, and we turned the corner and walked together down Lexington Avenue. We were headed for a shop owned by Mitch Starnes, a cousin of some sort to Pink. Mitch was a famous banjo picker who earned his daily wage repairing pistols and rifles. Pink had said that there were always a few unclaimed weapons behind Mitch's counter that he'd be glad to part with, and the back closet was full of ammunition that he'd collected over the years.

Turns out that Mitch and Levi knew each other from various dealings, some involving alcohol but mostly just life on the edge of town, for Lexington Avenue was the border, the place where country people were most comfortable. Mitch sold Levi a .45 caliber Colt "government" pistol made since the war, plus a box of

.45 shells. Best pistol in his place according to Mitch. A retired judge had dropped it off for repairs to the trigger mechanism and never returned for it. We put the pistol and shells in a brown paper sack and walked on down to the Kings' Store, the large, rambling structure made up of at least a dozen different rooms and as many more stalls, where farmers come in from the country bought, sold, and traded produce, livestock, and everything else.

Levi wanted to talk to Cal King, the owner, about whether he would buy or trade our whiskey if we brought it to him. Whether there was a way to use Lexington to help transfer the goods, as we liked to call them, into town. As we strolled down the street, enjoying the sound of voices like our own, the voices of his childhood and mine, men sidled up to Levi twice and, while I politely looked the other way, asked him for a loan. One asked for two hundred dollars to buy twenty acres of good farmland while it was so durn cheap, the other for fifty dollars so he could get married to his sweetheart and have some sort of start with her.

He turned both away, quietly, suggesting they ask Mr. King. Both said they'd already tried the Kings and got shown the goddamn door. It struck me suddenly that since the crash, this was the same thing that always happened to Pink Starnes when he was on the Avenue, the constant give and take about money, as if he was a walking bank but a bank with a human face and a forgiving smile.

55

I STOOD OUTSIDE THE FRONT DOOR of the store while Levi went inside. He claimed some distant relation to the Kings through his mother, and so would approach as kinfolk as well as businessman. While I stood there, quietly enjoying the spring sunshine and listening to a young woman across the street strum a guitar, yet another man came sidling up to me and offered me an apple—a Pippen, or so he said, grown up in Anderson Cove, where Papa was born. I was cradling the heavy paper poke in my arms—I didn't want the pistol to break through and fall out on the sidewalk—and didn't have a spare hand for the apple. So I nodded and smiled. "I have to hold on to the baby I've got in this sack," I said.

He grinned and nodded his head abruptly, almost as if he had a tremor. "My name is Sole Buckner," he said quietly. "I was awful sorry to hear about your Daddy. Lewis was a fine man and a good Christian."

"Probably a better man than he was a Christian. Didn't care for them preachers always lurkin' about." I could feel myself slipping back into the fine, old English of home. Slipping easily, happily. "Did you know him well?"

"His daddy was a brother to my grandma," Sole allowed. Which was how we all explained relations in the country.

"Up in Anderson Cove?"

"Yep, yep. That's just right." Another spasmodic nod of the

head. "Listen, Mrs. Arrowood, I was a'wonderin if you would consider a little loan. I got a chance to purchase me a pure Plott hound pup for only a hundred dollars. It's a wonderment for a bear dog, and his Mama was in on a dozen kills confirmed."

It was the second or third time that day I'd been called Mrs. Arrowood, so that didn't so much give me pause as did the nature of his request. "Well, Sole, just how in hell do you aim to pay me back? If you buy this pup, you ain't never gonna sell it cause you'll soon come to love it, and some day, a bear is going to bury it for you under a rock." I could sense Levi walk up behind me to stand at my shoulder. "When I think on it Sole," I added, "I believe your hound pup is a better investment for you than for me."

That brought him up short. He swallowed audibly and jerked his head. "Well, Mrs. Arrowood, I guess I thought the purchase of a dog was such a sacred act that it carried its own requirement. It's own . . ."

"Rationale?" Levi suggested.

Another jerk of the head, in agreement. "That's right, Mr. Arrowood, that's right. Its own . . ."

"Rationale."

"Yessir. And I wonder if you could reason with Mrs. Arrowood fer me. She has done turned me down fer a loan of just a hundred dollars for the finest Plott puppy you'd ever see. It's tied to a tree right down at the end of the street if you'd care to see it. I believe the owner, that son-of-a-bitch, might take ninety dollars if it was cash."

"Not today, brother," Levi said and reached out to grasp Sole Buckner's shoulder. "I grant you that a dog is a mighty thing, more faithful than . . . well, just about anything, but Mrs. Arrowood here watches over the money, and if she turned you down, I can't say different."

Sole walked off at that point, his head hung low in dramatic disappointment.

"So, it's Mrs. Arrowood now, is it?" Levi was smirking. "Did we get married while I was inside?"

I shook my head. "Apparently. At least here on the Avenue, folks are trying out the sound of it . . . And by the way, you were going to say that a good dog was more faithful than a woman, weren't you?"

"I considered it," he admitted. And took the heavy sack out of my arms. "But then I reconsidered." He nodded with his head on down the street, north, toward the edge of town. "Cal King says we want to talk to a fella name of Rogers . . . first name Norman. Big produce stand a block down on the other side."

As we strolled on down the Avenue, filled at six o'clock on a Tuesday evening with wagons and trucks, plus the occasional car—people everywhere, talking, laughing, swapping this and that—including lies. I asked Levi exactly what it was he was looking for.

"I'm looking for a way station," he murmured, "for the liquor. Rather than drive the roadster straight into town and right on up the mountain, leading any stray deputies or curious police straight to the Club, I'd rather have a place to drop the load and let it cool off for a while. I've been . . . antsy ever since the night we got raided. I'd rather not . . ."

Just at that moment, a woman round about our age stepped out of a bar halfway down the block and reached out toward us. Her lipstick was drawn broadly over the lower half of her face, as if a child had gotten creative with a crayon, and her blouse was unbuttoned far enough down in front so it must always hang off one shoulder or the other. No bra strap to be seen.

"Why, Levi Arrowood, as I live and breathe. Where the hell you been, honey? I still get the hots thinkin' about that night over at the Langren Hotel."

"I've been busy," he said. "Ah . . . Betsy."

"It's Nancy, you . . ."

"Listen honey," I said. "He's been busy with me. Get your ass back in that bar and forget about Langren's Hotel."

She stared at me for a long moment, trying to sort out if she knew me. "Why, shitfire," she said and stuck her tongue out. At me. As God is my witness, she stuck her tongue out, like we were both eight years old. "Didn't mean nothin' by it," she muttered. "Just bein' friendly." She tried to spin on her heel and almost fell over, but then tottered safely back through the swinging doors into the bar.

"I will be damned. Levi Arrowood, did you see that tongue? It was gray, maybe even black."

"Can't say as I noticed . . ."

"If you let that woman's tongue anywhere near you in or out of Langren's Hotel, I'm . . . I'm going to . . ."

"To what?"

"Scrub you all over with lye soap."

He was grinning. Apparently, I was a little louder than I realized. "From what little I recall of that encounter," he said evenly, "her tongue had nothing to do with it."

"Well, thank God for small favors. Just how long ago was that . . . encounter . . . anyway?"

"Three years at least. Growing hazy even now."

"You sure? Levi, if you're lying to me . . ."

We had an audience. "Give him hell, Mrs. Arrowood. Old Levi's slicker than you know what." . . . "Give it up, Levi, she done found you out!"

"I am not Mrs. Arrowood," I announced to the small crowd. "And after seeing one of his former hussies, I'm not sure I want to be!" And with that I stomped off down the sidewalk, half mad but mostly trying not to laugh.

"Hey." A few minutes later. "Hey, Jo!" It was Levi, behind me. And when I turned around to stare him down, he motioned me back with his hand. "Come on, Jo Belle, this is where we're going."

I had stomped right on by Rogers Produce Stand and had to backtrack.

I tried to keep up some spark of anger at Levi but the closer I got to him, standing there, holding our paper poke under one arm and the ancient screen door of Rogers Produce for me with the other hand, I had to smile at him. Still, though, I was shaking my head.

"Did you see that poor woman?" I whispered as I slipped past him.

"Her name was Betsy when I knew her," he whispered back.

The front of Rogers was a large open area covered with a shed roof and screened in on three sides to keep the flies and such off the fruit and vegetables. The back wall was solid, hammered together out of mismatched boards, with a door propped open in the middle and several windows that let outdoor light into the back room.

We found Rogers himself inside that back room, sorting early season corn, using a butcher knife to cut the wormy ends off of ears that looked suspicious.

Norm Rogers was a big, square, happy man. Tall, thick body; square, blunt-fingered hands. A mostly square head with a buzzed-off haircut and big, smiling lips. Introductions went around . . . Rogers, Arrowood, Salter . . . and he allowed that he knew my Papa but hadn't heard about his death. Knew Will, my oldest brother.

We all three had to talk weather and season and kinfolks near and far as prelude to the business end of things, but eventually Norm, for he insisted we call him Norm, turned the conversation.

"What can I do ye for?" is what he said.

"Well, Norm," Levi began, "we're looking for a friend down

here on the Avenue who has some handy storage area. We're engaged in a little bit of business that involves hauling corn and apples in from Spring Creek and Big Pine and need a place to drop off those loads kind of secret like. We would pay rent on such a place if we could find it."

Norm chuckled. "You mean in the middle of the night, nice and quick, when them shurfs ain't around." That's how he said it . . . *shurfs*.

"That's right. And then we'll come round now and again to pick up portions of the produce, the corn and apples, and distribute it ourselves. You wouldn't have to be involved in that part at all."

"Reckon the apples and corn you're speakin' about don't come by the peck or the bushel, do they?"

"More by the quart or the gallon," I offered, with a smile for the big man.

"Air you both involved in this haulin' business you're talkin' about, Miss Salter?"

Levi nodded. "Full partners, except that Jo here doesn't do any driving."

"Well," Norm said, "I can't recommend you do much either, friend Levi. I recognized you the minute you came in, even if the light back here ain't the best. And if I recognize your mug, then you can bet them shurfs know you on sight." Oddly enough, that had never occurred to me before.

"We'll work that out, Norm," Levi said. "You won't even have to worry about that. What we're looking for is a nice, big warehouse place, with a back door that locks."

"Inconspicuous like?" Norm asked. And when we both nodded, he said, "Well then, let's take a look. Back of this place used to be a livery stable, and I think I might have just what you need."

56

"NO. I SAY NO."

"Yes!"

"Hell no!"

We were lying in bed together at first light, my room, not his. As there was enough pearly glimmer through the window to see by, I threw the covers back and leaned on his shoulder to keep him from sitting up.

"What caused this?" I asked, touching a jagged scar on his shoulder.

"Knife. Back alley in Marshall."

"This?" Long thin scar on the front of his hip, perilously close to his groin.

"Another knife. Side of the road. Jupiter, up on the county line."

"And this?" A deep puckered scar on the inside of his left thigh, six inches above his knee.

"Oh that. Fell out of a cherry tree and landed on a tobacco stick when I was a kid."

"Never mind that one then. How about this?" The purple furrow along the outside of his upper arm. Right arm.

He winced. "Pistol. Back of a pool hall where I was making a delivery in Canton."

"I already know about this one." Pointing to a new scar on the side of his jaw. "Police lieutenant." Mocking with my voice the nonchalant way he described the violence of his life. "Parking lot of the Sky Club while we were being raided." Then in my normal tone: "I rest my case."

"What the hell do you mean, rest your case? I'm not teaching you to drive."

"Yes, you are, Levi. You have to. Everybody in three, no four, counties, knows who you are. Sheriff Bailey essentially told us that night at the country club. Like Norm Rogers said, them shurfs know you on sight, along with every other hijacker, robber, and drunk along the road. If you're there, then there's booze or money or both."

"Well, then, Miss Logic 1931, why in God's name do you think I would let you take my place? Just what kind of man do you think I am! Why would I let the woman I love get shot or stabbed? That's . . ."

"Did you say love?"

"I did not," he grunted. "Like. The woman I like."

"I'm not going to get shot or stabbed, Levi, you moron, because they don't know me. I'm just some silly girl driving a car down the River Road. The last time we went up home, I saw one."

"A woman driving a car . . . in Madison County?"

"Well, actually it was a truck. But it was definitely a woman behind the wheel . . . Listen, Levi, as long as you are you, anybody and everybody who sees you running the roads knows what you're doing. You've either got a trunk full of liquor or a wallet full of cash or both. I, on the other hand, am invisible. I'm nobody. People will just wave, and I'll drive right on."

"Maybe, but I'm still not going to do it."

I stood up. "Why the hell not?"

"Because I like your body just the way it is. No wounds and no scars." He gestured toward me, where I stood naked as springtime in front of him. "I'd shoot *myself* if something happened to you!" he added.

"Nothing is going to happen to me. All I'm going to do is make the run from the Rock House on Big Pine to the back of Rogers Produce. All you have to do is teach me to drive."

"What if I refuse?"

I picked his thick, wool robe up off the floor and slung it across my shoulders. "If you refuse, you can sleep in your own damn room till hell freezes over . . ." I was all but screeching.

I slammed the door and stomped off down the hall, forgetting for the moment that all my clothes were in the room that I'd just left. But be damned if I was going back for them.

So that was the rational and reasonable conversation that led to the driving lessons. Levi held out for a week before he gave in, and hell did not freeze over, so far as I know.

We began one mid-morning in the parking lot at the club: Levi and me in the roadster, Mack and Pansy watching nervously from the side porch.

I'd been watching Levi drive for months, even asking questions from time to time about the clutch and the brake, the gear shift on the steering column, and how was it to turn the wheel. That morning, he took me for a ride around the parking lot one more time, describing carefully what he was doing with his hands and feet. I have to say, he was as smooth as silk. He even put the Plymouth in reverse and backed it into its normal spot just by the back door.

Then we switched places, and for the first time in my twenty-eight years, I climbed into the driver's seat meaning business. I pumped the gas pedal, cranked the ignition switch, and the engine roared. I did everything just right, I swear, just like he said, and the crazy thing jumped forward six feet and died. Somewhere behind me, I could hear Mack laughing and Pansy screaming.

We tried again. And again. Finally, we began to make slow, tentative circles around the parking lot. In my defense, I have to report that there were obstacles in the lot. Three or four metal trash cans left out by the side porch steps. I crushed a couple of those. Two rock pillars that framed the entrance to the parking lot at one end. I only grazed them, both of them on separate passes. A low stone wall that separated the end of the parking area from our garden plot. I pretty much hit that sucker head on. I think Pansy cried and Mack sprained himself, both from laughing—laughing at the car leaping around the lot and at the occasional look of horror on Levi's face when we spun by.

But in the end, I was driving. Second gear and, for a few glorious minutes, third. I even tried reverse and, with Levi standing outside the car directing me, I backed that Plymouth right into its usual parking spot. More or less.

That was lesson number one. A few days later, after Levi claimed to have recovered his nerve, we drove down to Pansy's house on Valley Street to pick her up for work. On the way back, I drove, with Levi nervous in the front and Pansy cowering in the rumble seat. A few mornings after that, Levi and I went out and practiced stopping and starting on College Street, which is to say on the steep hill leading up to the Sky Club. That was not a smooth day, at least not for the first dozen times I tried to get that damn automobile moving on that damn hill.

Gradually, though, the whole process became less terrifying for me and Levi and less hilarious for everyone else. Then, one fine day, I drove the Plymouth down the mountain to work, parked it proudly on the street in front of Imperial Life for eight hours or so, and drove it home that night. All by myself, and I even stopped to pick up chicken and steaks from the butcher on the way home. Turns out that a woman could become an accomplished motorist. You didn't see many women behind the wheel in the '30s, not in our little mountain town, but by God, I was one of them.

Now all I had to do was convince Levi that I could help move the product from out on Spring Creek and up on Big Pine into town. And as you can imagine, given our previous conversations, the man could be a lot more stubborn than first gear on a steep hill.

57

As levi had promised me the night before we buried Papa, our first trip together with me behind the wheel for some of the way was up to Spring Creek to visit his Uncle Nathan and for me to meet his father. His father, whom he'd barely seen to speak to in thirteen years. And then there was his stepmother who rode a broomstick. We might lay eyes on her as well.

On a Sunday in May, the traditional visiting day in the mountains, we left early, crossed the river to West Asheville, and drove on out the Patton Avenue. Before we got to Haywood County, however, we turned right onto what Levi and the map called the Leicester Road. From there we drove through communities like Sandy Mush and Luck and Trust. No, I did not make up these names. There was a fine country store in Trust, where we pumped gasoline for the Plymouth and drank a cold Coca-Cola each from the ice box.

After being on the road for two hours or more, we came to the Spring Creek Valley. I had visited there as a girl and young woman by walking across to a dance or a revival from the upper end of Big Pine along steep mountain paths. I'd never come to it from below, up the main road so to speak. And as you can imagine, I'd never come to it in an automobile. We'd taken turns driving that morning, and even Levi had to admit I'd done passably well, but he was behind the wheel when we reached the old schoolhouse that marked the center of the Spring Creek community.

He pointed out various landmarks and then we went on to his Uncle Nathan's as he was too nervous to approach his father's place straightaway. Uncle Nathan, or Nat, as he kept insisting I call him, was a happy little elf of a man. He had a lame leg from a logging accident, so he hopped and limped along but always with a wide grin on his weather-beaten face. He patted Levi on the back or grasped his upper arm hard every few minutes, and it was obvious that he loved him like a son. We loaded twenty-five jars of prime white liquor into the trunk of the Plymouth while we were there, and I made sure that Levi, and not me, counted the $125 in payment out of his leather wallet. I didn't want the sweet old man to think his adopted son's woman friend was the controlling type. I figured there was already one witch in the equation, and neither he nor Levi needed another.

Nat gave in to the spirit of the moment as we were getting ready to leave and threw his arm around Levi's shoulder and punched him gently in the chest with his other hand. The gesture of love from one country man for another, though you wouldn't have known what it said if you weren't from up home. Nat didn't hesitate with me at all but hugged me like a long-lost daughter and, given that I'd just lost my own Papa to the ages, I hugged him back just as fierce.

From there, we drove back down the Spring Creek Road for five miles till we came to the turn off that led up to Levi's father's place. I'd never seen Levi nervous before, but there it was. He grew quieter and quieter the closer we got, and his leg was jerking almost spasmodically when he threw in the clutch to downshift the Plymouth. To distract him, I asked him what his father's name was.

"What?"

"Your daddy's name . . . what is it?"

"Jeter, I think it's Jeter."

"You don't know your own daddy's name?" I was teasing but I regretted it the second I said it. That's how anxious he was.

"The hell yes, I do. It's Jeter. What's wrong with that?"

"Nothing, honey. Nothing at all. Jeter is a fine name. And your brother's name is Gordon."

He nodded. "That's right. Older than me by two years, Gordon is."

We came to a steep place in the road up to the farm, which by that point was little more than a gravel and dirt trace through fields of knee-high corn. Levi pulled the roadster off under a stray apple tree, and we got out to walk on up to the house.

It was a hard few hours, I'd say. One of hardest. Levi's father was alive but only just. He'd suffered a stroke or perhaps two, according to Gordon, and his mind was gone. He spent his days rocking quietly either beside the fire, in winter, or on the porch, in summer. He rarely ever spoke except about events that had occurred decades before. Tildy, the wife, had her mind, such as it was, and spent her days cursing at Jeter or at Gordon, or both. Sadly, she was the picture of health, and it appeared that she might live forever.

Levi's father did not recognize him.

There it is. The stone-hard truth of it. He didn't know him. Oh, he didn't even bother with me, which was just fine, but that he didn't know his own son was heartbreaking. Tildy recognized Levi immediately and cursed him roundly for abandoning her. Not the family . . . her! And after a bit, for abandoning the family as well. *Witch* might be too kind a word for Tildy. There are women in the world who have outlived their usefulness to man or beast. Tildy was such a one. Bowed up tight with a humpback and snuff dribbling down her chin every time she paused to give somebody—you, me, her husband—hell.

This was all hard on Levi.

But to witness the reunion of Gordon and Levi, two lonely brothers, caused me to stare in happiness. One who had stayed; one who had gone. One who had suffered the wrath of the step-mother; one who had absorbed the wrath of the world. One who had loved the father as the father had slowly lost his mind; one who had secretly, silently missed his father for years. In five minutes' time, ten minutes at the most, they rediscovered each other. Poking and prodding and punching each other. Laughing and cuffing and talking; barely able to stop telling each other things, they just talked over and above and around each other. Even so, the understanding was immediate and complete.

Gordon didn't pay much attention to me; he was entirely taken up with Levi. And vice-versa. While they carried on in the yard, I slipped into the house to study Jeter Arrowood's face. His gentle, lined, leathery face. Quiet and reserved, an unlit pipe clenched between his teeth. The thing is that I could see Levi in his father's face. Indeed, I believed that I could see Levi in another forty or fifty years, could trace what he would look like, how he would hold his shoulders, how he would shake his head as stray thoughts troubled him.

And were it to come to that . . . Levi, with his mind or not, slowly rocking before the fire, I would care for him. If I had any mind of my own left at that point, and any strength at all, I would care for that man as if . . . as if he were the dearest thing in the world. And at that moment, my heart went out to Papa Jeter. I wished that we could just tie Tildy to a handy tree and leave her to screech, while we drove Jeter Arrowood home with us. Where I could care for him the way he deserved. I wanted this so badly that my hands trembled in a sort of agony. *Why can't we love whom we love?* I thought. *Why?*

I did all I could do. I borrowed Levi's handkerchief and wiped the drool from his father's chin. And when I did, I leaned over to whisper to the old man that we'd be back. I'd see to that. We'd be back.

When we left, Levi promised the same to Gordon. We'd visit there and Gordon must come to town. "The hell with Tildy," one whispered to the other. "She can stay right here."

And when we finally walked back down the hill to where we'd left the roadster, Levi carried a thick envelope in his hand. It was a letter, he explained, that his father had begun writing to him after he left a dozen years before. And continued adding to off-and-on during the intervening years. The letter of the many things he wished to say to his prodigal son, and now Gordon had passed it along to him to read.

What did I say when he told me this, looking away so that I wouldn't see the pain in his eyes? Here is what I said. I said . . . *"Oh, why can't we just love the ones we love?"*

"This is love," he said back to me, shaking the envelope roughly. "This right here . . . is love."

58

We were mostly quiet as we left Spring Creek. It felt as if so much had happened in the previous few hours, and that the weight of loss and wonder was stacked on top of everything else that had happened to our two families. Our two families that seemed to be crashing to earth before our very eyes.

We stopped again in Trust to fill up the gas tank. The proprietor's son—dressed in overalls but no shirt—pumped the gasoline manually while Levi held the nozzle in the Plymouth. When we were full up, the young man straightened and while staring off across the road, told us quietly that there'd been a deputy in the store not long after we'd passed through that morning. Cousin to his mother, who ran the place. And his mother had got to running her mouth about this and that.

"About us?" Levi asked quietly.

The boy stretched his back and pointed across the road at nothing in particular. From the store, it would have looked like he was talking about anything, a stray dog. "She did happen to mention you by name," he allowed, "and that you'd likely be coming back through this evening."

"Shit," Levi muttered.

The boy nodded and turned back toward the store. "Sure is nice to see y'all. Be safe on the highway."

The discussion as we drove was short and sweet. "What does that mean?" I asked.

"You know what it means."

"Maybe I should drive . . . You could . . ." I had started to say hide in the rumble seat but stopped myself in time.

"Too late," he growled. "They know the car."

"Did you bring the pistol?"

He glanced over at me. "Under the seat."

That was it. We passed through Luck just at twilight. Half-moon rising over the jagged, blue ridgeline to the east.

Then there were headlights behind us, two big, white eyes glaring. Almost immediately came the howl of a siren along with the eyes. Levi downshifted and slowly pulled over to the side of a lonely stretch of road. "What are you doing?" I hissed. "Run for it."

He just shook his head.

The Sheriff's car pulled over as well, maybe twenty feet behind us. The siren suddenly clicked off, and I could hear the creek to my right, splashing over rocks. The grumble of the automobile engine behind us went dead as well. Only the glare of their headlights remained. Somewhere close I could smell the sweet stink of a skunk, maybe run over in the road.

Levi reached down between his legs, pulled a dark object out from under the driver's seat and handed it to me. It was the .45 and God, it was heavy. Slippery in my hands.

I twisted around in the seat and watched not one but two deputies get out of the Sheriff's car and walk toward us, the one off the shoulder of the road to the right stumbling and cursing quietly. I didn't know what to do, so I used both thumbs to cock the .45.

When the two deputies were just beside the car, the one on my side even leaning his hand against the fender to keep his balance in the gravel, Levi gunned it.

From first to second to third like nothing I'd ever seen before, the engine screaming at the height of each gear, and we hit a sudden steep climb, the road winding against the side of a mountain like a snake. The car was clawing up the road, and Levi was laughing.

"Let the hammer down on that thing, Jo," he said when he finally stopped howling. "Before you jerk the trigger and shoot one of us."

"What the hell was that?" I yelled at him over the whine of the engine.

"County line," he yelled back as we flashed past a roadside store and then the crazily tilted brown sign that told us we were **Welcome to Buncombe County.**

"You mean they can't chase us over the line?" Still shouting at him. I slowly let the hammer on the pistol back down and searched till I found the safety and clicked it on. My hands hadn't stopped shaking.

"Can't cross that line," Levi shouted gleefully. "Oh, they'll find a phone somewhere and call ahead. See if the Buncombe County boys are bored tonight and want to join the fun. But that'll take a while, and we're going to use some backroads that you've never seen before . . . Stick that pistol back under the seat, Jo." He was still grinning like a fool. "You scare me with it."

WE UNLOADED THE LIQUOR THAT night from the alley into the back of Rogers Produce Stand. Closed and locked the barn doors on the back of the old building. In the glare from the Plymouth's headlights, you could still make out the faded words **Livery** and **Stable** in the paint peeling from the doors.

When we got ready to climb back in the Plymouth, Levi asked me if I wanted to drive. I shook my head. "Just take me home," I whispered. "It's been a long day for both of us."

I SLEPT IN LEVI'S ROOM THAT night, curled up in the blankets on his bed, while he sat up late beside me, propped against the headboard with pillows behind his back. He was reading the rambling letter his father had left him, many pages long and written over the years. The lamp lit beside the bed kept me from diving too far beneath the surface, and I was dreamily aware of him there while I dozed.

At one point, when I floated close to wakefulness, I could hear him sniffing, his breath catching, and I knew instinctively that he was crying as he read. My drowsy thought was to swim on up into consciousness and to speak to him, comfort him, but then something—my own father's spirit perhaps—shushed me, and I let go to drift again in sleep.

I say my own Papa's spirit hushed me because later in the tidal pull of the night, I did see him and speak with him. It was after the lamp was put out and Levi himself had eased on down beneath the covers, curled with his stomach and chest against my back.

In my dream, full of sunbright and light . . .

I am working up home on the farm, repairing a fence beside the pasture that lies just there below the Rock House and along the creek. I don't know where the brothers were for normally it would be a two- or even three-man job, but . . . *that shiny day, it is just me, at work to brace the locust posts and stretch the barbwire.*

I am sad in my work for I know that Papa is dead, gone on up to Crooked Ridge to lie beneath the tall grass with Mama. How could he be gone from this, my mind cries, his homeplace, his fields? His voice should be heard calling out to summon the boys from the fields and singing to me the old ballads.

As if in answer to my cries, my prayers, I see two figures coming along the dirt road beside the pasture, ambling down from the horse barn where they have been brushing Papa's old horse, Moses. A man and a woman strolling together in the yellow sunshine. The woman has Moses' curry comb in her hand, the man a long walking stick.

When I straighten and shade my eyes, I see Papa grinning at me as they come along past the old farm truck parked under the lean-to. The woman nodding in a friendly way. Who is the woman . . . not my Mama?

Why, it is his *mother I see . . . my own Grandma Salter . . . who went beyond us years ago. She is waving a gnarled hand in greeting as she did when I was a girl. She is calling out to me though I cannot hear the words. Bird song and the creek's rushing cry, yes, but their words are not . . .*

Except . . . inside my head. In the depths of my mind, *I hear them both . . . their words and their laughter . . . letting me know that they are walking the countryside together now. As they are used to do, checking on a favorite tree, combing the burs out of Moses' tail, petting the dogs as they sleep by the fire, and freshening the fruit when it is slow to ripen.*

They tell me that they are there, always there, and they are together now. Working the bedland. I ask where Mama is, and Papa turns to point with his stick up the ridge toward the cemetery and beyond. Berry picking . . .

That is what I remembered when I woke. The sure knowledge of their existence did not leave me when I woke to the morning. They were safe—*are safe*—and they were all of them together—*are together.*

You may say what you will, you who do not know our country ways, you with your sharp and doubting words, but I know what I know.

I was smiling when I sat quietly up in bed, readjusted the pillows against my back, and while the morning light came streaming in, watched my dear Levi sleep.

I watched him for the longest time and was not the least bit lonely, for I retained the sense that my Grandma Salter along with my Papa were in the room with us. They were chatting, pointing, laughing, and I could hear them just beneath the register that people call real.

Here, just here, was my Levi, lying on his back asleep, gently snoring, and there, beside the bed, were my forebears, floating with the dust motes in the morning light. That is the best of all knowing, when the evident past is woven into the apparent present. In the pure light of morning.

When Levi began to stir, I slipped down into the covers so that I could hold him as he woke. He groaned and stretched his limbs against the bed and against me. I sang to him just a bit as he woke, some silly song that came to me on the spur of the moment.

Where have you been and why did you go? . . . Where did you come from and how do you know? Some half-words that sounded like that.

Just some small sweetness so he wouldn't be afraid as he woke to the world. After he got through moaning and blinking his eyes at the light, I asked him a question and then shared a thought.

"Levi," I said, "could I read your father's letter sometime?" I placed my fingers over his mouth so he wouldn't answer me *no* too quickly. "I promise to honor . . . you and him."

He was nodding at me from where his head lay half-buried in the pillow. "I'll do you one better," he said and paused to cough, clear his throat. "I'll read them to you some night when we've had an Old Fashioned. Out loud. Though it cost me."

"Cost you what?"

"Tears. Cost me some tears."

I leaned over and kissed him ever so lightly on the lips.

"I have another idea," I said to him . . . there, where he lay. "It came to me in the middle of the night. Part of a dream I had. You remember that old farm truck that's parked under the lean-to next to the cattle barn?"

"At the Rock House?"

"Yes! That one. The very one. What if we used it to . . ."

"Haul the product, while we use the roadster as a decoy?"

I grabbed his chin, raspy with beard, and shook it.

"What? What did I say?"

"That is my idea, Levi Arrowood. My exact idea, and I had it while you were still asleep."

He smiled groggily. "I had it last night, while I was reading Dad's letter . . ." And then he added, ". . . had it first."

"I can beat that," I said. "I had it in my dream, and all you did was read my mind."

We stared at each other, and then started laughing, tickled at ourselves.

59

We talked with my brother Bobby over the phone at Worley's Store, and he laughed through the static when we asked about Papa's old farm truck. He allowed as how it was sitting on blocks under the lean-to and there were weeds growing in the floorboard. "The engine has mice in it."

Still in thrall to our idea, Levi and I roamed up and down Lexington Avenue, looking for a farmer who wanted to sell his truck as well as what he hauled to town in it. After a week of looking, we bought a 1928 Ford AA along with five crates of chickens still lashed down in back. Two hundred dollars for the truck and twenty dollars for the chickens.

We found someone on the Avenue to paint Salter Brothers Produce on both doors in bold, block letters.

We had a plan and we had a way-station warehouse. And in the evenings, a few pages at a time, Levi read his father's rambling, years-long letter aloud to me over a drink. Five or ten pages at a time, stopping when it seemed natural to do so.

Dear Son,

I am torn by the grief I feel since you left us. I know that I have not done right by you & Gordon because I have let Tildy run wild in the house, punishing you for no good reason. The woman has an adder's tongue, I admit, & it seems never to stop hissing & spitting.

Often, I would sip my own drink while Levi read—the bourbon rich on my tongue—but he would save his for after. For when his emotions calmed again.

I have spoken to her sternly & with many words & she has promised to do better if you should return to us. I took her famous razor strop that she is so proud of & threw it into the fire on the day after you left. When she objected, I raised my fist to her & would have struck her had Gordon not held my arm.

But oh son, it is you I miss today, & I am afraid that the break between us will not heal soon. If it was given to me to say, I would find you where you are & bring you home.

Your Father, Jeter

"Why don't we just bring him here?" I finally asked one night. "I'll take care of him." But Levi just shook his head and looked away. The thought was too large for him, I realized. Too great a leap into the past . . . and the future.

The club took on a new rhythm that summer. Since Levi and I had bought the place, we paid everyone a bit more, enough to keep the best waitresses, to keep Mack from working a second job, to keep the best musicians with us on Friday and Saturday nights, blowing a crazy horn and burning the piano keys into the night. And, by the saints above, we paid Pansy what she was worth. Which took some getting used to on her part, as she claimed it was riches.

I walked up to sit by your mother's grave, as I often do when I can get away. On this day, I asked her where you was & what was you doing. The crows in the trees cackled at me. Say you are alive. Working your way.

How I wish I could see you & help you. How I wish you might forgive me.

Your loving father.

With my paycheck from Imperial and the business we built up four nights a week, we were starting to make something, build something. But still and all, the Sky Club was not just happy families chewing hamburgers on the first floor. It was steamy jazz and branding-iron liquor on the second. On Friday and Saturday nights in particular, it was where people went to forget the depression that was slowly chewing the town down to its bones.

It was the sort of joint where men cut loose their wallets and women cut loose everything else. We had to have a steady stream of liquor whether we could lay hands on the last of the bottled and bonded stuff or not.

We had to have the greased lightning that Levi's Uncle Nat and my own brother Mike were cooking up home. That river needed to flow out of the mountains south into town.

You left here with barely the clothes on your back & few pieces of corn bread wrapped in a rag. Sometimes when I try to imagine your life, I can only see you in that way. Thin to the bone & hungry for anything at all to eat. Ever so often, I send Nat five whole dollars sealed up in a paper to use for you. To give you something more. I do not know what he does with the money.

We made an experimental run up to Big Pine, with Levi driving the Plymouth roadster and yours truly the Ford truck. We stopped for gas together in Marshall, just to signal any curious body that the famous liquor car was going up country, with the famous bootlegger behind the wheel.

We loaded up the truck and drove back down after dark, only this time I came down fast in the Plymouth, while Levi followed in the truck. I got stopped well before the county line on the river road and flirted with the deputy while he searched the car. Levi puttered right on through a half hour later, and nobody even blinked. The liquor buried in a pile of field corn in the back of the truck.

Son,

Just this June day, I saw a jack-in-the-pulpit flower in the edge of the woods & longed to show it to you. You will think many winters have gone by. You will not think of me today. I don't blame you. You are young & have a life full of days. But I have not so many, and often I think of you. Well, here is this flower that you would like to see if only I could take you by the hand to bring you here.

The second time I asked Levi why we didn't just bring his father to live with us, he listened. I could tell that the thought had grown inside him. He couldn't quite imagine it, nor truthfully could I. But here was a wound, a gash in who we were, and perhaps it was something we could heal. "What about Tildy?" he finally asked. "Do you plan to just leave her there with Gordon?" What he really meant was would we just leave Gordon there with her. I had no answer.

At night, I sit up by the fire for I have not hope of sleep. Gordon sleeps & that woman. But I have not any rest. So I keep watch & feed the fire. I can see your face, my son, in the flames. Not because you are on fire. Confused as I am, I know better. But because firelight is the only light I have left to see.

We made a second trial run, this time up to Spring Creek. Levi's Uncle Nat had only ten jars of brandy for us this time and promised Levi another load of whiskey by late summer. It takes time, he explained to both Levi and me, takes God's own time to do it right. We packed the brandy carefully in the truck bed and covered it over with a pile of burlap sacks.

When we went by Levi's father's place, I was as nervous as he was. The letters had sunk into me for now I knew what Jeter Arrowood's voice sounded like. The lilt, the rhythm, the words. I had begun to know the old man through those letters, as if I'd watched him age.

And when we got there, we discovered the strangest thing. Gordon met us on the road up to tell us that Tildy, the witch, had disappeared, and their dad was feeling better. We walked on up, Gordon and Levi talking excitedly about Tildy going off with her oldest daughter after cursing one and all. Then, slightly out of breath, we walked into the yard before the house and saw the strangest thing.

Levi's dad, Jeter, was sitting on the porch, shading his eyes with one hand to see who was coming. You need to understand what I'm saying. He was sitting in the sun, rocking himself slowly. Then he waved.

I gasped to see it, I confess. I'd thought him little better than a corpse the last time we were there. Unaware even of human touch. I stood stock-still in the yard and let the two brothers approach.

I could tell that Levi was afraid to speak, but Gordon called out a hallo. They walked closer and stood just below their father. "Dad, this here is Levi. You remember him?" Gordon asked.

The good old man stopped rocking to stare and began to nod, faintly at first and then almost spasmodically. Then he lifted his hand off the arm of the rocker and motioned the boys up onto the porch. They climbed the steps together and knelt down on either side of the rocking chair so that their heads came roughly to his shoulders. He looked slowly back and forth at the two faces as if to compare. He was smiling then, still with a faint tremor, a tremor he would always have.

He reached out with the same hand—he seemed to have only one good arm—and touched Gordon's face. "Gord . . . un," he said clearly. Then again, "Gor-don." Satisfied, he turned and reached with the same hand to touch the other face. Only this time, he let the tips of his fingers rest there, soaking up sensation from the skin. And surely, there was some dampness on that cheek. "Lee," he said, his voice still strong. A longer pause. And then, with some effort, "Le-vi. I believe you . . . are Le-vi."

He was alive. He had come back to us.

He was drawing breath and turning it into speech. Raising his hand and turning it into touch. I stood there in the yard and wept to see it . . . because by living, he confirmed some deep suspicion within me.

60

We paused for a few weeks before our next trip down into Madison County. Slept late on Sunday mornings, enjoyed quiet meals together or with Mack or Pansy or both—Sunday, Monday, Tuesday. I worked in the garden on late afternoons with Pansy, and we all played with Bodie the hound pup.

Bodie, who wasn't so much of a puppy now, but a long-legged creature who would run laps around us as we walked or worked or sat in the shade. Pansy and I would often sit and talk, whether outside in the garden or inside by the stove. We continued as friends, unlikely though that be, offering one secret or another to feed our shared understanding.

All our lives took on the shape of summer as the days grew longer, the nights warmer.

Even so, we knew we had to soon make a trip up to Big Pine. Michael had been busy with Bob's help and even Tony's from time to time. They had fifty jars of pure corn liquor and two dozen jars of apple brandy waiting, with more to come as late summer ripened more corn and more apples.

And so, one Sunday morning in July, when the Sky Club was closed for several days ahead and I had the day off from Imperial, we set out again . . . Levi driving the Salter Family Produce truck with me behind the wheel of the Plymouth Roadster.

We stopped together on Main Street in Marshall to fill up the tanks of both automobiles and chatted for a few minutes with my brother Will who was in town to see Lawyer Gudger and pick up a few items from the Penland General Store.

Then on ahead to Walnut, down the long, winding gravel road to Barnard at the river. We left the Plymouth parked beside Gudger's store there, intending to pack the liquor into the bed of the truck along with suitable produce to cover it. I didn't mind taking a break from driving, for the curves down from Walnut to Barnard had left me queasy in my stomach. I stretched out on the truck seat while Levi drove, with my head lolling out the window so the cold air rising off the river would blow on my face. By the time we reached Worley's Store, I was some better and agreed to tramp up the road to the Rock House to visit with Michael and any of the others who were about.

It was fun to sit for a bit on the steps at the Rock House and watch Levi and Bobby load the liquor into tow sacks slung over the backs of the mules. Six mules, four of which were borrowed from various brothers. It's the Salter Brothers Produce train, I thought and smiled to myself. A joint stock company, which was a phrase I'd picked up at Imperial. When Michael walked up from the barn to where I sat on the steps, he teased me for looking like a man since I was wearing my new pair of trousers. Lightweight cotton for summer.

"You're the man around here," I replied, gesturing at the farm. "How does that feel?" He blushed and stammered, pleased to no end.

I walked back down the Big Pine Road—or what we jokingly called a road—behind the mules, listening to the glass fruit jars clink together in their sacks from time to time. It was late afternoon but still and hot, flies buzzing over the mule droppings. I stopped at one point and vomited into the dusty weeds beside the road, which was a relief, for I felt better.

When we reached Worley's, Bobby and Levi loaded the jars into the bed of the truck, carefully padding them with the sacks. Then they threw a canvas tarp over the jars and set crates of chickens on top of the tarp. The chickens were clucking and clattering, which caused a rooster up behind Worley's to crow about his concern.

Dave was there at the store to collect payment for the family, since he was second oldest after Will, who was still in Marshall. Seventy-four jars total, at five dollars per jar, so I paid brother Dave $370 cash, first by explaining the math to him and then by counting out the dollars loud and clear. I didn't ask him for a receipt. I would have had to write that out too and wait on his laborious signature.

After we crossed the river bridge, Levi and I both had a cold Coca-Cola at Gudger's, which again settled my stomach. I was ready for the run home. Ready to unload and settle in for a hot bath at the Club. We sat down there by the river and watched the darkness enfold the eastern sky.

We drove together up the steep road to Walnut by starlight, where Levi parked the truck beside a church and killed its engine. I waved and drove on, using the half-hour advantage we'd agreed on to attract any curious sheriffs and gobble up their attention.

It was uneventful right on down through Marshall and out along the river road. The moon was up by then, almost full, and the light glittered on the French Broad River where it was torn by rock and shoal. For some reason I was jittery, almost scared. I couldn't imagine why because I didn't have nary a pint of whiskey in the roadster, and Levi had the .45 with him in the truck.

Haunted? For some reason I couldn't name, the night felt haunted. I drove on, glad for the moonlight on the empty, curving road.

Finally, when I was into the long, straight stretch just at the county line, the Sheriff car pulled out behind me. It was almost a relief when he flicked his headlights on and off and touched the siren. I took a deep breath, realizing it was what I'd been expecting all along.

I looked for a place to pull over, but I was a hundred yards past the stone lodge that landmarked the county line before there was room between the road and the river. I pulled over into the gravel and mud and killed the engine. Then I just sat there, reminding myself that not only was I cold sober, I carried no contraband. I was a law-abiding citizen.

I watched in the side mirror for someone to get out of the Sheriff car, for a door to open and slam, but the headlights from behind half-blinded me, and suddenly, he was standing there, right beside my door. He carried an electric torch in his hand, and when he held it up to show me his face, it was horrifying. Thin and almost skeletal, with a jagged scar pulling up on one cheek. Then the light was blinding in my eyes, and he opened the car door without asking.

"Step on out, Mr. Arrow-wood," he said. "We got business here, and we need to search this piece of junk auto-mobile to start with."

"I'm not Mr. Arrowood," I said. "My name is Josephine Salter, from up on Big Pine."

"Even better." He cackled. I know how strange that sounds—cackled—but the sound he made was even stranger. "I hear you're Arrowood's whore, and once we've finished with the car, we might better search you." He grasped my upper arm hard and jerked me out of the car. When I was on my feet, he shoved me into the fender. "Bend over the hood and stay put."

He stood behind me with one heavy hand on the small of my back, pushing me down onto the hood of the Plymouth, the metal hot against my chest and stomach. All the while, he was talking away to somebody named Jimmy, who was ripping into the rumble seat and throwing everything in the back floorboard out onto the ground. "Glove box," skeleton head said after a minute. "Check the goddamn glove box and under the seat. I don't care if it's a bottle of cough syrup. Something's there."

I twisted my head around on the hood to where I could see his belt. There was a holster, I could tell that, which meant a gun.

When it was apparent that Jimmy had found nothing, skeleton head ordered him back to the Sheriff car. "What the hell, boss?" Jimmy whined. "They ain't nothing here."

Just at that moment, I could hear a truck coming up behind us along the road. Please God, I thought, let it be the Ford . . . And then, I thought, please God not. Not with that load of liquor and Levi plus a pistol.

"Go on back and have a smoke," skeleton head said to Jimmy. "I got to search this suspect, and you ain't old enough to witness such."

Jimmy went. I could hear his bootheels sucking in the roadside mud. The truck was getting closer, but . . .

"What the hell kind of a woman wears pants?" skeleton head said to me. He shoved his free hand on up to my neck and grabbed a fist full of hair. Banged my head on the hood and shoved my face down hard on one cheek. "I misbelieve you're a woman anyhow. Some kind of dis-guise, ain't it? You're trying to fool me, ain't you?"

He dropped the torch on the ground and reached around my waist with his right hand. Fumbled at my belt buckle and pulled it loose. "I believe it is my sworn duty to determine if you are a man or a woman. Hell, you might be any kind of a thing." He tore the button and zipper, ripped them apart with his clutching fist.

The truck was close on us now, close enough for the headlights to bob around us as it bore down.

Skeleton head stood up straight and used his ripping and tearing hand to wave the truck on by. "Sheriff business!" he shouted as it puttered slowly by. "Get the hell on."

Skeleton head leaned his hips against me as he was yelling at the truck, and Jesus help me, I could feel the bulge in his pants against my ass. I prayed for Levi down in my gut and prayed that he wouldn't stop, all at the same time.

The truck passed on, and after a moment, its red taillights blinked out.

"Now then, where were we?" skeleton head muttered. "You man bitch, where the hell were we?" Still shoving my face down hard on the hood again, he pushed my torn trousers and my panties down over my ass. When they were down to my ankles, he kicked my feet apart and shoved something up between my legs from behind.

At first, I thought it was his hand and the hard appendage was his thumb. Pressing against my ass and beyond, against my sex. Hard, too hard for . . . it was a gun barrel. Son-of-a-bitch was jamming his pistol almost into me, the sight on the end of the barrel cutting me. "Nope," he muttered. "I was wrong, I was. They ain't no balls and they ain't no cock-a-doodle. You *are* a woman! Just what I been needing . . ."

"Fuck you," I muttered against the hood of the car. "Fuck you and . . ."

He jerked up on the gun, lifting my feet off the ground.

"Talk nice," he said. "If you want to live through this . . ."

"Back off." At first, I couldn't place the voice. I was hurting so bad that I couldn't . . . "Pull your hands back where I can see them and step away."

"The hell with you, whoever you are." Skeleton head. "This here is sheriff busi . . ."

The .45 sounded like a bomb when it went off, and gravel flew everywhere. Suddenly the hand on my neck and the gun barrel up my crack were gone. That fast.

"I said step back and throw your piece in the river." The voice was shaking, quivering in anger. And only then did I recognize it. Realize it. Cherish it.

I bent over and pulled up my trousers. Held them clutched with one hand at my waist. "Levi . . .?" I said. Terrified. Relieved. Trying to breathe.

"Go get in the truck," the shadow that was Levi said. "Go on now and don't look back." I could feel a great crash looming over us. The crash of the .45 shells exploding, our lives burned down into the cemetery ground.

I stumbled toward the voice and as I passed the shadow, reached out to touch its arm. "Please don't," I whispered. "Please don't shoot him."

The shadow shook its head roughly. "Why not? Needs killing."

"Just don't." I was still touching his arm. Afraid if I touched him anywhere else that he might cut loose. "I need you . . . Not in prison. Alive."

"Did he . . .?"

"No, no. I promise. He was just about to . . . and you came."

"Lay down on the goddamn road," Levi growled at skeleton head. "Lay down and say your last prayers. Pray for a long time, maybe an hour or two. And while you're at it, you'd better pray I don't come back and blow your damn head off."

I limped on the way to the truck. When Levi took my arm, I could feel the steel in his grip. Gentle even so, nothing like what I had just been through.

I was terrified that skeleton head had hurt what was inside me. But how could I tell Levi that? . . . Not yet.

Not beside the dark and glittering river.

61

WE WEREN'T CAREFUL ENOUGH."

"That's an understatement if there ever was one. I can't believe I let you get into that."

"That's not what I mean."

It was the next morning, Monday morning, and we'd carried our coffee out onto the terrace with a pan of biscuits I'd made. Levi brought some butter and jam, so that it felt like a real breakfast. I intended to call in to Imperial later and tell them I was taking the morning off. Not feeling well, which was true enough.

"What do you mean, Jo? I tried to stop you from driving, but hell no, you had to have your way. I wish . . ."

"Driving's not what got us into trouble," I said and blew on my coffee before sipping it.

Considering I'd had a pistol shoved almost inside me the night before, I felt fine down there. A couple of scratches up high on my inner thighs that must have come from the sight on the barrel, but my insides, the parts that mattered, felt normal.

"Trouble how?" Levi was staring at me, his coffee cup halfway to his mouth.

"Levi . . .?" I paused, not sure how I could say what was on my mind. "Would you marry me if I asked you to?"

His hand jerked and half the steaming coffee in his cup splashed into his lap. He was up and cussing like a jack-in-the-box. Mopping at his lap with the cloth I'd thrown over the biscuits. "Damn it, Jo. Trouble how . . .?"

"What do you mean?" I was still carefully blowing and sipping . . . while trying not to laugh at him.

"Just . . . what kind of trouble?"

"A good kind. At least I think so. So, would you? Marry me if I asked you to?"

"What if I say no?"

"Well then, I won't ask you."

"That makes not one damn bit of sense. Are you asking me or are you not?"

"Not sure yet. If I were to ask you, what would you say?"

"I might say yes. If I hadn't just scalded myself half to death."

"What would your terms be? What would you bring to the marriage?"

"If I said yes?"

"Yes. I mean . . . if you said yes, what do you offer and what would you require?"

"That you would honor and obey me for the rest of your life, my life, one of our lives, whichever came first."

"Honor . . . yes, fair enough. But obey?"

He picked up his coffee cup and carefully sipped from it. "What if I swore to obey you??

That gave me pause. "I'm not your ball-and-chain, Levi. I don't want anybody obeying me, especially you."

"No *obey* then. I'm fine with that. What financial resources would you bring to the marriage?" He was getting into the flow of the negotiation now.

"Well, I'd bring my salary from the Imperial Life Insurance Company—or wherever I happened to be employed at the moment—and I'd bring my considerable skills as an accountant to our common enterprises." It was hard not to laugh at the man, or at least smile.

"Skills is it?"

I nodded. "Considerable ones. That you need, given the plain fact that you can neither add nor subtract and get the same answer twice in a row."

"Humph!" he snorted. *Snort* is by far the best word for it. "That might be fair. Notice I said *might be* . . . In exchange for your skills, I'm willing to throw in that dog over there. Bodie Arrowood."

"Wait . . . ! You can't do that. Bodie is half mine already."

"Which half?"

"The front half . . . cause you're being an ass. Can't trade with a dog you don't even own all of it . . ."

Now it was him trying not to smile. "Well, every other thing I have, you own half of already. Except for the truck . . ."

"Both our names are on the truck, Levi."

"Damn it. What was the question again?"

"If I asked you to marry me, what would you say?"

"I might say that I love you."

My breath caught in my throat. "Do you?"

"Do I say it?"

"You already said it, do you mean it?"

"Hell, Jo Belle, I've loved you ever since you came sashaying in that door on the arm of some no-name man and lit up that dance floor like a thunderstorm in August. I've loved you ever since the night I suggested to Mack that he pour you an apple brandy. Not the stuff out front but brandy from the saved-back jar, the good stuff from Uncle Nat. I've loved you ever since you cornered me out here on this very terrace and later made me tell my story. I've loved you crying and laughing. I've loved you hurting and happy. I don't know that there's been a minute since I first met you that I haven't loved you. Though then and now, now and then, you scare the ever-loving hell out of me because I love you so much. It feels like my fulltime, lifelong job to keep anything from happening to you. I'm afraid you'll disappear in a puff of smoke right this very minute."

"We're going to have a baby, Levi."

He must have suspected because he didn't pause. "Do you want it?"

"Do you?"

"I want it like I want air to breathe. Don't you dare tell me you mean to lose it."

I shook my head. My eyes were full. My mind burning, burning like the biblical bush. "I want it cause it's yours," was all I managed to say.

"Ours," he said quietly. "I believe it's ours."

"Ours then. Yours and mine, like the truck." Can you laugh and cry at the same time? I can.

"Yes, girl or boy, it is ours. Will you . . . What was it you wanted to ask me, Jo?"

"Will you marry me, Levi Arrowood?"

"Edgar."

It took me a breath or two to cipher what he'd said. Then I tried again: "Will you marry me, Levi *Edgar* Arrowood?"

"Hmmm. I believe I will . . . Josephine Robbins Salter. Just you name the day and the time, and not all the deputies in three counties will keep me away."

I nodded at him. Still laughing; still crying. "Who gets to name the baby?" I asked, just for something to say.

"You do if it's a boy," he replied. "I do if it's a girl."

"Isn't that backwards?"

"No," he said. "It's not. After learning to put up with you, I believe I'd prefer a daughter."

62

In making a life, what matters and what doesn't?

Death matters . . . and birth.

Sex matters . . . and love.

The ability to be naked before someone without fear. That matters. And in saying that, I'm speaking of your skin, but really, I'm speaking of something more. Something deeper. The skin of your soul, perhaps.

To be able to bare your mind to someone. That matters. And how he reacts when you share it . . . that matters even more.

Work matters. When the crash killed or crippled most people, Levi and I caught fire. Mountain bred and determined.

In that 1930s world where meaningful work had all but disappeared, our work came to matter more and more. It mattered just for the money, of course, what little money there was. Salter Brothers' Produce survived, and the Sky Club thrived—despite the crash and what came after. I never drove liquor again nor did Levi. We found other, less conspicuous cousins for that.

We were never rich—thank God—but we always ate, and the music . . . well, the music never stopped. That's the death and sex of work.

What mattered most to me, however, was doing something you enjoyed with someone you liked and understood, who understood you. As Pink Starnes predicted, the Club was another, different child to Levi and me, something we shared, proving over and again just how lucky we were to have each other. That's the birth and love of work.

When my mother said good-bye to me in the winter of 1929, she bade me make a life for myself elsewhere. Make a life that she couldn't imagine. The season of her death and my birth.

Could she have imagined my life in the late summer of 1931? Me a working woman wearing trousers to the office several days a week. Partner to a bootlegger and nightclub owner. Pregnant with a baby that I wanted. Desperately wanted, truth be told.

Her firstborn, my oldest brother, William, was birthed when she was seventeen, and by her account, nearly killed her. His head was the size of a pumpkin, according to family legend. She swore on the Bible she'd never bear another. But he was the first of seven, and as I've told you, she died of exhaustion. Birth and death wrapped around work hard enough to crook your spine.

So was I different? Had I created that life she couldn't imagine, as I went day-by-day to my work, carrying my baby in my belly? Our baby . . .

I was twenty-eight years old, a decade and change older than my Mama when she first bore. Plus I worked with my mind, mostly, not my back. And my mind was stronger than ever, my number sense as sharp as a new pencil. Sharper.

My body was changing. When I left Big Pine for Asheville, I had a boy's body, at least according to Sissy, who knew what she was talking about when it came to bodies. I kept that body, plus or minus a few pounds, a few inches, until the summer of '31, when Levi and I got ourselves into trouble. Then I began to grow real breasts for the first time in my life. At first, I wasn't quite sure what to do with them, but Levi liked them. Once he got over being afraid to touch them.

As you can imagine, as summer turned to fall, my belly took on a life of its own.

⋄⋄⋄

So here's what we decided. And having decided . . . set about doing. We got married twice. The first time up on Big Pine in the yard in front of the Rock House. My brother Tony stood above us on the steps with a real preacher—meaning the local boy who had taken the correspondence course and carried on every Sunday morning at the church by the creek—and together they performed the ceremony. The preacher boy couldn't stop frowning, and Tony couldn't stop smiling.

When Levi kissed me, there on the steps, my other brothers fired off shotguns and pistols into the air. Out came the banjos and fiddles, and the food was the best you ever ate. Country food in late summer will always be the best you ever ate.

After spending the night at the Rock House—the boys hung a cow bell in our bed springs just for frolic—we drove back to town. The next day we got married at the Sky Club, by an Episcopal priest who occasionally ate dinner on the second floor, cocktail in hand. The country service was the legal one, as it came first, but nobody really cared. The priest had fun and so did we. Bodie was on hand for the second ceremonial, and he added his own howls to the proceedings. Second time around, the food was fair—city food—but the music . . . The music was that jazz they play in heaven. Or just outside of heaven after midnight. Dark and blaring and hot as a skillet. I couldn't fit into my moonlight on the river dress by then, but Lord God above, I could still dance the strong Black Bottom.

What was the same in the two places, mountain cove and city club? The booze was the same—the best pure white liquor and the sweetest apple brandy, made by family. In both places, what you call the wedding party was the same. Mack and Gordon stood up by Levi, and Pansy stood arms linked with me. She and Mack nearly jumped off the porch up home when the boys fired off their guns but then settled down after that and ate more than anybody. Drank more than some. Pansy showed us how she played the banjo . . . which no one expected.

Why get married twice? Enough have asked me that question, that I suspect you might also wonder. Here's my answer. We got married twice—Levi Edgar Arrowood and me—because we are neither of us simple people. We're country and city. Lonely mountain fiddle and sweat-hot jazz. Hell, we're every kind of music you ever heard.

We come from death *and* birth . . . sex *and* love . . . work *and* play.

Food *and* drink. Double down on the drink . . . Out of the ruin of winter and the crash, we built a life with our bare hands.

HERE AT THE END OF this story, I'll leave it for you to decide. To judge the quality of my imagined and created life. Say of it what you will.

I already know what I think.

ACKNOWLEDGEMENTS

I have wanted to write a novel about the November 1930 bank crash in Asheville, North Carolina, for a long time. I thought that the "day the banks closed" represented much of the what the entire country experienced during the Great Depression, and what happened on November 20 of that year, the dark of the moon, crippled the city, and indeed, the entire region for generations.

I also wanted to tell the story of the especially gifted and adventurous mountain people who went out into the world of the twentieth century and made very successful lives for themselves despite the widespread misconceptions about their backwardness and ignorance. In many ways, that is the story of my father's family, and that is why this novel is dedicated to the memory of my father's mother, Belva Anderson Roberts. Grandma Roberts, as I called her, was passionate about education and determined that her seven children would make a better life. She was my best friend when I was a little boy.

Which brings us to the historical places and people who appear in this novel. Mayor Gallatin Roberts (no relation), Bank President Wallace B. Davis, and the men who built the mansions of Lake View Park (Sinclair and Campbell) are all based on historical models. Indeed, the plea for understanding that Gallatin Roberts wrote for publication before he committed suicide is taken word-for-word from the Asheville newspaper. Pinkney Starnes and the Imperial Life Insurance Company were also part of the Asheville landscape; although, I had to manipulate the timing a bit to bring Pink onstage at the same time as Jo Salter.

The original Sky Club does sit high above Asheville on Beaucatcher Mountain, but it didn't begin operation as a restaurant and dance club until the late 1930s. It was still a private residence at the time of the novel, when Jo meets Levi Arrowood for the first time and falls in love with the sound of his voice. Thanks to my son, Jesse, for the photo on the cover—of the building as it exists today.

Writing *The Sky Club* was always a labor of love. That labor was made possible through countless conversations with Lynn, who offered good advice on everything from hair to hosiery. Among the several friends who read part or all of the manuscript as it developed was Wendy Ikoku, whose sharp editorial eye caught my miscues in draft after draft. A deep and sincere bow also to my agent, Margaret Sutherland Brown, and the team at Turner Publishing, who make this whole process both easy and fun.

And finally, there is Bodie, the little hound with a wild heart and huge voice. Not only is he real (see him posing with me on the back cover); he sat patiently with me throughout the writing, and so became the hero of the night the Sky Club was robbed. After hanging on for many years, Bodie has left us and gone over to visit with Grandma Roberts, where they walk the mountainside, discussing the changing seasons as grandmothers and dogs are wont to do. They are the spirit of this book.

ABOUT THE AUTHOR

Terry Roberts' direct ancestors have lived in the mountains of Western North Carolina since the time of the Revolutionary War. Many of them farmed in the Big Pine section of Madison County, a place that to this day is much as it's portrayed in *The Sky Club.*

Roberts' debut novel, *A Short Time to Stay Here,* won the Willie Morris Award for Southern Fiction, and his second novel, *That Bright Land,* won the Thomas Wolfe Memorial Literary Award as well as the James Still Award for Writing about the Appalachian South. Both novels won the annual Sir Walter Raleigh Award for Fiction, given to the author of the best novel written by a North Carolinian. His third novel, *The Holy Ghost Speakeasy and Revival,* was published by Turner in 2018. His newest book, *My Mistress' Eyes Are Raven Black,* a literary thriller set on Ellis Island, was published by Turner in 2021.

As well as being an award-winning novelist, Dr. Terry Roberts is a lifelong teacher and educational reformer. Since 1992, he has been the Director of the National Paideia Center, a school reform organization dedicated to making intellectual rigor accessible to all students. Born and raised near Weaverville, North Carolina, Roberts is the Director of the National Paideia Center and lives in Asheville, North Carolina with his wife, Lynn.